The Secret Magp
Gary J Mack

The Secret Magpie

Dedicated to Jacey. Here's to the next thirty years.
The main character of this book is named after my maternal grandfather Harry Morton. There are no further similarities. It's just a cool name.

Edited by Catherine Cooke
Cover Concept Gary J Mack
Cover Design David Collins

Chapter One
A Tale of Two Magpies

It was Lady Bell who named him the Magpie.

He wasn't sure if she had said it, or had transferred the name directly into his brain, although surely that would have been fantastical to say the least.

She had come to him in the secure unit, an angel in a wheelchair, broken halo of white hair shimmering through the bars of his partly padded room.

There she was, confidently explaining how she was going to set him free. One brief chat with the registered manager, one arthritically challenged signature and he was out. Lady Bell, it seemed, had influence.

"My last Magpie failed me," she confided, on the drive back to her stately home. "But I think you will be magnificent."

During that short journey, he learned she was a woman of power in the world of business; she promised to use that power to help him recover.

He then broke down, which was unusual. In his despair, he told her that his family had abandoned him, that he had nowhere else to go- and even if he did, he wouldn't have the means to travel there. He said he was vulnerable – an undeniable fact, but one that he hated admitting.

Lady Bell seemed to fully understand. "I *will* help you, *my Magpie.*"

She threaded one wizened arm through his own like an ancient aunt as they nestled in the back of the big old antique Jaguar Mark 2, as it purred its way through the countryside.

With trees rushing by, Lady Bell outlined what she expected from her new Magpie; by the time they had reached their destination, he had fully accepted both the challenge and his new name.

The next day, as he settled into his new opulent home, he researched the Cordivae family of birds: magpies, crows, ravens and rooks. He investigated their behaviour, how they lived and how they hunted. He attempted to spot magpies as he walked about the farm that had once been part of the Bell estate. He expressed his disappointment at not finding a magpie, Lady Bell just laughed without humour, then became very stern indeed. There had been no magpies on Magpie's Farm for an exceptionally long time, she had said. Her tone firmly suggested that any further probing on the matter would not be tolerated.

The Magpie spent the next few weeks improving his mobility. His limbs had atrophied all the time he had been in the secure hospital bed. Lady Bell's tall physician had given him an exercise sheet, which he followed religiously. It was hard at first, but soon his strength began to return. Not so long ago he had been a strong and healthy man, he *would* recover. For the first time in many years, he felt a tangible sense of positivity.

A few days into spring, some six months after his arrival, Lady Bell called him to her office. The time had come for him to do the work for her that she had outlined on their first journey together. He wholeheartedly agreed.

He knew he would rather enjoy the tasks she demanded, however gruesome.

Lady Bell then said she instructed the doctor to repair the regions of scarring around the Magpie's face and to restore more of his sight. The scar tissue and cataracts from his original accident meant his vision and orientation had worsened over time.

Unfortunately, they found his scars were beyond even the trusted doctor's medical skills. The doctor

4

did see to removing the left cataract, which improved the Magpie's sight no end, but was no expert plastic surgeon. Moreover, the Magpie would likely require further visual correction over time, the doctor had said.

With plenty of cursive disdain for the medical profession, Lady Bell vowed to take matters into her own hands.

She brought in a prosthetic make-up expert to develop a latex mask for the Magpie to wear as he went out and about on his practice runs. It was hot and sweaty, but wearing it brought him the reassurance that people would no longer stare at him, horrified.

It was regrettable when he heard that the make-up expert had met with a tragic accident a short time after the delivery of her amazing product. It was truly life changing, it was a shame others would not benefit from her skill.

"A stop-gap until you are ready for permanent change, my dear," the Lady had said. "You will know when it's time. In the meantime, I have taken delivery of your contact lenses."

Enveloped in the euphoria of being able to see so well under cover of his artificially normalised face, the Magpie planned his first killing.

He then researched it perfectly, capturing his actions in detailed notes, from the first time he wrote down the victim's name all the way to the final blow.

The Magpie felt like a playwright, a murderous Marlowe, beating out stage directions for the lead actor to bring the part alive- through someone else's death. He often laughed at the irony.

The first murder went so well that he repeated the process a second time, only deviating from his timetable for a few minutes to stop off at Tesco and buy some jars. He did, after all, need somewhere to store the victims' eyes.

Soon, he was in full flow. Up and down the country he raced. A total of twelve murders. Every time, he felt the cycle of elation then regret, but every time, as he watched Lady Bell's face - as he recounted the details, his remorse lessened. She positively glowed at his recitations. They transformed her.

Lady Bell appeared to be flourishing. She could walk now, her stoop straightened, and she looked younger. It seemed to him that each killing had made them both stronger. He laughed at his overactive imagination. She had probably just recovered from a long, debilitating illness. She had never been that old. Had she?

By the time he had walked her through his twelfth murder from start to finish, a few years had gone by. Lady Bell had lavished him with gifts and money in that time. He wanted for nothing.

One evening, he met her by chance in the ballroom.

He had passed the large, chequered dance floor many times during his stay, but it had always been cordoned off and in a state of disrepair. But now the room was glowing and resplendent. It looked entirely renovated – yet he'd never seen a single builder, architect, or tradesman on the estate.

That evening the two fires and the myriad candelabras had been lit and they crackled, the smell of burning wax hanging heavy in the air. A warning of what was to come.

Lady Bell looked at him across that vast space in a way she had never had before. They were about to begin a different dance.

She looked younger than ever, bathed in the firelight, a far cry from the old-looking disabled woman who had rescued him from the institute. She was dressed in a fine green silk gown, ready – she had said - to go to a police benefit, as patron of the Police Mutual Society.

She looked beautiful. The Magpie had never had such an immediate erection in all his life. He shuffled awkwardly in her presence.

"I know a young man who once asked to be my Magpie." She said, pondering a while on her own words it seemed. She put a hand on his chest. She stroked him silently before her hand snaked down his body until she was touching him *there*.

"My last Magpie didn't make the grade. He was a policeman and he thought he could kill for me, but he had mixed allegiances. Doubts. Despite my efforts, he did not carry out the act. He was nothing like you. *My new Magpie.*"

The Lady stepped back and undid her dress. The shimmering shift fell away, like a green skin shed by a serpent, to reveal her lithe body. Well, that must be it, he thought, she had been undernourished due to her illness and it had made her look much older, caused her to be disabled.

His mouth was suddenly dry, and he licked his lips. She was *so* desirable in that moment.

"There was no dedication from him," Lady Bell continued. "Not like the dedication I get from you." She moved to him and gently touched his face with one cold hand. She put the other arm around his waist, she pulled herself towards him. Naked. Touching.

He gasped.

"I want you to spend time getting to know Constable Marcus Vincenzo. The thirteenth victim. A Judas. I want you to find his flaws, mimic them. I want you to impersonate him in every way, your next round of killings will be with his face, not your own. Unfortunately, achieving that is going to hurt."

"I have lived with pain for most of my life - what is a little more discomfort?" Looking back, he didn't know if it was nonchalance, or bravado.

She led him to a nearby bedroom and bid him to take off his clothes and lie down. Then she laid her hands upon him. His body shuddered with the pain, but he tempered it as she climbed atop him.

The pain became excruciating, but he wanted more. He felt like there was a noose around his neck

7

and about to snap his hyoid. Every limb felt like it was going to be pulled out of its respective socket.

They were now bonded in the most personal way a couple could be.

"This temporary disguise will help you carry out the acts." She whispered in his ear as he shuddered out his lust. "Once you have killed my next set of victims, your transformation will be complete."

Later, when he had showered, after she had left to go to the benefit, he looked in the steamy mirror. He rubbed the mist into droplets of water, cleared the reflective surface. His vastly different, perfect face stared back at him. Was this some kind of sorcery? He laughed, dismissively; his mind must be playing tricks on him.

At first, Lady Bell just smiled when he mentioned his changed appearance at breakfast the next day. The smile then melted into a laugh – a sound tinged with something else. Madness? In the open breakfast room that morning, it rang out like the squared-off echoes of a tomb or an open grave.

Police Constable Marcus Vincenzo had just finished his last shift. He had finally left the police force.

He had nothing left in England: his mum and dad were now both dead and there was no woman in his life worth staying for. There had been no relationship since the brief, almost inexplicable fling with Lady Bell. When they had met at the function and she had asked him to sleep with her, he did so despite her age and infirmity. Marcus had always liked an older woman, although possibly not that old. Lady Bell wanted too much more, however.

She had asked him to go and kill someone – put a pillow over their head in return for a good reference, for his application to the Italian Police. His record wasn't exactly clean, but after much deliberation he had refused.

Lady Bell's proposed victim was supposedly a relative of hers. She had said he was an old man. But Robert had looked about forty when Marcus had carried out some initial investigations, not an old man at all. The whole prospect had made him feel sick. Nothing like how sick he had felt though when he saw Lady Bell the first morning after their lovemaking. She was ninety if she was a day.

Marcus had told the sarge what Lady Bell had said. Sergeant Laney said *he* was dealing with it. No doubt that meant sweep it under the carpet. Lady Bell was a police benefactor, an angel in their eyes. Marcus didn't care, he was out of it. He would start again in Italy at the bottom and work his way up. Who needed a reference?

That had been a week ago.

Marcus had just dropped off his house keys at the estate agents in Brum and collected his tickets for his flight to Milan from Co-op Travel. He picked up his car from the car park outside Lloyd House, then drove home.

He passed the Birmingham City Football ground, turned left off the island and drove up Hubert Road. He pulled up outside his house.

Clarence Samuels, his neighbour, was sitting on an old sofa in the next-door garden. Clarence was a man of few words; they tended to just nod at each other. As was his habit, Clarence was nursing a long cigarette, its ashen end dangling precariously.

As Marcus fiddled for his keys, the caw of a bird made him look up. A magpie, siting on his garden fence, looking from him to Clarence and back again, as if making some sort of decision about who to watch. Beautiful things, magpies.

"Morning Mr Magpie," he saluted.

Front door eventually unlocked, Marcus entered the hallway and dumped down his work bag on the brown and dark blue tiles with a flat concussive thud. He went to call for his mother, then stopped short with a still-grieving sigh. She was with her Marco

9

now. No more the sound of her singing in the hallway and up the stairs.

Gripping the lounge doorhandle, Marcus paused, changed his mind and headed for the kitchen. He scrolled through the news on his phone as he waited for the kettle to boil.

Mug in hand, he moved to the lounge door again, opened it.

The magpie cawed outside again, startling him. He looked towards his front door, towards the noise. A funny feeling in the pit of his stomach overcame him. Marcus shook his head. He wasn't superstitious; Mrs Magpie was probably about somewhere. He stepped inside his lounge.

He let go of his mug in shock.

Tea spattered down his legs and ankles, scalding them through his jeans. He didn't notice the pain.

Then someone grabbed him from behind, arm around his throat, something pressed to his mouth, and everything went black.

Marcus awoke sometime later. He felt like he had a massive hangover. *What the hell was I doing last night?*

Then a terrible comprehension dawned, like the sun rising behind a nuclear detonation.

His heart began to race. An immediate stress reaction.

Marcus had been trained to resist panic as part of his core anti-riot skills, but despite such expertise, alarm still claimed him. He tried deep breathing. It did nothing. It was too dark and far too quiet.

He remembered.

Coming home, making a cup of tea. Opening the lounge door, everything covered in plastic. *Plastic.* Like a scene from a horror film, like the curtains of an abattoir. Too clean, ready for surgery, torture. Death?

His mouth was taped and gagged. *That will hurt when it comes off.* Gallows humour. And then it was torn off, he gasped.

Then suddenly a strong hand pinched his nose whilst another covered his mouth with a rag that tasted strongly of alcohol. He resisted for a few fleeting moments…

Marcus awoke for the second and final time in his life. It was bright now; he felt the midday sunbathing him with welcome heat. He was still in his living room, still lying on the table.

He was also naked.

The bastard had stripped him.

Marcus fidgeted. His back was sticking to the plastic sheeting now. He must have pissed himself as his groin and upper legs were wet, and he could smell the staleness of his own urine, it clogged his throat and he gagged.

Don't vomit or you will choke.

Plastic. Still. Everywhere.

He knew he was going to die.

"Morning Marcus." The voice *was* lively, familiar, full of joy, but he couldn't place it. It was coming from behind his head, but he could not crane to see, due to the restraints.

He struggled from side to side, trying to loosen his bonds, expecting to see a table with surgical tools on it like in a Frankenstein film, or an episode of Silent Witness.

He'd watched too many horror films. Christ, he was going to die. He was certain of it. How long would it take, would it be painful?

"Nice day today, Constable Vincenzo!"

The voice was so familiar. Bizarrely happy, with a screech of fake-real madness.

"I can't wait to go to Italy for a break. Write a suicide note, leave a trail of breadcrumbs to a river or the sea, then return pretending to be your twin. Such fun."

Then he recognised the voice.

11

The voice was *his*; or a close enough approximation of it.

"You have lovely eyes, Marcus. I've got a jam jar with a blue lid on it, just for them."

What the fuck?

A figure came into view: as naked as he, same height and build, but unadorned with tape. The scar on *his* shoulder was the same as the one on Marcus's from the pellet gun attack. The appendicitis mark from his operation at the age of eleven. The ink and pin tattoo on his left arm of a badly drawn tear. As if triggered, one tear trickled down Marcus's face. Then another traced its way down the other man's face too.

Snap.

Facts. This man is doing an incredibly good impression of me - even our genitals are of an equal size and shape. What are the chances of that?

He recoiled as he noticed the shock of white hair amongst the black. The man was a mirror image of himself. Even Nanna wouldn't have known the difference. Nanna had named him Gazza. Magpie.

"You would not believe the number of times we have met, Marcus Vincenzo. God, that is a mouthful. Talking of which…"

He felt the tape ripped from his mouth for the second time, the gag removed; the sting of ruptured blood vessels, the taste of rust.

"What do you mean? We've never met! I've never seen you before."

The man giggled, then snapped his face into a serious expression.

"Oh." The man whispered. "The old Magpie has a voice. A loud voice. Magpies can be known to mimic, you know."

"Lady Bell called me her little Magpie. That fucking bitch. You've come to kill me, haven't you? If you are going to kill me. Just get on with it."

Marcus Two - his brain had labelled the intruder already - put a hand on his brow, caressed his face. Moved a hand down his body, finger edging slowly

12

over a nipple, glided past his balls and his groin and massaged his right inner thigh.

Dear God, please, not that. Just kill me.

Marcus Two must have read his mind.

"Don't worry, Marcus. I'm not into boys. Just getting the feel of you, so I can imitate it." His "t's" were accented, delivered distinctly with a "ta" sound. "Aren't we getting along? Unfortunately, it's time to interrupt this news programme."

Then, with a flourish, his doppelganger produced a large knife from the air.

It was a most clever and magical trick.

In less than a second, it was flashing through space and sticking out of Marcus's sternum.

That hurt.

He tried to take in a breath, but his lungs were already filling with blood.

Marcus knew enough about physiology to know that he would most likely drown before he bled out.

The Magpie had attended both Marcus's mother's and father's funerals. He had seen Marcus shower many times at the gym. He had broken in and installed cameras in bedrooms and bathrooms; he knew Marcus's intimate, private thoughts. He had watched him for such a long time. Now, he could replace him and begin part two of Lady Bell's plan. Marcus would be a great cover story for his next movements. The house on Hubert Road would be a great bolt hole.

He paused briefly though, as he shoved the old Magpie's corpse into the furnace.

"Lady Bell will not always control me," he declared, out loud.

The thing was, he had watched and waited for so many years. And he *was* a very clever man. He knew there was something not quite right about Lady Bell. He would need to be careful. He had two plans: one for his own ends and one for Lady Bell. They would remain mutual at first – but then, who knew what he might do?

As he left the foundry, he dropped an envelope containing one hundred pounds onto Leonard, the security guard's, makeshift desk. He hoped Leonard enjoyed the cash and spent some on his kids. Lenny would be dead by the end of the week after all.

He glanced up at the newly disabled security cameras and smiled, before driving away.

The Magpie glanced over to the passenger seat where a bag lay; in it a blue-lidded jar, containing Marcus's eyes.

He and the former policeman could have a chat later. The Magpie was looking forward to it. He felt elated. Things would slowly come to a head.

"Catch the Magpie if you can – Harry Morton."

Chapter Two
The End of the Last Case

Pain.

DCI Harry Morton's head was throbbing. It was either old wounds, or a new movement of the bone fragment that was eternally lodged in his brain.

Harry lived with a daily half-promise from death, a constant reminder that there was a sluggish missile slowly moving towards a high-collateral target. One day he would just switch off, like a badly wired TV.

Harry's bitter laughter broke the rumination. Laughter helped him to take pot-shots at his demons. It also turned the heads of a couple of fellow senior officers, who thought he was laughing at the Chief Constable's dirge of a presentation.

Martin Rivers, Chief Constable of Central England Police, stood at his podium, metering out death-by-PowerPoint. Harry sometimes wished his brain would choose one of these speeches to go bang, put him out of his misery. His commanding officer had all the personality and presence of wet cardboard.

Rivers was in his late fifties. A tall, thin man, with unfashionably tousled grey-black hair and an ale-enriched pot belly that looked like he needed to iron his shirts over a wok.

Rivers was espousing governmental cuts again, insisting their necessity would be the case under any incumbent government, not just the Tories.

The topic of austerity always made Harry nervous; he had voiced this in the networking break. Rivers had been quick to assure the room that the Cold and Complex Team would continue for at least another three years, but only if Harry got its case-closing threshold up to a level that was pushing the right buttons with the Commissioner.

It was at this point that Harry's head had started to throb. Maybe more related to work stress than the bone fragment, after all.

His team worked hard enough as it was, through strange and challenging circumstances. They did not rush arrests or cook-the-books like other teams or departments. Getting his threshold up would be a massive challenge.

Harry had been in the police for sixteen years and he'd loved it – overall. He'd enlisted at nineteen and he felt he had achieved a lot in life and work, despite his history, or lack of it, for the first eighteen or so years.

Harry had been involved in an accident in Lichfield Cathedral. He had fallen from a great height, resulting in a catastrophic loss of any prior memory. All he retained was his name. When he tried to trace his origins, there were no records. Nothing.

If it hadn't been for his adopted father, Wally Smart, the DCSI who had investigated his case, he would never have joined up, never emulated his dad. It had been the talk of the force – policeman takes in mystery boy- but Wally was still respected, despite his illness and his actions were rarely questioned around Harry. Up until six years before, when the dementia first claimed him, Wally had been Rivers' boss.

Head still throbbing, Harry spent the coffee break with DI Sally Worksop, an old Vice colleague. Their conversation had focused on all the new faces in the room. Lots of young, newly graduated coppers.

Harry had been a young graduate once - a high-flyer. He had paused his ascent, however, to develop the Cold and Complex Team- a labour of love and one that had Wally's full support.

The mystery surrounding his origins gave Harry an almost legendary status amongst the force. A man with no memory of his childhood, adopted by a Police Commissioner. When he took over from

Owain Pleasant as new head of all that was strange in the world, his status as an enigma was complete.

The probability of an early death gave Harry purpose and an almost terrier-like need to solve cases. That was his advantage over these youngsters. He needed to solve as many cases as he could before his brain switched off.

Harry's phone buzzed noisily in his pocket, jolting him clumsily back into the present. Rivers was speaking again, and Harry had obviously dropped off.

Harry pulled his phone out to silence it, but not yet quite awake, he fumbled it and watched horrified as it skittered noisily under the chair in front, still buzzing like an angry bee. Pushing back on his chair with a horribly loud scrape, he recovered the handset.

"Set-up call Morton?"

Rivers looked over at him in annoyance. Sally looked back and smiled. It was the oldest trick in the book, get blue-lighted out of the Chief's briefing. Just make sure you had something serious to do, as the Chief would catch up with you eventually.

Rivers paused momentarily, then resumed with an icy glare at Harry. Harry's phone chirruped a text alert before falling silent once more.

Gov, its Mo. We have found him. Leek is hiding out in Bordesley Green, 24 Wilson Road. Maisie is on her way.

"Anything you'd like to share, Morton?" The tone was resigned. All eyes in the room turned from Rivers to Harry.

"Sorry, Sir. We think we've got Leek."

The blood pounded in Harry's ears as the other officers focussed on him, expressions ranging from wry smiles to envy, or annoyance.

The Chief sighed wearily. "Can't Steve Rolleston bring him in?"

"I've deployed him elsewhere. I've got a sergeant coming to get me."

Rivers dismissed Harry with a wave. "I'll expect your report."

Harry nodded, grabbed his coat and headed out of the briefing room towards the lift. He popped a couple of ibuprofen along the way.

Detective Sergeant Maisie Price was waiting for him on Steelhouse Lane next to the Queens Head Public House. She was sitting in a plain service vehicle, a BMW M2. It was a beast of a car, sleek and beautiful, all curves and sheen. Wasted on his team. It would just get battered like all the others.

"Nice wheels, M. What did you have to do to get this one?"

"Guv." She acknowledged as he took his seat beside her. He clunked the door shut and belted up. "It's one of the new ones. Hotter than a pound a time whore's doorknob. I really had to chat up Leroy in logistics. I've got to go to the shit police quiz next month as payback."

DS Price was a handsome woman: tall, blonde, athletic, a good five years or so younger than himself. She was about to make Teddy Robson incredibly happy when they married later in the year.

Harry loved Maisie for her brain. She was quick, logical, and thoroughly well-considered, not to mention naturally funny. A huge contrast to her twin, Detective Constable Daisy Price, who was in his logistics and analytics team; equally clever, but a miserable cow.

Maisie was his new team powerhouse; the leading contributor to his case-solving numbers. It wasn't lost on Rolleston, his lone inspector, who was more than a little peeved. Rollo needed to pull his finger out though. He'd been slack of late.

"What have we got?" Harry asked Maisie.

Her side profile lit up with a smile, like the brightest of beautiful lights. Maisie was one of those people who was good-looking, but stunning when they smiled.

"Tip-off from Charlie. He said Leek has been seen entering the house of Bobby Clark, his cousin. I've got our teams set up in situ, and armed response is on the way. As a precaution." Maisie added.

He knew Charlie – not his real name- was a confidential informer, who'd been on the police books for a while. His personal use of crack-cocaine meant his information was often useless.

"Is Charlie sober enough to make sense?"

"Called in by neighbours as well. Lots of shouting last night apparently, "crashing about" and report of "gunshots." He raised an eyebrow at her lifting her hands from the wheel to mime the quote marks.

Maisie took the island quickly, but carefully, flicking her blue lights on.

They entered Wilson Road, one of the long, almost Roman-straight roads of the Edwardian development that was the top end of Bordesley Green. The road was flanked with two rows of trees, leaves already turning Autumn yellow.

"Your radio and ear-piece are in the glove box," Maisie said as she pulled up and applied the brake. "I've tuned them to the control frequency."

"The boys are here too, then?" Harry noticed his other sergeant's Ford Focus. They would be spitting feathers that Maisie had the Beamer. He fitted his earpiece and switched on the radio.

"Unit two. Ready?" Maisie spoke after she too had fitted her in-ear comms device.

"Ready, over. We will stay put unless asked."

"Unit Three?"

"We are in the garden of the rear-facing neighbours. Over." That was DC Miles, their newest recruit. A big lad and fast. Leek was a runner, so they might need Pete before too long.

"Ok. Teams, listen." Harry said across the channel. "Don't go too heavy-handed in a residential area or there will be media hell to pay. Let's lock it down quickly. See if we can get this bastard with the minimum of fuss." The armed response would be on the way, but they would only move in if Harry called on them as senior investigating officer.

"Fools with the tools are here, gov." Maisie referred to armed response.

"Is Teddy on today then, M?"

"Nope." She said bluntly. Then, opening her door, she added. "He's off." It felt like she was angry. Probably with Teddy. Harry knew he had form for being a bit of a dick.

Maisie climbed out of the car, and he followed suit. Now was certainly not the time to dig further into Maisie's relationship woes.

Together they moved up the garden path to the front door. The house was in disrepair; front garden a concreted-over graveyard for two rusting vehicles of undiscernible variety and age.

The caw of a bird sounded to their left. Harry looked over as Maisie knocked on the front door. It was a bloody magpie. He hated birds. Its black, marble-like eyes blinked; he was surprised there was no audible click. They moved like little birdy robots.

They waited for thirty seconds. Unsurprisingly, there was no reply. Harry banged harder. "Open up Mr Clark."

Unit Four had arrived. PCs James Matthews and Karol Wojcik had the battering ram.

"One more time, Mr Clark. Open for us. Or I will knock your nicely painted front door through your living room."

"Sarcasm, sir?" Wojcik asked; he liked to learn. He'd only lived in England for the past five months, a transfer from the Polish Straż Miejska Municipal Police. Although his accented English was amazing, Karol felt a little embarrassed that he didn't always get the nuances of British humour.

"Yes, Karol."

Matthews's laugh quickly subsided on the nod from Harry and he bashed the door as hard as he could. Once, twice. It went on the third go.

"Ya bastard." Matthews extorted as he followed through with the ram, his use of English language and grammar somewhat cruder than his Polish mate.

Harry patted Matthews on the back and indicated the ram bearer and Wojcik to withdraw with two quick hand signals. He motioned to DS Price to stay behind him.

The stench of weed hit his nose immediately – sweet, but cloying. The lounge was more like a building site, a knock- through that had never been finished.

There was a dusty couch opposite the front bay window. The curtains were drawn but, in the gloom, Harry could make out a grey-faced man lying on it. He was very dead. There was evidence of trauma wounds to his face, hands, and abdomen.

A bullet hole through his forehead.

The man's eyes were looking past the natural vanishing point of their focus, at something his brain could no longer decipher. Behind him on the wall a spatter of blood and brains, like an angry little Hubble-sought galaxy, populated with tiny, ivory white, star-like bone fragments.

Harry glanced back at Maisie - she signed a C. It was Clark. Leek had apparently killed his own cousin, not satisfied by the ritualistic, sacrificial black magic-influenced murders of his own wife and daughter.

Suddenly, there was movement up ahead at the back of the long room. Harry could make out a figure, heading towards what was most likely the kitchen door. There was a flash of light as the door was pulled open, a cackle - a mad, stomach-churning giggle- and then the figure slammed the door behind it.

"Unit Three. Miles, be ready." Maisie was one step ahead, as ever.

"I'll go in pursuit, M. Get SOCO on standby."

Maisie was going to warn him not to exert himself because of the thing in his head. Harry didn't stay around to listen and took off after who he presumed was Leek, into the kitchen, then through it. He had to turn right at the downstairs bathroom and into the yard.

He paused, edging forward carefully. Leek could very well still have a loaded weapon.

Harry's eyes scanned the long, narrow garden from the relative shelter of a gazebo wall. There was a small lawn, an ornamental pond, and a shed. Leek was behind the shed; the man was raising his hand; it held a gun.

"Shitting hell!" Harry felt the rush of air and a stinging feeling bloomed on his right ear followed by the concussion of a close bullet and the sound of a ricochet behind.

The wanker has only gone and fired at me.

Harry dropped like a stone in front of a randomly placed aluminium bin. He scuffed one knee and a hand on the rough concrete. It wasn't as painful as his ear.

"Leader to team three. Shots fired. Leek is armed. Repeat, Leek is armed. He's just shot at me. Bring in armed response."

Harry put a hand to his ear. It was wet with blood; he rubbed it between his thumb and forefinger. It wasn't that thick- the bullet must have just clipped him.

It was a bizarre situation. Leek had been a small-time crook. He wasn't known to be dangerous, but he had then killed his wife and daughter- more than a bit of a shock.

Leek was more of a seller of knocked-off goods, than a murderer. He sold the odd hooky pair of Adidas trainers here, a Nike top there, nothing more.

Leek's behaviour seemed to have escalated shortly before the murders. The police had been on the way to arrest him for GBH on another ex-con,

Marty Wilkes, when they had found the bodies. Leek had been long gone; his stash of mystic east-Asian and Haitian voodoo paraphernalia had brought the case to Harry's door.

The bleeding from the nick had almost stopped, so Harry made his way down the garden, as ever, thinking little of his own personal safety. He wasn't overly heroic, and he didn't particularly want to die; but he did seem to have a limited fear threshold. He kept vigilant as he moved, eyeballing a ginger moggy that hissed at him before scooting off.

Harry reached the bottom of the garden, noticing the gap in the hedge that Leek had taken, judging by the trampled greenery. The gap was behind a wizened cherry tree that seemed to have shed more fruit than had been picked. The rotting fruit made it slippy underfoot.

Harry was soon in the neighbour's garden. He locked eyes with an old lady and a middle-aged man, looking at him from their conservatory.

"Police, get inside." As he spoke, their back gate opened, and three-armed response officers piled in. One ushered the couple into the house. The other two came down the garden.

"Leader, this is Team three. He's in the alley. We have blocked it; he can only come your way or go into another garden."

"I repeat, he *is* armed," Harry knew that stating the obvious was important in situations like these.

Harry made his way into the next garden and then the next, pushing through gaps in the hedging and fencing. Chris Compton, an old Staffordshire colleague, sidled up next to him. Comps had gone into the armed division when Harry had moved to the Central team over twelve years before. They were acquaintances rather than mates, but knew each other well.

"Chief. What are you doing in the field? You should be behind a desk at your age," he patted Harry on the back.

23

"Comps, mate. I'll leave the field when I'm dead and not before. Less of the old too, you cheeky bastard, you've at least five years on me." He clasped Compton's offered hand. The large black man grinned back from a broad and pitted face.

Compton nodded at his ear. "Another war wound, H. That baby face of yours may look like it belongs to a twenty-year-old, but you'll look like a twenty-year-old potato if you're not careful."

Harry laughed sardonically. "We can add my mutilated ear to his charge sheet."

"We have secured the area, sir," said the second armed officer, Patel.

Martin nodded his thanks.

Suddenly Harry heard the sound of a gun going off. It wasn't far away.

"DCI Morton, step back, please. We are going in."

Reluctantly, Harry nodded. He liked the chase. He liked to catch his prey. He also knew that getting in the way of armed officers was stupid.

"Gov." It was PC Worth, Miles's back-up and another newish recruit. "The fucker's got me. Shit. Bastard. Upper leg, my inner thigh. He's into the garden of number thirty-two. Pete's in pursuit."

Damn. What was Miles doing? One dead, one injured. Harry was going to make sure no one else was hurt. He followed Compton and Patel into the garden of number thirty. It was empty, but there was another break in the fence. He would be able to get to PC Worth. If Leek was in the garden of thirty-two, he should be okay in the alley.

He squeezed through the broken panel and into the narrow, rubbish-strewn alley. Harry had to climb over rusting bikes and decomposing bin bags; there was barely enough space for two people side-by-side.

There was Worth. Sensible lad. He was using his belt as a tourniquet. He was pale and panting when Harry reached him -- he'd lost a lot of blood. Hopefully, the femoral artery had been missed, but by the look of him, it was a life-threatening situation.

He had never lost an officer; he wasn't going to start now.

"Maisie!"

"Yes, gov. I heard Worth, is he okay? I've called another ambulance; the paramedic is moving to you. I'll send him on his way down with another armed response officer, but only once the scene is safe for them to enter.

"Worth... Hayden, stay awake." Harry switched his attention to the burly officer. He wouldn't be turning out for the Police Rugby team at the weekend. Hayden would be missed too; he was a good tight-head prop.

"I had a fucking date tonight," Worth slurred, as if he'd just drank two bottles of wine. His eyes closed and his head lolled. Then he snapped to attention. "Sorry, sir for the language," he apologised, this time much clearer.

Harry laughed despite the situation. "No worries Worth. There's a paramedic on his way."

"I'm fine sir, you carry on." Worth said, knowing his gov liked to get results.

"Armed division have it. I'll stay with you for now."

There was a crash- someone bursting through the fence lower down the alley. It was Leek. He didn't have his gun, or he had stowed it. He looked Harry in the eye- and the bastard smiled, before clearing the fence. Harry raced after him instinctively, but Leek hadn't got far before he tripped and fell with the grace of a demolished cooling tower.

Harry reached Leek just as Comps and Patel arrived. Compton aimed his rifle at Leek, whilst Patel turned the fugitive over and cuffed him.

"Martin Leek. I arrest you for the Murder of Monique Leek, Ettie Leek and Bobby Clark. Not to mention firing a weapon at a police officer......"

Leek just stood there and giggled insanely for a moment. Then went quiet.

Later in custody, when the custody officer wasn't looking, Leek pulled out his eyes, one by one and told his custodian to give them to the Magpie.

In the horrific aftermath, stupidly, no one wrote down Leek's words.

Chapter Three
I Don't Love You Anymore

The water flooded down Maisie's body and splattered to the floor of the walk-in shower. She wasn't washing with any purpose; just letting the spray cleanse her thoughts, as much as her physical being. She wondered just what the hell was going on in her life.

Get a grip Price!

With new purpose, she soaped herself, anger dirtying her inner thoughts as suds cleaned her outer body.

She needed to wash away the smell of Teddy, the smell of his body, the smell of sex.

Teddy had dumped her. The bastard! She had cried and then they had ended up in bed together.

For fuck's sake Price, so weak!

Why couldn't her work professionalism flow into her personal life? If she could have controlled the situation a little more, even a touch, she could have managed things a damn-sight better.

Much of the time, Maisie was a swan at work, all elegant and cool on the surface but paddling furiously underwater like the devil was at her heels. Why couldn't that swan be replicated at home?

Teddy had told her he didn't love her almost as soon as she had got through the front door of their flat, the evening before; after the day she'd had. *My flat*, she corrected herself.

He had said he couldn't possibly marry her.

Maisie had screamed at him, thrown things, called him names - as was her wont- she never did hold back in a personal argument. Then she started to sob, lost her angry advantage, reneged on her rage and ended up accepting his embrace after crying some more. Then she had shagged him again.

Successful police officer caves into emotional weakness.

She had studied so hard for her inspector's interview. She had chosen to stay with the Complex Team for now, but would have changed assignment at the drop of a hat for Teddy. Maisie had always bent over backwards to make things better for him because she spent so much time at work; she had always felt she owed it to him. And this was how he repaid her. It seemed now she would be wedded to work, a spinster married to a police career. She wouldn't be leaping into a relationship again anytime soon. Harry would probably be pleased; they were very short-staffed. *No honeymoon.*

Rising police officer's slightly perfect world comes to an end.

Maisie had a headache, and the shower wasn't helping. The headaches had been frequent in recent months, particularly when things were not going right. She'd assumed she was heading for a breakdown. She had always worked long hours, spent little time at home, didn't sleep much. She had felt it coming a long time, waiting like a monster to jump out at her from a closet, ready to eat her up.

Maisie's GP, Dr Patel, had said there was nothing to worry about. Her blood pressure was fine and other tests were negative, or within acceptable parameters. Common stress was the diagnosis. Well, Dr Patel looked about fifteen sitting behind her desk. She wouldn't know stress if it slapped her with a prescription pad.

Maisie was being unfair again.

A precariously wrapped towel hung off her body as she returned to her bedroom. Teddy was still there, naked, dozing on the bed. He was the wrong side of flabby now. To think he often held the power of life or death in those hands, with their thick sausage fingers.

He had been an armed response officer for six years, but she couldn't envisage him running in a tense chase-off situation without gasping for his breath. How would he be able to gain a perfect shot if he were puffing like a steam train going up uphill through a snowstorm? It was cruel maybe, but that's how she currently felt.

Twat.

Maisie had loved Teddy, despite his snide remarks and bitter quips about sleeping her way to her promotions. It was all over now, though. The fat fuck hadn't even had the decency to leave.

"You okay babe?" he asked, sleepily.

She ignored him and sat down at her dressing table in a little bucket chair and dabbed her legs dry.

"Thought you were asleep." She was just making conversation. Conversation meant time would go quicker and he would be out of the door sooner, she hoped.

"I was, but you were crashing about like an elephant."

Fuck off.

Don't give him the satisfaction of seeing you're riled, Maisie. She didn't even pause, didn't acknowledge what he'd said.

"When are you moving out? You've got a lot of crap here to shift."

There it was. Blunt. Like a command to a subordinate. Soon to be inspector to special weapons constable. She heard him gasp. There was a pause.

Her confidence took a boost from the realisation this was over, and she was back in control. No more wedding plans. The dress could go back, and she would spend the thousand pounds refund on whatever she bloody well liked.

"I..."

"What did you think you would happen? You'd stay here? Sleep in *my* bed? Fuck me when it suited you?"

Teddy went bright red at her profanity. She hoped he'd taken his blood pressure meds; she didn't want him dying before she had had her say. She stood up and turned to him then continued to towel herself, naked in his gaze.

Look what you could've won.

She was growing in power now; showing him what he would miss. Maybe he did not want what she had got. Maybe he liked boys. *No Maisie, please don't be stupid.*

The bedframe groaned, and squeaked like a bag full of rats in a cider press, as her father would say, as Teddy hoisted himself upwards on his flabby arse.

"I'm sorry."

She dropped the towel, looked him in the eyes.

"You will never, ever get into bed with me again. You can come back at the weekend and collect your belongings. But that's it. No-one tells me they do not love me and then fucks me like that. Never again Ted. I'm worth so much more. I want you to leave. Now."

She left him spluttering as she went to make tea and toast, without a backward glance. She was going back to work, even though she had only been home a few hours.

She did not know at that point she would never see Teddy again. He'd never come back to fetch his belongings. He only had a few days left to live.

"You okay, M?" Mo Hyatt asked.

Maisie smiled at her friend of over ten years. "Teddy and I split up, but I'm fine about it."

Mo sighed sympathetically. Older than Maisie and already a sergeant, he'd met her on her first day as a PC in the Staffordshire police.

Stoic and sensible, but with a wicked sense of humour, Mo's Muslim faith was like an invisible badge on his arm. It was there, but he wasn't evangelical about it.

Mo was a strong supporter, listener and non-judgemental friend. Okay, he took the piss out of the things she wore when they went out on the town, tutted theatrically when she ordered that final double vodka, but he never, ever judged her.

30

Mo gave good advice, and she loved him for it. Adara, his wife, was a lucky woman to have such a loyal, dedicated husband.

"He never deserved you. Even if you are a wayward infidel."

She smiled at the banter. She was a Catholic girl on the quiet, albeit spiritually a long distance from the church. She still said her prayers - and Mo knew and respected that.

They were sat in the Complex Case workspace, an open office, large and full of mismatched desks and filing cabinets. A casual observer wouldn't have known the difference between it and any other public service office. It was only when you delved into those filing cabinets you saw that this was quite a unique place, even for the police.

It was nine p.m. There were a handful of officers about, finishing off their daily activity. The core non-uniformed Complex Case Team didn't work the same sort of patterns uniform did.

"Fancy a beer?" Maisie attempted a mood change.

Mo raised an eyebrow. "You are away with the fairies again." His forehead was narrow, framed by thick black hair. His eyes were brown but alight, his nose broken by a wayward ball at a six-a-side tournament. Mo was five feet six inches tall in his boots. Small of stature- big of heart.

"What would you do Mo, if you were in my situation?"

"Honestly? I liked him, but he wasn't right for you. Twice the man he was at the training centre where we met, half the love for you when I last saw him. He was rude, put you down. You're so full of life. You don't need that. It's Edward who's lost his way. Not you."

"I could kiss you."

"Leave it out, M. I'll settle for tea. I'm going home soon. So should you."

***

31

A few hours earlier, Harry Morton sat in the waiting room of the Maxillo-Facial department at Queens Hospital.

It was half-past four and he was quite obviously the final appointment of the day. He was awaiting the pleasure of Mr Prendergast.

Prendergast was the specialist in charge of his case and had been since Harry had been found on the floor of Lichfield Cathedral, unconscious and bleeding. The constant encephalograms had since offered no clues as to why he could not remember anything before that time. They were just tracking the movement of the piece of bone, as it slowly led him toward oblivion.

The waiting area was long, thin and smelt faintly of disinfectant. Harry straightened up as one of the doors opposite him opened and Lacey, Prendergast's assistant emerged. Nice girl, but he could never get past her eyebrows. They looked like they had been drawn on by a blind make-up artist with a roller.

"Come in, Chief Inspector."

"Please, just Harry." He said this every time, but the petite Irish nurse just smiled; the twinkling blue eyes that lived beneath the two huge eyebrows only hinting at the humour that lay within.

He followed Lacey Letts into the small, warm office. It smelt of cheap aftershave, cigarettes, and body odour. Lacey beckoned to a seat, smiled at Harry once more and then left.

Prendergast was as large as his name – a towering giant. Mr William Holton Prendergast, the Second. The son of an American surgeon who had settled in the UK, he had never quite matched the genius of his father - according to terrible hospital gossip.

Prendergast was probably thirty stone, but at six feet seven it spread on his frame well - although he *was* sweating like a jail-bound nonce, Harry noticed.

And it was no surprise he was sweating. Prendergast was wearing a rich bespoke three-piece suit that looked like it had been fitted by a twelve-year-old trainee tailor. His thick, greying hair was a mess; those large, fidgety hands must have been through it several times that day. Harry didn't want an examination.

"I see you have been in the wars." Prendergast's accent was received pronunciation, with a hint of Derbyshire. He'd gone to Eton, but had practised most of his career in the East Midlands.

"Yes, a little reward for bringing my latest case to a conclusion."

"Anyone we know?" the surgeon asked, eyes bright for a bit of news. His old-fashioned pencil moustache twitched when he was curious or intellectually aroused.

Harry just smiled and apologised that it would put him in a difficult position if he disclosed anything.

"You are a busy man." Prendergast paused as he was about to deliver some difficult news. "The latest set of tests didn't give us anything else, I'm afraid. There's no change to the hippocampus. The region that's damaged although minute is, as I have stated before, probably the cause of the long-term memory loss. I just can't find anything else that would explain it better."

Harry sighed. He had expected this response. "What about the fragment. Any movement?"

"No. It's all safely secured. No worrying movement. Although, if you are going to roll around apprehending criminals, Detective Chief Inspector, however young you feel, it will not help. I cannot express with any more clarity the need for you to take a more sedentary role." Prendergast's wheezing voice grated on Harry's nerves.

"Not going to happen." Harry replied, "I need to know what is causing the memory block and I need to deal with it the best I can. It's nearly eighteen years since the accident. I know you say I might never get my memory back, find out who I was, where I came from… but the only way I can sleep at night is to live in hope. I have to believe that one day, I will wake up and I will know my true history."

"Harry," Prendergast began in a very calm tone. He could play the game, this one. He would be a good hostage negotiator. "You need to live your life. You have a lovely partner in Ellen." *The dirty get licked his lips.* "Enjoy yourself."

Harry stood up. "William. Thanks for your time and patience. I'll see you in a few months when, no doubt, this merry-go-round of scans and tests and no further information will begin again. I'll see myself out."

The stress and bitterness of years of not knowing hung heavy in his heart, washing away the success of the day, like so much of his life experience since he awoke that first time in Lichfield Cathedral, profusely bleeding from the ears.

After his last appointment of the day with Harry, William Prendergast made his way from his office, through the corridors, past Patient Advice and Liaison and out toward the hospital car park.

Shuffling through the revolving door, trying to make sure none of his once muscly bulk got trapped, William heard a ping. He pulled out his phone and saw that there was a payment pending. Fifty thousand pounds via bank transfer.

It was his price. The price for sitting on his hands and at times for doing nothing. And yes, the price for falsifying medical records.

The medical records which should have clearly stated that there was nothing physically wrong with Harry Morton. There had never been any bone fragments left in Harry's head.

All this time, Harry had only suffered with amnesia, but the massive trauma had not been the cause. William did not know what the cause was. The money prevented him from looking any further.

It paid for his cocaine habit and his thrice yearly visits to Bangkok to satiate his lust for transsexual girls.

He had kept this secret for eighteen years and it was worth it.

Chapter Four
One for Sorrow

Harry awoke from his dream, trying to cling onto the images and feelings that always felt so real upon waking. He reached sleepily into his bedside drawer, pulled out his notebook and spent ten minutes - at least - trying to jot down any remnants of the dream. His session with his psychoanalyst wasn't for a while, but if he didn't note the details, he would soon forget.

Ellen was already up. He knew he was a fidgeter when dreaming and he knew his dreams seemed to crescendo early in the morning, so he guessed he had probably woken her by thrashing about in his sleep – maybe even calling out.

"Coffee, H?" she called from the lounge below. His sleeping area was on the mezzanine level of his large flat. All designer chic, totally impractical, Ellen Roux had said when she had stayed over for the first time.

"Please, sweetie."

The complex's air-conditioning made it artificially cool. He put his pyjama bottoms on, picking them off the floor where he had discarded them after their "cuddle" the night before. Harry then retrieved his t-shirt which had ended up on Ellie's side of the bed. He pulled it over his head and made his way down the thick oak steps into the minimalist living room, which linked with the kitchen as part of the open-plan design.

The aroma of scrambled eggs floated over to him, and he heard the toaster ping. Hopefully, muffins and salmon would accompany the eggs. Ellen was standing by the kitchen counter in just her light pink underwear, despite the coolness of the room. For a moment, he took in the beauty of her from a distance, then she turned her head towards him and smiled.

Wow. He might not tell her he loved her enough, but he knew how lucky he was every single minute of the day. His angel. Their four-year relationship went from strength to strength.

He was a busy policeman, and she was a busy sister in accident and emergency department at Queen's; it was rare they were together in the same place or the same time for long, but they made the most of it. They adored one another.

It was only six a.m. She would be on duty by seven, but still she took the time to make him breakfast. *Or you would never eat,* she would often say. She had come back to his flat the night before; it was gone ten when she landed, and he had only been in for minutes himself. They had ended up in bed soon after they had grabbed supper and here, they were again ready to get back on the hamster's wheel.

"Scrambled eggs and salmon. Without the salmon though, as you have none in your fridge." Her smile lit up her entire face, transforming it and filling him immediately with hope, energy and positivity. Ellen was a lot like Maisie in that respect. *Sergeant, soon to be Inspector Price*, he corrected himself, dismissing the thought immediately.

Ellen plated up and deposited the food on the breakfast bar; coffee was also waiting for him.

"You didn't tell me how your appointment went yesterday?"

He'd got a mouthful, so he quickly chewed and swallowed. "Same old, same old."

"Prendergast is a prick and a sleaze."

His eyebrows raised. "Interesting insight. Is there anything I need to worry about?"

She laughed. "Nothing we can't cope with. He just tries to touch up whoever he can, mainly the bank nurses who don't tend to hang around to file complaints. They don't return often, either."

As ever, he clearly did not want to talk about his medical issues further; she knew not to pick at him.

He loved that more than anything. It was like she could read his mind.

"What are you doing today?"

She put her cutlery down with a clinking noise. "Workshop, on admission avoidance, so I'm not on the ward. Should be free by six as they have covered me in A and E for the day. You about later?"

"I'm hoping so, unless the balloon goes up. Haven't checked my phone yet."

They finished their breakfast in silence and he stacked the dishwasher.

"I suppose you don't need to go in until a bit later then," he said, with a twinkle. Ellen suddenly looked thoughtful and didn't answer him. "El?"

"You were shouting a woman's name last night H. Do you remember?"

That stopped him in his tracks. He didn't recall dreaming about a woman. He could feel his face redden. He didn't know why. Then he remembered. The woman in yellow on the station platform, like a solitary jigsaw piece floating in his mind.

She laughed. "Don't worry, I'm not accusing you of an affair." Her tone became more serious. "H, you were shouting the name Edith, repeatedly."

Edith? He had never dreamed of an Edith. He normally dreamt of being a little boy and of the bully.

"Maybe she was your mother, or more likely grandmother.

His mood clouded. He didn't like it when things happened that he had no control over. Ellen got up and gave him a hug.

"I'm here for you baby. The facts will come in their own time."

He enjoyed her arms about him, he felt safe, even though he was the big bloke and Ellen was the petite figure she was.

Then his phone rang and the bubble burst. "It's the Bat-phone, better get that."

***

Uniform had closed the roads, so Harry parked up and walked the rest of the way through the hustle and bustle of a crime scene.

It was breezy, but it was warm; the sun was trying to hold on in there, even though it was early October. The sun had moved behind the clouds as if felt embarrassed, or saddened, to shine on the morning they had found someone dead.

DI Steve Rolleston met him on the grassy verge outside of the old medieval church.

Rollo was tall and rangy, suit jacket, no tie. He was a brilliant officer in some ways, but prone to long bouts of silence and moodiness. He'd transferred from Manchester Police two summers ago. He was only ever seconds from a cigarette, and recently he'd looked tired and worn out. Up all-night chasing "broads," as he liked to say in that fake irritating American accent.

Rollo pushed his jet-black hair out of his eyes. It was longish in a nineties rock-star kind of way. Probably dyed, Harry thought. In an era of short back and sides, the women seemed to love Rollo's individuality.

"Lichfield's first murder in a while, gov. Papers will be fucking loving it. Follow me." His long, precise Mancunian, like a Gallagher brother who had been to elocution lessons.

There were SOCOs everywhere, but Rollo cut a path through them and together they wove in and out of the paraphernalia with more than a little difficulty. Harry probably knew many of the officers personally, but they were all dolled up in their paper suits and almost anonymous, like upright white caterpillars.

Harry stooped under the blue and white tape held up by a baby-faced uniformed constable who was probably glad to have perimeter duties.

"Morning gov." Mo Hyatt, his diminutive DS, passed by them, obviously carrying out some sort of errand or another. "Hope you've not eaten lots of breakfast."

"Get us some tea, Mo." Rolleston barked with mock bluster.

Harry laughed. Hyatt just shook his head and made his way forward. They were unlikely to get their tea anytime soon.

Grace Hodgson leant on the church wall, like a scruffy amazon dressed in a noddy suit. She was the lead pathologist linked to the Cold and Complex Team. She ran a police officer affiliated team, nominally under the direction of Harry; but in reality, the Institute was her business and she exploited it. Harry let it go because they were such good friends and because Grace was brilliant. He didn't like having weak links in his chain.

"Dr Hodgson." Rollo shouted, "The gov has arrived. May I say, incidentally, you are looking as beautiful as ever."

Dr Grace Hodgson was just lighting a cigarette and gave Rollo a look that could kill, before offering him a fag. It was the only commonality between them.

Grace's straggly blonde hair was tied up in a failed attempt at formality. At six feet one, she cut an imposing figure, taller than Harry and could easily look Rollo in the eye. And as his inspector said, she had something about her.

"Rollo, you irritating bastard, are there no girls here you can go chase now the real gov has put in a show?" Grace said through her cigarette, as it teetered like a car on the edge of a precipice.

Rollo lit up too. "Your wish is my command. I'll leave you two to have a look at the victim in all his glory. I'm off to see the local Vicar of Dibley, she's early thirties. Worth a go." Rollo moved off towards the front entrance of the church.

Harry waved his hand to clear the pall of smoke that occluded his view of Grace.

"How are you?" he asked.

Grace sucked the life from her cigarette with one long drag, then dropped and ground it under one plastic covered boot before stashing the butt in an evidence bag full of discarded dog-ends.

"Living the dream," she said dryly. "Seriously. We've never had anything like this. Follow me."

They flowed past one incident tent and another and into the churchyard proper, down towards the wishing well, a feature he remembered from the regular fetes they held here; he usually bought tomato plants off one of the stalls. There was no fete today though, no happiness, only sorrow.

Harry stopped suddenly as the early daylight was blocked from his vision, the contrast causing him to cover his eyes.

Harry had seen many strange things during his career, and more recently in his dreams- but nothing prepared him for the horrific tableau before him.

A grassy area lay before Harry, filled with graves and memorial stones, some elaborate and beautiful, others like rotten teeth poking through the mossy green gums of the cemetery. The air smelled of dirt, as you would expect, but also of vomit and blood.

A wooden cross had been erected in the middle of the grass.

A man had been nailed to it.

The man was naked except for his underwear, middle-aged, grey hair soaked in crimson blood giving the appearance of pink dye, wispy curls blowing in the warm breeze, mirroring the weeping willow off to the left of the cross.

"As you can see it's a St Andrew's Cross rather than a Christian one. His eyes were taken, and his gag removed before he was killed, I think, although I can't be certain until I've carried out the post-mortem." She sighed. "We've got the gag for testing."

She continued, her voice sincere. "I just don't know how this was done without anyone hearing or seeing it. Even if it was constructed off-site and brought here, this is a bloody heavy thing to set up. If you look around the bottom of the cross beams, you can see the ground has been concreted and the cross seems to fit perfectly into rebates in specially made foundations. It is skilled work, prepped over a few nights at least. Fatal stroke was a knife to the sternum, and he bled out, or probably drowned from blood entering the lungs."

Harry had been in the force a long time, he'd seen many dead people in horrific situations, but this was something else. Even worse than the Leek girls? Maybe.

"Footprints?"

"Only one set, but sole-less. No imprint." She sighed again. "This is simply wrong. It's as if…"

"… he has been prevented from getting to where a dead person should be?"

"Yes. Symbollocks, as Professor Hunterton used to say on my profiler's course. Like he's been prevented from the assured dignity of a burial." Grace was more eloquent than he would ever be.

"Symbolic murder, indeed," Harry sighed, looking up at the victim. The gouged-out gaping eyeholes. The blood collecting in unnatural crow's feet around the eye sockets.

"I'd bet my mortgage on it," Grace said. "Albeit it's a shitty divorce settlement mortgage. It's bait."

Harry looked at her. So, the rumours were true, she was on her own again. She might be striking, but she was a pain in the arse to live with, as he knew only too well. He'd spent a few weeks lodging with her in Moseley, Birmingham, almost thirteen years before. Harry had just moved out of a long relationship. Grace had inherited the large house from her grandmother. They had worked on a few cases together and struck up a friendship. He loved Grace, but he could neither enter a relationship with her, nor live with her again.

"I know Bob's a friend of yours. Doesn't stop him being a house-stealing twat."

Harry held his hands up in mock surrender.

"Probably not a dignified way to conduct ourselves in front of a departed victim, Grace."

She sighed again. "Maybe not. You sensible, thoughtful man. Preliminary examination tomorrow morning. Will I see you at the Institute?"

"Me or Rollo."

"Please let it be you. You won't try to chat me up whilst I remove and weigh the deceased's lungs."

Harry made his way back to the Cold and Complex offices, deep in thought. Murder in Lichfield? They usually had to go further afield for murder. Birmingham or Derby. Now it was happening on their doorstep.

Originally a joint initiative between Staffordshire and Central Police, the Cold and Complex team had grown recently to include Derbyshire and Lincolnshire. The Lichfield offices were relatively new, based on a reclaimed site at the back of the main Eastern Avenue drag, cheap land, no doubt. His team didn't advertise themselves as being a police department. All officers were plain clothes and entirely independent of the local Staffordshire police department further up the same road, although there was plenty of liaison and partnership work.

The building was a new and half empty, a two-storey orange brick open-plan office block, with one small suite of rooms for him, his inspectors and the Super. The two inspectors who worked under Harry shared their offices with their other staff, much to their chagrin- well Rollo's chagrin, as DI Marsh was on the sick.

Gone was the time where your status was reflected in your office size. There was plenty of working space though, as the building was sensibly laid about around the plan Owain Pleasant, Harry's predecessor, had stipulated.

Maisie made a beeline for him. "Gov, any chance of a word?"

He nodded and she fell in with him as he headed for his office, immediately opening the blinds as he entered. Artificial light hurt his head. He flicked on the coffee machine, which gurgled like his stomach. The smell of coffee always relaxed visitors. Harry's visitors were usually more senior and generally vexed.

He plonked himself down. "You can sit Maisie." He smiled but she didn't catch it. She looked upset, nervous.

"Sir."

"And you can call me Harry if we are alone."

She sat down flushed. This wasn't like her. "I might need some leave soon, Sir. Harry. To go to see my parents in Spain."

"Of course. You have your entitlement. You could have asked Rollo this, though."

She let out a long sigh. "Teddy's left me. No, I threw him out. He doesn't love me anymore." She looked at him trying to fight back the tears. "You know what Rollo's like. I can't tell him about my personal life. He'll not stop mentioning it until I go out with him or knock him back. Daisy doesn't know either."

Who would call their twin daughters Daisy and Maisie?

"Tell Rollo you might want a bit of time. I'll back you up. When are you going?" He didn't want to go anywhere near the Teddy bit of the conversation unless he had to.

"I'm not sure if I am, definitely. Just wanted you to know so you understand why I'm a bit pissed off today."

"Will you be up for the PM tomorrow? Rollo and Mo are trying to track down the man's identity."

She nodded. "I'm not squeamish, just a shock seeing him like that. Oh, there's something else, gov. We've just had a delivery from Reynolds Solicitors.

Addressed to you. You'll need to sign for it in the post room.

He sighed; the coffee would have to wait.

Harry refused to open the large envelope until he was at his desk with a large mug of coffee. He'd had his late morning banana, part of his regular daily routine, then finally tore open the envelope. It was a letter on official paper, in a beautiful copperplate, accompanied by more documents in a similar hand, although evidently more aged.

Dear DCI, Morton,

The following information has been in our possession for many years and has been released to you following the receipt of an instruction from your office, regarding a client who died in 1948.

With the impending systematic appraisal of the case of the disappearance on the Thirty-First of October Nineteen Forty-Eight, of one Nancy Wright from Birmingham, a thorough review of papers belonging to George Wright has been carried out.

It seems that during the initial investigation in the late forties, papers were requested but not pursued after Mr Wright disappeared himself and his trial was shelved for lack of evidence, following a later decision from the Crown Prosecution Service.

Enclosed is the entirety of those official papers, but does not include Mr Wright's diaries, for which a warrant will be required. The official papers, should you subpoena them, also include the deeds for two properties which have been looked after by the same managing agent for well over seventy years.

The management agent has been informed that you may wish to view the property - number 42 Legend Street Edgbaston B15 9OO - which remains in the estate of Mr

George Wright, who had no known family alive at the time of issue. Whilst this office has no objection to viewing of the property, you will still have to formally issue a warrant whilst we try and establish an heir or whether the building will be received by the government as an unclaimed legacy. The additional property details will be forwarded to you; however, the address is 46 Howell Lane Dywol's Cove nr Bude.

Yours, Giles Reynolds, Solicitor.

Harry read the letter twice to ensure he had understood it and then called Maisie back in.

She entered his office looking worn, the day was obviously not getting better. He had his sympathies, but she would be better here than moping at home.

"Maisie, will you read this? Then, can you find Rollo and ask him to get over to Legend Street tomorrow – the address is referenced in the letter. Go have a look. You might want to join him if you are up to it?"

She just nodded and left the room, closing his door behind her.

He unfolded the manila cover and took out another handful of tracing paper-like correspondence. It reminded him of Izal toilet paper.

Mr Cyril Reynolds
Reynolds and Son
1176 Calthorpe Road
Edgbaston
Birmingham
B15
2nd November 1948

Dear Cyril,

I hope this finds you well. I am sorry but I am having to go away, immediately and for some time. I have a friend who needs my assistance. I wonder if you would be so kind

*as to enter into an agreement with a management agent to
secure and keep clean the properties of 42 Legend Street,
Edgbaston and 46 Howell Lane Dywol's nr Bude until I
return. I have put in trust a sum of money that could
secure their services for a hundred years if necessary,
however, I really do hope it will not take that long. If you
are wondering about the term, please do not. The attic area
is not to be accessed.*

*In the envelope enclosed are the trust details which can
be verified at the Trustee Savings Bank, 1 Calthorpe Road,
Edgbaston.*

I will be in touch.

Yours, whatever word you should put here,

George Wright Esq.

There were other documents in the folder but
nothing relating to Nancy's disappearance. Her flat
in Corporation Street had been found empty on the
1st of November 1948. George had vanished a few
days later and had never reappeared.

Maisie had asked to open the case when they had
been a little quieter over the early summer, to try and
make headway with the massive list of unsolved
cases their ally forces had sent to them. Harry
sometimes wondered what sort of beast his
predecessor Owain Pleasant had created. He must
catch up with him someday. The Cold and Complex
Team went from strength to strength, solving many
ancient and bizarre crimes, but Pleasant had set the
foundations with his "strange case" review team.

He returned to the documents. His instinct told
him this would be another dead end. They would
have a scoot around the house formerly belonging to
the Wrights and then they would be able to go no
further, no doubt.

How wrong he would be.

Chapter Five
The Woman in Yellow

Rollo was not happy. Maisie could tell. He normally didn't speak that much in the morning, but today, of all the days when she could have done with the silence, he would not shut up. She knew she had caused this case to be opened and she knew Rollo was venting about her promotion – well, in a roundabout fashion.

"I'm a DI. Not a constable," he'd spat, for the umpteenth time. "If we acted on every historic letter, we got... Look I love H, he's a great boss, but he does like his flights of fancy." He sighed. "Let's get this over with and then go for something to drink, Maisie. Hair of the dog."

The rest of the journey from Lichfield into Brum down the A38 had been torturous, he'd just rambled on. She neglected to admit she had asked to open this case. Something hadn't felt quite right.

Rolleston was one of two DIs on the Cold and Complex team; DI Marsh, who was a complete control freaking cow-bag, thankfully was on long-term sick. She *was* extremely sick though.

Rollo was okay, Maisie mused, despite his bouts of silence, the perving over every woman and the obvious complexity of his ever-chugging genius brain. Yes, he was opinionated and self-assured, but he was also wise and quite a good copper. Just a complete letch. Today, he looked more tired than ever. Clearly still burning the candle at both ends - hitting the pop and shagging whatever fell for his chat.

Maisie pulled into Legend Street, a road brimming with three-storey townhouses and slipped the automatic BMW into park. Number 42 appeared very normal. She had expected a yawning Stephen King-style wreck; but it was in excellent nick.

The agent was standing on the drive in a hard-hat, holding two other hats in her hand. She looked about forty and too thin for her clothes.

Maisie did not wait for Rollo but leapt out of the car into the close grey morning. It had just started to spot with warm rain.

"Hi, DS Price?"

"Hello, Miss Barnes, thanks for meeting us here."

Rollo strode straight past them both and muttered "I'm not wearing a hat." He was really not in a good mood.

"Sir, I must insist. Its health and safety. The integrity of the house remains unchecked."

"No hats. And you aren't coming in. My warrant gives the DS and me access, not you. Keys please."

Miss Barnes looked at Maisie but all she could do was shrug her shoulders. Rollo was the gov today.

Miss Barnes held out the keys. "The Yale's the front door. I believe the Chubb lock is for the outhouses and the small key is for the loft access lock- it's padlocked. Looking at the plans, the attic's quite extensive too."

"Kindly wait here, or go for a coffee, we might be a while." Rollo offered a kind smile, but it didn't reach his eyes.

Maisie raised her eyebrows but took the keys. "Whatever we find and further warrants we have applied for may impact upon whether we keep the keys or not."

Miss Barnes nodded, shot a half-angry look at Rollo and went to find her car.

"Yapping on about health and safety and those poxy hats. Not as fit as she thinks. " Rollo offered. "Would you do the honours?"

Maisie inserted the key in the front door, which had expanded in the frame a little. Rollo gave it a shove with one hand, and it not only opened but bounced off the right-hand hallway wall.

It was a long hallway that stretched past a flight of open, carpeted stairs with an elaborate banister.

The floor was a mosaic of red and blue tiles. What was clear was this house had not been lived in recently, but people had been in to clean. *Hopefully with hard hats on*, Maisie thought.

There was a huge pile of post on a side table, some of it ancient by the looks of it. An old black Bakelite phone sat upon the ornate phone table with Queen Anne legs. The velvet seat looked brand new. Someone was carefully keeping the place free from dust and dirt.

They explored further. There were two reception rooms on either side of the stairs, each with a varnished oak door, one to the left next to the phone table and another to their immediate right. Rollo took the left-hand room; she took the right. She turned the square handle and the door creaked open.

The room was dark. Large, crushed velvet lined curtains kept out most of the light, a single chink slicing a mote-casting beam upon a long dining table, surrounded by chairs upholstered to match the curtains. The table was set as if awaiting a planned, but long-since forgotten meal. The rest of the crockery was housed upon a large tallboy, with six equal drawers which would have held spare cutlery, table settings and napkins no doubt. There was nothing else in the room. It had no other exits.

"Clear," Rollo shouted from the other room. "Clear" she concurred. "I'll do upstairs, gov."

"I'll carry on down here. Shout if needs be."

Each stair creaked like an old ship's decking, she thought, despite the thick Axminster carpet held in place by ancient-looking brass runners that were shiny-new.

The stairs turned left or right through ninety degrees either way. A large stained-glass window of yellows, blues and greens depicting a sunrise over a waving sea - cast patterns from both sides of the stairwell.

Maisie took the right-hand turn and at the top appeared a corridor of rooms. She could have

50

continued up another set of stairs that appeared opposite her on the landing, but she decided to try out the first-floor rooms.

The first was a traditional bathroom, tiled enamelled white. Royal Doulton at its best. No towels or toiletries.

She approached the next room, guessing it must be a bedroom and was amused to realised that, instinctively, she'd knocked on the door before opening it. She was well brought up. Let the ghosts know I'm coming; in case they were in a state of undress.

The bedroom was empty. The shutters were locked, but light permeated through narrow cracks and dappled across the varnished floorboards.

George Wright had lived here with Nancy. What had happened to her? To him? Would they ever find any clues to their disappearance?

The house was nicely proportioned, immaculate. What had gone on here? She could have happily lived here with Teddy, once upon a time. *God, I'm sounding like a shitty fairy tale now.*

With thoughts of Teddy temporarily banished, she zoned back in on her search. Absolutely nothing here other than a beautiful, well-maintained time capsule.

She headed back to the stairs. There were another two bedrooms on the opposite side of the first floor. She checked both, they were the same as the first. No furniture. Had George lived here since 1948? Had it been cleared out, was he about to receive new bedroom furniture just before he died? In 1948, surely Nancy's womanly, know-your-place touch would have been all over this house? *Ugh, sexist.*

Suddenly she heard a door slam. It dragged her from her rational mind into her irrational thoughts. *Ghosts? No. Squatter? Too clean. Cleaner?*

She raced out of the room, back onto the stairwell and the turning landing, nearly colliding with a young woman. Maisie screamed, uncharacteristically. It was the shock.

The woman also screamed shrilly and was off down the stairs like a whippet after a rabbit. A yellow blur, trying to land each step in high heels that matched her outfit and hair bow, Maisie in hot pursuit.

"Gov. We've got a runner!"

The woman had reached the front door and was struggling to open it. Throwing a glance back to Maisie descending the stairs, fear was clearly etched on her face. She was beautiful, not a hair out of place. Where had she come from? Why was she here? Was she the one keeping the house clean? What had happened to the house after George Wright had died?

"Stop. I'm a police officer."

Maisie was nearly down the stairs, as Rollo entered the hall, but the woman wrestled the door open and she was out into the street, slamming the door behind her. Maisie yanked the door open and spilled out into the street, looking this way and that. The woman had apparently disappeared. Where had she gone? *I couldn't have run that fast in heels.*

"What was all the screaming about?" Rollo had sauntered to her aid and caught up with her by now.

"Woman in yellow. She was on the landing. Did you not see her?"

"I didn't see anyone, sergeant. I didn't hear anyone, either."

"She was in a yellow 1940s A-line skirt, golden bow in her hair with matching shoes? She looked straight at you, Guv."

"Are you taking the piss?"

"Well…" She started, but then thought better of it. "I saw her. She screamed. I screamed. Then she ran down the stairs and I followed. She looked at you. I swear it." *What the hell was going on?*

"You look tired, sergeant. Let's finish up here and we'll go and get something to drink."

Maisie nodded. *Had she imagined the woman? Was this the start of an emotional episode? A breakdown?*

"I was right down the other end of the hall. My line of vision was blocked. I did hear the door slam. I probably just missed her. We'll put out an APB call. I don't think you are crazy."

But for a split second, she thought he didn't mean it. His face looked conflicted, pained. Then the events of the afternoon overtook them.

An hour later, they were in the attic of number 42. They had searched all the rooms in the house and associated outhouses and stables.

It was a large, expansive attic, floor-boarded, filled with chests and boxes. Here and there were tailor's mannequins half-lit by the sunshine that carved through little cracks in beams, illuminating them like an undisciplined Midas.

The wall at the opposite end to the entrance was solid.

"It seems there's nothing else here." Toys and games mostly, clothes and shoes too. All years old.

Rollo was eye to eye with one of the dummies as she looked up. "It's not big enough," he said pushing the dressmaker's dummy away from him on its castors. Her nan had one; she had been a tailor's assistant as a girl, and she'd kept up her dress-making skills for years.

"Sorry?" she asked, only half catching what he said, lost in thoughts of Nanna Price, who would have loved this house.

"Each house is about forty feet across. There is only about eighty feet of space here. There has to be a false wall."

Rollo made his way through the attic. One of the skylight beams split him in two momentarily; Maisie followed, feeling the radiating heat momentarily bathe her skin, even though her clothes.

Rollo was at the far wall. It was made up of yellowing plaster in between the beams. There was no visible door.

"There's got to be at least two times this space behind here." He began to tap. She took out her pencil torch and shone it around, illuminating a series of archways. They looked like they had been made by the coming together of the apex of supporting beams, one after the other. The one she had her torch on didn't look quite right, somehow. Darker, maybe?

"Gov. Look."

Rollo joined her, so close that she felt his breath upon her neck. She shivered for some reason, even in that heat. He moved in front of her and started to tap the floor with his shoe.

"Check for a springboard. It might have a switch under it. Hang on- got it."

With an initial creak, the archway swung inwards with a moaning groan. *Not at all creepy.*

Rollo went in after he had clicked his own torch into life, Maisie right behind.

"How did you...?"

Rollo grinned. "History major. I did my dissertation on Tudor houses. Some of them had priest hidey holes."

There were no skylights in this part of the attic, but it was also broken up by stud walls. The initial twenty feet or so was alcove after alcove of nothing. She followed Rollo into another space. That was when it started to get sinister.

A large table appeared out of the gloom. Made of porcelain or enamel, purest white. It had holes at either end which sat over two metal drip trays. Next to the table was a set of instruments, tools, they looked medical. *Shit. A post-mortem slab.*

"That was unexpected," Rollo said and then disappeared into the gloom again. She tried to keep pace, but it seemed that Rollo had gone down a corridor, stud-walled again, but much narrower.

54

"Take the room on the right, *Sergeant*," Rollo hissed. "I'll do the left."

Dick, he knows I'll be an inspector soon. Putting the little woman in her place.

She reached an unpainted wooden door. She took a deep breath and opened it.

She was hit by a terrible sickly smell. The stench of meat from a butcher's shop on a hot day. There was a chemical tinge in the air too - a thick, cloying miasma.

The door behind her slammed. Her torch went out.

"Shit." Her batteries must failed. She had spares somewhere in her pocket. *Be prepared. Gosh, where did that come from?* Maisie was struck with a pervading sense of danger.

Blindly, she felt her way to opening the torch battery housing and as it was a single battery the changeover was easy. She clicked the beam back on and raised it to eye level. Then for the second time that day, she screamed like a soon-to-be victim in a horror film.

There was a face looking back at her. A face looking out from a head, upon a naked body that was dead and preserved in some form of liquid in a large glass tank. It was a woman, that much was evident. The liquid was viscous and yellow, but her view of the deceased wasn't occluded. Maisie realised the dead woman had no eyes. She looked left then right and gasped. They were all missing their eyes. There were six of them in the tanks. Six silent, eyeless statues.

She dry-heaved noisily, just as Rollo entered the space.

"Don't puke on me." Rollo's torch illuminated the room and its contents. "Dear God."

By now, Maisie had noted that there were more of those separate tanks lining the walls of the room, they could have housed many more dead.

Without another word, Rollo disappeared again, leaving her in the room with those well-preserved, eyeless corpses.

When he returned, moments later, he was grim-faced. "There's another room of empty tanks. And another one full of jars. Six of them with two eyes in each."

An hour later she was perched on the low garden wall of the property, drinking sweet tea. DC Pete Miles had arrived the soonest, and had gone off to a café around the corner as soon as he saw Maisie's pallid face. Rollo, stoic as ever was leaning on the car, having a fag while on the phone. Harry would most likely have his head in his hands. A crucifixion in Lichfield and now this. All of them with their eyes missing. Surely there was a link? It was certainly becoming a week to remember. *Wait till I tell Teddy.*

No.

Maisie thought about the woman in yellow. She had put a call out to the local Central Police team; a grumpy desk sergeant had promised to pass the issue on.

Then she'd phoned her sister. Daisy had always been the pragmatic one. Surely the woman in yellow was the cleaner? Maisie could sense that something had upset her twin – and it wasn't just that Maisie had pointed out no-one cleans in their best clothes. Her mother had spilled the beans about Teddy and Daisy was angry that she hadn't been the first to know. "Twin to twin first," Daisy had repeated and again, as Maisie got more and more wound up.

"Bitch," she said aloud.

"You okay, Sarge?"

Pete Miles was a massive bloke, but a lovely lad. For a moment she wondered what his strong arms would feel like wrapped around her. Then she broke out of her inappropriate thoughts. He must be about twelve.

"Sorry Pete. Family issues."

"Enough said." Pete flashed a Cheshire cat smile at her. A beautiful smile.

"Your tea all right?" He asked kindly. His Lichfield tones were reassuring and familiar, a mixture of Brummie and something a bit more northern.

"Had a row with my brother the other night about whether there had been three or four Bee Gees."

She couldn't help but smile. Why was a twenty-odd-year-old man discussing the Bee Gees with his brother?

"Stayin' Alive is on one of the PlayStation racing games he was playing. He reckoned there had been four Bee Gees. One of them died. I said there were three and two of them had died, the twins. He got all shitty and started to skim CDs at me. He might be only thirteen, but he's a bugger."

She laughed aloud. It was a bit of inane conversation, sure, but it was someone to talk to. With Teddy gone, she had felt so alone in her flat. And now Daisy was being a cow and after the events of the last few days and the horrific things she had seen…

"There were four Bee Gees, Pete. Three in the main group and their brother Andy." She drained her cardboard cup and put the plastic lid back on.

"Yep, I Googled them last night. I'm not going to tell him he's right until he apologises. Look!" Pete pointed to the side of his face, where there was a V-shaped cut. "Do you have any idea how much the edge of a CD hurts?"

She laughed again and then wondered what it would be like to touch the cheek of the big man in front of her…

"I'm finishing in a bit. Rollo wanted to go for a drink but he's trying to crack onto the local team's inspector. Do you fancy a pint back in Lichfield?"

"I don't actually drink alcohol in the week when I'm weight training. But yes, I'll come for a quick non-alcoholic drink. Need to get that horrible formaldehyde taste out of my mouth. You can buy, sarge-nearly-inspector, you're the one with the stripes."

"Tap water it is then, Constable."

Chapter Six
Legend Street

Grace was driving Harry to Legend Street.

Harry had been in with his Chief Superintendent, Claudine Taylor, discussing the crucifixion case, when he got the call about the preserved bodies in Edgbaston.

Rollo had been as descriptive as ever. *Bodies in big jars - come and have a look. Never seen anything like it. I've said that twice in two days too. Bring Grace and you'll probably need that other one. Posh one? Horace? He'll love this."*

Mo was waiting for Harry outside the house in Edgbaston, on the evening liaison shift with PC Crabbe from Central Police. Harry had wanted one of his team close to this, but the locals weren't having any of it.

Luckily, he knew Ian Crabbe. Crabby was an eternal constable. In his late thirties, he had just plodded along avoiding promotion like it was a terminal illness.

"A royal visit." Harry couldn't help but smile at Crabby's irreverence.

"Evening Crabs. Still climbing the corporate ladder, I see." Harry's smiled at his old friend. Ian Crabbe had taught him how to be a decent copper; as brilliant as some of his high-flying colleagues, but he liked a simpler life: the pub, going to the football, and checking his fantasy team score before he even looked at police work for the day.

"How's El?" Crabbe asked, crushing Harry's fingers in that strong grip as they shook.

"Who the hell is he?" Harry heard Horace Parkes ask Grace in his cut-glass tones. Horace was a public-school boy who had been wrapped up in cotton wool, until he embarked upon his career as a forensic officer backing up the Institute's pathology team. He spoke with at least three plums in his mouth.

"He's a good man. One of the best." Grace answered, lighting up and offering a cigarette to Crabbe who took it with a nod of his head.

"Right," Horace pulled a protective suit out of his over-sized bag.

Mo Hyatt began his brief. "I've not seen anything like this Guv, well since yesterday at least. It's horrible. Maisie and Rollo found them." Mo didn't want to be here, looked like he might retch if he thought about things too much, so Harry cut him off.

"I've already spoken to Rolleston; I'll check in with DS Price tomorrow. Can we go in?"

"Suited and plastic booted." DS Hyatt responded, pointing to a bag on the ground. "I've already been slapped by the SOCOs." Horace and Grace had donned their gloves, suits and shoe covers and were ready to go in.

Grace and Parkes moved inside the house. It was well-lit now. Operations had connected bright incident lights to the mains, blowing the 1930's ring main, so now the put-put of a portable generator provided the soundtrack, as Crabbe followed them in to show them the way.

Mo put his hand on Harry's arm. "Hope you don't mind me saying, Sir, but Maisie, DS Price I mean, will need a bit of support. Said she saw someone flee the scene, but Rollo's denying it. She's a bit flat."

Harry sighed. *Bloody Rollo, he's winding everyone up at the moment.* "Okay, Mo. Noted. You're keeping a watch tonight whilst the SOCOs work?"

Mo nodded.

"More will arrive. There are six bodies to get back to the Institute." He patted his junior colleague on his shoulder before moving into the house.

"Take tomorrow off, or come in late Mo. I know what you are like with the overtime. I'm not sure I'll have any budget left by Christmas."

Mo laughed, good-naturedly. They were a close team, and they knew each other well, had grown together. DS Hyatt was the embodiment of that. An incredibly professional and thoughtful man; he'd watch the site like a hawk, surveying its surroundings, watching its prey.

Rollo and Mo were right; Harry had never seen anything like it. Six adults, eyes removed, suspended in a viscous liquid in glass tubes, preserved for who knows how long. He couldn't even imagine how this had come to be. How long had they been there? *God help them.*

There was, however, nothing of God about the setting. Under the glare of the big temporary lights, the ghoulish nature of the scene was accentuated. The growing heat of the lingering Indian summer made it stifling up in the attic. The arc lights in the loft space were also contributing to the sweat rings under his arms- and a new headache. He would have to report into the Chief Constable just in case anyone leaked anything to the press. He could vouch for his people, but he couldn't be so sure about the local team, or Grace's lot.

One after another he looked at each of the dead, his sorrow growing face by eyeless face. The bodies were like waxworks, like yellowing Greco-Roman statues. So very well-preserved, you might think they were sleeping, if they'd still possessed their eyes. His own eyes drifted to the nearest victim.

The woman looked strangely peaceful. Not like the man they had cut down off the cross the day before. Harry hoped the eye removal had been achieved post-mortem; he was grateful she couldn't look back at him. He had seen the dead many times in his job, even in his various lucid dreams, never like this. It was as if they had volunteered to die. No visible trauma wounds about their necks or bodies. How the hell were Grace and her team going to get them out? How could they protect the dignity of these sleeping naked statues from the media scrutiny that would inevitably descend? It would only be hours before this was all over the internet, no doubt.

"Thought I'd seen it all," Grace said, almost choking with emotion. He had never seen her so moved. "I've picked up bits of children after car accidents, excavated war graves, but this? Collected like specimens, murdered presumably, their eyes removed and placed in glass jars. How has this gone unnoticed? Slap bang in suburban Birmingham, for however long?" Grace smelt more strongly of smoke than usual. She had always chain-smoked in times of stress: when her exams had been approaching, when she had gone to interviews, or after she had ended a brief fling with someone.

"Any ideas?" he asked, breaking his own thoughts.

"Shouldn't be so well-preserved. Even in a preserving liquid, there is always decomposition. I do think they have been here a long time. Their clothes have been recovered - wrapped up in paper parcels, as if they were going to be sent back to their homes, possibly to their families. The garments need to be dated, but I would say they range from the late 1930s to the latter part of the 1940s. Whoever did this did it without being disturbed. They built this preservation site up here." She ripped off a latex glove and pulled her now-gloveless left hand through her hair. "Where the hell do you buy glass tanks or tubes that big? How did they get the preservative chemicals in such quantities? We are going to have to draft more staff in. I need another pathologist, forensic scientists, technicians. And we still have to do the work on your namesake."

"Who?"

Another wave of stale smoke hit him as she exhaled. "Angus Morton. Our crucified man.

Reported missing by his wife. They were visiting relatives in the Midlands."

"You think they're linked? But the time lapse…" He looked back at the eyeless woman, a creeping horror building in his guts.

"He had his eyes removed, too."

The woman moved very, very slowly in the liquid, a dance of death, slow like the movements of tectonic plates, her hair flowing about her as if she were in the vacuum of space - as if her eyes had shattered in that cold and deadly place.

"Morton worked for a funeral home. Up in Fife." Grace continued. Harry felt a growing unease.

"Morton. Why couldn't he have been called something else?"

"Coincidence, Harry? And how dare he die on our patch the bastard? Come on H." She was worked up now.

"There's about to be a shitstorm. Be easier without the press pointing out I share a surname with that of the victim. Not to mention linking the modus operandi of Angus's killer to six dead preserved bodies here."

"Worried about leaks?"

"Someone has tipped the press off about Martin Leek removing his own eyes. Another link Joe Public might question?"

"Leek was a nutter, there's nothing to link him to this case. There needs to be a lockdown on this, then. We've got to get six people in body bags out of this house by morning. I'll talk to comms over at Central."

"I'll get uniform to go house to house tomorrow, but in the meantime, let's temporarily evacuate the immediate area."

"Good luck with that."

"Rivers," the voice filtered through Harry's hands-free system.

"Sir, It's Harry Morton." He was ready for the barrage he knew he would get. He'd stayed at the scene most of the night with Grace. He'd pissed off Ellen, Claudine and probably the CC by not putting the calls in. It was now nearly six in the morning, and he was driving home from his departmental offices.

"Why the fuck did you not call me before now? Have you no awareness, Morton, of how this is going to look, off the back of the Lichfield murder? Leek pulling his eyes out, then Angus Morton, then six bodies with missing eyes."

"We have twelve of the eyes Sir, in jars." He regretted saying it as soon as it left his lips. What a stupid thing to say. Thankfully, Rivers was just ranting and not listening.

"It was a good job it was Claudine who got to me first and not the Birmingham Mail."

Harry knew exactly how it looked; he had some sympathy for Martin Rivers, who would have to pull the curtains on the press over the house in Edgbaston. Nonetheless, he felt his hackles rising.

Thank God Claudine was supportive. He would have to buy her a drink, dinner, maybe. He had, after all, failed to brief her too.

"Look, Harry. You and I go back a long way. Your father and I were- are- good friends. However, the high profile you have nurtured around your department will not help when this lands. People will want answers. The people of that street, of Edgbaston, of Birmingham, will want to know why there have been dead people under their feet, over their heads, for God knows however many fucking years, despite us having had the case files on the homeowner for most of that time. Not to mention how the fuck someone constructed a crucifix in the church grounds of a suburban area of Lichfield. Cement foundations, for fuck's sake." As ever, the staccato delivery of Dalek-like proportions rose at the end in a stunning crescendo.

"Sir. We will need to lock it down."

"The crucifixion is out of the bag, son. The Express and Star have already splashed it. One of the residents had provided a lovely shot of it, both with and without the body. Staffs CC Tim Rogers is spitting feathers. He wasn't briefed either, so I've got to kiss and make-up with him too, with tongues. Sort out your fucking comms, Morton. Or I'll have to hand it over to them. I needed a pair of clean hands after Pleasant dropped himself in the shit, marrying Cobden's daughter. You don't have the luxury of failure too. Not on my watch. Solve this, Harry. You can have what you need but don't drag it out. I'm no moneybags."

Rivers rang off. It was a matter of seconds before his phone was ringing again. It was Ellen. The beautiful photo from their first date came up on his phone screen. He swiped to answer.

"Morning, stranger." She spoke. "You nearly home?"

"Yes, you off to work?"

"Unfortunately. I've put some coffee on. You will get some sleep, won't you?"

He laughed. "Try and stop me. I'm dead on my feet."

"You don't sleep enough. What with the nightmares and all?"

"I know sweetie. I will try."

"Good. I'll be back by four. Will you be home?"

"Possibly not."

"Don't forget we are going to see your dad. The care home called last night. They want a word about the funding."

"Okay." He said not wanting to think about that any more than he had to, or he would never sleep.

"Got to go. Bye. Love you."

"Love you."

His angel.

Maisie woke with a start, goose bumps on her naked flesh, despite the Indian Summer morning heat that caressed her like a lover's breath from the half-open window. She could feel something touching her back, so she turned to look at Teddy. They must have made up the night before. Although through a foggy head, she couldn't be sure why they had made up. He had dumped her, and she had promised herself she wouldn't do *that* with Teddy again.

The duvet was in the way of his head, but she could feel the warm nakedness next to her own skin. She put out her hand and touched something hard, a broad naked back. Then she realised it couldn't possibly be Teddy. Teddy was flabby, and he had left her.

Then it came back. Drinks after work. Shit. It was Pete Miles. Detective Constable Peter Miles. One of her subordinates.

Bollocks. Her hand recoiled in horror.

A handsome face appeared, angular and strong, dark hair a mess. A chiselled face like the statue of a Greek god loomed into view. *Greek god, where the fuck had that come from? Oh god, what would Daisy say?* Daisy had gushed about Pete when he had arrived.

"Morning." he said, sleepily. As if this was the most natural thing in the world. Shagging a senior officer and just popping up from the duvet afterwards to say "morning."

Double bollocky-shit-bags.

"Do you know how many rules I've broken?" she offered. He shrugged, a smug smile creeping across his lips. She threw back the duvet and revealed rather too much of their bodies than she could cope with. Twisting away from Pete, she sat up, her back to him. Embarrassment and self-consciousness were riding over her in waves, adding to the headache and nausea of a half-remembered night that had ended up with downed shots, lots of them and a forgotten shag. Only she had drank the shots though. He had only been drinking coke.

"You haven't done anything wrong. We were off duty. We're consenting adults."

"Pete, you are about twelve."

"I'm only two years younger than you. I just have good skin."

"A recruit in my team. Thankfully, I'm not your line manager."

"I won't say anything." He had got up, naked, without a care in the world and came and sat beside her. He put his naked arm around her naked shoulder. She so wanted to shake his arm off. It was wrong. Yet so right. *What about Teddy?* One half of her brain asked. *Fuck Teddy*, the other side answered.

"We're going to be late for the briefing. I'll drop you home to get a change of clothes. We will have to talk about this later," she said, trying to retrieve some sense of authority.

He turned her head with his hand and looked into her eyes. *This is wrong.* Then he kissed her.

They both missed the briefing that morning.

Maisie was thankful her sister had gone to Fife the previous evening with Rollo, to liaise with the family of Angus Morton. Morton's wife was understandably in a bad way; she'd had to be sedated during the visit apparently.

Maisie swung by DCI Morton's office, peering through the glass before she knocked on the door. He was sitting with his head in his hands, coffee cups and paper breeding upon his normally tidy desk. She glanced at the clock. It was just after eleven; he could only have had four hours sleep at most. He looked dreadful: eyes were ringed like a panda, normally well-groomed face culturing dark stubble, ash-blond hair a tousled mess.

"Morning, Price. Hope you got more sleep than I did. Rollo said you might be late. Shut the door."

How the hell did Rollo know she would be late in? Then she recalled him telling her to miss the briefing and come in later. Her brain was as furred as her mouth. He gestured for her to sit, poured her a coffee and handed it to her.

"Firstly, those two crime scenes you've been exposed to were horrific. The Edgbaston scene was one of the worst I have ever had the misfortune to witness. How are you bearing up? I've asked Rollo to set up some counselling."

"The soft squad? Thanks a lot, Sir." she said ironically,

He smiled picking up on her intonation. "Come on Maisie, don't knock it."

"Never mind that, Harry. I saw someone at the scene. A woman in yellow. Her clothes were kind of vintage looking. Just like the clothes recovered at the scene." There. It was blurted out.

"A cleaner?" He thought about how a woman in yellow clothing had featured in one of his dreams recently.

"She was immaculate. Like she was going to a party. Unless she had some matching yellow marigolds and a duster in her pocket." Maisie began to twitch her leg up and down, almost spilling her lukewarm coffee. "Rollo didn't believe me. Thought I was mad."

"Rollo is getting all the shit jobs now and he's a little brusquer than ever, if that's possible."

"I saw her, as plain as I can see you. Rollo accused me of being tired, insinuated I imagined her. What about you, Harry? Do you agree with him?"

"I've asked Central to pull surrounding CCTV and do a house to house in the area. I've got comms to drop something surreptitiously into the press, see if we can trace her. I believe you, Maisie."

"Thanks." She let out a great big sigh.

"With Rollo away, I need someone to attend the PM with me on Angus Morton. Are you up to it?"

She nodded appreciatively.

"And I've got some good news. I've had Marsh's resignation. I've approved your promotion to begin in a week or so. Taylor just needs to sort the budget."

Maisie clearly wasn't expecting that. She seemed elated, but also a little deflated.

"Maisie. You, okay?"

"What? Oh sorry. Yes, I'm made up," she said.

"Good," he said with a confused smile on his face.

The PM room at the Institute was all white walls and grey floors, as if the dead were not allowed colour. There were three stainless steel mortuary tables, each with a trestle side-table laden with equipment. Two of the mortuary tables were empty. On the first lay Angus Morton, the naked old man, with only a small towel covering his dignity. He looked pale in death, as you would expect. His eyelids were closed thankfully. They had not recovered his eyes at the scene.

Harry looked at Maisie, who was sitting writing notes, seated at a table in the viewing lounge. She was as professional as ever; her conduct this morning proved he was right to have recommended her for the exams. Her questions had been sensible and to the point. They had been there for over four hours.

It had been a long morning.

The door opened and Grace entered. She had changed out of her scrubs and was now in her civvies. Blues and greens, jeans tucked into long boots.

"Quite straightforward then. He died about two days ago, about three hours before he was put upon that cross, judging by the pooling of blood in his body. Killed by one heavy knife blow to the sternum. He would have bled heavily for a short while. It's likely his eyes were removed as he lay dying. They were removed perfectly. Possibly by someone who knows what they are doing or someone who has watched a particularly good YouTube video."

Harry noticed Maisie shaking her head. As ever, Grace was courting controversy. They had argued many times over this in the past; today, he chose to ignore it. Grace had six other bodies to get through and he needed her to keep up her momentum; he bit his tongue accordingly.

"Any ideas why him? A mortuary assistant from a funeral home?" Grace asked. Maisie had put down her pen.

He noted she hadn't said *with the same surname as you*. Grace wasn't stupid; she would be wondering.

"Rollo has gone up to Fife to speak to the family, try and get more detail. All we know about his movements was that Angus was visiting relatives. He went out for a pint on his own and did not come back. His wife didn't know he was missing; he quite often came down to visit his elderly aunt. He had Power of Attorney over her health and finances. Maisie will set up an incident room for this case and the six other people we have found. She will be here for the ongoing tests along with Rollo when he gets back."

He suddenly felt a sharp pain in his head, and he winced. Grace raised an eyebrow.

"I think it's long past our clocking off time. I've got to get home." He needed to go and visit his adoptive father. "Maisie, are you off?"

She nodded. "Once I've checked in with Rollo. I'll make a start on the incident room tomorrow."

"Good. Grace- I'll see you later this week once we know a bit more about the people from the attic."

"Say hello to your dad. I need a fag."

Walter "Wally" Smart was the man who had taken in a seventeen-year-old homeless lad he had found with a severe head injury one day in Lichfield Cathedral. Many said Harry had probably climbed up into the choir and thrown himself off to commit suicide. Wally disagreed.

Wally had been a DCSI at the time and was lambasted for his actions. Nevertheless, Wally had risen to the rank of Chief Constable and until only recently, was Deputy then Acting Commissioner. Early-onset dementia had ripped Wally's life apart just eighteen months ago. Joan, Harry's adopted mother, had died three years before the start of Wally's decline. The grief had probably stolen Wally's memories and functional ability to live.

Harry looked at his dad. Wally was staring vacantly into the unknown distance. A trail of drool ran down the side of his mouth, residue from the cup of tea that Harry had given to him with the help of a two-handled plastic safety cup.

Ellen had her hand on his back, as supportive as ever.

Harry wasn't legally adopted; he had taken up the offer to live with the Smarts after he had reached his majority. It was good he had been able to choose. Those few weeks as a seventeen-year-old in the hostel had been difficult and dangerous. Of course, the officials had only guessed he was seventeen. They couldn't be sure. If they had said eighteen, he would have avoided a year of physical and mental abuse.

The nursing home dayroom was scattered with people like his dad, sitting in a square of chairs of varying types and colours, as random as the lives of those they seated. The television dealt out episodes of old programmes from ITV3; with the radio on too, albeit quietly, it was an annoying cacophony only cognitive dissonance could keep at bay.

A care assistant came over to let them know that it was time for Wally to be showered and readied for bed. They had got there later than usual; many of the old folks had been taken away for their evening ablutions already.

Harry got up from his plastic chair to give his dad a hug when the old man grabbed hold of him and whispered in his ear.

"Edith. She is here."

Harry pulled away to look at his dad to see if there was anything else forthcoming. Wally Smart's face had its usual vacant expression.

In the car on the way home, Harry was bemused. Who was this, Edith? He'd already checked with the care home – no one of that name currently there. His father had no relatives called Edith; he'd established that with a quick call to Patrick, an ageing cousin who had a subscription to Ancestry and was tracing the family tree.

"Penny for them." Ellen broke through his pensiveness, like a healing balm. "What did Wally say to you?"

"It was nonsense, love." He felt instantly terrible in the lie; but he was trying and failing to internalise the coincidence of him shouting a name out in his sleep and his father whispering the same name to him in turn.

"You've had a difficult week. Let's go and get something to eat. My treat. I'm off rota tomorrow- I can have a lie-in." She sang the last three words as a taunt.

"Cow," he laughed - and she laughed along with him.

Chapter Seven
A Jar of Eyes

The early hours were still warm, even though it was well into October. The Indian summer had bleached the grass and cracked the roads; they'd only just lifted the hosepipe ban. According to the forecasters, the following week would be even warmer still.

The man who had assumed Marcus's identity had left the house in Small Heath and had travelled in papa Marco's car towards Lichfield. The Magpie had taken good care of the car too; it was quite classy to have such a vehicle when one looked like Marcus. People often looked twice. If he had been minded, he could have taken advantage of many of those looks. But it wasn't often that sexual activity figured as part of his plan.

The Magpie had a lock-up on one of the industrial estates by Trent Valley railway station. There he kept equipment and other bits and pieces – and it was there that he stored Marcus's car. He swapped it for a little yellow Vauxhall Corsa, which he used whilst he was out and about around Lichfield.

The Magpie had been feeling tired. It was not surprising. He had been travelling backwards and forwards from Birmingham to Lichfield with little sleep in between his nocturnal and daytime activities. That crucifix had been difficult to set up and he had been discovered quite early on; but thankfully the old curate had a short-term memory issue and would have forgotten him cementing in the foundations in the ground by now, especially after Lady Bell's doctor had paid him a visit.

He had subsequently locked Marcus' house up as his plans would keep him in Lichfield for the time being.

The Magpie changed out of Marcus's clothes into plain, black overalls; he'd swap them for his everyday things later. The Magpie liked to be tidy and organised, so he began to arrange the items he would need for the coming few days.

Standing upon an Avery filing cabinet at the back of the lock-up was a safe. He followed the combination from memory, turning the dial this way and that until the tumblers clicked and he could pull down the handle. He had dropped the lock-up shutters, so anyone about this early - or late depending on your view - would not attempt to enter.

He pulled opened the heavy safe door to reveal his latest collection. He had others, but they were in safe keeping elsewhere. Upon the top shelf were three jars. Two were empty but the third held, suspended in fluid, a pair of eyes. The eyes of Angus Morton.

"Morning, Angus." He spoke aloud, in a clear voice, as if the recently deceased Angus were in the lock-up with him. He took out the jar and offered up a prayer. Not to God, but to fate. A fate that he hoped would see him mete out justice to his enemy. Harry Morton. That was his secret plan - and the less Lady Bell knew about it, the better.

"Just going to put you in a bag for a bit, Angus. Don't worry about the dark. Won't be for long."

He pulled up his black hoodie, even though it was far too warm; it would give him more cover in the half-light, less identity for any computerised CCTV to search against. It was part of the costume of the Magpie.

He switched to his black trainers, putting the ancient Sambas under a bench and found an old Adidas bag he used for such occasions. He put the jar into his bag, closed the safe using the handle, then spun the dial. He reached towards a bookcase that sat next to an old hat stand, pulled out a roll of plastic from a shelf and stashed it under one arm.

He had soon locked up and was on his way in his yellow car across Lichfield. Eventually, he would head onto the A38 towards Burton; his destination the maternity wing of Queens Hospital, but not before he stopped off at Chrissy Parson's house on the Victoria estate, to lay a few sheets of plastic on the living room floor.

Chrissy was tired. The evening shift had been a busy one. Life as a midwife was like that, always on call, always ready to jump into action when you were needed. Babies rarely picked the best times to arrive.

It was twenty past ten, her night was nominally over, and she was ready to go home. Her routine took her past the vending machine to get a can of Diet Coke to drink on the journey back, as well as a little bit of chocolate.

Chrissy had been a midwife for seven years and enjoyed it most of the time. Sometimes the job could be incredibly poignant; miscarriages, still-birth and health complications - but most of the time it was utterly joyful. It was a bit pants working for the NHS with a pay freeze, and the worst of COVID, but the love of it kept her going.

Whistling the latest Take That tune which had been rattling around the wards earlier that evening, she made her way out of the hospital and turned right, walking the hundred or so yards back to her vehicle in the staff car park. She undid her cardigan. It was unusually warm outside. Normally you felt the cold, coming off duty at this time of the year.

She blipped her car when she was quite far away from it, so she could run and jump in should there be anyone following her. It was all fear fuelling fantasy; in all the years she had worked at Queens, no-one had approached her after a night shift.

The inside of the car was stifling. How could that be? Maybe it had been so hot in the day that the night hadn't had made any difference at all yet.

She wound down both front windows and slid the key into the ignition, having to react quickly to turn down the speaker volume at such a late, or early hour- depending upon how you looked at it. Again, it was Take That on the radio. She should order the album from Amazon. It would piss Rob off, if nothing else. Make a change from Pink Floyd.

She stuck her card into the exit barrier, and it swung open. She pulled down the exit slipway, passing only one other car that let her go by at the narrow point of the road. Some people were still kind. Chrissy did not notice that the car, a yellow one, followed her most of the way back to Victoria Park. Her new-ish house had been built on the site of the old maternity hospital, where she had once been a trainee healthcare assistant.

The Magpie had overtaken Chrissy's car partway down the A38, near Alrewas and had been careful not to pass her on camera. He had been watching her for weeks and he now knew she was a dawdler, hesitant maybe. Once he got past her, he'd have time to reach the back of the estate, go through the park, climb over her fence, open her back door with the key that was under the gnome and be waiting for her when she returned home.

The Magpie wanted to be there in situ. Chrissy always had a bath when she got home. He prayed to Fate that she would not change the habit of a lifetime. This was part of the thrill for him. Human nature, even for the most routine-led people, could suddenly cause them to change their minds and decide to do something slightly different. Once he was done, he would have to remove the small cameras he had set up some six months before. As usual, research and preparation were key. He knew Chrissy and her husband intimately. She had some strange kinks for a respectable midwife.

He listened from the living room as she came through the front door. If Chrissy checked her front room immediately, he would have to strike there and then.

There was a click, then the sound of a latch turning and of the front door opening. The distinct creak of a new door resisting the frame and slightly moving the hinges. Then the ultimate thud of the door closing, which would have been quieter if Rob had been in bed. The Magpie knew that Rob was off on a planned trip to Germany and would not be back until later the next day. The Magpie had timed his strike to perfection.

It took her an hour to have her bath, but finally she was coming down the stairs. He waited patiently for her to enter, gripping his favoured anaesthetic-soaked cloth in his hands. It was crude, but just like the old horror movies.

Chrissy had almost fallen asleep in the bath; she'd dragged herself out before she pruned. She wouldn't want Rob coming back and finding her drowned or maybe dissolved. She dried quickly and put on a cool set of cotton pyjamas with shorts.

She opened the lounge door and stepped onto the carpet. No, not carpet. Plastic. And she was sticking to it. *Plastic? What the f…*

Then she was grabbed from behind and locked in a vice-like grip, not even having time to react or scream as a cloth was pressed over her mouth. Something innate told her she was about to die. Then the alcohol smell like hand sanitizer. Then she faded.

Chrissy woke up, her mouth dry, a tense headache across the left temple. It was even warmer, obviously later in the day. It seemed that she was taped to a pasting table set up in her living room. There was plastic all around, covering every surface, diffusing the light. *What sort of sick thing was this? Oh god. I am going to die. Today.*

"Chrissy." The voice whispered. "Let's have a bit of a chat."

She jumped, even though the voice was softly spoken.

"How are you?" Like it was a conversation. Like they were on their first date, or had met at a train station, by the timetable, like casual acquaintances.

She didn't answer him. Why would she? *Dear God!*

"God's not going to help Chrissy."

It was a coincidence; he couldn't read her mind. Could he?

"Are you going to kill me?" she asked. *May as well get it over with. To the point. Come home early Rob, please rescue me.*

"No of course not. I like my women subdued. Rather than meet them in a bar, I capture them and tie them up in a plastic-covered room. Then we will go out on a date." He paused as she was tried to understand his sarcasm. "Yes, of course I'm going to kill you."

That was the point she felt in her heart that her life had ended. There was going to be no rescue, Rob would still be in France, on the way home from Germany. The realisation that she could do nothing about it. They would never have the children they wanted, she would never see her parents or sisters again.

"It won't hurt, mostly. I'll deliver the killing blow with aplomb, then I'll perfectly remove your eyes as you die. We can then have a chat later when you are in one of my jars."

She choked on a sob. He was an absolute maniac. "Why?" She had to know.

"Why kill you- or why collect your eyes? Firstly, I collect the eyes of my victims. Serial killers should have an affectation, collect something, according to the books. Obsessions. Obsessive behaviours. Believe me, I find no joy in it. A means to an end. Although I've always liked talking to the eyes, I'm going to need a bigger safe at this rate. It seems I am cultivating an M.O. all-ready for my conflict with Harry."

He came into view for the first time. She looked him up and down. God, he was naked. *Weirdo.*

"Secondly," he continued, after a dramatic pause. "Your original surname was Morton. I know you haven't used it since you left the refuge, after your first husband beat you up that final time and you plucked up the courage to leave him. Rob doesn't know you have changed your name, does he? You kept that from him. You naughty sausage. I know everything, Chrissy. I know how you and your husband tick. Or rather whip, you dirty girl."

"Please. Don't hurt Rob."

The naked man laughed. "Why would I hurt Rob? He is not part of the plan."

Thank God. Momentary relief, then she remembered her predicament. How could she forget? The snot and tears should have kept her grounded, at least.

The light coming through the plastic that now adorned the living room windows caught the reflection of something metal and shiny moving quickly through the air. She felt an unimaginable force hit her in the chest. There was pain, briefly. She wandered in and out of consciousness for some time as the light diminished painlessly in one eye then the next. Then Chrissy left the world- never to return.

The Magpie deposited Chrissy's eyes into the jar before cleaning up her body. He packed the sockets to soak up residual blood; he did not want that to ruin the eventual tableau. With his unnatural adrenalin-spiked strength, he carried her plastic cocooned body up the stairs still naked, out of practicality rather than perversion, depositing her corpse into the bed she normally shared with Rob. What a surprise he would have. The Magpie let himself savour the amusement for a short while. Then he was back on task.

He laid her out in the foetal position, stuck one thumb in-between her lips and teeth before she seized up with rigor mortis. He cleaned her up as best he could, then re-inserted the killing tool in between her breasts.

He dressed back into his dark clothes as he stood on the plastic. The house backed onto a park. He had a British Gas jacket he would wear to aid his disguise. He might even read the meter for authenticity. He wouldn't leave any clues. He wasn't stupid.

He said his see-you-later to Chrissy's eyes. He wished there could have been another way, even though he had enjoyed his morning; there was still some regret at taking yet another life. Chrissy was fated however to die at his hand and so be it. They were Lady Bell's orders after all- and the Magpie wanted to keep his new face.

He returned downstairs and cleaned up all the plastic, putting it into a strong refuse bag for disposal later at another random furnace miles away. Then he retraced his steps to check that there was nothing of him left in the house.

The little boy was trapped in a cage. There was another little boy sitting outside. The one outside the cage was smiling; the boy in the cage was trying to stifle tears.

Harry knew he was the boy in the cage. He knew he wouldn't get out until he had solved the riddle. He knew the answer to the riddle, but couldn't get out until he had said it.

"Why do birds fly south in the winter?" the boy on the outside asked, as he always did.

Harry knew the answer was, "because it was too far to walk."

The cage opened and he stepped out. The other little boy smiled and then punched Harry right on the nose.

Harry chased after him and they grappled until they were both on the ground. They fought for a time, as ever- and then they stopped.

The outside boy moved away. "I hate you."

He always said this. As well as "Mummy should not have gone away. Did you kill her?"

Harry wanted to say he hadn't killed Mummy, but just as the words were about to issue from his mouth, he stopped, confused. Always confused. What was he about to say? He had forgotten. He had forgotten everything....

Harry woke and immediately tried to control his heart rate. He regulated his breathing, as discussed with his counsellor: panic attack, find the five points of connection. It was dark, the bedside clock read five forty-six. El was fast asleep; her measured breathing as ever a comfort to his regular awakenings. He needed to pee and decided to get up rather than try to go back to sleep.

He made his way into the en-suite still in darkness and relieved himself, then he washed his hands and made his way from the mezzanine downstairs, where he boiled the kettle and made himself tea.

The dream was the same again. Always the cage, always with the other boy or sometimes one of the other characters. Never a conclusion to it. Always open-ended, always wanting to shout as the other boy screamed, without having to answer the riddle. He was never, ever on the other side of the cage. He was always the little bird trapped there. Waiting to be set free. Always accused, of killing Mummy, whoever Mummy was. Had his mother died in childbirth? It was unlikely his dream and his past forgotten life were linked. His therapist said it was his conflict dream. Not able to solve the riddle, not able to solve the crime.

He sat and drank his tea, although that just made him warmer. When he went to bed, he found he could not sleep for a long time. He was thinking about the call just before he had retired to bed the previous evening. Grace was doing the first PM the next morning on one of the six bodies from Legend Street, and he wanted to be there.

Harry had a feeling of utter unease, as if the next day would deliver new mystery.

Chapter Eight

Caught on Camera

Maisie now had too much to do and too much on her mind to take any time off over the weekend, let alone go to Spain. She had taken great pains and pride in setting up the incident room, but the boards had needed to be made bigger, as there were seven victims now.

She was at Birmingham Council to talk to the Zonal CCTV Control Commander, to ascertain if any of them had picked up the lady in yellow. She couldn't get her out of her mind.

The more she thought about the woman, the more she was convinced she had seen her. Firstly, could she have imagined the woman in her 1940s clothing? Maisie had researched the clothing of the period again the previous evening. Was she retrospectively linking her memories to the belongings and clothes of the six preserved people? Her mental image of the woman in yellow was perfect. Secondly, she remembered the woman bumping into her on the landing of Legend Street and screaming. She had physically felt that bump, her teeth clattering together, the primal scream that came out of her like some fight or flight response.

The CCTV officer had three clips to show her. Let's hope the third was promising. The first had been the feed from the bottom of Legend Street – her running out into the street followed by Rollo - the woman in yellow nowhere to be seen. The second was the feed of a neighbourhood CCTV, angled to cover the shops and their forecourts, so it wasn't focused entirely on the street; again, it showed nothing.

Further down the Hagley Road was a long row of shops. If anything, the woman would have gone this way if she had turned right out of the house, down the street onto the main highway.

"Right, this is at the exact time you wanted." Marky Hayes, the operator said. He was a nice, nondescript man, although he smelled faintly of cabbage and chewing gum. "This is from the bus lane feed- it's on most of the time and not operated as a flash camera."

Maisie watched carefully as the ten minutes of footage he had retrieved slowly played out. The camera mainly caught cars breaking minor traffic laws, but also had a good view of the route the woman would have taken. At six minutes forty seconds, she asked him to pause the recording. There, on-screen was *the* woman dressed in a 1940s yellow dress with matching shoes- running quickly. *Bingo.*

He looked at her as if she were mad. He couldn't see any woman in yellow, at all. Clearly, cabbage and mint Marky thought she was imagining it all. Like Rollo.

"This would have been thirty seconds; give or take from the time she ran from the scene." He pointed at the screen half-heartedly. Maisie could clearly see the woman. Marky could not.

Maisie went cold. Why could she see the woman on film, but Marky couldn't?

"She can put quite a pace on in high heels," she said, trying to mask her nervousness with humour. She asked him to play the third clip again. The yellow woman was gone.

"I'm sorry, it's all I've got," he said.

It wasn't a good start. He handed over a CD of the footage, with a half-smile that made him look like a reluctant shrink who had come across his thirteenth no-hoper with mummy issues of the day. Maybe she was going mad, after all.

By two pm, Maisie was sitting in a meeting room at Lloyd House, waiting for the Police Historian to take her through information they had on disappearances from the 1940s. The records were sparse and patchy due to their age and the destruction of some records by the German Luftwaffe during World War II.

Inspector Greyson White (retired) of Central Police was the official historian to the Midlands force- a lovely man. He'd helped her with various cold cases in the past.

Greyson- or Grey as he liked to be known- was just over sixty, a grandfather and the descendant of his Windrush Father and his white mother. He had worked as a Cold Case Inspector for many years under Owain Pleasant, but had taken a Local History degree at the University of Birmingham upon his initial retirement; he was as well known for his local Windrush talks as his Police History orations.

Grey was still very handsome and only looked to be in his forties. Maisie had worked with his wife Louise, now a desk sergeant at Sutton Coldfield Police Station. Louise was only in her late thirties and had met Grey when she had been a recruit and he had been forty. Their relationship had been much maligned by colleagues on many levels, but they had come through. Unlike her and Teddy, it seemed.

Grey looked at her across the table with that beaming smile of his.

"I take it this is initially a confidential discussion, Maisie Price?"

Maisie nodded as she added sugar to her tea.

"Are you sure they all went missing around that time?" he started, sipping from own his cup of tea, leaving his biscuit on the saucer.

"Not sure. Grace is looking into it. She's completing the PMs as we speak. The bodies are incredibly well preserved; I've never seen anything like it. The fluid composition tests have come back

85

inconclusive. Carbon dating of one of the victims suggests that they were born in the late 1910s. The approximate age of the first victim, a female, suggests they are in early adulthood, between twenty and early thirties."

Grey nodded, putting his cup down. "That gives us something to go on. Luckily, the records after the war of missing persons should be relatively complete and not skewed by the war itself. Detail always varies, though. The more important a person was in society, the more there would have been noted. If they were from more common walks of life, or ethnic in origin, then the records are almost always going to be few and far between. I can compile a list of all the people who went missing between 1938 and 1948, if that's your range. It might be a long list. The more we can focus it down the better."

Maisie nodded. "I'll get as much information for you as possible. My SIO, Harry Morton, has asked if you would do a few days with us freelance? Probably a couple of days over a six-week period in the first instance. To look at some of our other cases with similar historic relevance. It might mean a trip or two to Lincoln."

Grey laughed. "I'm twice retired, darling. I'm not cheap."

"I thought you might say that. The offer is in this envelope, as well as payment arrangements as agreed last week. Give Harry a shout if you fancy it."

"I said I'm not cheap- I didn't say unavailable. I'm not so busy as to pass up the chance to work on a strange. There's only so much daytime TV I can watch, and Louise says that I'll start to get old if I'm sitting down too much."

Maisie nodded. "That sounds like Lou. She, okay?"

"She is. The love of my life. She is the best."

"She is lucky to have such a gentleman as you for a husband," Maisie added with a nod and a smile, enthused by his words.

"Louise told me to behave and help you out. I hear on the grapevine that you have nearly made inspector."

Gosh, news travels fast, she thought.

"You know what the jungle drums are like, particularly in Louise's department. She said you wouldn't mind if I told you."

Maisie wasn't offended. She could learn a thing or two from this man.

"Would you like me to mentor you?" he offered, with a smile. "Whilst I support the department, I could throw in my considerable coaching skills for free."

"Do you know Grey- that would be wonderful." He could read minds, too.

"That is settled then- if your gov agrees. I'm not free until late January next year; I still have a few things to do for the Chief of Central Police, so it will most likely be on your next case."

Maisie nodded. That was fine.

They chatted for another half hour or so, but then she realised she needed to be at the Morgue for 4:30 pm and made her excuses. She shook his hand and said she would wait for Grey to contact Harry.

She picked up the BMW from the car park and made her way back to Lichfield.

Harry was waiting in Claudine Taylor's office. He needed to build bridges; he'd forgotten to call her last Tuesday. There was a comms issue they needed to iron out before Rivers popped a vessel. They had applied for a court injunction against releasing the details on the six corpses from Edgbaston, but they would need to manage it strategically. The local hacks had already been in touch with both Harry and Taylor, fishing for information about Birmingham and Lichfield crime scenes.

"Harry, how are you?" Claudine's familiar mixture of Parisian French and West Midlands drawl met his ears as she wheeled herself into the room. She'd used a wheelchair since she'd been in a road traffic accident – ironically, she and her family had been hit by a stolen vehicle being pursued by the police. Her husband and mother were both killed at the scene. Claudine was now married to the job: a popular, charismatic Chief Superintendent. She'd always been one of Harry's champions.

It was Claudine who had supported his swift rise to DCI; the naysayers had not objected because of his ability, but there were a few raised eyebrows at his elevation at such a young age. Some inevitable murmurings lingered over the potential influence of Harry's father – although the former commissioner had been retired by the time the promotions board had made their decision.

"I'm fine, Ma'am. Sorry to drag you into the office."

"It's not a problem. I was bored at the senior officers meeting anyway. By the way, cut the Ma'am shit. It's Claud to you unless Rivers is sniffing around."

"I always forget." He remembered saying the same to Price.

"Linda Palmer's been on from the Birmingham Echo and a visitor from Midlands Tonight whose name I can't spit out at present. Been bending my ear, although their intel's a bit off - they think we've dug up six bodies in a house in Birmingham as opposed to finding them in preserving fluids in bloody big glass tanks. We've got to manage this though, Harry, so we have an answer when we tell the public the good news."

"I've prepared a briefing for you and the CC."

"Yes, I've seen it, it's good, although we might want to ensure that we make it clear the Legend Street victims are cold case victims, historic crimes. I have been summoned to the morgue tomorrow morning to speak with the Coroner. He can smell a university paper at ten paces. I've set Grace on him in the meantime."

"Poor old Partridge," Harry said.

Colin Partridge, Lead Coroner for the Central Midlands was old school, but Grace had a way with him. Even Rivers phoned Grace before discussing cases with Partridge. It was his links to Whitehall the chief was bothered about and how much shit it would cause him if he gave the wrong answer.

"I'll meet with Palmer and whoever the BBC wants to send my way, so just keep feeding me with the information I require to keep Rivers happy, and my innate curiosity satisfied." She smiled and changed the subject. "What's the craic with DS Price, does she have her Inspector's commission yet? I've signed the budget off."

Harry nodded. "Just waiting for internal services to do the paperwork. I've got Marsh's note."

"I'm doing her exit hearing later this week. Likely it will be full medical retirement due to an end-of-life diagnosis. She's an evil bitch, but I wouldn't wish brain cancer on my worst enemy. Start Maisie next Monday."

Losing DI Marsh to such a horrible prognosis was unfortunate, but what she caused his team in backstabbing didn't make up for her skill at the job. Marsh had been incendiary, and he had lost a couple of good lower grade officers because of her bullying. Rolleston's predecessor had resigned after months of harassment accusations from Marsh, despite the charge being unfounded. In fact, Internal Services had reflected it back upon Marsh and she had received a final warning for her behaviour. Maisie would do a much better job.

"How are you? Any news from your specialist?"

"Same old same old. No more detail than before. They are keeping an eye on the bone fragment, but it's not going to affect anything operationally."

"Too right, it isn't. Come the New Year, once this case is over and Maisie is established as an inspector, you can step down from field duty. I need you with me, not out catching murderers and rapists."

"Isn't that my job, Claud?"

"No, you count them and sign the paperwork. I have no worries about Price. Let Rolleston pull his finger out. Where is the lazy shit by the way? Probably helping out HR with induction programmes so he can leer at the female DCs."

Harry laughed more out of nervousness than agreement, "Bit harsh, ma'am." He accentuated the "Ma'am."

"He's a good police officer. But not effective in terms of his figures. It's like his mind is elsewhere."

"I am probably to blame. He's effectively doing a sergeant's job."

"Because you can't trust him. Keep an eye. I want him on report if he's not getting his numbers in. I know your department is a strange one, it's not like you will get lots of arrests on an ongoing basis, but the figures are reduced for that reason. Rivers isn't impressed."

"Rivers…"

"…is never impressed. I know. He's the gov though- and my gov. So, the shit lands at this desk. Let's not have Rolleston drag us down with him, Harry. We're too good for that. If his numbers aren't up by the next performance count, I'll have him in to talk to."

"I won't argue with that."

"So," Taylor said in the tone of voice that strongly hinted she had finished that conversation. "Can you pour me a coffee. I'd get it myself, but they have put the disabled police officer in the smallest, shittest office and I'd have to run you over. I am honestly not treating you like I was treated by most male superiors for the first twenty years of my career." Her smile was precious.

He was sitting just in front of the cafetière, so he stood and did as he was asked.

"I'm amazed you have stayed in this office, Claud."

"Yes, considering, yours is twice the size of mine."

"Want to swap?"

"Do I fuck. I'd have to listen to you lot talking like the X-Files all day every day. It's quiet up here, other than the toilets flushing every ten seconds. Access rights for me meant they made this palace out of the original fucking disabled toilet, so now I have to go downstairs in the lift and use the one next to the gents. Which doesn't stop them all sneaking in and pissing on the seat."

He put the coffee down onto her desk on a Star Trek coaster next to her computer.

"No comment."

"*You* are obviously a gentleman," she laughed, then changed the subject again. "Had a quick look at the incident room earlier. Do you have enough for the body count? Partridge agreed to co-resource the preserved bodies PMs. Do we need more people on the ground out in the community?"

"I've got Miles already and DC Shaw starting in a few weeks; we should be ok. Losing Worth was terrible, but Maisie will run the A-team; I'll have Rollo over here."

Taylor raised an eyebrow. "Talk of the devil."

There was a knock at Taylor's door. Rollo entered.

"Sir, Ma'am. We've had a call. Another body. Victoria Park. No eyes."

"Shit," Taylor said.

"Get hold of Hyatt and get over there. I'll follow."

Harry ordered, getting up. "I'll catch you later Claud. Duty calls."

Taylor shook her head. "I'm just thinking of the shit storm. Brief me as soon as you get there. I'll inform Rivers. He's on the golf course with the Commissioner. He'll be spitting curses our way from the nineteenth hole, no doubt."

As soon as Daisy had told her they'd found another body in Lichfield, Maisie had hung up and called Rollo. To her relief, he'd told her to stand down; not that she didn't want to be involved, but she'd sat in traffic on the Hagley Road for the last hour after reporting to the scene at Legend Street first thing that morning. Harry had wanted to be sure the SOCOs were on the button, as it were. And now there was no way she'd be able to make it back to Lichfield in a hurry. There was some hold up at Five Ways and the traffic was backed up. The car had a blue light, but she wasn't authorised to use it in Birmingham. It was a Complex Case car in the Central region; she could end up on a charge.

There was some rubbish track on the radio that cut off as a news report started. Maisie turned the volume up.

"I'm sorry to interrupt the new single by Jay Z and Beyoncé, but we are getting reports that police in Birmingham have found six bodies in the same house in Edgbaston. Initial reports suggest that the remains date back to the late nineteen forties. There will be more in the main bulletin later."

As usual, it was a half-arsed guess by the press.

She continued to navigate the tight traffic. Loud sirens could be heard in the distance; the sky had darkened; it became close and humid. The first spots of rain that were the beginnings of a storm started to pitter-patter on her screen.

Maisie clicked on the wipers. She watched them for a while as they hypnotically scraped the windscreen free of the deluge. The downpour was getting stronger and stronger, the sky blacker and blacker.

She glanced back up as a flash of colour passed her car on her nearside. A flash of yellow. A woman dressed in yellow.

"Shit," she said to only herself. Instinctively, she clicked on the blue lights that were housed in the forward and rear grills. She would have to blag any charge.

She manoeuvred as best she could out of the traffic and managed to get park in a nearby bus stop. The rain fell in sheets as she got out of the car. She had no umbrella, but it would have been useless anyway.

She could see the woman running up ahead and gave chase. How the hell did the yellow lady run so fast in three-inch heels?

"Ma'am, stop! Police! Lady in the yellow, please stop."

The yellow lady did not stop. An old woman, soaked to the skin, turned at Maisie's shout; but the running lady just ploughed on ahead, ignoring Maisie's calls. Instead, she darted down a side street. Gillott Road, the sign said. Maisie followed, turned the corner into the long street that disappeared into the distance, flanked by a row of trees each side and a row of cars on the inside track. Hundreds of tall Victorian townhouses disappeared off into the distance. But there was no sign of the yellow lady. No sign at all.

Chapter Nine
Adding to the Collection

The Magpie watched as Harry Morton talked to the PC standing on guard outside the home of his latest victim, Chrissy Parsons. It was early days, but he hoped Harry and his team were befuddled, struggling to piece the mystery together, still lacking that lucky break. He had left no clues. This would be fun.

He stifled a belly laugh. Being this close as Harry dealt with another eyeless corpse was so exciting. The beautiful Chrissy in her foetal position, grey voids where her eyes had been. He looked forward to their conversation later: Chrissy's eyes were beautiful.

He imagined the effect of discovering her body had on Rob, her husband, and he felt a frisson of positive energy- maybe sexual. Not because of the kill, he wasn't a monster. His reaction was more about his ability to manipulate, to control people from the side-lines. The plan coming together, the quota for her Ladyship.

The next stage of his plan was complicated, and it required some considerable thought, so he turned the key in the ignition and drove back towards the lock-up. There, his Escort Mark II would be waiting for him, ready for a brief trip back to Birmingham and his insular life as Marcus- who had come back from Italy after all. Well, as far as the neighbours and estate agents were concerned.

He did just enough as Marcus to make sure no one started to meddle or poke their noses in. He couldn't have them finding out.

***

Harry left Rob Parsons in the hands of a family liaison officer in the lounge and trudged his way back upstairs. It was such a nice clean house, they had both taken exceptionally good care of where they lived-nothing out of place. Floors hoovered or swept regularly, surfaces gleaming; it smelt nice and welcoming, but he knew that where he was headed would be far from pleasant.

The carpet on the stairs was deep and plush. The paintwork under his hands on the stair rail was smooth and without bumps. The curtains framing the turn-landing windows were bright and newly washed. A wonderful home - torn apart.

The bustle of the two SOCOs and Grace brought him to his senses. She was taking photos of the scene for her records and for reference during the PM, as well as any possible court proceedings- if they found the bastard. The click of the aperture -despite the digitised camera- rang out loudly, invading this solemn, yet undignified situation.

Chrissie Parsons lay on the bed in the foetal position. A knife protruding between her naked breasts- the tool that had separated her from her life. Her eyes were gone. It was obviously the same MO. A serial killer was at large. They could say that now.

Two bodies, four days apart. But what was the connection, if any, to the bodies they had found in Edgbaston? Was it serendipity that he had received the letter about George Wright's property, or coincidence? He was scientifically minded: there was a reason for every action everyone made, whether it be it conscious or unconscious. He couldn't help thinking that it was some sort of test. A test from God? Harry wasn't a religious man. Fate was the only ethereal presence in his life. Why would a forgiving God cast such horrors on the world he created? How could a benevolent God subject his dad to the curse of dementia, take away his mum, leave him without memory of his natural family?

Disease, famine, pestilence and war. The four horsemen of evolution. All human reactions and interactions. And this was how he felt about Chrissy's murder. His human side wanted to scream aloud, curse, cry. The scientist in him needed to discover the links in the chain of events that led this person to kill in such a way.

He pondered the eye collecting. Profilers would probably say the murderer is subconsciously trying to prevent the victim from ever seeing heaven. Or something more prosaic, that the eyes were the window to the soul. Was the killer capturing the souls of his victims or was he just a messed-up bastard? Did he get rid of the eyes, or did he collect them? Was he definitely he? Could be she, but usually he.

"Penny for them?" The clicking of the camera had stopped. Grace had spoken, in softer tones than usual. He could smell her usual perfume mixed with tar. He wished she would give up cigarettes, but he knew she probably wouldn't.

"We have started a profile on this killer, but it seems there will be more victims and a pattern are emerging. It obviously someone who will do it again."

"Whoever it is, Harry - and it's probably a male-they're covering their tracks perfectly. There's not a drop of evidence anywhere. No third-party prints, other than the couples' family as far as we can tell, although that will need further study. No hair or clothing fibres, he doesn't rape them or abuse them in any way, so no bodily fluids. Other than the obvious killing blow and harvesting of the eyes, it seems he is just killing for killing's sake."

He looked at Grace. He had never seen her so concerned. "I'm worried about a link to Edgbaston."

She shrugged. "How could there be a link? We carbon-dated most of the samples. None have the nuclear signatures we would expect in people from the sixties and seventies. Some of the dental work is early century- if there is any at all. Cavities and poor oral health in one or two. We are looking at an event window for the Edgbaston dead between 1920 and 1950. The clothes, although yes, they could be planted, match a period pre-second world war to the late 1940s. We could fit a pair of shoes to each corpse, Harry."

He shook his head in frustration. The SOCOs had left the room, leaving them to their discussion.

"If it is the same man," she continued, albeit with a heavy pause, "he would be over ninety years of age. The force with which Angus Morton was hit shattered his breastbone and most of the ribs below. No ninety-year-old man could do that."

"Father and son?"

"It would be a seventy-year-old son doing the killing."

"Copycat?"

"Do you think our killer has had access to the house in Edgbaston? Has anyone been up there since the 1940s?"

As ever, Grace wasn't just useful for her scientific and professional expertise, but also as an effective sounding board, challenging any assumption he might make. He didn't mention Maisie's mysterious woman and apparently Rollo hadn't spoken to Grace about it over a cigarette.

"We will need to go over the house in Edgbaston again, the scene at St Peter's and obviously here."

She summed up their conversation- the habit of a procedural clinician used to detail. "I would say he's a strong man. Perhaps he has seen the bodies in the attic in situ? Fascination? It can't be the same man, because of age. Or it's coincidence. And I know what you would say to that under normal circumstances. These victims may not be his first. He's a trophy hunter, obviously. No eyes at his scenes, although we have all the eyes of the historical victims."

Harry's head hurt. "Let's get one of the SOCO teams over to the Edgbaston case. We'll need to excavate the grounds, so we will need some direction and help from your team. I'll get Maisie to set up control at the scene. I'm going to have another word with the solicitors and do some digging into George Wright. See if there are descendants and rule them out- or otherwise."

It was at that point his phone rang. It was DS Price. "Price? Were your ears burning? Yes, I am, I'm at the scene with Grace. Further work on the six has been suspended so don't attend the morgue. Listen, I know it's a ball ache, but can you get over here for an hour? Make sure the Edgbaston site is secured over the weekend. We will probably have to bring the diggers in. I need us to work on the George Wright slant and rule out any links to direct descendants. Yes, it's the same MO here, it seems. We can discuss that later too. Thanks."

"She is a good officer and she'll make a fine inspector, better than the other idiot. Where is he, by the way?"

"Rollo's back at the office."

"Shouldn't he be here?"

"Got an early finish. He's going fishing with mates apparently, up in the Lake District."

Grace made a noise. "Fishing the gene pool, more like. Drinking his way around the Lakes, shagging anything that moves…"

Harry laughed wryly. "I'll leave you to it. Keep in touch." He touched her arm affectionately.

"Later, H." Grace winked.

The journey back to the office was uneventful. He phoned the solicitors back- Giles Reynolds had left him a voicemail wishing to see him urgently. He agreed a meeting in an hour. There was something more going on there; he felt it in his bones, or rather his currently aching head. He popped a couple of ibuprofen and washed them down with the cold McDonald's coffee he had bought earlier.

Back in his office, he retrieved the solicitor's letter. He couldn't help but feel that there was something missing. Maybe this was what Reynolds wanted to see him about. Grace had confirmed that none of the Edgbaston victims bore any resemblance to the photos they had of George Wright's missing wife, Nancy. Her birth certificate was not in the records found in the house. He hoped the solicitors might have it, otherwise he'd ask Maisie to get on to legal for a copy.

At 1:30, DC Miles informed him that Mr Reynolds had arrived. Harry went out to the waiting area outside his office and welcomed him.

"Afternoon, DCI Morton. Giles Reynolds. Good to put a face to a name."

Reynolds was a tall, hugely broad mixed-race gentleman, probably in his late forties, in a tight-fitting navy-blue suit and expensive scent. His grip was over-strong, but not meant to intimidate. He clearly looked after himself.

"Nice to meet you. Follow me. Coffee?"

"No, thank you. I think my assistant explained I have to be brief - I have another meeting in Birmingham shortly." He sat down in the chair that was offered to him, over the desk from Harry.

"How can I help you?" Reynolds smiled the smile of a man who looked like he was going to be no help at all.

"How long have the property deeds for 42 Legend Street been deposited with your firm, Mr Reynolds?"

The big solicitor shuffled a bit, his bulk uncomfortable in the small bucket chair.

"The firm was started by my great grandfather in 1926. We are a small firm with associated partners, but the name has never changed. There has been a Reynolds Solicitors Office in Birmingham since. We are highly respected and highly regarded."

Harry laughed, if only to cut the man's sales spiel off. "I have no doubt you are a diligent and well-regarded firm of solicitors. My questions are more about how the property has been managed. Why has it remained in the legacy of George Wright and never been offered up to the Crown, as no beneficiaries have come forward? Why do the managing agents maintain it the way they do? It's a clean well-maintained property, if somewhat old-fashioned?"

Reynolds started to vigorously nod. If he did not stop, his head might fall off. Harry frowned and the man picked up on this.

"The last will and testament of George Wright said the house should remain as it is, well-maintained and in order, so if he returned home, it would be available immediately. There is also a substantial sum of money awaiting his return."

"Yet he has been missing and never found. Missing since 1948."

"Assumed dead after seven years. His will states that- and I quote- "the property should be maintained in its present state until at least 2048.""

"Yet he was an only child. His parents were dead, and he and Nancy had no children. So, no aunties or uncles, nephews nor nieces."

"The will is clear. One hundred years. Since 1948, only a select group of the managing agent's cleaners and handymen have been allowed access to the house. I have just this morning instructed the cleaning company concerned to release the names and addresses to DS Price. We would have been in breach of my client's wishes if we had changed any aspect of this."

Reynolds had a point. "Yes, well. I am sorry for a wasted journey, but I was determined that we should meet each other. I need to ascertain if there are any other papers kept by your firm regarding Mr George Wright. We are a little busy at present."

"I think it may be serendipitous to visit his property in Bude. There is a suggestion in his writings that there are possibly papers regarding Nancy and her future there. There is a clause in his will that his papers were never to be released. Now, only a warrant pertaining to criminal activity can release them. However, no papers at all were requested by the original investigation, but in consultation with my father, we have decided you should be free to go and search the property in Bude to see if you can find anything of relevance. You would still need a warrant to enter, however."

"If we can find them."

"From his forensic record keeping, we believe there may be a journal, a set of letters and his diaries, which may relate to his work with an organisation called the Cordivae."

"Do you think the papers are relevant to the case? Or to Mrs Wright's disappearance?"

The solicitor shrugged.

"I don't know, not having seen them myself. We have not investigated his papers, DCI Morton. I am going on inventories and notes on file from past conversations. Retrieval is up to you, courts permitting."

"Thank you for your time, Mr Reynolds."

"I am sorry if you feel we have hampered the investigation in any way; I would like to add that as soon as we deemed these papers relevant, we cooperated. We did have very definite instructions to follow - Mr Wright was incredibly well-connected. There is a letter from the Attorney General himself to instruct us that the will was to be executed in its entirety - in the strictest confidence and to the letter."

"The cooperation of Reynolds' solicitors is thoroughly appreciated. I commend you for coming forward."

Harry stood and offered his hand.

"Thanks." Giles Reynolds said, getting up so quickly he knocked his bag onto the floor. He shook Harry's hand and departed quickly, as if his feet were on fire.

"There's nothing Harry. No signs of trauma. I can't be sure when her eyes were removed, but they were taken out expertly. Surgeon-level skill."

"You think the perpetrator could be a medic?"

It was Saturday morning; he hadn't attended the Institute at the weekend in a while. But with a serial killer apparently still at large, the pressure was mounting for Harry and Grace to come up with some answers – and quickly. They agreed another look at one of the Edgbaston corpses would be beneficial, considering the precarious links between the two sets of murders.

"She is quite beautiful, even with her eyes missing. Someone's daughter, sister, mother or wife. She may have been taken away from her family, never knowing whether she would return. Her family may have not known what happened to her. A missing person. All that grief. Did she suffer, did she scream?"

"Could she have donated her body to science?"

"There were protocols, even then. Donations are normally dissected; every inch of a body is looked at to help advance science and medicine. I do not think these bodies are donations."

"Shall we move onto the next one?" Harry asked.

"I will, but on Monday, you are going home to that gorgeous girlfriend of yours."

The other boy was throwing stones through the cage again at Harry. They pinged off the bars, the sound echoing, grating on him, the clanging hurting his ears.

"Why are you doing that?"

The other boy did not respond. Every now and then, a stone would pass through the bars and strike Harry. He would move around the cage, but the other boy would follow.

Harry felt hot salty tears trail into his mouth. He cried a lot in these dreams.

"Stop it!" he screeched. His back was against the bars, always keeping the other boy in his sights.

Clang. Clang.

The boy seemed to have an infinite number of stones in his pocket.

Clang. Clang.

Harry looked down at one of the stones. It was shiny and white. He leant forward and picked one up to throw it back, to give the boy a taste of his own medicine.

In his hand, it was smooth and surprisingly warm. He investigated his palm where the very white and very round stone sat. Far too warm for a stone. Wait - it had other colours, patterns. Concentric circles, white, green with flecks of amber, a black centre. No. Not a centre. Pupil. It was an eyeball.

Harry screamed.

"Baby, it's alright. It's okay. I've got you. It's me, Ellen."

The room came into sharp relief. He was in his bed, on the mezzanine of his flat. Harry investigated Ellen's face. So beautiful. Ground yourself, Morton, you are panicking. Five things to see. Ellen, the clock, the bed, the lamp, his wardrobe. Four things to touch, Ellen, himself, the quilt, a pillow. Three things to hear, his breathing, Ellen's breathing, the noise of cars through the open window. Two things to smell, his sweat and Ellen's beautiful womanly scent. One thing to taste. Ellen kissed him knowing exactly what he was doing. Delaying his panic.

He only fell asleep again because Ellen was rocking him. He had no further dreams.

Outside, on a dark Saturday night just before midnight, a figure sat under the dancing beams of a flickering streetlight. A train went on its way to City station, staccato rhythms on the track. The Magpie laughed and as he did so a voice in his head said, *Come to me. I need to commend you on your work.*

How did she do that?

Chapter Ten

A Flickering Flame of Pain

Maisie left her car at the bottom of Legend Street and walked up the road. She was on her way to have a cup of tea with PC Crabbe, who was still on duty, whilst she waited for Harry.

She hadn't slept at all well last night.

She'd had yet another altercation with her twin. Daisy had come over and let herself in to find Pete there. Pete had done the manly thing and cleared off, leaving Daisy plenty of time to make her feelings about the situation abundantly clear. She'd called Maisie all the bitches under the sun. She'd been out of order; it wasn't like they had done the dirty on her. Daisy wasn't seeing Pete. She'd still managed a pretty comprehensive character assassination of Maisie though; needy, high-maintenance, shallow apparently.

Daisy had always had a chip on her shoulder about Maisie's appearance. It wasn't her fault that they looked so different, that Daisy had inherited the Price nose. Daisy outlined her theory, not for the first time, that Maisie might get the blokes because of her looks, but none of them hung around for long once they found out what she was really like. Teddy being the latest example. Daisy always did know how to go for the jugular. Maisie shouldn't have risen to it, but she ended up telling her sister that if she wanted Teddy that much, she was welcome to him – and that Pete was worth ten of Teddy any day. That much was true. Pete was the opposite of Teddy; strong, loving - incredibly good at loving in fact - and intelligent too.

If she was honest, though, it wasn't the mess of her relationship with her twin that was keeping her awake at night. It was knowing she had been so close to finding the woman in yellow – and that she'd slipped through her grasp again. Maisie felt identifying the woman was crucial to the case; even more now the gov had filled her in on his meeting with the solicitor. And yet, she was still worried that her promotion was doomed to failure before it had even begun. What if she was wrong about the woman in yellow? What if she didn't exist? Perhaps she was really going mad. Her self-doubt was not exactly helping her sleep.

The only way forward, Maisie decided, was to throw herself into her work. When the gov summoned her for a catch-up, she was straight in the car, despite it being the weekend. Why he would come all the way over to Edgbaston on a Sunday she was unsure. Maybe he was at a loose end – his girlfriend was probably at work - or maybe he was doing it in support of her, even though he probably thought she was bat-shit crazy.

She was washing the night duty team's cups in the makeshift bowl in the narrow kitchen, when she heard Harry's voice.

"Morning Maisie, you, okay?"

"I think so, gov."

"Are you sure? It's your weekend off and you are still looking for the woman in yellow."

She went to the fridge they had got on loan from Central Police stores and grabbed the milk.

"Guilty as charged. Think I'm going slightly bonkers. You may have employed a duffer as your new inspector. I can't stop thinking about her." Maisie handed him his drink.

Harry looked great as ever. Young looking, fresh-faced, ash blonde hair falling over his very green eyes. Most of the girls agreed he was fit, but he was the gov. Work and pleasure don't mix. Then she thought of Pete.

"You don't think I'm crazy, do you?"

He shrugged.

"There's video evidence of the woman, isn't there?" Sipping his tea, he beckoned her towards the lounge. They perched on two of the old-fashioned chairs. Hers was hard -uncomfortable. Which was genuinely how she felt.

"I've heard a rumour about an office romance."

Shit, he knows. Daisy, you bitch.

"Gov. I'm sorry. I..."

"Look, M. You are the best I've got. I can warn you about conflict of interest, but I'm also aware of how things have been for you recently. Losing your grandmother and the split with Teddy - well, you deserve to be happy. God knows it's not easy in this job." He put his mug down on the wooden floor, pushing it carefully under the chair so he couldn't kick it over. "I'll move Pete across. Rollo's complaining about doing too much of the grunt work and from what I know of Pete, he doesn't mind a bit of hard graft. You'll need to work on a different pattern to him though. You'll see less of each other, but it'd mean no complications from the Chief if he finds out. That okay?"

Well, that was a surprise. She liked him even more for that.

"Thanks," was all she could manage, more than a little choked up. "It's early days, though."

"I went out on a limb for you, not because you're not good enough, but because you're not hugely experienced. Rivers wasn't totally convinced. I need you on point -- can't have you affected by this. Vice is pissed off that I've got another DI and they're struggling. Don't let me down."

And despite him being wonderful, you still know who the gov is.

"I won't."

"Now. What about the woman in yellow?"

"I saw her again. Did I tell you? The Council officer said he couldn't see her on the video, but I definitely saw her when I was driving away from here yesterday."

"On Hagley Road, running between the cars?" He was teasing her, smiling as if taking the piss. His eyes sparkled, like those of a kid. She took a moment to scan his face: no lines whatsoever. Colleagues frequently commented on it - the more bitter ones suggesting he'd had work done, but that was ridiculous. Barney in Stores reckoned the gov was on the other bus, using make-up and moisturisers. As if that was what made you gay. Barney was a Neanderthal. No, it was more fundamental than that as if he aged slower than other people. Pete liked his moisturisers and skin treatments too; he had a bigger toiletry bag than she did. Maybe the gov was just lucky with his genes. Wherever they'd come from - she'd heard the rumours that he didn't know who his real parents were.

"Tend to repeat myself a lot these days. Like I'm convincing myself she exists."

"It seems she doesn't want to be found. Or not *yet* anyway."

"Think she has anything to offer the case?"

Harry mused. "Grace can't find any evidence of anything other than natural deaths in all of our six preserved bodies - aside from the removal of the eyes, of course. The eyes were taken pre-mortem, just like Angus and Sally. So, the actions of our "killers" are the same. But it can't be the same person - he or she would be ancient now. Could be someone who had access to this house, or was here as a child. A copycat, or maybe the unconscious resurfacing of a repressed horror. The tableaux of our two current victims are different. They seem to be like messages. I'm worried I'm missing the clues."

He turned his gaze back on to her, leant forward, almost conspiratorially.

"Angus having the same surname as me has really freaked me out. Are these killings messages for me? Am I the connection? Maisie - if that does turn out to be the case, I'm relying on you to take this forward. If it's a grudge or payback for something I have done, someone I have taken down... or even a link to my past..."

108

He left it hanging. If she was reading this right, he was taking her into his confidence.

"The woman in yellow may be able to tell us about this place." He pointed upstairs towards the attic; his meaning clear. "Even if she is a cleaner, even if there is a distant link to George Wright, I need to know. She might be the key. Or she might be the killer." He didn't seem convinced about the last bit.

"I've looked at the photos of the St Peter's scene, guv. She would not have been able to construct that on her own."

"Whoever carried out the Lichfield murders had help. I went down with Pete the other day, tried to lift the crucifix. No chance. Did he mention it?" Then he winced, visibly. "That is out of order. That would imply I don't trust you either of you to remain professional. I'm sorry."

She laughed. "You are allowed to be suspicious."

He shook his head vigorously. "I trust you implicitly. I'm a good judge of character. I trust and then if I'm betrayed, I am a bastard." Her laugh tailed away as he became serious.

"I've got some photos. A team of local officers is going to join us going house to house. We will knock on as many doors as we can today - more tomorrow if necessary. Let's split up and see if we can find this woman in yellow."

Harry spent the afternoon with PC Chandra, a lovely young woman whose family hailed from the Indian subcontinent of Bangladesh. She was a Birmingham graduate. He'd been so impressed he made a note of her details, should his team have a vacancy in the future.

It was almost 6 pm and he was in the pub. They hadn't found the woman in yellow and to be honest they would have been lucky to do so. This was only the second house to house sweep, with a further planned the next day and more throughout the next week.

He had arranged to meet Maisie at the Dog on Hagley Road for a pint or two. But she'd phoned to say they were following up a lead and that she would be with him soon- probably about six-fifteen.

As he sat there, he sensed he was being watched. Harry had carried out enough undercover and surveillance training to know that prescient feeling of eyes boring into the back of your head.

Behind the bar was a long stretch of mirror tiles, reflecting the scene behind him. He looked up and then – he saw it. Yellow. Sitting at a table, there she was. Out of focus; like a crackling light, or the edges of a flame in the gloom.

Her dark hair was dressed in a style he could only guess was from the forties. He studied her for a moment; she was engrossed in a book, but suddenly, she looked up from the page and met his gaze. Well, he thought, she was becoming very blurred. The pain started to shoot behind his eyes, as if someone were sticking pins in his eyeballs. Not a great metaphor at present, he conceded.

"Hello, Harry." Looking at her was difficult, but he could sense her eyes were full of tears.

He went cold. "How do you know my name?"

"A guess, I suppose." Although she seemed uncertain.

Things cleared a little. She was probably late twenties; wide, green eyes shone out of a heart-shaped face, slim, like her frame. Her yellow dress was plain but stylish; she wore a tallow cardigan, light stockings, and yellow shoes with a thick heel.

"I think she's coming for you."

"Who is?" He grabbed his drink and phone and moved over to sit with the woman.

"The Lady and her Magpie." Her tone was quiet. Fear etched in lines on her face, as if drawn suddenly by a sharpened pencil. She was blurring out of focus again, yet the sense of fear coming from her was so stark, he was surprised he couldn't touch it.

"Who is the Magpie?"

There was no response. Then, approaching from the side, the boy appeared. The boy who threw stones. He just stood there. Was Harry now dreaming?

What is your name?"

"I can't tell you," she said.

"Yes, you can. He softened his tone from his usual to-the-point manner. "Go on, I won't bite."

"I can't tell you."

"Can't or won't?" he asked.

"Can't. Can't remember."

"You can't remember your name?"

"No. They took it from me."

"Who? The Magpie?"

"No, the Lady."

Then suddenly he felt searing pain behind his eyes again. Stabbing, thrusting pain. Pain like he had experienced once before, when he had awoken in the Cathedral. It intensified - he lost his vision. Bright white lights exploded, a myriad of prisms sparking in his head.

Then a familiar voice cut across the room and his thoughts. "Gov, gov. I have a lead." Maisie's voice. It had sliced through the pain momentarily, but now it was back.

"Gov, are you all, right? Harry. Harry, look at me. Your nose is bleeding. Who were you talking to?"

Then time stopped and the world went black, but not before he saw the little boy laughing and reaching back, ready to hurl a stone.

Maisie had chosen to go it alone with the door-to-door interviews. It had been a long and boring afternoon, where the distant promise of finding the woman in yellow had slowly petered out.

111

The final house she had come to was grand. A sprawling complex, set back from the rest of the street. The gate had slowly swung inwards after she had shown her warrant card to the lens on the access panel.

A long gravel drive led up to the house. More glass than brick and surrounded by trees, which dappled the light that fell on its vast glazed panels. The double-fronted entrance looked like it had been carved from those magnificent oaks, sturdy and expensive. Off to the left of the house a Bentley was parked; to the right were outbuildings, old stables that echoed the history of the site.

She was about to raise her hand to the ornate eagle-headed knocker, when there was a deep, drawing thump and the left-hand door opened inwards.

A man stood there, tall, and lithe. He had blond, unruly curly hair that reached to his shoulders. He looked strong - not bulked up, but well-built. A youthful, yet unhandsome face, craggy through expression, rather than age. He looked like he was dressed in his grandfather's suit.

"Detective Sergeant Price? William Beaton. Pleased to meet you."

Posh Brummie. Nothing could take the accent away. Not even money.

"Professor Beaton." She held out a hand and he shook it with a vice-like grip. "Thank you for sparing me a few moments."

"It's not a problem. I am due at the University in an hour or so, but I'll have half an hour or so to spare. Did I hear that you are trying to locate information on George Wright? I was going to contact the senior officer. Oops. Sorry, where are my manners? Please come in."

She was led into a massive open hallway. Greenish light filtered through the stained olive and yellow glass above their heads, reaching up to the first-floor ceiling. Panelled oak walls, well-lit by the

112

same green light, spread through the space. The doors leading off the entrance hall were just as sturdy, but each had a beautiful image of a bird set in stained glass. An owl, a raven, a peregrine falcon. She knew her birds. Her dad was a twitcher; he had taken her out in all weathers to spot them. She treasured her Usborne book of British birds, with as many pencil ticks as images in it.

"Beautiful house."

"My father was an architect. I got left this in his will." He stopped at a door which was to the left of a set of ornately carved stairs, balustrades sweeping upwards, carved acorns and oak leaves on every strut. "It's a bit too big for just me, but I made a promise. Come in."

He did not expand upon the promise, and she forgot about what he had said as soon she entered the library.

Immediately her eyes were drawn upwards to the domed glass ceiling. The same design as the ones on each door; all blues and different shades of green, the sky, hills and fields covered in so many birds. The light cast a rainbow of colours on the bookshelves that encircled the room on two floors, the first accessed by little ladders.

There was a large round table just in front of them, covered in paper and books, pens and other ephemera and surrounded by chairs at regular intervals,

"This is my home. I have a bedroom upstairs, but this is where I really live."

"It is breath-taking."

"My father bought the land with the help of George Wright. My dad designed this house himself." Professor Beaton pulled a chair out for her to sit.

She did so, then retrieved her notebook and pen from her large bag.

"Coffee?" She had noticed the aroma of coffee as she had entered the room. Unusual for a library.

"Please, just milk. Your father was friends with George?"

"Sort of, from what I can gather. They both worked at the University. The only one in Birmingham in those days. My father was a lecturer in Medieval History as well as a freelance architect. George was also something to do with estates, always mixed up with property deals, apparently. I was born in my father's dotage, so I never met George. Is it true they found lots of bodies in Legend Street?"

It was in the public domain; she could not deny it.

"Yes, we knew where Wright worked. But what we didn't initially know was that he was also involved with a group of scientists?"

"Yes, they both invested in a project. A group were carrying out experiments with soldiers following World War One, focusing on shell shock. Father helped to fund the work as it was dear to his heart, having served in his youth. He developed some of the early evidence for PTSD, but the links were only really made in the last year of the study. My grandfather was one of their subjects. He came back from the war a broken man."

"When did your father last hear from George, do you know?"

"The last letter my father got was in January 1948. George had invited him to re-model a house in Cornwall for him in nineteen forty-six. He obviously completed the work, as the letter was an invitation to the housewarming. I have the sketches."

"Did your father ever speak to the police? George and Nancy Wright went missing in 1948."

"No. He did report the letters to West Midlands Police in the 1990s just before he died, but they were too busy for cold cases. They said someone would be in touch. No one ever was."

Maisie shook her head. This was incredible. There was a lead for a suspect in a major disappearance case and volunteered evidence had been ignored. She needed to tell the gov.

"Do you know a Robert Waterfield?" It was a long shot, but the name had come up in the solicitor's papers a few times.

"I believe George Wright bought 42 Legend Street from Mr Waterfield. My father was going to rework the house for him. However, I have never found any records pertaining to the man after 1948, and what came before is closed by the Official Secrets Act. It was as if he too vanished."

"Would you be happy for us to look over your father's papers to see if there are any other clues?"

"Yes of course, happy to help. I can courier the papers over. There's quite a lot of them."

Maisie shook her head. "No, if it's okay, I'll get a couple of colleagues to come over at your convenience. Thank you, Professor Beaton. You have been incredibly helpful."

"Are you going to throw stones at me too?" Harry asked the beautiful woman who approached the cage. She was dressed all in yellow. She had dark hair and green eyes. She looked friendly though, not like she would throw anything.

"Don't be silly, Harry. I'm here to let you out. My name is Edith.

"Pleased to meet you, Edith." It was important to be polite, even if you were locked up. I'm sure his parents, wherever they were, would expect it.

The woman in yellow came over and opened the cage door. She didn't even have to unlock it, it just creaked open as she pulled.

"Come on, Harry. You don't look like you have eaten in days. Are you hungry?"

"A little, yes."

"Let's go and see Cook and then we shall take you up to the nurse. She needs to give you an injection."

"An injection. From the nurse? Matron gives the injections. I don't like needles."

Edith stopped, turned, and took both his hands.

"The nurse is an absolute angel, beautiful inside and out. She will give you the once over and then you and I can go back to your room and talk some more."

Harry wasn't sure. "I don't want to go to the nurse."

"It's fine, she is lovely. Her name is Nurse Ellen. She will look after you and give you the injection. It will sort out the thing in your brain, Harry."

Harry shook himself free of Edith's hands. The woman in yellow had looked so nice, but she was going to take him upstairs. Take him for an injection. It couldn't happen. He was starting to panic.

"No!" he screamed. "Noooooooooooo!"

"Edith. The woman in yellow is called Edith."

"Are you okay, love?" Ellen's voice. They were in bed. It was nearly four o'clock in the afternoon. He'd been discharged from hospital earlier that morning and was still feeling groggy, so they'd both decided to have a nap.

Ellen had been asleep herself and he wasn't sure she had heard what he had said. Although he now knew the link between the name Edith and the woman in yellow, he didn't want to share it with anyone before he told Maisie.

"Harry, you've have had a difficult few days. It's not surprising the dreams are affecting you even more." She was soon holding him tight, comforting him as he came down from panic.

"I just wish I could remember. Remember who I am, who I was. I am sure there are clues in my dreams." He deliberately didn't mention Edith's name again just in case Ellen thought he was going mad. He kissed Ellen gently.

"Harry. I'm helping in Prendergast's department this week. I've been moved from A and E because of my seniority. They need someone to focus on the electives. With the good weather, the hospital is quiet. I could have a look at your records. See what's what. I'm not sure they are telling you the whole story."

"Ellen. No. You would be risking your job. I would rather file a freedom of information request."

"That could take forever, they fix those things and bury them in statistics."

"You could lose everything; your profession, and so could I, by association. Don't go anywhere near those records. I'll apply for them once this case is over."

Harry kissed Ellen mainly because she was frowning. The frown that sometimes led to anger.

"Okay. Sorry. I just want you to know." Ellen said.

"I don't want you to get into trouble on my account. There's a process I will need to follow. I just can't concentrate on that now."

"Okay."

If only Harry could have seen the look on Ellen's face as she turned away from him; one that suggested that she was going to find those records anyway.

Chapter Eleven

Price Leads A Briefing

The Magpie stood in the reception lounge of Bell Manor, looking up at the portrait sitting over the fireplace. It looked very much like the Lady, but she was dressed in Victorian clothing, all black with a bustle, like a Victorian widow.

He hadn't liked returning there. It was no longer welcoming. The oppressive heat and the yawning maw of the entrance to the old house made him feel like a cooked meal. The weather continued to be hot and smothering outside, as the Indian summer festered onwards, the air seeming fit to burst. He was sweating heavily - unusual for him.

"My new Magpie." Lady Bell said, appearing as if from nowhere. She often seemed to do so.

New? We have known each other years.

The Magpie had always thought of himself as alert. He usually had a great kinaesthetic sense, always ready for action. But around Lady Bell, he felt like a blind man in a maze. He could never forget the helplessness he had felt when he had first met her; he felt like that now. The slow dripping dread seemed to be returning, much like the sweat that dripped beneath his shirt.

"Lady Bell." He took her proffered hand and kissed it, as was her way and expectation.

"Have you carried out my instructions?"

He found himself swallowing, his throat dry.

"The plan is all in-train, including your... tweaks. I *have* been planning this for many years, as you know. The last-minute changes are... troublesome."

He could feel his hackles rising as he challenged her, like touching a Van Den Graph generator.

She smiled at him as if he were an errant child.

"It cannot fail. Your petty vengeance, your random acts of murder, are of no interest to me, but you know I must have my payment. It is essential; I have helped you to remain looking as you are, in deep cover, as it were. Now you must repay that gift."

"Why do you need an increase in numbers? We agreed on five deaths in this second tranche. Now you want more?"

"You haven't earned that confidence yet, my little Magpie. Rest assured when the time comes, if you don't figure it out yourself, I will let you into my plan."

"I'm guessing it's based on that inane rhyme, if you want me to kill seven in total?"

"It might be inane to you, but rhymes have power. They build power. Power that I need. The eighth victim will give us a boost. A binding as it were. "

The Magpie wasn't sure what she was talking about. He knew she wasn't like most people, but surely, she derived power from her business status, not killing.

"Murdering police officers was not in our original scope; their deaths bring more attention. More investigation. Do I really need to do this?" He didn't name the potential victims. It was as if it might all unravel if he did.

"More attention than the discovery of the bodies in Legend Street?"

He looked at her in surprise.

"You think I have no way of finding things out? Do you think my reach goes no further than rural Staffordshire? Interesting what happened to those poor creatures. How it mirrors your own ways of working." The last was said with disgust, as if she wasn't the one who had commissioned further deaths. "It is as if you killed them. Yet that would make you ancient. No one lives that long. Do they?"

Lady Bell was pouting, as ever. She was incredibly beautiful on one level, but it was as if she was carved

119

from stone. Like the Witch from CS Lewis's Lion the Witch and the Wardrobe story. Her age could only be gauged with difficulty, somewhere between an old-looking twenty-five and a youthful sixty. She was taller than most men now, her once ashen hair, now blonde, was presented in ringlets that cascaded down each side of her face. She was dressed in a plain red shift dress, tied with a rope belt. It was simple but did not detract from her beauty.

"Has Harry Morton caught the bait yet?"

He paused just too long.

"I know your history, Magpie. I know there is still revenge in your heart."

"One of his subordinates is looking for the woman in yellow," he answered rather quickly. He didn't like her mentioning Harry. Harry was his project. Her murders just happened to tie in.

"Excellent." She gave a little laugh. How strange. None of it touched her face. "I think I may know who that troublesome yellow bitch is. Although she is not part of our plan, she could become a useful lure too."

"Who is she?" He didn't expect an answer.

"You just concentrate on your victims. Leave the rest to me." She said quietly, as if deep in thought. "I need to know as soon as the policeman is dead. Nothing more. Be gone."

And that was it, he was dismissed. He left her presence quickly, why would he tarry? He travelled back to his Lichfield flat pensively. He wasn't happy that she knew so much about him, but what could he do? She had once been his carer, then his confidante. When she had become his murder patron, their relationship had shifted slightly initially, but over time, his early privileges were like melting diamonds, once so solid, but now not much more than ice.

The Magpie had prided himself on being able to cover his tracks. Lady Bell, with her ever-changing instructions, was introducing more random acts into his plan. She was testing him. Testing his loyalty or usefulness, no doubt. But it was chaos that got you caught. He needed to plan more, spend the next few nights allying his onward steps with her additions. For the first time in years, he felt nervous and sick to his stomach, even after leaving her presence.

He needed to talk to his collection of eyes. Angus and Chrissie might be able to help.

"Right. Simmer down. Oy!" Maisie almost screamed.

The whole team were in for the briefing, except for the gov, who was still poorly and wouldn't be present.

It should have been Rollo leading the session, but the lazy get was AWOL when she had tried to contact him the evening before.

"I need to bring you all up to speed." Surprisingly, they calmed. Spotlight on her - her throat dry. Harry had told her to take her time when she had briefly discussed things with him that morning. A call that she wasn't going to answer because Harry should have been recuperating, but he'd phoned repeatedly until she'd picked up.

The room smelled of cigarettes (Rollo and Grace), nervous sweat - probably half the blokes- and perfumes, both male and female. She gagged. *You don't want to vomit in front of this lot. It would be a massive faux pas.*

"As far as Dr Hodgson can tell, the first bodies she examined from the Legend Street attic were not murdered. However, there is a mystery surrounding their demise. Dating of the remains is still incomplete, but according to dental examinations of the first three victims, they died circa 1935 to 1948."

Some eyes turned to Grace who nodded her encouragement, but did not add anything to help Maisie, not even a customary inappropriate comment. Maisie knew they were looking to someone to affirm what they were hearing.

121

Maisie took another deep breath. "The latest victim Christine was killed, like Angus, by a single stroke to the chest. Like Angus, she suffered a blunt trauma hemopneumothorax. This was not the cause of death, however." Again, she looked at Grace who just nodded. "In both cases, the blade was inserted with such force that it went through the sternum, bypassed the heart and into a lung." She paused for effect. "They would most likely have choked on their own blood."

Another deep breath. *Come on M.P. You are doing well.* DC Price and DC Miles are now tracing the last movements of both victims. It is essential we piece together as much as we can about where they both went and what happened to them during their last hours and minutes. Oh. And just to warn you - the next presentation will not be pretty."

Nodding at Mo to turn off the lights, Maisie flicked on the projector. The first visuals that were cast on to the screen were received with obvious horror. After that initial collective gasp, silence fell.

"Only a select few of you have seen pictures from Legend Street, aside from those of you unlucky enough to be at the scene. There are similarities to the Lichfield victims. This is a photo of one of what we now refer to as "The Six." Her eyes have been removed."

Maisie clocked the uncomfortable looks passing between the team. Pete caught her gaze with sympathy, Wojcik too. Hayden Worth sat at the back, shaking his head. Mo was muttering under his breath, probably a prayer; Daisy wasn't even looking.

Maisie clicked the remote control. "Up next are the post-mortem images of the latest victims. They have similar facial injuries. Both Chrissy and Angus had their eyes removed, possibly before they breathed their last. Yes, he removed their eyes as they bled out. It goes without saying that he's an evil bastard." She let that sink in. There were further gasps.

"So, we have The Six from Legend Street, Edgbaston. We have two more victims, seventy or so years later, also with missing eyes. Is it a copycat killer? Who knows? Those responsible for the six bodies at Legend Street did not kill their victims, but they did take their eyes. If this were the same person, they would be well into their nineties -if not older- by now." Again, she paused to let that sink in. Maisie could almost hear the cogs.

"The situation and environment at Legend Street suggest there would have been more than one person at play. We are currently looking into connections only because of the missing eyes. The results will be on a need-to-know basis." Maisie clicked the laptop remote.

"There is no third-party DNA on our recent victims, nor on the Legend Street Six. Nothing that could remotely be called evidence has been found at any scene. Whoever killed Angus and Chrissy knows what he or she is doing when it comes to removing eyes. They are professionals, or they have read up on the procedure and are very well planned. It's weak, I know. The eyes of the Legend Street Six have also been precisely removed – but no later than 1948 and we have those jars which present another angle.

"In short, we have nothing but eight victims. We are waiting for the perpetrator to slip up, which means we are sadly waiting for him to strike again."

"This week, Team A - led by me, will be looking into The Six. Mo and Karol will support me. Team B will be looking into the details surrounding the latest two victims, led by Inspector Rolleston, aided by Pete and Daisy. Team C will be helping the Guvnor to look through the paperwork we have received from the solicitors. George Wright, as you may recall, was the owner of Legend Street, who went missing shortly after his wife's disappearance. Is Nancy one of the six victims? We think not, but we are also looking into a mystery organisation called the Cordivae, who are named in papers belonging to Wright and Professor

Beaton. The Professor's father Paul we now know was an associate of Wright's."

"Finally, we are also looking to identify a woman dressed in yellow, who was seen running from the scene."

"We're not still pursuing that nonsense, Price?" Rollo had finally contributed.

"The woman in question was also seen by the gov shortly before he was taken ill."

Rollo's eyes narrowed. He hadn't been informed. Whoops, she would no doubt suffer for that, even though she was already de-facto Inspector, much to Rollo's annoyance again.

"I think you and I need to talk, Sergeant. I am not happy about being kept out of the loop."

"With respect, Inspector, we tried to contact you last night and you refused the call. I would have been happy for you to lead this briefing had you arrived on time." *In for a penny.* She wasn't going to put up with him. There were a couple of gasps in the room.

Rollo gave her a withering look and walked out of the briefing. They would no doubt talk later.

Maisie took a deep breath. She noticed Grace who had a smirk on her face

"Back to the facts. Angus was an undertaker. Chrissy was a midwife. Is there a significance? We are looking for someone called the Magpie."

There was a tangible frisson in the room. Karol snapped upright on his seat.

"That's not in the briefing pack."

"It's a working title, Wojcik. Magpies take shiny things. Eyes are shiny things." She knew that was not the reason; the reason was that the gov had been told by the woman in yellow.

"Let's keep it to ourselves, though. If that hits the press, they will have a field day."

"One for sorrow. Two for joy," Daisy offered.

"Sorry?" Maisie frowned at her sister.

"Undertaker. Midwife. Death and birth. Sorrow and joy?"

"Fucking genius." Grace offered - the only irregular thing she had said all briefing.

Maisie nodded. It was. How had she not put that together? "It fits. Maybe there's more to the name than we know. Let's keep going through the evidence."

"Three for a girl and four for a boy. Jesus. He's not going to kill kids, is he?" Pete's words stilled the room once more.

"It may not be that literal." Grace countered. "However, we do need to brief all colleagues that the rhyme may be part of the M.O."

"Daisy, can you re-set the incident room focusing on the victims and the evidence we have. The current information needs to be combed through in light of the discussions we've just had."

Daisy nodded, apparently able to follow an order without being a bitch.

"The Magpie name and rhyme are just guesses though." Daisy reminded them.

"DCI Morton has received information suggesting that this is what he or she is called. More likely to be him."

"Information? What information? Daisy asked. She was as difficult as Rollo.

"Any questions?" Maisie rounded off the discussion, determined in the face of her sisters rising negativity. "No? Let's crack on, then."

Rollo didn't take long to confront her after the briefing was over. She was absorbed in spreading out some of the background information in Harry's room when he burst in, evidently straight back from a fag break, judging by the stink of smoke.

"What sort of ambush are you trying to pull, Price? Going over my head with the gov. Are you fucking him? You ditched Teddy are you doing the gov as well as Pete?"

125

Maisie stood quickly. The bastard wasn't going to look down at her.

"Is this about you having to go up to Fife?" She was too exasperated to respond to his vile accusations.

"No. I expected that. This is about you continuing to walk over your colleagues to get to where you want to go. Your sister included, no doubt. All these cosy meetings with the gov."

"I have just been about when he was."

"On a Sunday? I have friends at Central . I know you were over at the scene then. You both went to the pub after. "

"Proper detective work." She retorted.

"Don't get funny Price. I'm still de facto SIO with Harry out."

"I know. Sorry, sir." She deflated visibly. His mouth twitched, sensing victory. *Fifteen love.*

"And although the gov has asked me to keep quiet, I do not condone the fact that you, soon to be inspector, are fooling about with one of my new PCs."

"I don't line manage him; Marsh did. He wasn't my new PC, but he's now yours. I did report it to the gov." *A slight white lie, he had found out.* "You should be glad of the help."

"That doesn't make any difference. Harry is a good man, but he is soft. If it were me, I would have transferred you, *sergeant*, with immediate effect."

"Good job the gov is not you then, Rollo." She deliberately did not use his honorific.

She would not cry. Not in front of Rollo. Instead, she stared at him. He rarely made eye contact; she knew he would back down eventually. He did so and made to leave.

"At the end of the case, if Pete and I are still together I will ask for a transfer. It's early days for us." she called after him. That was a spur of the moment reaction - but she knew it was wrong to think she could go on like this. "Until then, you are stuck with me."

You supercilious twat.

Harry was in the cage, but the other boy wasn't there. The woman dressed all in yellow looked at him. She was sitting in a chair in the space outside the cage.

"Hello again," she said. "Back in the cage?"

"I've been naughty, or at least that's what they tell me."

She was a pretty lady, although she looked no older than early twenties. He had no concept of attraction yet, he was just a boy, but she looked a little like Snow White from his Ladybird book.

"My name is Edith. I thought you were looking for me?"

"Yes, I know who you are. No, I don't think I am looking for you. You aren't going to take me to the nurse again, are you?" He asked. He did recall something about a woman dressed in yellow. It was meant to be important. He just couldn't grasp the facts.

Edith walked up to the cage and opened the door. How could it have been so easy? He could have reached through and opened it himself, if he had known.

"Little boys should not be locked in cages. Come on."

Harry hesitated; could he just walk out? Would the other boy come back and start to throw stones until he went back in? There was no sign of the other boy, however. He started to sob tears of relief. He couldn't help it.

"The dream is like a story, El. But it's developing."

She had been there when he woke up. He'd been saying Edith's name again. The memories of the woman in yellow - just wisps of ethereal memory clinging to an image half-remembered.

"Edith was there again. She let me out of the cage."

127

Ellen looked at him with concern in her eyes - and something else. Disbelief? No, maybe not. It was more than that. It was as if she felt he was having a breakdown. She believed what he said, but it was clear what she thought were his musings were symptoms of a mental illness.

"My therapist said she was jealous of my ability to have concurrent dreams."

"They aren't unusual, then?"

"It's the lucidity of them. I can write more and more of them down each day."

He moved his head down, kissed her hair. She moved her head upwards and kissed him on the lips.

"I need to get back to work." He'd decided hours ago, but did not want to broach it with his angel.

"Harry. It's too soon. But I know what you're like."

He kissed her again. This time, she didn't let him go.

Chapter Twelve
The Moribund and the Dead

Pete had gone home; he was on an early shift. Maisie decided to take a walk into Lichfield to clear her head. Pete would get the cold shoulder tomorrow, working with Daisy; no doubt she'd be prim and disapproving towards him too.

It was still very warm. Middle of October and in the high twenties. Everyone was blaming global warming; Maisie felt a pang of guilt that she was too damned busy to get involved in any of it. She was a shit ecologist - her children would hate her for it.

She stopped at one of the myriad coffee bars and ordered a cappuccino. It took ages to come and that pissed her off too, as did the barista spelling her name with a 'y' on the side of the cup. She took the coffee with a grimace at the exhortation to "have a nice rest of your day." That was highly unlikely.

Rolleston had wound her up good and proper over the last day or so. She hadn't expected the volley of spite he'd kicked at her like a fast-spinning rugby ball of misshapen vitriol. How dare he question her about her private life? She wondered what Daisy's role in all of this was. Was it her who'd told Rollo about Pete? It had better not have been.

"Excuse me Miss, can I join you?"

Oh God. Who was that? She had wanted some time on her own. She really did not want to speak to any strangers. She seemed to attract strange people. Always had done, ever since she had been a girl. She remembered seeing a man in Lichfield Square when she was visiting her Nanna. They had said she had imagined him and put it down to a migraine. Yet she had seen Edward Wightman quite clearly. She had researched him afterwards too - the last man to be executed for heresy in England and in Lichfield.

Something about this encounter reminded her of that time. Her head began to hurt, like it had back then. Maisie looked across to the table opposite. There, large as life, was the woman in yellow. A jolt ran through her, the shock was like nothing she had ever experienced before.

"Shitting hell. It's you." She knocked her drink over as she stood, the contents flew out and the cup shattered on the floor. The woman had not been there before. How could she be here now? How did she know where Maisie lived? How had she just appeared?

Maisie felt eyes upon her; the other patrons in the coffee bar clearly thought she was mad – she was inclined to agree with them. The waitress was clearing the table where the woman in yellow was sitting, oblivious to her existence. Edith, Harry had said. She was just sitting there.

"I nearly said that when I first realised you could see me. Although I would not have used such language."

"Sorry?"

The waitress frowned at Maisie as if she were a complete loon, a dial short of a radio, but continued to clean up.

Maisie's head was throbbing, she felt faint. She felt above all else that she needed some air. She weighed up her options. Stay in here talking to an invisible woman or get the invisible woman to follow her.

"Follow me." Maisie whispered.

The woman in yellow winked then disappeared.

Maisie's heart went in her mouth again. She was going mad. Maisie left the coffee shop with another heartfelt apology leaving a tenner in the tip jar.

Despite the heat outside, Maisie felt cold - bone-numbing cold. She shivered. Goosebumps pricked up and down the bare flesh not covered by her summer top.

Concentrate, M.

Edith re-appeared right beside her.

"Oh, my fucking God, Mary, and baby Jesus!" she gasped. It was lucky the city was quiet. She might be sectioned by the time she got past McDonald's.

"Don't react. They will think you're mad." Edith said, with thick sarcasm.

Maisie gazed at the woman in yellow, completely terrified, but unable to avoid raising her eyebrows. "I think I'm already mad."

Edith carried on oblivious. "When I saw you at Legend Street, in Birmingham, well, that was such a shock."

"For me too…"

"Let me finish, please. No-one has seen me for such a long time. Not since I was properly alive, that is. Oh, and you do realise if you talk back to me, people will think *you* are mad. Few can see me. So, whisper."

I am completely mad. What was she saying? Not since I was alive?

"Let's go to your house. We can talk there."

"You are a figment of my imagination," Maisie said, more to herself than Edith. "Aren't you?"

"Could be," Edith admitted, pensively. "I'm not quite sure why I'm here myself."

"Harry saw you," Maisie whispered.

"I tried my hardest to make him see me. He has a block. That thing in his head seems to block his ability to see. You don't have such an impediment. You can see the dead. Whereas with Harry I have had to invade his subconsciousness."

"Dead. You keep saying dead. I bumped into you. I felt you."

Scared, Maisie started to run across the small city centre, up past Boots, then up Bore Street. The ghost would probably be able to follow her again, no doubt.

Ghost?

Reaching her home, she opened the door, lungs bursting, then locked it behind her. Only then did she allow herself to pull in deep gasps of air, like a half-drowned woman.

"I'm sorry, but you can't run away from me. We need to talk."

Maisie screamed, then clamped a hand over her own mouth. She felt the urge to vomit, just a little more strongly than the pressing need to lose control of her bladder. She screwed her eyes shut, as if that would get rid of Edith. The woman for whom she had spent so much time searching; the woman who might hold the key to what had happened at Legend Street.

Slowly she opened her eyes. The woman in yellow was still there. Brave heart, her Nanna always said when she was tearful. Oh, Nanna what is going on?

"Are you a ghost?"

The woman in yellow smiled. "It's a little more complicated than that. I think I'm a soul-echo. I'm not sure. An old friend called Robert named us the Moribund."

"The half-dead?"

Edith shrugged. She really was beautiful, perfect in every way, as if she had been sculpted by Michelangelo or painted by a Pre-Raphaelite artist. She was tall, nearly as tall as Maisie. Her body was an hourglass of yellow, full, and flowing like the fleeting sands of time. She had seated herself on one of the breakfast-bar stools, her legs crossed, her tanned legs smooth and long. Maisie hadn't looked at a woman like this in such a long time.

"Edith?" Maisie asked, "Is that your name?"

"It seems so, although I'm not certain. I need affirmation. Harry needs to dream more."

"How did you know where I lived?" Dear God, she was interviewing a half-ghost. In her own living room. What was that Edith had said about Harry? Were his dreams linked to this?

Edith smiled. "I didn't. I just knew you needed to speak to me. I went to the market square. I came to Lichfield many times during the war. It has changed so much since then, but there are still many restless souls in this city. I met Edward Wightman in the square. He said he's met you before."

Deep breath. Maisie thought, *turn on your professional head, don't be a piss-your-pants girl.* Was she asleep somewhere and dreaming all of this? Was her mind giving her answers to the mystery woman in yellow? Was it the split with Teddy causing her subconscious stress? Was it that breakdown finally coming?

"What were you doing at Legend Street? When we bumped into each other on the stairs?" Maisie found herself a chair opposite Edith. "And when I asked you if you were a ghost, you said it was more complicated." Maisie felt tears on her cheeks. This beautiful woman dead, yet not dead. It defied the laws of nature. Nanna believed on the other side, the supernatural; she went to seances, practised the Ouija as a girl and laid the tarot cards. Her father had said it was all mumbo jumbo, but Nanna had been serious. Nanna was always serious when she spoke about parting the veil. Why had it taken this to make Maisie realised her Nanna knew things, possibly how people could appear after death? *Oh, Nanna how much I'd love to call you up and ask for your help with this ghostly woman.*

Although Edith looked as solid as Maisie and more beautiful than any dead person had a right to be.

"It was my first appearance in such a long time, at Legend Street, that is. I had been there before, with my friend Nancy. I know that much. I came looking for Nancy the night she went missing. Died. I wanted to see Mr Wright, ask him where she had gone, but he'd disappeared. After eight o'clock on the night of the 31st of October 1948, I can recall no more. I knew I must have died to suddenly reappear seventy years or so later. I would be very old by now, not looking as I do now. Nancy and I were going to a Halloween party in Soho. Obviously, neither of us made it there."

"There were bodies at Legend Street. But we have no way of knowing if Nancy is one of the six."

"I saw them." Edith interrupted. "I have never seen anything so vile in all of my existence. Their eyes. Nancy isn't one of them. Nor in fact, am I."

"You said that to Harry before he collapsed. What does it mean?"

"I don't know." Edith was sobbing. Her tears, the handkerchief she took from her clutch bag looked real. "I truly remember so little. I just feel this evil. And the one who controls it."

"Another moribund?"

"I don't know, but I can feel her. She is near. She is there, like a distant un-graspable memory, like a forgotten word forever on the tip of my tongue."

Edith was very well-spoken, clipped, almost received pronunciation. Maisie had studied drama as well as politics at university; the dialect coach, an older woman called Ruth Davies, spoke like Edith - like an announcer from 1960s BBC.

"So, you aren't one of the bodies at Legend Street, Edith?"

The ghostly woman, the Moribund woman, if that was really what she was calling herself, looked up. There was great sadness in her eyes. Then she shook her head.

"My death, whether natural or unnatural, remains a mystery to me. I do not recognise any of those faces behind the glass in that tank. Only you and a few others I have come across can see me. Most think I am an oddly dressed woman. Only you seem to have derived some significance from seeing me. My purpose here is linked to you - and Harry. I don't know why. I don't know why I know about the Magpie, the one you are searching for. I don't know why I know about the evil one. I just know."

The woman stood and moved towards Maisie.

"If I am truly a ghost, how do you explain this?" Edith grabbed both of Maisie's hands in hers. Solid. Warm. How could that be?

"How...?"

"I'm testing a methodology. When I *am* here, I can touch things, interact with them. Most do not feel me. When I touch your hands, you do. I can see it in your eyes." Edith smiled, tears coming again. "That's why I think they call us the Moribund. We are between life and death, on the cusp. Why? I do not know."

"Who are they?"

"I'm not sure. I feel them. I have not seen them. I briefly met Robert Waterfield in a place of nothingness before I forgot."

Could ghosts cry? It seemed Edith was something other than what centuries of supernatural writing had drummed up; she wasn't a poltergeist, nor a thing of conscious presence, she was here in Maisie's living room. Who was this Robert Waterfield too? His name repeatedly came up in documentation, William Beaton cited his name, and now Edith.

"How can I do this?" she spoke, before vanishing. Not fading, vanishing as if she had never been there.

There was a knock on her front door. Maisie jumped again - she was a bag of nerves and quite rightly so. Her life, her world, her belief system had turned upside down in a matter of moments.

She answered the door, already knowing who it would be. Edith stood with half-dried tears on her cheeks.

"Come in." She said it automatically and then laughed. Edith's face curled into a smile.

They talked about nothing for a while. Maisie made tea. Edith was able to drink it and said nothing else that would answer the obvious questions in Maisie's head. How can she drink? Does she need to pee?

Edith suddenly straightened.

"I can feel someone nearby. It might help if we speak to her. She is walking in the park, just as she did when she was alive. She has recently passed, fifteen or so months ago. I know that much. I would like to speak with her. I think I knew her in life. Would you like to join me?"

Maisie physically recoiled. More ghosts? It was bad enough dealing with Edith.

"She is known to you. She wants to say goodbye. She never had the chance."

Nanna. Nanna used to walk in Beacon Park. *Fifteen months.*

"Oh, dear God no. I mean, of course, I would like to. Oh God, I'm not sure what I want." Maisie was cold again. It was the cold of her last resting place calling her. She could feel it. This was not just an encounter with a strange woman from the past and yet appeared to be as alive as any living being - this was directly linking Maisie to her own past. She could feel it.

"Is it Nanna? My Nanna?"

Her voice was childlike, she could hear herself as an eleven-year-old girl. She would always visit Nanna on one of her family's regular trips down from Yorkshire, before they moved back seven or eight years later. She had been the only one who wasn't with Nanna when she died, and she had regretted it. She had been with Teddy.

"Come," Edith said. "There can be no answers without further questions."

Edith was a philosophical moribund woman, it seemed.

Edith led her out of the flat by her hand. Maisie snatched her fleece from the rack, despite it being over twenty-three degrees in the shade. The cold of the past had filled her. The goose bumps rose all over her body again. She was going to see her Nanna.

They came into Beacon Park on its eastern side. Edith led the way, as if she knew where to go all along. Through the children's play area towards the pool, where children pedalled in ladybird boats as their parents looked on. It was midday by the time Edith sat her down on one of the park benches by the coffee shop. She knew because a nearby church was ringing its bells. Or were they tolling?

"Look," Edith said and pointed.

And there was her Nanna.

She wasn't solid like Edith. Nanna Price was flickering like an old image captured on celluloid film that was partly decomposing. She was there and she was not there, at the same time. She was slowly walking, and she was not – because she was dead and had been so for fifteen months or so. Disappearing every few steps, but then catching up with the perceived distance as she reappeared.

And although it was Nanna, it wasn't an old woman. She looked no more than twenty. Clara Keats, as she would have been known then, was a handsome woman; short, a little plump - or cuddly, as Grandad had called her. Her hair was styled in a bob, flapper style. Nanna had been born in the early 1920s

Although Nanna Price was flickering in and out of existence, Maisie noticed she was approaching them. She remembered seeing a video from her mum's collection by a band called A-ha. There was a song that had a video of the singer and his girlfriend drawn in pencil, looking real, but not really. Nanna sat next to them, looking like that. Flickering. There and not there.

"Hello dear. It's been a while." An old voice spoke from the young visage. It was doubly disconcerting.

Maisie felt herself crying, her tears like the rivers of grief she could have cried but had never had the time. The pent-up grief that had been trapped in her heart for her Nanna. Nanna -Clara Price, or Keats as she would have been.

"I'm glad of your tears, girl. However, I don't need them. Pack them away. I know how much you, Daisy and your parents loved me."

Nanna's voice - as far as she could tell - was as she remembered in her head. For all intents and purposes, especially to the casual onlooker, Maisie looked like she was sitting on a bench on her own, crying, talking to no-one in particular. Something deep in her knew she should not draw attention to herself, as a senior police officer, so she took her phone from her pocket and put it to her ear. Anyone looking on would just see a woman making a call.

"You and Daisy were always clever girls. You are more so. Although Daisy could do those number puzzles. You were so good at finding the words in the word searches. Edith, you were the same."

Maisie heard Edith gasp; that made two of them. Nanna had equally surprised the half-ghost. How could this mysterious woman in yellow have links to her own family?

"How do you know things about my past, yet I struggle to peer through the fog?" Edith asked Nanna's ghost.

"My recollections are limited, but everyone remembers their little sister. You were adopted by our family. Here - let me gift your memory, but it is only a strand. It is not for me to reveal your secrets." Edith gasped again. "All I know, Edith, is that you disappeared on Hallowe'en night in 1948 and we cried for decades."

Edith vanished – but this time she flickered first, as if reeling from the shock of the memory given by Nanna. She reappeared in front of Maisie and the ghost of her Nanna. "Sister. Clara? Thank you."

"You are welcome, sister. I have one last gift for you both before I go. Edith first. Your friend Nancy will be found. George did not kill her, but she died the night you disappeared, dear. For reasons, only George or his writings can explain."

"Thank you. I think." Edith said, sitting down next to them again with a sigh.

"Now dear Maisie, to you. I don't know why you can suddenly see the dead. Or the Moribund as Edith's kind are called. All I can say is you have been chosen. Chosen to carry out great work here in the living world. As you look for the Magpie."

138

"Who is he?" Maisie asked.

"That I cannot tell you, my dear. The living world is not open to the dead."

"Is there anything else?"

"Yes. That young man you love. Make sure you love him and tell him you do. Life is too short. Your life, however, will be long dear. Do not have any regrets."

"Pete?"

Nanna shook her head.

"Teddy?"

"You will know him when you find him. I need to go."

Riddles, Nanna?

"Can I kiss you goodbye, Nanna?"

"No dear. I am as insubstantial as a wisp of smoke. I take the sentiment, with me though. We might meet again, given your new skills; however, I cannot promise. So, this may be our final goodbye."

And with that Nanna Clara Price flickered out of existence.

A great, wracking sob grabbed Maisie as the last of her grief for her Nanna came flooding out. Moreover, the shocks of the morning's events came flooding out too, as the more solid ghost – now known as Aunt Edith -held her, like a dead guardian preventing her from moving on.

Not far away, the woman known as Lady Bell stirred in her uncomfortable rest. A powerful woman was nearby; a woman who could jeopardise all her plans if she let her. She would have to speak with the Magpie again. He did not like the unplanned though, so, once he had dealt with Harry Morton, he would have to help her deal with that woman. Although even Lady Bell didn't know how to kill someone who was half dead.

Chapter Thirteen
Talking to My Eyes

Harry still felt a little groggy, but he had hauled his sorry arse into work. The revelation of knowing they were looking for someone called the Magpie was intriguing- although that information was dependent on the mysterious woman in yellow. Edith, the woman from his dreams.

Of course, no one knew about his dreams; that side of things would remain secret, however bizarre. He had Google searched the name Edith, along with other terms including Lichfield, Edgbaston and Legend Street and missing whilst in hospital - and had come up with nothing familiar.

He had put that aside for a minute and had taken a call from Grace, who wanted to see him and Maisie later. She was being coy on the phone, which usually meant she had a big reveal for them. Then he decided to start to rifle through other evidence sources.

By lunchtime, Harry had got through the paperwork supplied by Professor Beaton and had found two things of interest. The first was related to George Wright's property redesign portfolio, which had been managed by Paul Beaton, the architect father of the professor. George had other houses up and down the country, but the one he visited most according to his documents and diaries was the one in Bude, Cornwall. This correlated with what Giles and Maisie had said. They could look there for clues regarding Nancy Wright, although the excavation at Legend Street could still reveal her remains.

The second revelation was the discovery from the papers and diaries that George had been donating to a secret agency called Cordivae. Based at the University of Birmingham, the group appeared to be linked to the ongoing support of servicemen and women injured in the First World War- particularly those who had been alumni of the university. Harry would need to have a look into that later. He would get DS Hyatt onto it.

There was a knock on the door - it was Maisie. She looked tired and worn. The split from Teddy must be affecting her. Harry had good news for her, however; her promotion would be effective immediately.

"Gov. You, okay?"

"Yes M. A little groggy, but better none the less. We've still got the team talk later. I've found a few other important things in the Wright evidence, so I'd like everyone to know about it. I've also decided to open an investigation on Edith, but only you and I will be privy to the detail for now."

Maisie understood his secretive nature. "She came to see me."

"What?" Now, this was strange indeed. He dropped the papers in his hands and cast all his attention on his soon-to-be inspector. Things had taken a really bizarre twist, even for the Complex Case Team.

"She appeared yesterday. Came looking for me."

"How?"

"I'm not sure Harry. There is something really strange going on."

He stood and thought for a while. He wasn't going to reveal his dreams, but this revelation made it necessary. Maisie was looking at him in anticipation. He *was* going to have to tell her. "Listen M, I need to take you into confidence. You must keep this to yourself." He paused, at once reluctant, but knowing it was now linked into the investigation. "I dreamt about Edith. The woman in yellow. She's been there all the time, in my dreams, ever since I woke in the Cathedral all those years ago. I just did not remember her or her name."

"Edith Keats, she said her name was." Maisie added, slowly. "She said as much to me, but she

141

knows nothing else. Says she's a friend of Nancy Wright."

Harry was flabbergasted.

"How can Edith Keats, the woman in my dreams, be both a friend of Nancy Wright and alive in 2022? She would be ancient. Not a woman who looks like she is in her late twenties."

Harry pulled a hand through his hair, a nervous response.

"Can I meet her again? I need to ascertain if this is all a hoax." He could have demanded it, but he felt there was something Maisie was not telling him.

"She will not reveal herself until she knows more. She left me without a forwarding address, Harry. I'm not even sure where she lives, even if she has a house. How long have you known?"

She smiled, trying to put him at ease. She really was quite beautiful when she smiled. A Yorkshire beauty.

"I've always had dreams. Since they found me. Normally I am fighting with another boy. They are so vivid, so detailed. They progress too like a story. My psychologist tells me somewhat rare to have progressive dreams." Harry sighed, but thought damn it. In for a penny. "I started to dream about Edith, but would not remember when I awoke, then in the last few days, she let me out of the damned cage."

"Cage?"

"I am invariably in a cage; another boy is always throwing stones. The location is the same, but our conversations move on. Then I remembered that Edith has been there, all along. Not when the boy is, but consoling me afterwards." He paused, amazed that he had said so much. "I'm trusting you here Maisie. This is personal, but if I didn't discuss this with someone, I would burst. If you see her again, if she reveals where she lives, I need to speak with her as a matter of urgency."

Maisie nodded. If he were a betting man, he'd say there was something she was holding back.

Harry had opened up to her –a positive thing. Why couldn't she have reciprocated? It didn't feel right – it was too soon. Edith was her great aunt, a Moribund soul. She was woven into both of their lives. What was the link between Harry's dreams and Edith appearing to her?

"Shit." Edith had appeared in the office. She was standing by the door. Maisie did not react further, quickly regaining her composure.

"M?"

"Sorry. Lot to take in. Yes, of course, I'll keep it to myself. We both sound as mad as each other." It spluttered out of her, and his frown softened into a half-smile.

"Thanks, M. Maybe we could go for a drink later in the week and discuss it further? I'll try to make sense of the notes I've made about my dreams. I'll show you. I'm sure this is all subconscious on my part, but how can that woman have the same name, look exactly like the woman I have been dreaming about? Edith Keats. I've just googled her again and there's nothing."

He smiled that wonderful smile of his.

"Are you coming over to the Institute later? Grace wants a word with us. Rollo will be along too. Hope that doesn't present any difficulties. I hear he was a bit of an idiot at the briefing."

"Yes, he was. Accused me of sleeping with you as well as Pete."

Harry reddened – with anger, or was he blushing? Maisie couldn't tell. "I'll see you then." She just wanted to get out now, withholding evidence was weighing heavy on her soul. She hadn't told him Edith was a half-ghost. And the woman linked them both. It wasn't time to admit it; or rather, she wasn't ready to admit, even to herself, that she could see the dead.

"He needs to know I'm dead." Edith offered. Her voice echoed in Maisie's mind. She did not respond as she walked past the ghost of the woman in yellow and out into the corridor.

If you keep appearing like that, I am going to go mad. Sorry.

Harry looked up again as someone else walked in the office, another disturbance. It was Rollo. He didn't look too well either; what the hell was going on with them all?

He would not be telling Rollo about the dreams yet, or any of the dots he and Maisie had just joined. He liked Rollo but he didn't trust him, not like Maisie. When Rollo had transferred over to his team it had been under an investigative cloud, hush-hush. Harry had no idea of the detail. He just knew this taciturn, intelligent man still hadn't integrated into his team after two years. He would probably ask Rollo to think about a transfer. Particularly after his snide comments to Maisie.

Rollo stood before his desk with his hands on his hips.

"How come Price took the lead when you were away?"

"I needed the briefing to go ahead, I couldn't track you down. She called you herself. You didn't answer"

"It could have waited a day or so, I could have led it and not lost face."

Rollo looked scruffy, like he had not changed his clothes for days. It was so unlike him; he was usually well-groomed, not a hair out of place, if a little on the casual side. There were rumours he had been an alcoholic, liked a spin on the horses, but nothing substantial. Police gossip was terrible. They were all criminals if you listened to it, they were all worse than those he and his colleagues locked up. Was Rollo in trouble? Alcoholism or gambling? Drugs?

"I'm not going to have a stand-up row with you Rollo, I'm not in the mood. I want the team together in an hour. I've found a couple of things in the detail of the papers we got from Beaton. You and I need to go down to Cornwall to do some more digging. I'll buy you a few beers and you are going to tell me what's wrong. You look like you're burning the candle at both ends. You need to iron your clothes and you need to brush your hair." His voice was rising in volume. Rollo was getting redder and redder. Harry was determined not to give him a chance to respond until he had finished his lecture.

"If there's stuff going on outside of work, I don't need to know the detail, but I need to know you are at the top of your game. You, Price and I need to give ourselves a good shaking. We are the senior team here, but we look like a bunch of amateurs. Eight dead bodies and nothing to show for it and you coming in here all bruised ego. You don't have to like Price, but you *will* work with her. Now go, and set the next briefing up.

Rollo took a breath.

"Yes gov, sorry. Lots on my mind. I'll tell you about it when we go on our road trip."

He looked worse than when he had first come in. The adrenalin had clearly leached out of him. Rollo looked deflated, a man on the edge. Harry would find out what was at the bottom of this eventually; he always did.

"And if you ever accuse Maisie and me of having an affair again, you will be suspended."

Rollo nodded, almost imperceptibly.

An hour later, Harry surveyed his senior team gathered in the incident room. Surrounded by boards and loads of paperwork, but no leads. It was a mess.

145

He would have to have a word with Maisie - it was hurting his minimalist head.

Mo, Maisie, and Rollo were there, with Daisy Price and Pete Miles in attendance. They were working on tracing the last steps of Chrissy and Angus.

"Right, I have some more information on George Wright. It seems he had properties up and down the country- most of them designed by Paul Beaton, the Professor's father. Paul Beaton was an architect but also involved in a group in the 1930s and 1940s called the Cordivae. That's Latin for a genus of birds, by the way for those of you not classically trained like me – which includes magpies. Our suspect is known as The Magpie. Daisy has made a connection with the Magpie rhyme. It's a potential link, although we're not totally sure whether it sheds much light on the killer."

Daisy Price smiled; it was unusual.

"George Wright regularly visited his renovated property in Cornwall, which might suggest it could be his second base. DI Rolleston and I are going to go and do a recce."

Rollo immediately started to fidget.

"DI Price will take care of things here whilst we are away for a couple of days. She is the gov when Rollo and I are not here. The SIO. She will maintain the key lines of enquiry and liaise with the Super and the Chief. We will be going Thursday and Friday, so we have time to cover off a few things first. Right... onto the detail. Where are we with the last steps of the two deceased?"

Daisy lifted her head from her notes.

"We have Chrissy's journey on tape, down the A38 all the way home. There are no clues as to whether she was followed. I would suggest not, or she has been followed at a distance, although I'm happy to be contradicted. We haven't got the Lichfield City feeds yet, but the images of the main roads show nothing- it's a total blank. There's no

146

CCTV in or around the part of Victoria Park where the Parsons live."

Mo piped up. "I've been back in touch with Angus Morton's family. He went for a walk the evening before he was found. He just wanted to clear his head - he'd had a few to drink watching the football with his brother-in-law, Michael Reilly. The Reillys live in Burntwood and having looked at CCTV and having asked around these last few days, there is no evidence of him past the Star Pub at 1 a.m. of the morning he was found."

"He was abducted and killed and then put up on that cross in the churchyard sometime between say one-thirty and seven a.m." Maisie added. "Let's keep tracking them. Pete and Daisy will continue to do so."

"Yes, ma'am." Miles snapped a little too enthusiastically. He was a good officer. A good-looking boy. He could understand how Maisie been drawn to him.

"Mo, where are you with family liaison?"

"Mrs Morton and Mr Parsons are quite obviously distraught. Mr Parsons is being encouraged by the press for a response however."

"Thanks, Mo, he is entitled to speak to the press so long as it doesn't impact upon the investigation. Maisie – can you give everyone an update?"

"I've just come off the phone from Grace. The gov, Rollo and I are going to see her later about the Six from Legend Street. However, following a detailed post-mortem on Chrissy and Angus and after follow-up tests, we can conclude that there is no evidence of third-party DNA at either scene. Nothing in their bloodstreams, only faint traces of chloroform. Neither Angus nor Chrissie were users of non-prescription drugs, nor did either have any underlying health conditions. There is no evidence of financial issues. Angus was about to retire; the Parsons had already cleared their mortgage. Both victims were killed, as we all know, by a single blow to their diaphragms, under the sternum, piercing their lungs. The only physical evidence we have is the killer." She paused. "The Magpie knows how to kill quickly. This would suggest he may have been trained in combat, or medically trained, which fits in with the expert removal of the eyes. Grace would lean towards him being a medic. What is beyond dispute though is the killer has taken their eyes shortly before death occurred. He has either discarded them - or has them in his possession."

"The windows of the soul." Daisy offered, but it was lost on everyone but Grace, who raised her eyebrows – and Harry. Daisy was a well-read girl. That was Shakespeare, if he remembered rightly. He wasn't a big fiction fan, but he liked the Bard and some of the other classics.

Harry watched Maisie as they finished the review. Her eyes were darting all over the place. What was wrong with the girl? It was like she was on speed. He couldn't afford his newest senior officer to fall apart. He would have to try and get to the bottom of her demons, after he and Rollo had travelled to and from Cornwall. The sooner they went, the better.

"Okay, team. Good work. It feels like we are getting nowhere but keep going; there are links. The bastard *will* slip up. Let's have another update later in the week, led by Maisie, if Rollo and I aren't back. I'll be briefed remotely, if necessary. Have a good evening, all? I'll see you soon. Rollo, Price - with me."

Grace was full of life at the Institute briefing; that might be invigorating for some, but Maisie felt so tired, so in need of sleep. She'd cancelled her day off to be there after all.

Edith had appeared and disappeared throughout the briefing; she was with them still, which was very disconcerting. Sitting in one of the open plan offices at the Institute, listening to Grace with Rollo and Harry, Maisie was trying to not let it show that she was utterly freaked.

Harry had asked for some headache pills as they came in and Maisie had obliged. He was usually the first to volunteer to do the morgue duty, knowing how horrible it was for his staff, but he looked a little green.

"One of the corpses is not like the others." Grace started in a sing-song fashion, as if she were going to turn things into a Foo Fighters musical. The day could not get any more surreal. "She has something wrong with her DNA. Or I'm being told it has been re-engineered. Which was impossible in 1948. I could go into the details, but none of you is intelligent enough to understand. It means the body, a female, experienced changes to her DNA at some point in her lifetime. I don't have any answers to that bit. There are raised levels of certain hormones consistent with immunotherapy – the type one might give a cancer patient. Like the reaction a body would have after it has fought off a virus and is on the up, for example. I only sent three samples away. I'll send the rest now. There's nothing else. Dead ends. I just don't have anything else to go on. Like the policemen investigating the stolen lavatories."

Grace took a deep breath, as if she had delivered it all with a single lung full of air.

Maisie, ignoring the terrible joke, suddenly had an idea. "Was the Cordivae group linked to the university, or were the links elsewhere? Could they have been test cases? Professor Beaton said they were carrying out experiments on soldiers with PTSD – long before the current science had started to do so."

"Harry and I did consider that. But you don't normally kill your test cases."

"Unless it was very secret." Rollo suggested gloomily. "Or they died as a result of the tests."

"But there are no signs that they were poisoned, or had severe reactions that might have resulted in their deaths."

"So, they committed suicide?" Rollo asked.

Grace ignored him, although Maisie did not think he was being difficult.

"The medical testing is an avenue we could explore. Medical records from that long ago probably no longer exist." Grace explained.

"We have a potential connection, though, the Cordivae test cases. If George Wright and others were funding this Cordivae group, could the bodies in the attics of his old house be linked? Is it worth me catching up with Professor Beaton about his father's University days again? Does the Cordivae group still exist? I can do some digging whilst you are in Cornwall, gov. I'll see if Greyson has any information on historical medical tests."

"Good idea, Price; we need to pursue this line of enquiry. This is getting more and more bizarre, and so it's not going to stack up for Rivers, or even Claud either. Is there a link between those victims in the past and what this Magpie is doing?" Harry paused. "Let's get on and find it. We need to break this case and quickly."

In the flat he had owned in Lichfield, (bought for him by Lady Bell) the Magpie was sorting his collection. He had his three sets of eyes in jars in a row, all with their filaments of trailing optic nerve fibres and ligaments that had once attached them in their sockets and the victim's brain. The two globes in the first jar, so well-preserved from years ago, belonged to Marcus. Angus and Chrissy's more recently collected. He studied them all. He had spent the evening securing the latest eyeballs in place on webbing, so they did not move about in the fluid like errant planets under a bizarre form of gravity.

The Magpie liked to look into their eyes and investigate each soul, asking questions of each in turn. Of course, he never had a response. He wasn't mad, he just liked to converse with them. His victims' eyes were gateways for him, the gateways to understanding their personalities. Lady Bell had called him mad, when he told her about his collection. She hadn't told him to stop, though. That would have been the end of their relationship, however much she had supported his ascension back into the real world.

She had also told the large doctor to show him how to remove the eyes carefully and quickly too.

"It's a pretty queer hobby," Lady Bell had said, the last time he had mentioned his collection.

He apologised to his victims again for her saying it was a hobby. The Magpie did this regularly; it was part of the ritual of seeing them.

He also told the eyes that hadn't been born this way. God hadn't chosen him to be a monster. Revenge was the only thing that would make him whole.

"Well, will you look at the time chaps?" he said to his collection. "I need a little sleep. See you all in the morning," he added, entirely without irony.

The phone rang and Karol Wojcik picked it up. It was Mr Parsons, wanting to give him more grief.

"Hello. DC Karol?" The man never got his name the right way around.

"Speaking, Mr Parsons, hope you are bearing up okay, sir."

"Well, yes as well as can be expected. I've got some information for you, however."

"Okay, good, go-ahead sir."

"I've found a letter from Chrissy's late mother. I'd never seen it before, so forgive me. It was part of her private things. It's to Chrissy and me, but she obviously did not want me to know."

There was a pause. Karol's skill in these situations led him to pause too; Parsons was welling up, finding it difficult to talk.

"Take your time, Mr Parsons. I am here for you."

There was a loud snotty sniff from the other end of the line. "Chrissy, it seems, was adopted. She wasn't born into the Hughes family. Her real name was Morton. Wasn't that the same name as the first victim? Isn't that the name of your DCI?"

Drogi Bogu. Wosijc thought.

Chapter Fourteen
Magpie's First Mistake

Ever since the briefing the previous day, Daisy had decided that she should go and see Teddy. She had spent most of her working day with Pete Miles, who was a lovely man, but she really believed her sister would be better off with Teddy. Teddy was loving, kind and adaptable. Pete was so young in his outlook. Although undeniably fit.

Daisy had gone home, showered, then dressed and then got in her Volkswagen Beetle to drive the five miles over to Stonnall. She found herself nervously standing outside the door belonging to the Robson house. Daisy knocked. She had been here many times over the years. It was a beautiful Tudor farmhouse, massively extended, its footprint set on a good few acres of land.

Ralph and Maddy Robson were away in Spain, not far in fact from her own parents, so Teddy would be in the house on his own.

She couldn't understand how Maisie could treat Teddy so. Teddy had been a good friend to Daisy. More than just a potential brother-in-law. Why had Maisie let him go? She was such a fool. Teddy was a catch and Maisie needed him. Her sister worked too hard. Without Teddy she would likely have a nervous breakdown.

The door clunked as a bolt was drawn back, then the door creaked open. Teddy stood on the threshold. He looked rather scruffy, in a football shirt from some team or another, tight-fitting on his large frame and covered in food stains. Teddy was also wearing grey sweatpants, also stained. He wasn't looking after himself properly, it seemed. It wasn't a good look. However, he was grinning.

Daisy had expected him to be more down in the dumps, miserable, lonely, perhaps even suicidal. She had travelled over to give him support, words of advice about her sister, the promise of a night out when he was over things, or even if they got back together. Teddy actually looked nothing like a spurned lover; he just looked like just a lazy bloke.

"Hi, Daisy. I didn't expect to see you." His smile lit up his face.

"I thought I would check in with you see that you were okay after my sister dumped you."

He nodded although his face was confused. "Cup of tea?"

"That would be lovely."

"Come on in, Dee."

She hung up her jacket and joined him in the large, opulent kitchen, situated at the end of a short winding journey through the extension at the back of the property. The kitchen was wall to wall cupboards with a breakfast island, complete with gleaming halogen hot plates brimming with controls and next to it one of those posh hot and chilled water taps. It was like someone had parked a spaceship bridge in the middle of the kitchen.

"Sugar?"

"Just the one please."

"Okey-Dokey."

He finished the tea, discarded the tea bags into the composter and led her into the lounge, both mugs out in front of him like boxing gloves, before he set them down on a coffee table.

The lounge was huge too; a sixty-odd inch screen sat on a long low-set TV cabinet. Other than the leather sofas – three in all- there was little else in the room. Teddy's parents were the epitome of minimal. Well, it was Teddy's mum who was. She wore the trousers and had the obsessive cleaning habits.

"You do realise I broke it off," Teddy insisted, although she was only half-listening. "I said I did not love her. We have been together since we were kids. I've not been with anyone else. But I never see her. Other than the occasional night here and there."

Daisy could feel her face screwing up. This did not compute. She had thought her sister had been a bitch, as usual.

"She's always at work. Okay, I'm always on call, but at least I rarely get called in. Morton is always getting you lot into work. I surprised you stand for it."

"Harry's a good guy, Teddy. Like you. I thought Maisie had dumped you."

"Why did you think that? Can't a thirty-year-old over-weight balding man tell a beautiful woman he doesn't love her anymore?" Teddy had one eyebrow raised. Self-deprecating as usual - the art of Midlands sarcasm. Yorkshire lasses such as Daisy were so much more black and white - a spade was a spade.

Daisy's laugh was muted. "Are you sure it wasn't her?"

"No, Dee. It was me. Look in all honesty, I've been in touch with an old uni friend who I really get on with. I did not want to lead her on, but I also did not want to hurt Maisie."

"There's another woman involved?"

Teddy shrugged. "I'm not involved. We just talk. We have a lot in common."

Daisy placed her cup down on the table. "I see I have had a wasted journey."

Teddy sighed. He moved over and sat next to Daisy. He tried to hold her hand - he was creeping her out now. "Look. I wish it had been different. You would have made a great sister-in-law. We were good together, not in that way, you are probably pleased to know, I've never seen you in a romantic light, despite being Maisie's twin. We will always be friends, but you aren't my type."

Daisy had gone to see if she could save her sister's relationship. Didn't twins always support each other? She hadn't gone to get the rebound. *I've never seen you in a romantic light.* It was ringing in her ears. *Cheeky bastard.*

"Never tell Maisie I came here. And for the record, I wasn't making a pass at you. It doesn't look like we will see each other again, Teddy. I didn't realise what you thought of me. Did you think I had come here to fuck you on the rebound?"

He looked shocked at her use of the expletive. Good. "And for the record – you're not my type, either. I'll see myself out." And with that plain speaking, she left him with a quivering lip.

"Sorry, M. I misjudged you." Daisy said to herself slamming the car door with a sigh.

The Magpie watched Daisy leave Teddy's house, nerves building. Lady Bell would be happy, finally, after days of demanding that Teddy would be the next victim; but he was feeling like a pawn, too easily controlled. He wasn't comfortable carrying out this murder. Something could go horribly wrong where a policeman was involved. He hadn't brought any of his eyes with him either. Their closeness would have reassured him.

Killing Edward Robson will increase their grief, heighten your influence over them, pull them into our grasp.

The Magpie hadn't thought it was a good idea to kill a policeman at this point in the plan. Lady Bell had said this was a game changer, however, assuring him it was the right thing to do. He had argued with Lady Bell about it just the night before. Even though he had concluded he would have to kill one or two of Harry's team eventually, it was too soon, and Teddy wasn't even linked the rhyme killings either. It was too messy.

God, he would need to break free from Lady Bell's control. This was too irregular. He had carried out the first three new murders as requested. Marcus, Angus and Chrissy. Then *she* decided on more than seven. Then *she* wanted Teddy to die. Every time he had planned everything down to the last, minute detail, to the very last second - Lady Bell had changed her mind. The frustration he felt was outweighed by his growing unease at her increasingly creepy behaviour.

He suddenly felt a headache brewing. Lack of order and planning made him have headaches. It also made him remember Harry and what the policeman had once done to him.

It was no more than an hour later.

The Magpie had made his way back to his yellow car and retrieved his killing knife. He had sharpened it, after he had spoken with the eyes of his victims again that morning. Marcus had been most put out that he couldn't do the kill - or at least be present. Chrissy called him all sorts of names for not letting her know the detail, but Angus was silent. Angus wanted to wait. The Magpie knew it. They spoke to him in his head, of course. What else would they do? They no longer had any mouths.

As well as his weapons, the Magpie had a selection of outfits in his car. A police uniform was probably the best option. Teddy would know of him if he was on the ball, might even recognise him. He put his hand through his hair, trying to get the unruly- and a bit long for his taste - black mop into some order. He lifted the boot with the other hand. He donned the uniform quickly in the darkness of the country lay-by, where the absence of light didn't even show up the yellow of his car. Then he put the knife in the leather sheath he'd sewed into his inside pocket, to save him cutting himself. He also had a muslin cloth and a bottle of chloroform that he had treasured for years; he'd taken it from *that place*.

He walked back up the gravel drive. It was pitch black, apart from the light from Teddy's home. There was really truly little illumination in the area, the nearest neighbours were a mile away. They wouldn't hear Teddy scream.

Knock. Knock.

157

It took a while, but eventually, Teddy opened the door. "Hello, mate? What are you doing here?"

"It's Maisie, she is in trouble. Can I come in?"

"You've just missed her sister, should I call Daisy back?"

"No, I've just spoken to Daisy. She asked me to speak to you. She was terribly upset."

Teddy was now shaking with emotion. The Magpie liked that. It meant Teddy would be off-guard, it meant *he* could exert control. Bad news was always delivered by a door-stepping police officer.

He smiled sympathetically. Boy, Teddy was bigger than he had expected. But size did not always indicate strength. The act of grabbing him and pinning him down could be an easy one.

He followed Teddy into the hallway. It was a wooden floor and was creaking and uneven. Looking ahead he saw that the lounge was carpeted. Damn.

Too many problems with deposited DNA in a carpeted area. He hadn't had time to lay his usual plastic protection. He could, however, scrub this wooden floor with bleach if needed. He needed to move quickly. He caught Teddy around the neck in a death grip.

Teddy gasped, but then moved in a way the Magpie wasn't expecting. Neither was he prepared for Teddy's strength. Teddy easily broke the grip and threw the Magpie over his shoulder. As he crashed down, hitting the wooden floor with a thump, his head banging off the boards. Teddy screamed.

"What the fuck are you doing?"

Teddy's move away had given the Magpie enough space to get back up on his feet. He wasn't often bested, he was naturally strong, particularly when he was in a killing mood. Advancing on Teddy again, there would be no other choice but to floor him, probably break Teddy's neck - although he itched to plunge the knife into that chest. Quickly, he threw an uppercut that jarred even his gym-intensified right arm. Teddy wavered but he did not

158

go down. *Fucker.* Instead, Teddy dashed through the lounge. He was going for a phone. No. He was an armed response officer. He was going for a gun. *Shit.*

Lady Bell was the cause of this. These difficulties. The stupid fucking bitch. Teddy was obviously flabby but physically fit *and* had clearly trained in martial arts. Why had he not known that? Not enough time to plan.

He suddenly stopped, took a deep breath and then smiled. "Turn it into a challenge, my boy." He could hear his mother say. "Turn a problem into a challenge." How had he remembered that from such an awfully long time ago?

He was now desperate to have Teddy's eyes in his collection. He needed to be able to talk to him later, congratulate the man, get closer to his soul.

Despite his size, Teddy had raced through the lounge into the adjoining kitchen with impressive speed. The Magpie wasn't afraid of reappraising a victim, but he would rather have known how good Teddy was. The sisters had described him as podgy and slow.

He strode into the kitchen. There were no doors where Teddy was standing, but there was a way out through the main kitchen window, if necessary. He now would not put it past Teddy to jump up onto the surface and leap out. He was probably very nimble too.

"Where do you keep your gun, Teddy?" He sang, to a ring-o-roses tune, a menacing, growly nursery rhyme. *Let's put the fucker on edge.* "Obviously not in the kitchen."

"What do you want. Money?"

"Nothing so crude, Edward. I'd like your eyes."

"My what?"

"Peepers, ocular globes. Your eyes, for fuck's sake. I collect them, Teddy. I have lots of pairs." Was he being too theatrical? It was a slight flaw he had when he was in the killing mood. He would have made a particularly good actor. In fact, after Harry was dead,

159

he might just do that. He would make a fine Macbeth. Now he was contradicting himself. He had told *her* at the beginning that he would never be an actor. But he had been much younger then; since the day he had taken on the disguise things had changed.

Teddy obviously knew his surroundings and reached behind himself to grab a carving knife. He grasped a handle and pulled it out. It was a tiny paring knife. Of all the knives Teddy could have pulled out, it was the fucking paring knife.

Dumb fuck. The Magpie laughed at the face Teddy pulled. A face of realisation that perhaps this was it.

Then, in one well-rehearsed movement, the Magpie ran towards his would-be victim, pulled out his much bigger knife and thrust it just under Teddy's sternum.

Teddy's eyes widened in surprise.

"Whoops. Not so quick after all, Teddy!" A little Jack Nicholson emphasis there, he even used the eyebrow trick. Shame Teddy's name wasn't Johnny.

It was a powerful death stroke. Teddy was already dead. He watched Teddy's eyes lose that wonderful spark which he would try and recreate with the preserving fluid later.

Within minutes, he expertly removed Teddy's eyes, using the kit out of his other pocket. He fetched Teddy's handgun; it hadn't been difficult to locate. He put the gun in Teddy's hand and laid him out on the floor in the ridiculous pose of an eighties murder series victim - sans chalk outline. This tableau had been too rushed to fulfil its comic potential and there was no fucking chalk about he had looked in all the drawers and everything after a nice cup of tea.

The Magpie laughed as he downed his final gulp of Yorkshire and then cleaned up his cup with anti-bacterial spray.

What he didn't realise was for the first time in years of killing, he had made a stunning mistake. Yes, had worn gloves, a mask and a hat. He'd worn his tight-fitting overalls and similar multi-layered, non-snagging underwear - despite the heat - so he would not leave fibres behind, let alone a tissue sample. He had even worn shoes with unmoulded soles affixed; he had picked up some flip flops in a cheap pound shop and had swapped the soles of boots with them. He thought he had been careful.

The Magpie went home to his flat, stored Teddy's eyes in a display jar. He masturbated. It wasn't a ritual, he convinced himself, it just seemed to cap off the events. Then he had a bath.

Only when he got out of the bath, and he sat upon its edge to clean his feet did he notice the ever-so slight pain at the back of his head. Just below where his hat would have ended. Level with the base of his ears, at the back of his skull. The Magpie touched his head and scabbed blood came away. He hadn't realised he had cut his head. He felt something sore rubbing there too. He picked at it with a finger and thumb. There was a splinter of wood in the wound. With tweezers and with quite a bit of effort, he worked it free.

"Shit."

He dressed quickly and he drove back to Teddy's, forgetting his own rule about trails. For once, though, the man now known as the Magpie was desperate.

The floor hadn't been fully sealed. He had left DNA behind.

Bitch, you caused this, he thought.

Josette Parkinson had gone to school with Teddy Robson years ago. It was the last year of the sixth form that she had become distraught when he had got off with the Price girl at a party. Down from Yorkshire, visiting relatives and to steal her Teddy. Josette had to watch Teddy via Facebook for most of the last twelve or so years. Waiting for a sign that things might not be right between Teddy and the Price girl. Teddy deserved better: a good well-bred

161

Staffordshire farmer's daughter, not a common Yorkshire lass. He deserved Josette.

So, when Teddy had reached out to her to say he was fed up and asked if she would like to meet up for a drink – purely platonic, because she was such a good listener- Josette had snapped both his hands off.

They had organised a Facetime catch up that evening and when Teddy did not sign on, she thought, at first, he had been called into work. Then she had realised she had his rota, and he was neither on call nor on shift until the weekend.

She drove up the long driveway to his parents' lovely expensive house and parked up. They were on holiday; Teddy would be all alone. She would give him a piece of her mind. *Control your men,* her mother had always said. He had better not have made up with the Price girl.

Josette got out of the car and approached the door. Unbeknownst to her, she was Teddy's third visitor in as many hours. The door was strangely ajar. She did not know the layout of the house and presumed he was out the back. She pushed on the door and went in.

The house was silent. That was strange. Teddy had said how he now liked to play his vinyl records now he had the time. Now he wasn't fawning around the Price girl. Josette would let him have the records once they were married, so long as they were not on display. By the looks of the house, Martha had instilled some tidiness in him at least. Maybe, Josette thought, she would get to see what his bedroom looked like today.

There was no-one in the large reception hallway. "Hello?" she called up the great stairs. She walked over to the area where the Magpie had cut his head. Her shoe caught the minutest of wood splinters, poking up from the boards where something must have broken the surface; it in turn concealed the tiniest of drops of blood and the minutest clip of hair and flesh. The chip came off and lodged in her shoe.

162

"Edward?" She walked through the lounge, not noticing anything awry initially.

She was about to turn around when she noticed the paring knife. It lay off to one side, discarded. That was a dangerous thing to leave lying around. One could cut one's feet, she thought.

Then she saw a hand. The hand holding the gun. Teddy. She screamed more than she had ever screamed in her life, her despair as black as the pitted holes in Teddy's skull and chest.

The Magpie re-approached the scene in his car. He didn't get as far as Cooks Lane before he could see the blue and red lights twirling and flashing in the distance, silent but foreboding.

He had made his first mistake in years. He was seeing Lady Bell tomorrow and she would most likely know. She always seemed to know. He needed to finish his obligation to her and soon. He would kill Harry and kill her. Then he would be free.

Chapter Fifteen
Out on the Town

The last but one day Daisy Price would be alive had started well for her.

She was hanging around the water cooler when she saw Pete. Tall, dark and handsome Pete. He was a beautiful specimen of a man; his broad chest filling out his shirt, his biceps tight against the material, his trousers well-fitting about his arse. He was a vision. His only flaw - and this was very picky, hence her single status - was his ears stuck out a little too much. She supposed Maisie used them to hold on when they were rutting.

"Morning." Pete said, and she flushed. Was it obvious to him what she had been up to in her mind?

"Hi, Pete."

"You okay, Daisy? You look a little flushed."

God, he knows what I was thinking.

Pete was quite the fitness and healthy living freak. He spent his time, when he wasn't with Maisie, down the gym for hours, day and night, she had said. Obviously, that was how he got his wonderful body.

"I'm sorry to hear about Teddy."

It had been three days since Staffs Police had found Teddy and she had been missing from work for two of them, signed off by the gov. Obviously, she'd had to make a statement, as she was the last but one person to see him alive. And she had left him on less than good terms. Daisy would never have wished him dead, and would never forgive herself for the last words she spoke to him.

"Can we change the subject, Pete?" She could feel the tears welling.

"Yes, of course. I came over to say we are going to the pub tonight. Me, Rollo, Wojcik, Maisie - if she gets back from Teddy's in time, few others. We need to have a drink for Teddy. Pay our respects. He might have been Maisie's previous boyfriend, but he was also a colleague."

Now come to think of it, it might be a nice idea. Karol was a dish too. All football and nothing else in his brain though. She hated footy unless it was FIFA on the Xbox. But she supposed she could possibly manage a few live matches, for Karol. He was bigger, bulk-wise than Pete, not as pretty, more rugged, but similarly dark-haired and strong, another gym-head.

If she couldn't have Pete, she might stand a chance with Karol. God, she sounded desperate. But Maisie had always got the boys; Daisy was left with slim pickings. She wanted more muscly pickings. Karol would do very nicely on that score.

"Yes, great idea. We need to finish off looking at the CCTV footage, but I'm close to rounding up and putting my notes together."

"I've done mine already," Pete replied. He was leaning on the water cooler, and she could see past his shirt to his chest, through a gap at a point that showed the line between his pectoral muscles. She suddenly felt dirty, like an old man staring at cleavage. She swallowed and looked up at Pete.

"Five o'clock?" he asked.

"Yes, great." Daisy nodded. She needed to get away. She excused herself and went into the ladies, which was situated next to the photocopy room. She pushed a stall door open, sat down and started to sob, because of Teddy primarily, but also because she was a sad spinster sitting on the shelf.

A short time later, having dried her eyes and composed herself, Daisy made her way back to her desk. DI Rollo was standing there. He looked knackered. Bags under his eyes, clothes unruly. He

165

always used to look like a new shiny penny, albeit one you happened to find in your knickers by accident.

"Price, have you got the accommodation sorted for me and the gov for when we go down to Bude?"

Harry and Rollo were going to investigate the links between Professor Beaton's father Paul and George Wright.

"Yes. I've got you two nights at the Bude Holiday Express. Okay?"

"Coming out later?"

"Yes, thought I'd join you."

"You okay about Teddy?"

She sighed but he gave no reaction. "Yes. The gov and Maisie are over there. She shouldn't be, but you know what she is like."

"She should be off the case," Rollo said and there was quite a bit of venom in his voice. Daisy knew that her sister was pushing noses out of joint. But between them both, they had made a lot of improvements to Morton's team.

Rollo's performance was down; maybe it was why he looked like he did. He was either not sleeping or drinking heavily. Perhaps drugs. He wouldn't be the first officer to get hooked on dope, or Charlie because of the pressure.

"Fancy going clubbing after. Me and you. We could have a chat."

And there it was the legendary Rollo come-on. She had never experienced it first-hand. It was normally all the dolly birds he chatted up. Daisy was not in his normal catchment league. She did, however, feel sorry for Rollo and would be happy to go out with him later - purely as mates. Rollo was a striking-looking man, not handsome, something about him, but he was stuck in the eighties, judging by the almost mullet-like hair. He never aged either, just kept going with that shoulder-length mop and leather jacket - and his Samba trainers he always wore when off-duty.

"Let's see. It's been a mad few days, but I could really do with a blow-out. I'm off rota tomorrow, so can we play it by ear?"

Rollo nodded. "How's the CCTV evidence?"

"Nothing further to suggest any other suspects. Any cars near Chrissy at the time she travelled down the A38 all check out. All have destinations other than Lichfield. She was the only person to leave the A38 and end up in Victoria Park all night."

Rollo mused. "This Magpie is crafty, isn't he? Get it written up for Harry. We can have a look at the next steps tomorrow in the late briefing before we go to Cornwall. Has Pete done the same? I'm seeing him later, so I can check then."

"Harry has already caught up with Pete today."

Rollo nodded. "See you later."

Daisy had two further periods of crying in the loo. One of which was followed by a recce to the nearest shop for some fags. She chain-smoked three whilst she stood in shirt sleeves under the cigarette shelter. It was still twenty-five degrees in late October.

Karol Wojcik was there, puffing on his vape, the random smell of berries mingling with her Benson and Hedges.

"Ah. My favourite English teacher."

"Hi, Woj. How are you?"

"Daisy, Daisy, give me your..." He sang her name like that after Rollo had introduced him to the lewd rhyme.

"You know that's inappropriate."

He looked up puzzled. "Inna what?"

"Inappropriate, not right."

"Ah, nieodpowiednie! Don't do it, Karol! Sorry, is it not funny song?"

"It's rude."

"Ah, sorry Daisy just once. I'll not sing it again. How are you?"

"Shit."

"Need a hug?"

She looked at him properly. He wasn't handsome, he was a little goofy with an overbite that made him slightly whistle his s's. His almost black hair was a mess. He looked too pumped, and his fashion sense was a little erratic. He was, however, a genuinely nice person. Not at all what the bigoted force expected to come from the Polish municipals in the exchange.

"Please." She did really want a hug, preferably from Pete, but Karol would do. He almost broke her back. Nice and strong, though.

"You look sad."

Her tears started to roll down her face. She put the current fag out under the ball of a foot and pulled out another from its box, put it to her lips and lit up with a zippo she carried in her pocket. She had inherited it from her grandfather. He used to sneak her a single fag every now and then - her mother or her nanna would have lost their plots if they knew she was a smoker.

"I'm hugging," Karol said more forcefully, wrapping his arms around her again. "Back home we give hugs all the time. Even though we might not know each other that well."

Daisy nodded into his shoulder, holding her fag out away from them both. Karol seemed to realise this and then stepped back.

"My grandfather used to say that sadness is a rolling snowball. The more you keep it rolling, the bigger it gets and the longer it takes to melt. Smash the snowball when it is small, and it melts quicker. He was a wise man. I loved him. Unlike the other one who would hit me rather than look at me."

Daisy felt herself smiling. Karol was a dear man. She was lucky with her work colleagues. She had a group of male friends she felt safe with – despite Rollo's come-ons.

"Are you going out later, Karol?"

"Yes. I am going to skype my mother first, then I will be out. Possibly by six half-past."

"Six-thirty."

"Six-thirty. Yes. That's what I said." He said it in a goofy voice, and she smiled. They finished off their respective cigarettes, virtual and real and then went back to the office.

Quiz night at the Duke was always noisy. Karol had stayed out a few hours, but had gone home tired. Before that, Daisy had another nice chat with him and had promised to go with him to see the film IT, Parts One and Two at Tamworth Cinema, it was a special double bill.

Pete and Mo were soon talking about their gym regimes – so it was quite boring. Rollo was at the bar talking to Jennifer the barmaid, she was all fillers and implants and obviously his type. Jennifer wasn't biting though, probably because Rollo still looked a mess; he hadn't had a shower or changed his clothes after work. Dirty get.

Maisie and Harry arrived around nine p.m. They had been with Grace to cover off the teleconference with the locum pathologist, who had been drafted in by armed response to carry out Teddy's PM. Whilst their super had doffed his cap Harry's way, they had not allowed Grace to do the business. That was better for Maisie; at least she hadn't been in situ as the post-mortem had been carried out.

Harry got the drinks and Maisie sat down next to her sister. She looked fine, not look like she was grieving for Teddy at all. Not like how Daisy herself felt.

"You, okay?"

"I saw the statements, Daisy. I know you went to see Teddy just before he died."

"It wasn't a secret."

"Why was my name mentioned so much in the statements?" Maisie hissed.

"I was trying to make sure you and he were finished. I wanted you to get back together. Mum said…"

"Fuck Mum. I'm not interested in what she thinks. And you had no business interfering. Just because you haven't got a love life yourself you want to go around leading mine."

"You've got Pete. I wanted to make sure you were serious and not going to hurt him as well as Teddy."

"You can have Pete if you really want him, Daisy, I'm thinking of cooling things off, or at least having a break. Teddy and I did not have a future. He was seeing someone else, he…"

"He wasn't seeing her. Not until he finished with you. He did not want to mess you about."

"Did you go to see if you and he might have a chance? I know you held a candle for him, Daisy."

She could have got angry at that, but it was fair comment. "Teddy wasn't interested in me, Maisie. I am not - I wasn't–" she paused, "-his type." She knew her eyes had filled with tears again.

Maisie sighed. "I'm sorry kiddo. I'm sorry. I can't believe he's gone. I can't believe he's dead." Maisie hugged her tight, but her embrace was nowhere near as comforting as Karol's had been.

"You need to take some time off." Daisy dabbed at her eyes.

"Harry needs me. Look at Rollo, he's falling apart."

"You will too if you aren't careful."

"I need to help find this bastard. There are too many links. The Morton link, now Teddy. I get the feeling he knows us all very well. Either someone on the force or someone nearby."

"There's no evidence it's the Magpie, no links to Teddy."

"Deep down we know it is. Same use of the knife, missing eyes. Rivers is giving Harry and Chief Super Taylor a real hard time now. Harry and I have got to meet them in the morning before he and Rollo go off to Cornwall. Then it's me in charge for two days."

"You might not believe me Maisie. But I'm really proud of you."

Maisie leaned towards her and gave her another hug. She smelled of aftershave. Not Pete's.

"Thanks, Daisy."

"Ladies. I come bearing drinks. Gin and Tonic and a pint of Theakston's."

"Thanks, gov," Daisy said as Harry plonked himself down next to them. She caught a whiff of his aftershave. Distinctive. And the same as she could smell on her sister.

Both Maisie and Harry had offered her a lift home, but Daisy had said she would go with Rollo. He was a bit worse for wear, but they lived over the same side of the city, and she could make sure he was dropped off. He staggered out of the cab, still managing to proposition her on his way out. She fended him off with a peck on his cheek and then got back into the cab.

Her parents' house was not a million miles away from where Chrissy Parsons had lived, on the fringes of Victoria Park, nearer the Bowling Green pub, rather than the Saxon Penny. It was warm; she had been dropped off at the end of the road and made her way down the alley towards her mum and dad's house. There was no-one else about and she walked as you do when you are on the fringes of drunkenness, with one eye on your feet and your mind on your full bladder.

She arrived home, dialled the keycode that opened the large-gated drive and made her way up to the door. She put her key in the lock and turned it, stepping into the house, throwing her bag and coat down. She opened the door of the reception lounge and felt plastic underfoot. She walked further into the room and put on the light. Plastic sheeting on the

171

floor. Had something happened, had they had a leak? She checked her phone, no emails. She looked up, no tell-tale signs of water damage.

Then something was put over her face and for a time, she did not feel a thing.

Pete pressed his lips against her, slipping his tongue into her mouth. He tasted of coke and mints. His body, which was on top of her at present, was, as ever, hard and sinewy. He was inside her and her body was afire with sensations she had never experienced with Teddy; his mouth was kissing her breasts and she gasped.

Teddy. He had only just died. He didn't love you. You are disrespectful- he is barely cold. Killed by the Magpie.

"Stop. Pete."

"What's up, lovely? Aren't you enjoying yourself? I'm having a great time."

She forcefully pushed him off her and that was not easy. Pete was a big man.

"It's not right. This is not right. I'm sorry, Pete. Not so soon after Teddy."

Pete turned over onto his back and sighed. She hated doing this to him. He was a great guy, but she had no time for this. She'd rarely had time for Teddy. Teddy was now dead, and she felt dirty.

"Look, Maisie. We can cool it for a bit, if you like. Let's not call it a day, though. I really like us. I know it must be hard with Teddy's..."

God, Pete was a considerate bastard and had, as usual, read her mind. She turned to him, looked deep into those beautiful eyes.

"It's this case. This Magpie. I can't afford to be distracted; I need to be on my game. We've got to get him. Not just for Teddy's sake, but for the other victims too."

Pete sat up naked and put his big hands either side of her face.

172

"Let's cool it, until this is over, but when we have nailed this shit-bag, you are coming out with me. Ma'am."

He was a bugger; she knew his humour would melt her every time.

"Don't wait for me. You deserve better."

He grabbed her and pulled her to him. At that point, she could have wilted within his strong arms. He kissed her passionately.

"I'll wait for you, Maisie. I'll be here if you need me. You can call me any time. Any time of the day."

As she dressed and left the flat, she knew her time as Pete's lover was probably over for good. She could sense things changing. The death of Teddy was linked to her, the other murders linked to Harry, Edith. The Magpie. This seemed personal now. The Magpie was close by. He had to be. Pete could be in real danger. She could be in danger. Harry could be in danger.

She needed to focus. One loose thought or action could mean the difference between capturing this bastard or letting him kill again.

Chapter Sixteen
Ellen Takes a Risk

"Hi, Maisie. It's me. Dee. I'm feeling a bit shit. I've got Rollo to agree to a couple of days off last night whilst he was drunk. I'm going to extend it with compassionate leave. I've spoken with HR. I'm going to go over and join Mum and Dad for a week or so in Spain. Hope that's okay. I'll only be off rota for a couple of days. I'll be back soon. Thanks for the chat last night. Love you."

The answerphone message clicked off. Pete was with Maisie; he had come to get his things back from her flat after his shift. He looked at her, clearly unsurprised by what he'd just heard. "She's really feeling it. Did she hold a torch for him too?"

Maisie looked at Pete as he packed his man manicure and beauty bits and pieces.

"What's that supposed to mean?"

"She is obviously taking this harder than you. You seem fine about Teddy now. I know we haven't seen each other much aside from this weekend, but you are hardly grieving for him. He was a fat miserable git, you said."

Her anger was rising, but she knew he was right. She had said that but had felt terrible afterwards.

"I was angry with Teddy. I didn't want him dead. God. Not without his eyes." She caught a sob. She was trying to deal with this professionally rather than personally and here was Pete trying to pull grief from her.

"Maisie, I'm not saying that. Sorry, I can't put it into words. You don't seem to care as much as Daisy does. Was she in love with him? Was that why she went to see him before...?"

"I nearly married Teddy. We met at seventeen when I came down on a visit. We were going out by eighteen when I finally came to live with Nanna after the sixth form. He was sporty and slim then; then he was handsome and brave - a great officer and a great friend. I know he dumped me, I'm still angry with him for that but I am grieving. Have you ever lost anyone, Pete? You don't say much about your family, other than your brother."

"I've lost people Maisie." He almost growled. "People have done horrible things to me too. I am not good at dealing with it. I can't lock it up. So, I don't, and it eventually finds a way out. You don't seem to be like that. Thankfully, I have my little brother to look after since our parents died. He keeps me sane."

"Oh, Pete. Look at you. Balls-out, with not a care in the world. Twenty-odd with your whole life ahead of you. But..."

"I'm not the man for you now. Was I a rebound from Teddy?"

Maisie sighed. *Perhaps he was.* She had argued with her internal consciousness so many times to the contrary - but perhaps he was.

"I'll see you later in the week, Pete. Don't know when. It's not over. It's just..."

"Not right..."

"Stop finishing my fucking sentences. I can speak for myself. Go to the gym for a few days. I might have calmed down by then."

He just laughed; that made it worse. It was just like Teddy all over again. She wouldn't friend-fuck Pete though. That ship had sailed for the time being. She wouldn't do what she had done with Teddy. It was more or less over. She knew it.

"I'm off to see the boss."

"I'm on a late tomorrow covering for Daisy. I might see you then."

She nodded and he turned and got his things. Her eyes lingered greedily on his body, probably for the last time.

***

175

"If you do not get me some evidence that links a suspect to these murders, I am going to lose my fucking rag and put someone else on this."

Rivers was furious, foaming spittle edging his mouth. Maisie saw Harry take a sideward glance at Taylor, who looked like she wanted to roll herself right out of there, as fast as her well-oiled wheels would take her.

Maisie could see the chief's point of view. The press had seized the story like a terrier with a rat in between its jaws. The chief had no answers at his briefing at all that week, and it had been two weeks now since the first murder. Rivers was under pressure and the slaps were cascading like two pence pieces in an arcade machine.

"Nine dead bodies. One of our own amongst them." Rivers pointed at Maisie. "DI Price, congrats on the promotion by the way, I cannot begin to understand how you can continue with this case when Teddy is barely cold. Not to mention, Harry, the Morton link- which thankfully hasn't leaked, although it's a matter of time. Such a fucking mess."

"Martin, we are trying our best." DSI Taylor offered, trying to at least calm the chief.

Maisie had almost burst into tears at the mention of Teddy. She knew that normally she would probably be off the case, but with her predecessor off long-term sick pending a dismissal appeal, she was being catapulted into the role before everyone had got used to it. *Be professional. Don't cry.*

Harry stepped into the breach.

"The fact there is no evidence, is not unusual in a case like this sir. Serial killers – unless spree killers - are very clever. They plan, they cogitate. He's probably wearing and using all the right gear. He's probably someone without a record. Serial killers don't normally engage with petty crime and work their way up. Moreover, the six from Legend St died of natural causes, no suggestion of murder, so we are possibly looking at a copycat who has killed three other people. The killer knows about us as a team; he is almost baiting us. That suggests he is close. If not on the force, then affiliated."

There was a knock-on Harry's door. Maisie looked toward it, trying to ignore Edith, who was sitting in the corner filing her nails. Why did the moribund woman need to file her nails?

Grace entered, looking, as ever, dishevelled and weary.

"Better late than never." Rivers muttered, sarcastically.

"Martin, how lovely to see you. Just remember if you want to retain my services, can you please pay the invoices that have been pending for three months. Finding it difficult to pay staff and keep the fridges on."

Touché, Maisie thought.

"So," continued Grace. "Do you want to know the good news?"

Rivers gave a sarcastic thumbs up.

"You know I have said there was something wrong with one of the six?" She looked around waiting for someone to nod, like a comedian trying to find the right moment for the punchline.

"Yes?" Maisie nodded. Grace nodded a thank-you and then glared at Harry, who looked like he'd got another of his headaches.

"There was one individual who shows signs of advanced healing, even after she was deposited in one of the tanks. Tests have found high levels of proteins that wrap around the RNA, which could suggest the individual healed very rapidly. That her death had been mistaken. I have a friend who is working on cellular reproduction at the university who had a look at the sample. It was nothing like she had ever seen before. Cellular regeneration on that scale is unknown. She might have lived in that fluid for some time until she eventually drowned. Although her lungs would prove otherwise in later tests -no sign of drowning. It was as if she had lived in the fluid for a time."

"I wondered if that was linked to something the Cordivae lot were up to back in the day? Trouble is, they would not have had that understanding in the 1940s." Harry suggested.

"Indeed not. So, this evidence would suggest the victim had a naturally occurring metabolism that healed much quicker than most." Grace surmised. "In addition, we have found markers that would suggest the ageing in this individual had slowed. The victim is in the region of twenty-five to thirty-two. Her teeth showed no sign of decay, which in this period was rare. She looked no older than eighteen."

The room was silent. Grace sighed with the patience of a teacher in a remedial class.

"We can't go public with that. It's all mumbo jumbo." Rivers spat.

"Okay. If that's too much for your brain to take in. I have another bit of news for you, Martin. We have third party DNA from the home of Teddy's parents."

That immediately got the attention of the room - particularly that of Rivers. Grace continued.

"During Josette Parkinson's debrief on the night of Teddy's murder, we took her clothes for swabbing and found a splinter in her left shoe. It was a fragment of wood from the hallway floor. It had blood on it that did not belong to Teddy, Josette, or any of the visiting professionals or house visitors on the day of the murder. And we know his parents have been away for some time. It's a starting point. I personally went back and had a look; there was more residue under a thicker splinter that had been forced back by the weight of Josette's shoe. We have enough to be able to carry out a DNA profile and match it to known groups."

"Thank fuck for that, Grace." Rivers said. "A lifeline. Let's get to work on this. I've been here pissing in the wind so long my turn-ups are sopping wet."

Rivers grabbed his coat and was gone in moments, but not before asking Grace to visit his office the next day.

"Bye, Sir." Claudine Taylor muttered sarcastically. The door slammed and she rolled her eyes.

Harry looked up at Grace. "Thank you. Even if this is a dead-end, it buys us some time with the press and the chief. Get the samples processed, Grace and I'll catch up with you once Rollo and I come back from Cornwall. We'll all need to offer samples no doubt to rule out members of the team. We will need to speak to the team and the unions."

Grace nodded her goodbyes, nearly bumping into Pete Miles as he arrived with the tea.

"Are you sure you are up to this, Maisie?" DCSI Taylor asked, with real concern.

Pete put the tray of drinks down on the table and took his leave.

"Yes, ma'am. I need to stay on this."

"Any more on finding the woman in yellow?"

Maisie looked over at Harry for help, but his eyes were on the floor.

"I'm still trying to track her down, ma'am. She has made contact, but will only meet with me in future in a public place."

"Get on it. We need to know her links to all of this."

"I'll make sure that I go with Price next time, Claud." Harry offered.

Maisie angled herself so she could no longer see Edith, but Edith had vanished again.

It was then that Harry seemed to brighten. He stood up and inhaled, as if relief had imbued him from the ether. *Was there a link between Harry's headaches and Edith being in the room?* Whenever the ghost was present, Harry never looked himself.

Maisie had talked herself out of informing him about Edith being a sort-of-ghost. She was not ready to be taken off the case and being labelled a stress head. She wanted some time as an Inspector under her belt and the last thing she needed was to be taken off with supposed mental health issues or stress. Being away from the case would finish her. She would mourn Teddy later.

"I need to round up Rollo and get down to Cornwall."

Taylor nodded, taking the brakes off her chair. "Maisie, if you need me over the next couple of days, just yell. Keep me briefed if anything changes, yes?"

Maisie nodded. Taylor left.

"You sure you are, okay?" Harry's voice had softened. "I won't be gone long. Promise."

"I'll be fine. I'll call you if there are any issues. I'll go to Taylor, if necessary, but I'll let you know first."

"Fab. See you later."

That was Maisie's cue to leave too.

Edith was already in Maisie's new office when she arrived there. It had only just been released to her by estates and she hadn't even had a chance to box up DI Marsh's personal effects yet, but there Edith was, dressed in her yellow clothes as ever, grinning. Maisie didn't think she really wanted to talk to Edith now. Not after her words with Pete.

"He's dreamt about me again. In more detail," Edith cooed, like a lovesick teenager. "Harry, I mean. I remember now. Harry dreams of a little boy. He has been captured in the dream and I freed him. I don't know why. It seems I only remember things after Harry has dreamt them. You are going to have to tell Harry soon. About me being related and dead."

"Yes, I know." Maisie had put her phone to her ear to ensure no one thought she was talking to herself. "I just need to find the right time and not make myself look a twat."

"Are you having a bad day? Your language is a little saucy. Although that word sounds good in a Yorkshire accent."

Maisie laughed out loud. Adopted Aunt Edith might be some sort of ghost, but she was as good at picking up on bad language as she was at body language. Maisie found herself wondering about Edith's life. She must have had boyfriends. Did they say twat in 1948?

"Do you remember anything else at all, Edith?"

"Nothing at all."

"Then try to remember. Because currently supposedly Great-Auntie Edith, *you* are no use nor fucking ornament." Maisie said this in a thick accent.

Edith started to giggle, and Maisie joined her.

Ellen was on shift on the surgery wards; they were over-staffed in A and E, and the on-call director had moved her from overseeing the Onward Care Team to the busy electives department. The mild end of autumn to early winter meant the hospital was not (for a change) full, not like the COVID madness of previous years. Normally, as the kids went back to school, the germs festered and spread to their parents, siblings and grandparents. Yet it was strangely quiet on the infection front. So, Ellen was surplus to requirements and had jumped at the opportunity to work somewhere else, particularly as it meant she might be able to do some detective work.

When she had found she would be working late in the vicinity of Prendergast's office, she suddenly decided she would have a look at Harry's records. Harry was going to be down in Cornwall for a few days, so she could think carefully about how to bring up the fact she had broken into an office had a look at her boyfriend's medical notes without his - or his surgeon's -permission. It could lead to her dismissal if she were found out, it could also lead to a serious row with Harry, but it was worth the risk. Ellen *needed* to know why Harry was like he was. She was desperate to know what was actually wrong with him. It was essential she found out. She had never liked secrets.

Emotion bubbled up from another time in her life and she found herself smiling with a devil may care attitude.

Ellen knew the hospital very well. She had looked at where all the cameras were, planned it all meticulously. She had got through a lot of professional and personal scrapes, because she was so careful.

She was a Band 7 senior nurse; no-one was going to question her movements that evening. Particularly late at night when all the managers were at home and unlikely to be drafted in for escalation duties.

Getting into the office was the easy part. It was situated just off the main corridor of the hospital, next to the charity shop and voluntary sector reception. She opened the door and went inside. The lights came on automatically.

The files would be indexed under their lead physician – in Harry's case, Prendergast, as the more senior specialist. Prendergast distrusted computers: he would allow Lacey to upload the files, but he always had to have a paper copy. She knew the keys to the cabinet would probably be on Lacey's desk. After arriving from Ireland in the late noughties, Lacey had ended up under Ellen's wing at the hospital. They were still mates. Lacey had once spoken about how she had to keep all her keys in an easy to reach place, for fear of her losing them or leaving them at home. Prendergast apparently was a bastard to her, so Lacey had needed to be on the ball.

Ellen checked the index card box - they weren't there. She checked the drawers of both the desks, to no avail. Wracking her brain, she tried to work out where Lacey would keep them for ease of access?

Suddenly, her eyes were pulled towards a box on top of the first filing cabinet. She raced over – time was running out as her break was only half an hour – and fished the keys out of the box. She found a cabinet marked A to M, opened it, and rooted forwards through to the Ms: Martin, Merrick, Miles, and there it was: Morton, H.

Ellen pulled the file out and put it on Lacey's desk. She flicked through the contact and appointments section. At the back of the file was a clutch of interdepartmental memos. She started to go back to the point that Harry would have been admitted and his initial treatment. There were a lot of memos in the file.

Then she found something of interest. It was from Prendergast to the mental health liaison nurse.

I continue to inform Mr Morton that the fragment in his head is purely imaginary. It was all removed following his admission for the trauma head wound. I suggest he is worked with to ensure his understanding of the situation is that he is not incrementally dying; he is just imagining it. The verdict is that he is as right as rain, so you must now take this forwards and support him with psychological support.

Mr Prendergast 1/4/2005

Ellen almost gasped. So why was Harry continually informed he had a piece of bone moving slowly towards his brain. What was the cause of his headaches?

Then she found another memo.

Dear Mr Prendergast

We currently cannot pick up this referral due to capacity. It has been returned to you so you can inform community psychiatric nurses' team to support Mr Morton's rehab and recovery.

There were no further records about it. No community mental health team referral. Prendergast had sat on this. He had kept Harry believing he was potentially terminally ill, or at least at risk of a stroke due to the inoperability of the wound due to a foreign object. Bastard. Why?

She quickly photocopied the relevant pages, reordered the file and she put it back in the cabinet. She locked up and returned to the ward. All the time her mind racing: *Do I tell him or not?* Encouraging him to apply to view his own file under a Freedom of Information request would be one way forward. Trouble was, if he didn't, she would have to tell him.

Chapter Seventeen
A Trip to Cornwall

The Magpie sat waiting for Lady Bell in the East Wing reception room of Bell Manor. He felt hotter than ever - were the cool winds of Autumn ever going to arrive?

He'd heard a radio bulletin on the way to her abode which had suggested that there was third party DNA at the scene of Edward Robson's murder. Whilst *his* blood would not be on record anywhere, (he had paid due attention to that) it was sending him near crazy that he had made a mistake, that he had slipped up.

"Have you brought Daisy Price here, as per your orders?" The voice seemed to have come from nowhere; a trick Lady Bell was good at, like materialising from the shadows.

"Yes, but I'm not sure why? It's too soon to have captives in the plan, isn't it? You are causing me to change things. I need to kill Daisy. I cannot believe you have asked me to involve another police officer."

He had stowed Daisy in one of the vacant rooms in the servant's area in the attic, as ordered. He would now have to keep an eye on the policewoman, which unfortunately meant more visits to Lady Bell's estate.

Stupid. Stupid man. The look on Lady Bell's face said.

"You must admit, it helps to lure Harry further into your darkened web, my Magpie. You can have your obsession and I can have that person so very close to him."

"I have confused the trail a little as you asked. Daisy will not be missed for some time." He recalled the phone message he had forced her to record.

"Good. You are lucky you didn't kill her too soon. I would not have been pleased." Lady Bell was behind him now. He didn't jump, but his heckles rose, it wasn't right that she could creep up on him like that.

"I've told you before: I make my own plans, even in response to your requests for deaths. I want to know why I need to kill the others. Why can I not focus on killing Harry? I need to add his eyes to my collection. *If* this comes to a head too soon and you are powerful enough to emerge from your isolation, will you still support me? Will you be of help if the sun is over the yardarm? I'm not sure I've seen you in the light for some time." *Ever?* "Will you help me get Harry if I have delivered you your quota?"

All his visits had been in the evening. He had only ever seen her in the day once, back when she had brought him to Bell Manor from the psychiatric ward.

"I am not a vampire. Fool."

He had guessed Lady Bell was something more than human only recently - a witch then perhaps, if such things were real.

He could see her clearly now. She seemed to glow with power.

She hissed at him like an angry cat. He had guessed some of her secrets and somehow, she knew. He took a step back and that was when she smiled. There were flecks of spittle around her mouth as she approached him. Like a rabid animal. Nearer and nearer. She undulated like a serpent in that green shift dress.

"My talents *are* phenomenal, you cretin; they help disguise you. Your face is not glue and rubber, you know that, but you seem to have forgotten our pact. I pull the angst of those deaths through you and into me to strengthen me. I *will* be strong again, and remember, you hunt for *me*. I care not a jot for your mind's secrets. All I care about is breaking free of this accursed place, to be whole and hearty once more. To walk amongst the living and make them my slaves. As you are, my Magpie. You think you are so strong, so clever. Yet I could destroy you with one thought."

Lady Bell clicked a thumb and forefinger, and he jumped as if a thousand volts had coursed through his body.

"So, it is not just smoke and mirrors? Not just some hair dye over my white patch of hair and a little plastic surgery? What will you do with me?" He made himself sound more frightened.

"Ha." Lady Bell laughed, and he had a hint that once upon a time she had good humour. She pushed him lightly in the chest with both hands and they stung him with static current. He sensed that if she summoned all that supernatural strength, she probably could very well have crushed him after all. He rebounded dramatically.

"You are clever, my Magpie. Cleverer than I once thought you were. I *will* grant you that. When you have killed the children, I'll let you know more. You can send Daisy back to the arms of her sister once I have finished with her. Then I'll tell you why you have to bring me the new victims off my list - and why so quickly. I am on the cusp of greater things. A day of reckoning approaches and you must play your part. Then I will let you have Harry Morton, with pleasure."

That got him thinking. She had scared the absolute shit out of him and that wasn't an easy thing to do, but he had overreacted on purpose. He had seen horrific things as a boy that had fuelled a lifetime of fears and he had just used that fear to bait her. And sensing her dominance, she had revealed more of herself.

The Magpie had known there was more to his disguise all along, ever since the night he had slept with her; he knew there was more to Lady Bell than just magic tricks. Once an old hag, now a younger

187

beauty. He would eventually need her name, it seemed. He understood it would be unlikely that he could kill her without it. If she was in fact alive. Maybe he could add her eyes to his collection. A witch's eyes, perhaps? What secrets could he learn from them?

The Magpie laughed. He almost sounded mad.

Harry had asked Maisie to look through some of the other paperwork he had received from Professor Beaton and the solicitors. It seemed George Wright had once part-owned a farm not far from Lichfield, near Wall. It was called Magpie Farm and was currently, and ironically, owned by the previous DCI of the Cold and Complex Team, Owain Pleasant. Pleasant's wife had recently died in prison following her arrest and culpability in the murder of four or so victims found on the farm. Rollo's predecessor DI Charles had overseen it. Diddy Charles, a diminutive four feet ten formidable Inspector had retired last year, with that success the coda to a wonderful career.

The farm was on the Bell estate, although it had been privately owned, and apparently sold off to George Wright in the early forties by a Robert Waterfield. There was that name again. She could not find any evidence or further links to Mr Waterfield, even though his name popped up every so often. Was he part of this Cordivae group? Had George Wright known him? They needed to find out more. She would have to contact Grey.

Maisie had once seen the owner of Bell Manor, the strange Lady Bell, some years ago at a benefit ball. Lady Bell was an old woman – but clearly, she had been incredibly beautiful once. Bell was a contradiction: a strong businesswoman, but very frail, in a wheelchair at times, but with a powerful business acumen. Lady Bell's philanthropy had benefitted the police charities many times over. Why

188

the police? She had never found anyone who could answer that.

Maisie would not have been allowed to contact Lady Bell unless she really had needed to. So, instead she had phoned Diddy and had a chat with her, before deciding to phone former DCI Pleasant. He was away abroad, so she had arranged to give him a call at a respectable time his end.

"Pleasant, speaking." The voice was deep and resonant. Pleasant had been a bit of a dish, according to many of her colleagues, not overly handsome, but magnetic. He had had everything: a great career, beautiful wife who was an heiress - albeit of the estate of a famous career criminal, Terrance Cobden. Jennie Pleasant had been locked up for perverting the course of justice, as well as aiding and abetting a criminal – manslaughter through diminished responsibility and preventing the burial of human remains. She had died in prison under suspicious circumstances. Rumour had it another con had killed her, but it was never proved.

"Chief Inspector," she said, as pleasantly as possible. "You don't know me; I am Inspector Maisie Price from the Complex Team."

"Yes, your constable said you would be calling - but he called you a sergeant last night. Do promotions happen so quickly these days?"

Maisie laughed; he had put her at ease. "We are a little short-staffed."

"No, I don't want to come back thank you," he laughed.

What a nice man. "No, I'm phoning about the farm. It seems that before Terrance Cobden or George O'Neill owned it, a certain George Wright bought it. I wondered if you had ever found any information or documentation pertaining to him on the premises. Or to a Robert Waterfield? Did your late wife ever speak about any of this at all?"

"George Wright? Yes, he came up when I investigated George O'Neill and his abusive past. He

189

sold the farm to O'Neill's father and mother-in-law for a steal. It was a wedding present for George and Frances. I haven't found anything in the house, but to be honest, I haven't been into the underground office since the old man was brought out in his concrete coffin. Too bloody sinister, Maisie. Wasn't Wright's case one of the unsolved files we had in the store?"

"You have a good memory, Sir. When do you return to the country?"

"Not until next July. I'm developing a property portfolio out here. I do have someone staying at the farm, but he is rarely there. He travels to and from Lincoln for business. I could get the managing agent to give you access to the underground bunker. Although it's been searched before. There might not be anything of relevance left."

"That would be helpful. If it's not me going out, it will be junior colleagues. Can you send me the details of your agent? That would be great. Once again, I'm sorry to disturb you."

"It's not a problem, Maisie. Good luck. Let me know if you need to dig up the property again, won't you?"

"It shouldn't come to that, Sir."

"Glad to hear it, Inspector. Happy hunting as we used to say."

"Thank you, Sir."

"Oh. By the way. Don't go there on your own. And do not go in the dark. It can be dangerous down there. Let's say the building has been affected by decay. Oh, and I have never heard of a Robert Waterfield."

"I will bear that in mind."

She put the phone down.

"He's evil." Edith had appeared in the chair opposite. "That place is evil. Stay away."

"What are you talking about?"

Then Maisie's phone rang – Mo. They had found a box with bones in it whilst excavating the grounds at Legend Street.

190

"A box of bones?" She looked over at Edith, who looked sad. "Are you certain? Get in touch with Grace if she doesn't know already. Pardon? She does. Good. Ask her to crack on with the PM, then."

Edith nodded. "Nancy's bones. I can feel it."

"Can you reach Nancy? Like you did with Nanna?" Maisie couldn't quite believe she was actually asking the question.

"No. I'm blocked."

"Why does Harry get headaches whenever you are in the room?"

"I'm not sure, I caused him to collapse too, didn't I? He could see me in that pub, then he couldn't. I think he has a block in his head." Edith was almost triumphant.

"Yes, he told me. It's a bit of bone."

"No. Sorry, let me be clear, it's not in his head. It is in his mind."

Rollo was snoring. Apparently, he had spent the evening in bed, but by the smell of him, Harry could tell he had either gone out and hit the bottle - or he had stayed in and hit the bottle.

To be honest, Harry was glad of the peace and quiet - other than the inane tunes on Radio 1. He put on an Iron Maiden greatest hits CD; Rollo still didn't stir, even with Bruce Dickinson's growling operatic melodies.

The M42 gave way to the M5 to the A39. He pulled into the outskirts of Bude and found the hotel relatively easily.

Harry parked up and cut the ignition. Rollo awoke with a snort. Dribble coursed down from the left-hand corner of his mouth.

"Gov? We there?"

"Yes, Sleeping Beauty. Let's go and check-in. We have the agent on hand from 4p.m. We should gain entry around then. It's two now. "Harry looked at his watch. "See you at half three?"

191

Rollo nodded and they both made their way into the hotel.

Harry's room was basic. Nothing posh on police expenses, but it was comfortable enough. He checked his messages. He'd missed a call from Ellen. She was probably just off to work on a late.

There was an email message from Maisie. They had found more human remains at Legend Street, possibly Nancy's bones. Body number ten; they were racking up the corpses. Maisie had also spoken with Pleasant. Owain had given the team permission to search the underground bunker if necessary. Well, it wouldn't do any harm; there was nothing left in the evidence stores, he had asked his team to check.

He set his laptop up and intended to reply to some of the endless emails he received, but he decided to make tea and then he lay on his bed. In moments, he was asleep.

For once in the dream, Harry was a man, not a boy.

He was sitting in an infirmary. They had put him there as he really had lost his memory and wasn't able to tell anyone anything, other than about being a boy in that cage.

He remembered he had spent time speaking with a soldier called Fortune. Stephen Fortune had lost his left eye and most of his left hand to an explosive device on the very day the war had ended. They were playing cards when Fortune offered him some information.

It was unusual for the patients to speak about their situations, but Fortune had struck up such an affinity with Harry, that they told each other much about their former lives before they found themselves constant companions in Whittington Nick, as they called it. Well, it was mostly one-sided, as Harry could remember truly little.

Then the dream skipped, and Harry was a boy again, still in the ward, but it now seemed to be attached to a school.

He went to look for Stephen Fortune. Matron had said Stephen had gone for his injection with Nurse Ellen. Shortly after, Harry was called to Brigadier Scotland's office. On arrival, the Brigadier's adjutant marched him out of the building into the back yard. He was asked to wait and watch and not respond.

A man was led out by two soldiers and tied to a post. A file of six or seven soldiers followed them out and lined up opposite.

A firing squad. Oh No!

He looked back at the poor man. The soldier looked petrified and really not with it, as if he were mad, no, as if he had shellshock. Harry caught his breath. Where had he heard the phrase shell shock?

The soldier sagged against the ropes where they were secured to the post, his arms flailing. One of them was missing a hand.

The firing squad stepped up. They aimed. Then they fired.

"Why have you done this?" he screamed.

Silence. Then Matron answered. "It's because he wouldn't have his injection. He was a traitor. Stephen Fortune was a traitor.

Harry woke with a start as the phone alarm pinged. It was only a dream, he reminded himself - albeit a very vivid, ever-developing one. He quickly wrote down a salient description in his notebook, which he had brought from home, and then he sent Rollo a text, asking him to meet Harry in the foyer.

As he freshened up, Harry re-lived the recent strange events happening in his life over and over in his head. Who was Edith to him? Could she be the same Edith that Maisie was in contact with? What he did know was that although she hadn't appeared in his latest dream, he could still feel her on the periphery. Why had he not forced the issue and asked Maisie to arrange a meeting with Edith?

When he returned, he would have to do so. Harry did not like how there were links between the dream story and real life. Was there a true link between what he was dreaming and his current investigation? Was his loss of memory prior to him waking up in Lichfield also part of the mystery?

Yet his dreams were of another boy, years ago. They were dreams, weren't they, or possibly planted memories? He had discussed planted memories with his psychoanalyst, maybe she was the one to affect him. No, that was ridiculous. That would suggest people had got to him and modified his thoughts. No-one had messed with his memory. Had they? Prendergast? There were endless questions, and he was still thinking about them when he entered the bar and Rollo tapped him on the shoulder.

"You okay, gov?"

"We need to talk, Rollo," Harry dragged himself back to his present concerns. They had a short journey to George Wright's property ahead of them and it would be a good chance to find out what was eating at Rollo.

They belted up and Harry pulled off the drive of the hotel, heading back onto the A39 and towards their destination. Dyowl's Cove - Cornish for Devil's Cove. Wright's house was a gated property perched on a promontory in the Cornish hills. The agent would be meeting them there.

"So, what's up Rollo? You look like shit, you are quieter than ever, you look like you haven't slept properly for weeks. You reek of alcohol."

Rollo half-laughed, half-spluttered with indignation.

"I'm fine, gov." The usual curt hand-off.

"The fuck you are, Rollo. Your performance in recent weeks is on the dive. If Rivers sees our figures, we are in the mire, we won't get the funding next year. We will all be moved to regional teams or God forbid, uniform. When was the last time you closed a case? There's a pile of cold cases on your desk, it's not getting any smaller."

"Why don't you give them to Little Miss Sunshine?"

"Maisie is doing okay, particularly with Marsh off sick. I had to push her promotion through, so we had cover."

"She doesn't have the experience, yet she is allowed free reign."

Harry banged the steering wheel with one hand. "You've had your chance. You are meant to be progressing this side of the case, but frankly, I have dragged my arse down here to make sure we get what we want, and you don't overlook anything. Your hand-written notes from the Legend Street discovery were poor. I had to get someone to go back in situ to get a first-hand description. I asked you to get the grounds excavated and you forgot. A few months ago, I could have trusted you to cover things for me, but you are fading Steve." He didn't often use the man's first name and he felt that he hit the mark. Rollo flinched.

"I've told you, *Sir*, I'm okay."

"If that's how you are going to play it, I'll have to put you on leave until you can sort your shit out. I don't like playing the suspension card, but I'd prefer to have temporary cover if you're going to act like a zombie."

"Whatever."

Harry dropped it. He hadn't got the energy to sort it here, but he would raise it with DSI Taylor once he was back.

They pulled up to the gated property. There was the agent's car - Martin's Management Services emblazoned across the side.

Gemma was the agent; she was young, orange-skinned and shiny. "Afternoon, gentlemen." Her Cornish lilt was nice and smooth. He could feel Rollo eyeing her up, like a lion ready to pounce on his prey.

"Hi, Gemma, isn't it? Here's our warrant," Harry showed his papers, "although I believe the solicitors for Mr Wright's estate have given us full access. When was the last time someone was granted entry?" Harry asked Gemma.

"Not since the year 2000, Chief Inspector, when they fitted these gates. The house is kept in a nice condition apparently, although I have never been inside. Reynolds the solicitors pay for the upkeep. Our large estates division deal with that side."

Much like Legend Street then, Harry thought. "We'll take it from here."

"Be careful gents, won't you? Don't go into the cellar." She grinned, her slightly sarcastic tone lost on Rollo, but food for thought for Harry.

"It's the attics you want to be more scared of love, not the cellars. Oh, and before you ask, I'm not wearing a hard hat." Rollo replied and winked at her. To Harry's disgust, she blushed and turned darker orange.

"I'll leave you to it. If you would just drop the keys back through the agency door later, or in the morning. She held out a small card to Rollo. "That's my card Inspector Rolleston. It's my personal number. Just give me a shout if you need anything."

She got in her car and left.

"Right Lothario let's go and have a look. You can catch up with Orange Gemma later."

The grounds of the house were well-presented but not ornate, as if the maintenance contractors had just been intended to keep it ticking over, rather than enhance it - much like Legend Street, it seemed. George had certainly liked big properties, but he wasn't a show-off.

The house itself was probably built in the late nineteenth century, in the art deco style. The frontage was smaller in width than the house behind it - probably Paul Beaton's 1940s redevelopment. The building's facade was of dark orange bricks, three stories high. There were three sets of bay windows above and below, triple free-standing garages off to the left and a couple of small stable buildings to the right.

196

The building behind the façade was huge, extending over a large square footprint. They could see the threshold of the grounds; a steep drop or ha-ha that seemed to have a joke sign pointing downwards that said "Beach, 300 feet." It was as if Paul Beaton had just plonked the expanse of a mansion behind a two up and two down semi on the side of a cliff.

Harry opened the front door and they both entered. Rollo closed the door behind them.

The hallway was dark, despite the late afternoon sun which was trying to invade through large glass windows lined with heavy drapes. The layout inside was very much like the house in Legend Street. Two reception rooms either side of an entrance hall, a grand yawning staircase vomited garish Axminister-covered steps at them from a middle landing, which curved off to the left and to the right to differing wings on the first floor.

Down the hallway, they found two further rooms: a large, long dining room and what looked like a room of equal size that was clearly a small ballroom. That room alone was probably the size of Harry's entire flat.

"Rollo, you have a look for the library. It was on the plans just behind these rooms and next to the kitchens."

Harry took the stairs - it was darker up there. There were screens screwed shut on the windows at the top of the landing on the left. Three rooms lay ahead at equidistance to each closed door. He tried a door, but it was locked. Retrieving the bunch of keys, he picked a Yale one with the same serial number on it as the lock. The door opened with the creak of aged wood, and he peered inside. Harry flicked the switch - remarkably the room lit up, although the bulb was flickering. The Bakelite switches showed how long it had been since the electrics had been overhauled, if at all, since installation.

The room was grand. There was a matching four-poster double bed and double wardrobe, each with a curved scrolling apex and rich inlaid Verdigris laminate. There was a basin and an ottoman, but that was all. It smelled musty, but not damp. He left the door open and moved onto the next. There were four rooms on the left-hand side of the building and three on the right. Three had ensuite bathrooms and the large family bathroom was the fourth room on the right-hand side.

There were stairs at the end of both corridors that possibly led down to the back of the property but definitely went up to the second floor. Harry took the left-hand stairs up to what he expected to be an attic. The steps were not carpeted; they creaked and groaned loudly as he went up, originally towards servants' quarters, no doubt.

Harry found that the second-floor rooms were all empty, devoid of furniture drapes or carpets. He guessed that at the time this house ceased its usefulness, the servants had long since gone.

He then decided to go through to the right-hand side. He climbed the stairs and tried the handle which should have opened to a similar corridor to the one that had revealed the servants' quarters.

None of the keys fitted. Harry huffed and puffed a little, tried them all again in case he had missed one. Nothing. Then he felt a stabbing pain in his head that took his breath away momentarily and he had to hold himself up to stop from collapsing.

A male voice spoke to him. "Harry. Harry Morton. Is that you?"

It was coming from the other side of the door.

"Who is that? How do you know me?"

"Oh, it's George, George Wright. I have been expecting you. Get rid of the drunk so we can talk."

198

Chapter Eighteen

Happy Birthday

Rochelle was smiling. Tomorrow was her eighteenth birthday, and they were having one hell of a party. Kaden, her twin, had organised the DJ and she and her mum had spent the day dressing the hall. She was now off to see her girlfriends. They were all going to watch a rerun of Pet Sematary at the cinema - the first in a series of Stephen King films leading up to Halloween.

The nights were drawing in; she was walking through the industrial estate towards the back of the station to catch the train to Tamworth from platform two. It was still warm for the time of year, and she was feeling sweaty, despite her vest top being "too short," according to Grandma. Not to mention her tight shorts that would be a "come on" to any perverts and paedophiles who were going to attack and rape her. This was Lichfield though - nothing ever happened like that here. Thank God she would legally be a woman in less than six hours. She could then do what she liked - well, within reason - and not around Grandma.

There was a ping notification on her phone. It was Instagram, obvs: the girls had reached the cinema and were buying the tickets. "Hurry up, bitch," Megan had put under the photo of them all pointing at the film poster. Rochelle smiled. *Banter.*

There was another ping, this time from Kaden. He was over at the hall with the DJ - setting up. *Got list of songs sorted. We will set up and I'll see you at home later. Love K.X*

Rochelle smiled. Many of her friends were jealous of her relationship with her brother. He was her rock and had been ever since Dad had died of cancer the previous year. A brief shudder of grief went through her, and she held back tears for a moment, remembering her dad Royston, his handsome brown face fading to grey as his life ebbed away.

She was soon by the post office depot and thought about getting back on the main road rather than facing a lonely trek through all the industrial units, but she was going to be late for her train if she didn't hurry up. So, with a deep breath, she set off at a canter, as fast as her four-inch wedge heels would allow.

The shadows seemed to lengthen as a thick darkness approached. It was a grey early evening, the clouds keeping in the warmth. Thunderstorms were needed, but they weren't approaching any time soon, according to the weather. It was as if dark clouds had been drawn onto the late summer sky, like God's own curtains.

She tripped up the kerb, just managing to prevent herself from falling flat on her face but not stopping her phone from dropping with a crack. It could easily have been one of her bones if she had toppled. She retrieved the handset and saw that the screen – despite having a protector – had a mighty crack down its length.

"Bollocks." It was only a few weeks old. She had upgraded it because her old one was full of photos and junk.

She ran a finger over the crack, broken screen held in place by the thin film that was over it. She checked the time and began to run.

"I did that last week."

Rochelle jumped. Good job she had decent bladder control. She really needed a pee.

"Jesus, mate. You shocked me then." She looked at the man. He was slouching so it was hard to tell how tall he was. He stood next to a police car. It was unmarked, but the lights were flashing. He *was* fit though, if a little old.

"A young lady like you shouldn't be walking through the industrial estate at this hour."

"I'm in a rush. Sorry. I've got to go. Train."

"Just a minute. Are you Rochelle Morton?"

"Yes. Are you police?"

He smiled and nodded. "I am now. I used to work with your father Royston in the prison system, when he was at the Young Offenders Institute. We used to look after the naughty boys, years ago now when I was a trainee. I recognise you from his funeral."

She didn't recognise this man, but that had been a terrible day. She couldn't recall most of what had happened. He didn't look old enough to have worked with her dad at the YOI. The light wasn't great, though.

"Hi. Look. I'm sorry I need to get my train. I think that's it pulling in."

"Yes, sorry to delay you. I'm just staking out the place. There's been a spate of robberies. Off you go - you've got a minute or so to get there."

It was further than she thought and as she landed on the platform the train pulled away. Darkness had fully closed in and the weak orange light from the safety lamps gave the immediate area a sick glow.

"Fuck," she spat; everything was going against her, she was going to miss the start of the film. There wouldn't be another train for forty minutes. Despondently, she plonked herself on a bench.

Suddenly the policeman, her dad's alleged friend, ran down the steps onto the platform.

"Have you seen a lad about fifteen come this way? He hasn't gone down across the line, has he?"

"No mate. No-one at all, unless he just got onto the train." But he would have had to have overtaken Rochelle. No one had.

"Where is it going?"

"It's the cross-country line. Next stop is Tamworth."

"Are you going there?"

"Yes, eventually. I'm late for my film."

"I could give you a lift."

She looked at him. He looked kind of nice. He seemed older than he looked, she could tell, but his skin was so smooth. He had nice thick black hair, even if it was old-fashioned in style.

"I know your mum too. We all used to go out drinking with my girlfriend Sarah-Jane when we were younger. We worked at Winson Green together too. Roy used to be called Hot Chocolate because he looked like the lead singer. Probably too near the knuckle these days, but he didn't mind. He was over the moon when you and Kaden were born. Look, call Marion."

He couldn't be bluffing those facts, although his comment was just a little racist. She sent Mum a text. He sat next to her on the bench.

"What did you say your name was?"

"Marcus. Marcus Vincenzo. Your mum would know me as Gazza." He beamed. He really was quite handsome and youthful. Italian stallion. He'd definitely had work done.

She smiled at him and as she did, she missed the subtle movement of his hand coming out of his jacket pocket with something in it. She felt the jab in her leg, then she looked down as there was a sharp burgeoning pain.

"Three for a girl." He whispered. "Silly fucking rhyme. *Lady* Bell."

Those were the last words Rochelle Morton ever heard.

"Right, I'm off, K," Big Mick said. He had the last of the metal cases his equipment had been in. Kaden watched him go. They were starting early the next day, so they'd had to set up the evening before the birthday proceedings. Leo was meeting him in a bit, in the Spitfire pub for a cheeky drink. Kaden worked there, so the landlord was cool with his underage drinking. He was meeting Sam later and he was hoping he'd get some sex on the last night he was officially a boy.

His phone pinged. A text. It was Rochelle. "I'm not going to the pics now. I'm coming to you. I'll meet you at the hall if you like. Just walking there now. I'll be twenty."

"Okay." He texted back. That was cool. Sam was her friend, so he stood a better chance of getting in Sam's knickers if Roch could lure her out. *Kaden, you dirty bastard.*

Sam had been a bit hot and cold for a while, but Kaden felt like he'd had more of a chance lately. She was coming to the party, so if she said yes to seeing him, then he could have his way and then show her off the next night. Sam was a gymnast, very petite and fit. Just how he liked his girls. Flexible and supple. Jaden was at the gym day in and day out - he had worked hard to lose the fat he had carried until his fifteenth birthday.

He looked around the hall. It looked sick. Not what he really wanted for an eighteenth, he'd rather be at the Raze club, but he wanted his grandparents to be able to join them and his little nephews and niece, so they needed to be somewhere that would be okay for them all. Music could not be too loud for his ageing Jamaican Nanna and her flock of belly-laughing sisters.

Kaden's older half-sister Karen would also be coming up from Milton Keynes the next day to be with him and Rochelle. Karen was bringing the twins Billy and Jake and their sister Kayley too, so a club or pub party had been out of the question.

Kaden went into the kitchen, got a glass, and ran the tap. He was well thirsty; he had worked most of the afternoon at the pub and was still hot from helping Big Mick to lug the kit. Considering he was built like a brick shithouse; Mick was amazingly slow and lazy. Kaden had set up most of the P.A. system and rigging himself.

He drank deeply, then rinsed out the glass, dried it with a smelly threadbare tea-towel and put it on the side. He decided to turn all the kit off and wait for Rochelle.

Then he heard police sirens. Faint, but coming closer. He had a mate Ronnie who would shit himself every time he heard one. Probably because he was always up to no good, with him always lifting gear and selling his fenced reproduction goods.

Kaden was what they called a stiff in his friendship circle; he had never got in trouble with the law. He had never smoked weed. He had always been the peacemaker in fights or disagreements. He had never brought the police to his parents' door, even when he went off the rails when Dad had died. He never thought he would be able to recover from that, but he had. Now he was looking forward to his party and possibly slipping Sam a tickler. Well, he supposed he wasn't that much of a goody two-shoes.

He switched off the kit and then started to turn off the lights in the back rooms. Locking the back entrance, so it was secure, he made his way towards the front.

"Hello." A voice came from outside. Kaden froze for a bit. There was no one due to come here, other than Rochelle - this was a deep male voice.

"Hi," Kaden offered, as a tall man entered the hall.

"I'm Detective Marcus Vincenzo. I've just been called to say there has been a break-in here. Can you prove you should be here, sir?"

Kaden's heart lurched. Even though he was here legitimately, he knew the response of a white police officer to a mixed-race kid. Act first and ask questions later.

"I have keys, officer. I'm setting up for my birthday party."

"Name?"

"Kaden Morton."

Then something strange happened. The police officer laughed.

"Are you Royston Morton's son? Rochelle's brother? Marion's son?"

"Yeah," he responded, puzzled.

"Your dad and I used to work together. At the YOI. Up the road."

"Looking after the naughty boys?"

The man smiled. "Look, sorry. Busybody neighbours probably. Thought you had broken in."

The man walked up to him and offered a hand. "Is it your eighteenth tomorrow?"

"Yep," Kaden said, shaking the officer's hand. He had a surprisingly strong grip. He was pulling Kaden towards him. "Oy mate, steady on."

The officer ignored him. Kaden tried to break his hold, but it was crushing. The man pulled something out of his pocket with the other hand. It was a syringe. In one swift movement, he stabbed it into Kaden's neck. The pain was intense and spread to his head, but he was falling by now and watched distantly as the ground came up to eat him.

Well done, my Magpie. Three for a girl and four for a boy.

The Magpie stiffened. Lady Bell had never spoken to him remotely before.

Her voice was in his head. He felt sick and violated.

She had communicated feelings before, but never fully formed words. She must be getting stronger with each kill - as she said she would. *Witch.*

Clever Magpie. I can watch you now. I can watch your every move. I know what you are thinking, and I will be one step ahead. Do not let me down.

He shivered as her consciousness left him. He needed to be rid of her, but didn't have a clue how he would do it.

He looked at his latest tableaux. It really was a good one. The twins, yin and yang, male and female, so noticeably young. So very dead. Arranged on the tables with their birthday cake between them. What a party this was. He felt a little perverted when he had undressed Rochelle and Kaden. He didn't seek sexual gratification from his killing and arranging however, but he would soon get that from talking to their eyes. He imagined their first conversations. It would be so very modern and youthful, and on their birthday too.

He sat there munching birthday cake whilst looking between the corpses and the two jars containing each set of the twins' eyes. He bit down on the marzipan and icing and savoured every mouthful. He didn't eat much crap food; sugar interfered with his thought process. However, this was a time for celebration, after all.

The anaesthetic he had injected Rochelle and Kaden with had come from Prendergast. The Magpie had taken the twins' eyes quickly, as Prendergast had taught him, whilst they still drew breath, so they did not lose moisture.

He also found the conversations tended to be better, if he had harvested the eyes whilst his victims were still alive. But he wasn't mad. He *had* killed them both quickly. He wasn't a monster. He had felt his knife sliding into both effortlessly. The sighs of their final breaths, minutes apart, were satisfying indeed. They had both been oblivious to what he was doing to the other's twin.

Two more lives for the witch. Two sets of eyes for him. A good night's work. She was no doubt more powerful in their passing.

He needed a beer to help his bitterness at Lady Bell's intrusion into his mind, and to counteract the cake, overly sweet, unlike the old bitch witch.

Time to get rid of any evidence and roll up the plastic.

Marion Morton had got in from work and had gone straight to bed. Her stepdaughter would be arriving early doors, so she needed her sleep. She hadn't heard either Kaden or Rochelle come in the previous evening. They'd both messaged her to say they were going to the Spitfire.

206

The last of the messages on her phone puzzled her, though. It was Charles from the Community Hall. Kaden had not returned the keys and he couldn't get in. Could she ask him to give them back as soon as possible? Charles needed to be able to put the heating on well before the party.

The second last message was from Sam, Rochelle's friend, the one Kaden was sweet on. *Mrs Morton. Kaden and Sam didn't show. Are they okay?*

That message really threw her. She rang Rochelle. No answer. Then she rang Kaden. It was the same - straight to voicemail.

She started to panic. Maybe they went somewhere else, ended up at a party. It was the night before their majority, they probably ended up celebrating early. She would curse them if they had hangovers, if they had ruined their big day. It wasn't often she didn't get a message, but it wasn't unusual for kids to be self-centred , especially when they were drunk.

She made a cup of tea whilst she speed-dialled both the twins again. That was when there was a knock at the door.

Marion put her phone down and went to look through the bay window. It wasn't Karen, she thought. She went out to the hallway and opened the door.

"Morning. Mrs Morton?" A tall, beautiful-looking woman with a northern accent, dressed in a business suit, hair in plaits like a Viking Valkyrie. There was a small Asian man standing behind her.

"Hi. Is everything okay?" Her mind was reeling. She hoped her babies were okay.

"Marion Morton? I'm Inspector Price. I'm afraid I have some bad news. Can we come in and sit down?" the woman said, just before Marion Morton's world fell apart.

Mo had phoned Maisie two hours earlier that morning, and then all hell had broken loose.

DSI Taylor had been on the phone to say the local press was running a story about a George Wright, linking him to the murders of the six and could she draft a response in Harry's absence? Then Mo had called her over to the Hall in Bailey Park, just by the Co-operative store.

Grace had arrived around the same time, and they entered the hall together. The boy and the girl were laid out in a foetal position, like Chrissy Parsons had been. The birthday cake, with one neat slice cut from it, in between them both. The knives were both still in situ. Blood - lots of it - had pooled under the table. The air was filled with a sickly-sweet smell, tinged with iron. She couldn't get the idea of blood particles hanging in the air out of her mind for quite some time after.

"One young male and one young female. In the foetal position, knives protruding from the sterna, eyes removed. Looking at their skin and hair, I would suggest they are young adults, probably late teens."

"Grace," Maisie said and pointed to the two big silver balloons that were caressing the ceiling, bobbing in the subtle draft of the hall.

Grace nodded. "The victims, it seems were eighteen, or were about to be eighteen. If this is, in fact, their birthday party and not some sick representation of such."

Grace moved over to the bodies. She took a selection of pictures before putting the camera away and retrieving a pair of gloves.

Maisie did likewise; she had noticed clothing. She pointed at the two piles. Grace took photos. There was a phone and a wallet on one and a small handbag and phone on the other. One of the phones was ringing, silently.

Maisie looked at screen which said "Mum." As she watched, the other phone came alive and the screen said, "Badass Mother." It was the same number.

Mo had silently joined them in the hall. The small man was taking things in, horror writ large across his face, no doubt like her own, if she could have seen it. Grace at least had her professional shell to fall behind. Maisie just felt raw. The Magpie had struck again. Twice. They were kids. Dear God. Pete had hoped there wouldn't be kids in the briefing room the other day.

"Barakah Allah." Mo muttered. She thought she heard a sob. His children were this age.

"Can you do a trace on this number, Mo please?" We need to go and see their mum.

"Twins?" he asked.

It was Grace who answered. "I think we can safely guess so."

Then Maisie remembered what Daisy had said. Thoughts of her twin came through, almost suffocating her. "Three for a girl and four for a boy."

"It is exactly what we feared. Not young children, but not old enough to die," Mo whispered.

"Grace, I'm just going to call Taylor and then Rivers. You okay if we go and see their mum? I'd await liaison, but I'm fairly sure we will be crucified if we delay letting her know."

Grace nodded. "My team are on their way. You get off."

"Pete's just rolled up outside I'll come too, gov. He can hold the fort here." Mo offered. It was the first time he had called her gov. It didn't register, however. Her mind was elsewhere, with her sister. How would she feel if her twin died? She hoped Daisy was having a great time in Mercia with their parents.

Chapter Nineteen
Another Moribund Soul

Daisy Price was locked in an attic. It had skylights and irregular sloping walls that made it look like it was a solid A-line tent. It was damp and she had spent the last few hours asleep on a tatty mattress with just an old fleece blanket to cover her. She was almost certain she knew who had taken her. However, she could not grasp it, could not quite remember, probably the chloroform. Did they not know how dangerous that stuff was? Well, they probably did, actually.

The other girl in the room was rocking silently.

She had said her name was Lizzy. Lizzy didn't know how long she had been there and didn't know who had captured her. Daisy had quizzed her for hours. Lizzy just started to cry and scream and rock more.

Daisy had almost lost it herself when she had awoken in this place. She had tried to find a way out, but to no avail. There was the skylight high in the sloping wall but there was no ladder nor any way to climb up and even if she could, she would probably slide off an extremely high roof.

When she had eventually fallen asleep the first time, her voice hoarse from shouting, she slept deeply. Her dreams were full of thoughts of escape and a mad man who had come to hurt her, reaching out to grab her around the throat, a large knife in one hand – then she had awoken.

Lizzy had been there, then. She had been rocking to and fro ever since. Lizzy had screeched at Daisy when she first approached her. No number of questions she'd thrown at Lizzy had made up for the growing horror. She only knew the woman's name because she kept repeating it.

Lizzy is dead. Lizzy is dead.

Daisy knew all about these sorts of situations, human trafficking, human slavery, not to mention the possibility some sick fuck was going to abuse them, rape them and then kill them. It took a brave man to capture a police officer. Unless she was being used as a hostage, unless she had a price that could be exchanged by her captor, then it wasn't looking good.

If only she could remember who had taken her. It was on the tip of her tongue. He was... No, she couldn't remember what he looked like at all. He felt familiar. Strong.

Twice that day a door hatch opened, and food and drink were passed through. Her captor did not speak. He turned the lights out, so there was no chance of seeing who he was. Had Maisie thought she had gone to see her parents? He had made her record that message. Her parents were still away and not likely to be back for a while. So, they would not be overly worried. Teddy might have realised. Teddy, however, was dead.

She would miss his funeral. That was her first thought. She would be stuck in the attic, and she would miss Teddy's service.

"Teddy is dead. Teddy is dead. Teddy is dead."

Lizzy was chanting again. But Daisy had not told her about Teddy.

"What do you know of Teddy?" she asked the woman.

"Teddy is dead. Teddy is dead. Teddy is dead."

No number of words from Daisy could stop her. Daisy had shouted for her to shut up, but she only ceased the rant when she was hoarse. Lizzy then fell asleep, her light snoring soon filling the echoing room.

Daisy thought about her predicament. He would have to come to them at some point and then she would be able to challenge him. Or hopefully her sister would realise the message was a forced one and she was missing, and their colleagues would be coming to look for her. The latter was always a more

211

distant hope than the likelihood she would face her captor soon. If only she could remember him. She was sure she had recognised him. He had been familiar to her, hadn't he? The hair, the height, the strength, his smell. Like alcohol.

Then Lizzy sat bolt upright. She went from sleeping to awake in seconds.

"Daisy."

"Yes, Lizzy."

"I'm not Lizzy. It is your Nanna."

"You sick bitch, can you stop..."

"Is it better that I use my own voice, dear?"

Nanna's voice. How was Lizzy doing this?

"You and Maisie have the gift, dear. Like I had."

Daisy thought for a second. Gift? What gift did Nanna have? She was a lifelong housewife; she had brought up four kids. She could read the tea leaves and she had liked to think she was a medium, but Grandad always called her a small, because he always took the piss.

It had suddenly gone cold. She hadn't noticed it at first, but she could feel the goose bumps, feel her nipples pushing at her bra, hairs on the back of her arms and neck rising.

Nanna was a self-proclaimed medium, always talking about those beyond the veil. Said she talked to her own father regularly. He had died young, in the 1950s. Daisy had laughed along with her own father, who would tease Nanna. Daisy felt a pang of regret. She had not paid enough attention to Nanna, it seemed. She had always been in her Grandad's shed, playing with his trains as he watched. Surely this was nonsense, though.

"Grandad says hello. He is at peace." Nanna's voice, coming through Lizzy, said.

Tears came freely to her eyes. She must be dreaming, or, God forbid, she was having a complete mental breakdown.

"You are not dreaming, dear. I can't stay long. He's coming. You'll be free soon."

"Who's coming?"

"The Magpie is coming. Then we will be able to see each other again. And Teddy. He's here too, he sends his love. He always liked you better than your sister. He always harboured thoughts about you, dear. No matter what he said to you."

"Stop, Nanna or whatever you are. Stop."

"Look at Lizzy," Nanna said. "If you look closely, you can see through her."

Daisy had a good look at Lizzy. There was indeed something insubstantial about her. You would miss it nine times out of ten, if you didn't know what you were looking for. She had an aura; it crackled like a digital tv picture, around the edges Lizzy was pixelating. Yes, that was the word for it.

"She's dead too, dear. Lizzy died in 1782. The owner of the farm Cargill killed her here; he killed her little boy, Edward, too. He cut their throats in the night. She was his second wife, and she did not like him. Would not sleep with him. Spurned his advances. She would fight and bite and scream. Cargill was a Magpie too."

This was stupid. She was conversing with her dead Nanna, who in turn was telling her what appeared to be a tall tale. She was sure that she would wake up soon and all of this would be a dream. Please God, let her be in her own bed at home. Let this all be some sick, disjointed dream.

Then the door was unlocked and it slowly creaked open.

"Remember the necklace I bought you and Maisie? When we went to that show in London, the Lion King."

Daisy nodded; she always wore it. She treasured it. "Maisie had the one half and I the other. We still wear them, Nanna."

"Good girl. She will find you eventually. Maisie will find you. Or maybe you will find her. Don't judge her, dear. Hold your necklace tight and give it a rub. Your half a sixpence."

Daisy looked up as he stepped inside. Could she overpower him? She looked back for Lizzy and gasped. There was no sign of her.

"Nanna!"

There was no audible response.

Be a brave dear. Grasp your half a sixpence. Maisie will find you. Or you will find her.

Then the strong man caught her shoulder and wheeled her around and she saw his face again and recognised it. As he pulled the knife out, she started to scream, "No! Not you."

Harry had told Rollo to go back to bed, the inspector looked like he had not slept at all that night.

Harry decided to go back to George's house alone. They had spent the time wandering from room to room but to no avail, so they had returned to the hotel. They would leave later that evening.

Or that's what Rollo thought. He needed Rollo out of the way so he could return to talk to George Wright. Their brief discussion that evening had been bizarre.

"Do not tell your colleague I am here. Lose the drunk and come back later."

Harry had stood looking at the man who had appeared though the door. Yes, as if he had just walked through it. George looked no older than forty, yet he would be, even with a conservative estimate, one hundred and twenty.

"How can you be alive?"

"That's a long story. I cannot discuss it with your friend lurking about. I don't trust him. You shouldn't trust him. He is doomed. Possibly evil."

"You are one of his descendants. George Wright's grandson. His great-nephew?"

"No. I am the George Wright."

"How can you be alive?"

"This is getting a little repetitive. Lose Rolleston. Come back later and we will talk."

214

And that was that. George had walked back through the closed door and locked it. Harry had laughed, despite the strangeness.

Every part of Harry's rational being was screaming out to get Rollo to send for back-up, ready for when they cautioned and questioned this lunatic pretending to be George Wright. All his gut feelings were telling him to lose Rollo and return.

"Rollo. Take the rest of the day off. I'll look through the papers we have found. You take that girl out. I saw how she looked at you. It might help."

Rollo had smiled for the first time all trip, and had done as suggested. Harry then made his way back to the large house overlooking the Dywol's Cove.

He let himself in and wandered into the hallway. There, waiting for him, was George Wright. As soon as he looked at the man, his head began to hurt. Sharp pain cutting through him. Like shards of glass slicing through his grey matter.

George Wright moved over to him. Harry flinched as George laid his hands on Harry's head. He had to reach up, as Harry was much taller.

"You've got something in your head, Harry. It's stopping you from seeing."

"I can see fine. I've got a bone fragment in my head that's cutting through my brain."

"Well, you do have a blockage. It stops you from seeing us. But you have nothing physical in your head Harry, nothing. The block is a mental one. I am not the one who can take it down, as I didn't put it there. I can, however, stop the pain."

And suddenly at the touch of the man's hands, the pain stopped. Harry's head cleared. Like magic. In fact, it was clearer than it had ever been. He had never been this pain-free as long as he could remember. He was almost giddy with joy.

"What did you do?" he whispered, incredulously.

"You are suffering from a psychic block. I've just stopped it from resonating."

"Psychic block? Just hang on a minute - what the hell are you talking about? How can I be talking to a man who is allegedly over a hundred years of age?"

"One hundred and seventeen. Yesterday, in fact."

"Well, Happy Birthday, mindfuck. Hope you enjoyed your cake."

"I'm Moribund, Harry. I can't eat cake. That's not exactly true, I can, but I can't taste it. Well, not all the time."

Harry sighed. He was tired; he hadn't slept well. So much going through his mind. The case, no evidence as such. His health. The world was on his shoulders. The last thing he needed was some freak pretending to be a dead person of interest in one of the biggest cases in police history.

"I'm a Moribund ghost. You can see us know you are unblocked. Only a small percentage of the population can. An infinitesimally small percentage of them believe. Your friend Maisie, she can see us. Edith Keats, she's the other Moribund, a half-ghost. Maisie has kept it from you because she thinks you will think she is mad and take her off the case. Watch."

He looked at George. The man was probably five feet eight at the most, ash-blond wavy hair, balding and combed over. A pencil moustache like the spiv off Dad's Army. What was his name, Private Walker?

"Your mind is wandering, because it's not liking what it sees. Look closer."

George wasn't transparent but he flickered.

"I'm a half-ghost," George repeated, as if he were telling Harry for the first time.

"A ghost?" Harry was still not processing the fact, despite George's neat disappearing trick.

"Not technically, but I'm damned if I can explain it. I don't know why I am here. I just know I need to spend some time with you."

"So, what happened to Nancy?"

"Someone killed her, so I had a surgeon cut her up and buried her in the garden of Legend Street."

Harry couldn't believe what he was hearing. A confession from a ghost? Was he dreaming? He felt like he was awake though.

"Your team dug up a body from the garden this morning. I watched them. It's Nancy. We killed loads of the creatures like her. I was paid handsomely. They needed people to test. I found the people and then when they were finished with them, I made them disappear."

"Your own wife?"

"She wasn't my wife by then. She was one of them."

"One of what?"

"A creature of the Cordivae experiments."

"A what?"

"I don't know what they were, other than deadly. We just used to kill them. They wouldn't die unless..."

"You cut out their eyes?"

"I am not a freak. What kind of person would do that? I knew a surgeon, used to pay him. He would remove them under anaesthetic, then they would cease. That's what happened to Nancy."

"Cease?"

"Yes - they were already dead, so I couldn't say they were killed."

"Who were the Cordivae?"

"Not entirely sure. Need to know, Official Secrets Act and all that. They were led by someone from the government, from Whitehall. Paul Beaton was one of them; he had been my friend, but he double-crossed me. Led me here. He killed me on November 4th, 1948. I don't know what they were up to. I just got rid of the bodies towards the end. To think of all the money, I had invested."

"Who were the bodies at Legend Street?"

"Beaton wanted me to preserve the ones who lived after they were supposed to be dead. Apparently, it was leverage against Whitehall and the Cordivae board if they ever revealed the research

217

to the wider populace. I moved their bodies from the University to my house in Birmingham. They never found them. I've watched over them since."

"What do you mean - you can travel backwards and forwards up the M5?" Harry asked, an exasperated laugh escaping from a sewn-up sense of humour.

"You are struggling to believe I am a ghost then wonder if I can be corporeal in different places? Some of us are bound to our place of death. I am different. I don't know why - I'm guessing it's because I'm Moribund. Not a real ghost. I appear from time to time to carry out my duty. To those poor people in the tanks."

"What do you know of the recent murders? Do you have connections to someone who is killing people? Taking their eyes?"

"No. He is not known to me." George stopped, as if listening to something. "He has help from the dead. His help is clouded, however. I cannot see through the veil. It is a powerful block in your head. I think the source may well be the same."

"What do you know about Edith Keats? Do you know I dream about her?"

"I dreamt about her too - she was a doll. She will not speak to me, however. Probably doesn't remember I am here. She was Nancy's friend; she came looking for her the night I had to bury Nancy. Nancy had gone all strange. That's when I realised Cordivae had turned her and short of her ripping some young lad's head off, I needed to put her down. As it was the young man did it for me. Still not sure who he was. Probably a junior member of the Cordivae. They were animals, those Cordivae creatures. Animals. The woman I killed was not Nancy. Nancy was long gone. Edith had discovered what they did and tried to attack Paul Beaton, then she disappeared too it seemed, but I am unsure of events after my death. I am not sure if Beaton killed Edith."

Harry was pacing. "Tell me about the Cordivae creatures."

"They were the result of experiments they said. They hid it under the guise of PTSD, but it wasn't just ex-servicemen. They recruited drunks and whores too, anyone in debt, in return for wiping the slate clean. I don't know why, and I don't know how. I just would clean up the mistakes."

"Did you have any other contacts than Beaton?"

"No. Nancy was trying to find out for me when she was turned. She never got close."

Harry knew Wright was lying. It seemed a good copper could read the soul of a ghost too.

"Is she there? Where you are, I mean. Is she contactable?"

George shook his head sadly. "The Cordivae process took their souls."

"So, we can't find out anything else about the victims from your side? The secrets must have died with Beaton."

"What do you mean? He's not dead. He's still alive. "

"How can he be alive? He would be older than you!"

"I know for a fact that Beaton is still alive. I just don't know where."

"We have met his son. He said he had died."

George Wright shrugged his shoulders.

"George, can you return to Legend Street? I've not finished talking with you."

George nodded. "I'd rather drive with you in the car. Just call out for me, I'll stay invisible."

Harry pulled out his phone. He found Maisie in his recent calls list and called her.

"I need a favour."

"I need to talk to you first. The Magpie's just killed again. Twice. A set of twins, on the eve of their 18th birthday."

"Shit, shit, shit."

"There's more, gov. Their name. Their name was Morton."

Chapter Twenty
Inspector Mo

Harry was discombobulated.

Rollo was sitting next to him, as silent as the grave, whilst there was someone actually from beyond the grave sitting on the back seat. Whilst George Wright had said he could easily relocate to and from Birmingham and Bude, he also asked if he could have a lift back up the M5.

Harry had asked him to keep quiet; he did not want to talk to George in front of Rollo.

Rollo had met up with the management agent, Georgie, for a night on the town and looked in an even worse state than he had the previous day. Harry was silently fuming, he had allowed his inspector to go out, but didn't expect him to still be shit-faced the next day. He had already booked a meeting with DCSI Taylor to get Rollo suspended, pending occupational health referral, for failure to disclose issues that may impact upon day to day working. He had made this clear to Rollo, who had decided to give Harry the silent treatment. No surprise there, then.

Harry could have easily sent Rollo back on the train, but although he was many things, he wasn't a bastard. It would a blessing when he got Rollo back. He'd had a skinful of the man. *Ironic*. Despite the times they had both been out for a drink after work, Harry knew almost nothing about Rollo, his past, or why he was like he was. Harry just did not need it now.

Harry dropped Rollo off home, then made his way to the offices.

"He's trouble," George said, not for the first time.

"Yes, you have said," Harry replied, as he pulled into the offices on Eastern Avenue. "It's time for you to go, George. I have things to do. Maisie has agreed to meet me over at Legend Street later. No doubt you will be there?"

"As you wish." George vanished.

Feeling the wrong side of bonkers, Harry parked up in his reserved spot, put on the handbrake and got out of the car. He walked through reception, talking to no one despite nods and "hellos" and through the double doors into the office suite. He knocked on DSI Taylor's door.

"Gov," he said entering. Surprisingly, Mo was with her.

Taylor was all excited. "Harry, I've had a brainwave. I've drafted DS Hyatt in as an acting Inspector in order to support Price over the next few weeks whilst Rollo is suspended. Any objections?"

"That's fine." It was undeniably a good move. He was unsure of what else to say.

"Mo agrees that he's not quite ready for a permanent position, but this will be a good experience."

"Sir." Mo nodded, looking somewhat relieved. If he knew his officer and Taylor well enough, he would guess that she had railroaded Mo, and he had accepted out of duty.

"Acting DI Hyatt will run the day-to-day stuff on the Magpie case for you. It's the only way I can fudge you still being involved despite all the new victims clearly having the same surname as you. Although there's no direct family link, the Press are already sniffing. Maisie is too inexperienced to face the media on a regular basis, so I will do that whilst you and Maisie catch this bastard." Claudine took a deep breath. She obviously wasn't finished. "I've spoken with Grace this morning. There's no evidence from the latest tableaux that links to the evidence in Teddy's case. They took him over to Spain this morning by the way. Maisie is not happy, but it was cleared and out of my hands. "

"What? They are burying Teddy in Spain?"

222

"It was his parents wish. They returned him there with help from the Air Force. Wing Commander Robson still has influence, it seems. It's their second home and it's unlikely they will return with Teddy gone. He was an only child. Some people grieve in different ways, Harry. Just look after Price."

Harry sighed. Poor Maisie.

He needed to pull himself together though, no time for sorrow. "I'll see if Maisie is okay to head over to Legend Street later. Welcome aboard *Inspector* Hyatt. Pop and see me in an hour or so and I will brief you. Then we will hold a team briefing which you can lead."

Mo looked horrified.

"That's all for now then, Mo. I'll speak to you later." Taylor added.

Acting DI Hyatt nodded and closed the door behind him as he left.

"Good move, Claud. I think." Harry sat down opposite his gov.

"He's solid, Harry. Dependable."

"Yes, I suppose he is that. Still, it's your call. It's all a whirlwind anyway. Why not Mo?" He ended rhetorically. Mo would be fine. Hopefully.

"I've filled out the paperwork regarding Rollo. He's suspended for two weeks, pending a medical review. I've heard through the grapevine that he's drinking in work hours. I've had his office searched, but there's nothing to see. I've been in touch with his previous CO who is a jobsworth for data protection, so that was a dead-end, but I also contacted the Head of HR, who has had a look into his past. He's been suspended before for drug use. He nearly lost his job, but it was tranquillizers and linked to his wife and child dying in a horrific car crash. Know anything about any of this?"

"No."

She looked at him through narrowed eyes, noticing he hadn't used her name. He held up two hands in silent supplication.

She continued placated. "Me neither. I wasn't happy to have had to go digging for this, I like to know the history of my senior officers. You know I'll carpet you if I find out you did know." She was smiling but he knew she wasn't messing about.

Harry shrugged. "I knew nothing at all, ma'am."

"Good. Now, what happened in Cornwall, other than Rollo got drunk a lot and sampled the local talent?"

"The six corpses at Legend Street are a red herring. I've found papers at the Wright residence in Bude that suggest they were used by a project called Cordivae as test subjects. George Wright disposed of most of them after they died, under orders, but he kept some of them as an insurance policy." He was lying a little, but Claudine was not ready for the truth, not just yet.

"Six of them?"

Harry shrugged. George had said he knew where the documents were that backed this up, and they would be revealed.

"We might be able to trace their families; they all might have surviving family. Some of their descendants might be alive. Nancy Wright was also killed; George also disposed of her body. The remains dug up will be hers, I have no doubt. There was a reference to a diary entry in the papers to suggest this, which we also need to collect."

He left out how Nancy died as it complicated this nice temporary ending. He was certain he needed to find out more about the Cordivae.

"That would close that aspect of the case down. Except for any digging into the Cordivae group. Hold off with that until I can ascertain if it was covered by the Official Secrets Act. But none of this explains why the Magpie is taking the eyes of his victims."

"Unless he had access to the house in the past. If someone unhinged at a young age saw those bodies, the jars of eyes - I could imagine the transference."

"Are you going to do a sweep for DNA matched against the sample from Teddy's?"

Harry nodded. He had forgotten to order that before he went to Cornwall. Had forgot to speak to the unions too. *Shit.*

"Right. Off you go, then. I'll phone Rivers. He will be pleased this part of the case is closed, but we will need to spin a story for the comms team that Rivers will remember. Make sure you bring yourself up to speed with the Morton twins, Rochelle and Kayden, killed the night before their eighteenth birthday."

"Will do, Claud." He sighed again. It seemed like he was doing that a lot.

Was he going mad? It felt like he wasn't far off.

Maisie sat in the left-hand reception room at the front of Legend Street, sipping tea. Edith was there too.

"You seem nervous," Edith offered. She was dressed in a yellow trouser suit. *Did you get an infinitely varied wardrobe when you were dead? She wondered if it all had to be the same colour too.*

"Just worried that Harry will think I am mad."

"I somehow think that's unlikely, but you know as well as I do, you both need to be in on this. If he can't see me, then you can help him understand."

The door slammed shut. Maisie jumped. It *was* breezy outside. *Calm down, M.* She was very jumpy at present.

The Robsons could have told her about taking Teddy's body to Spain. Why were they so angry? What would Daisy think? She would never have gone away, knowing the funeral would take place in her absence. She had tried to phone her sister and her parents, but there was no response. After all, Maisie, Mum, and Dad were in Spain. Maybe they could have got to the funeral. Or at least sent some flowers.

Harry entered the reception room. Maisie noticed his eyes; they were not looking at her. They were looking at Edith.

He. Could. See. Edith.

Edith had noticed too, and she stood, shaking, emotional. What sort of ghost was she? She was crying. Tears fell but they never hit the floor, evaporating before they landed. Maisie could see them vaporising, as if they had been poured directly onto a hotplate.

Edith moved towards Harry and hugged him. He hugged her back. Maisie could see there was more to their embrace. She was the woman from Harry's dreams, if not a romantic link, important to him. His eyes were closed. Maisie guessed that Edith's would be too. They were holding back the tears. Maisie had lost that battle; tears streaming down her cheeks - whether they due to this encounter, or for Teddy, she was unsure.

"How can you see her, Harry? You collapsed the last time you were in a room together."

"George."

The room got a little colder, if that was possible. George Wright appeared, a smiling spiv materialising out of thin air. Maisie noticed he was in 1940s dress, too.

"You bastard," Edith screamed, flying at George, disengaging herself from Harry. "You murdering bastard."

Harry looked at Maisie shortly before leaping in and attempting to separate them. It looked like he was wrestling melting ice statues. They looked solid, he could grab hold of them, but they were slippery. She knew that his best bet was to just block them from one another.

"Stop!"

"He killed Nancy," Edith spat. "I can tell from your mind you dreamt about this earlier, Harry."

George held his hands up, the sign of a fair cop, but he wanted to speak, and Edith wasn't letting him.

"You killed your own wife. She was my friend." Edith went for George again and this time Maisie came to Harry's assistance.

"Edith, wait. Stop."

"He's a murderer. "

"You are both dead too. And there is an explanation."

"How can there be an explanation?"

"She was already dead when she died."

"Well, that's only plain stupid. Do you take me for a fool?" Edith almost screeched. She held her clawed hands out in warning.

"Stop!" Harry shouted. He pointed at George. "Sit." He turned back to Edith and showed her a seat with an outstretched hand gesture. "Thanks. There's more to this than meets the eye."

Edith and Maisie picked up chairs that had been knocked over during the fracas and sat.

"Edith, in my dreams, you let me out of a cage. Do you have any recollection?"

"I recall freeing you, but my memories are only returning as you dream. We share some link that is affecting both of us." Edith replied, still flustered, her cheeks red.

"George helped me to see. To see people like you. Dead people. He unblocked my ability. Obviously in the same way as you did it for Maisie."

"I did not unblock Maisie; she could always see; she just did not know where to look."

Harry sighed, exasperated. Weren't ghosts meant to chase you around, going "oooh" rather than disagreeing on the finer points of paranormal experience?

"The Cordivae were experimenting on people. The experiments were meant to offer people with trauma issues a way to rebuild their lives, much longer lives with better health. They wanted them to enter the military, spy on behalf of Britain. Go into deep cover. Unfortunately, some of the early experiments were not so successful. It turned the trialists into mindless creatures, which could be controlled to an extent but had a habit of going wild.

227

They experimented on Nancy; she was much younger than George when they met, she wanted to enter the military. According to George she enlisted your help, Edith, to do so."

"Yes, that much I now know. "

"Nancy was a mindless Cordivae reject when she died, because of them. George had the dubious role of disposing of the dead. The only way to do so was by taking their eyes. Or they would kill anyone in their reach apparently. They were all put down under anaesthetic, huge doses of horse tranquillizers, which would have been fatal to any other human being. Their physiology meant that their bodies processed the drug out of their systems at a faster rate than normal humans. Even after death, there would be no trace of the tranquillizers. The six were preserved by George for leverage should Cordivae put pressure on him. George couldn't do that to Nancy, so he asked the surgeon to remove her eyes and dispose of her. As it was someone took Nancy's eyes first. One of the Cordivae team no doubt. The surgeon cleaned her up and sent Nancy's dismembered body back to George, which he buried in the garden of Legend Street. She had to die, or she would have killed others."

"Why dismember her? Why not put her in the tank?"

"And forever look at her? We were worried she might revive." George almost choked. "Zombies can't walk in pieces."

Edith lowered her face.

"It's true, Edith. I would never have harmed Nancy - I loved her. I built the house in Bude for her. We were going to move there when I lost her to them. The divorce was a ruse to free us from prying eyes. Then only a few days afterwards, I was also killed. By Beaton."

"Why can't we see Nancy?" Maisie asked. Harry could see she was impatient to join in.

"You can't return from that." George explained.

"This is bigger than just a spate of murders. We are all entwined in this, our lives, our pasts and to some extent our futures, are all wrapped up in events that happened years and years ago. I need to give you a quick summary of my dreams from the last few weeks."

Harry outlined his dreams: the boy throwing the stones, meeting Edith, Edith setting him free and taking him to the barracks, then finally watching Fortune be executed. He didn't mention Ellen and the fear of the injections. That was still too raw.

"What I am not sure about is whether the events in my dreams happened? Is it me in those dreams? Is it this version of Edith, or is her presence haunting me? If it is me, how am I still alive? How do we find out more about the Cordivae group? Do we really need to? Or do we need to leave it in the past and focus on catching the Magpie? How is the Magpie linked to events in the past - is he just a copycat killer?"

George retrieved a sheath of papers from his inside pocket and unfolded them. "I've got the list of names of the six, Harry, as well as the other documentation that confesses to my storage of them and in effect what happened to Nancy."

"For the time being, until I am given clearance on the Cordivae investigation, nothing will come out, other than medical experiments gone wrong. I expect I will face the press about this with Chief Constable Rivers at some point. Once I have clearance, we can try to get to the bottom of the history of this project. Now our priority must be the catching of the Magpie - so if you can think of anything or remember anything that helps, please let Maisie and I know."

"So, the only question left worth asking is, why can we see ghosts and no one else?" Maisie asked.

"I think it's broader than that," Harry responded. "How can we feel them, touch them? What is a Moribund soul? This is nothing like what you would expect from a supernatural experience. And I can't believe I'm saying that, even with the evidence of previous cases we have back at the office. The room is a little cooler when you are around but nothing else, no reports of spinning heads or ectoplasm or the other ghost-related clichés I could name."

"I've seen my Nanna. Edith helped me to see her. She was walking through Beacon Park."

"So, it does extend past Edith and George. We seem to have some sort of gift?"

"Possibly," Edith added. "Why are we only half-dead? Could it be reversed? Could we live again?"

"I don't think we know enough. At some point we can do some digging, but first I need to catch the Magpie. Nothing more." Harry sighed.

"Oh. Did I say that Edith is my great-aunt?" Maisie said, cutting the silence.

Harry sighed for probably the hundredth time that day.

Chapter Twenty-One
Rollo's Girls

Steve Rolleston reached out for the bottle of Vodka, he tried his best to pour another shot, but his hands were so wobbly, he only managed to drop the bottle, sending both it and the glass to the floor with a shattering crash.

"Steve," the tall redhead said to him. "Careful. You'll break the floor tiles; they are expensive to replace."

"Silly Daddy." The little blonde girl was playing with her toys at the coffee table on the other side of the room.

Neither of them had been to this flat in their lives; and they only came there now as ghosts. They were not haunting him in a way that frightened him, they were haunting him in a way that was taking a toll on his already flimsy mental health. They were haunting his emotions.

"Why are you here?" he asked his wife. Angie had been thrown through the window of her car that horrible night her arm had been torn off and she had hit a tree and died as he watched. Chloe had died from a single blow to the head from the back seat passenger in the car, her grandfather, who had survived the crash, but with no higher brain function.

"I'm here to show you that you do not have mental health issues, Steve. You have been drawn here, drawn to your colleagues, because you have the sight. The ability to see some of us. Where there is a powerful connection or where there is a certain kind of angst, you can see the dead Steve. You are gifted."

Angie had said this more than once in the days since she and Chloe had appeared back in his life, on the night of the first Magpie murder. He felt that the trauma of that death, the hopelessness of that situation, had caused his current visions. Looking at Angus on the cross had opened his mind.

The day of the accident that killed them, Angie and Chloe had been travelling with Frank, Angie's father. Steve had been driving behind them in his car with Angie's mum and the dogs, as there was not enough room for all of them in the Zafira.

He had seen the accident. He had seen the car swerve on the ice, go off the road into the trees. He had found his wonderful Chloe as the life left her eyes, as she had the seizure cause by her brain injuries, her little lips foaming. He had also found poor nearly dead Angie. The trauma of seeing his beautiful wife in such a way would also live with him forever. At least the apparitions were helping him to remember his girls as they were, when they were alive and whole. He knew at times when he was low, he would see the image of Angie after the accident, but more often he would supplant it with the image of her on their wedding day, where she was the most beautiful, he had ever seen her.

He got up from the sofa as Angie watched. He had not been good to her memory recently - the drinking, the sleeping around. Angie had already said that it was fine and that he needed a way to get it out of his system, just so long as he didn't catch any diseases or killed himself in a drunken state. She kept telling him he couldn't die yet; he had something to do .

The previous evening, at his lowest after his failed attempts of making love to Georgia the estate agent, he contemplated ending his life. He had the pills in his case. His GP had readily prescribed him some after the girls had died. There had been no prescription review and he had kept on collecting them, taking them spasmodically, so that he had a supply that would help him to go to sleep and never wake up again.

He tottered into the kitchen to get a drink. It was a pigsty, mess everywhere. He hadn't washed up for at least two weeks and he was running out of crocks.

"I'll do it for you baby, if you like," Angie offered, and he shivered again. This was not right - what was wrong with him? He would go to the pub, eat there, carry on drinking for the rest of the day and then come home. Angie and Chloe wouldn't follow him to the pub. Angie had never liked alcohol; her beloved grandfather had died of cirrhosis when he was a young man. It wasn't ironic that he had hit the drink heavily after Angie was gone.

He swilled out a cup to fill it again. He was so thirsty; his lips were dry - he wasn't too far gone to know he had serious dehydration. He had only ever been like this before when he was on tour in Afghanistan, where he'd first had to look at terrible things, but nothing nearly as terrible as seeing your wife and daughter dying.

His head was ringing.

"Take some tablets, honey," Angie set about cleaning the pots in the kitchen. As he watched, only the ghosts of pots moved, the original corporeal ones stayed in place as dirty as ever. He sighed and went into his lounge where Chloe was playing. It broke his heart every time he saw her like that. A life cut short, so many prospects; he wouldn't see her get married, nor have his grandchildren. His family had ended with her. Both his parents were dead, and he had no siblings.

There was a knock at the door. Postman, probably.

He wandered down the hallway and opened the door. It wasn't the postman. It was Hayden Worth.

"Gov," Hayden said. Despite being a subordinate, Hayden was a good friend.

"What do you want? How's your leg?"

"I've just come to see if you are okay. My leg is fucking killing me."

"Any rugby?"

"No. Physio probably won't let me until after six weeks following the stitches coming out. He won't see me now. I have tried to call. Time for a coffee, gov?"

"It's a bit of a shit hole in here. Let's go to the pub."

"No. You need to keep off the sauce. Aren't you seeing Taylor soon for your review?"

"Not for a few days. Just the one. Come on. "

"You need to clean up. I've come to help.

"Who is it, Daddy?"

"It's Hayden, Tuppence," he replied automatically. Hayden would probably think he was mad. Big H, as he was affectionately known, did not bat an eyelid, however, so he invited him inside. Angie and Chloe had gone.

"Stinks like a tanner's yard on a hot day, as my gran used to say."

"I haven't had the chance to get sorted."

"I tell you what. I'll do some washing up before I make the tea, because it looks like you are growing antibiotics in some of these cups." He picked up a mug on the coffee table, pulled a face and put it down.

Rollo went for a shower and washed his hair, had a shave. Incredibly, he felt better already, as if the act of cleanliness was helping him recover a little. He had taken his time, and as he had shaved, he could hear the chink and splash of pots being washed. By the time he was in the kitchen again, Hayden had almost finished. It wasn't perfect, but it looked better. The big Welsh lad carried on drying the pots as they talked.

"You need to be back on form, gov, by the time your review happens. We need you. Too much going on."

"I'll be back as soon as Taylor signs me off. Harry's got his favourite girl in charge, no doubt."

"To be fair, her fiancé has just been murdered, but she is still on point. Still functioning. Look at your past, gov. You have faced worse - you can get back there."

Rollo shrugged. Hayden was right, although constantly seeing the girls was clouding his mind.

"We will stay away for a while, Steve, if that helps," Angie whispered. He almost asked Hayden what he had said, but he recovered. Hayden didn't need to know he was mad.

"Stay off the sauce, boss, you'll feel better. I gave it up for good a few days ago - best thing I ever did. Better mood, better health, better memory."

"I'll bear that in mind. I don't have any booze left anyway."

"Just stay away from the drinks aisle - easier said than done, I know."

He nodded. "Thanks, Hayden."

"No problem, boss. Let's go and get something to eat. And a mug of tea."

Harry was now in a garden shed. It was cold outside, but it was warm inside it. He had been asked to paint it, but he did not know who by. He had put on an old, oversized shirt, taken the plastic lid off the creosote and had started to apply the runny and very smelly brown liquid. After two sides, he was as high as a kite, thirsty, with tear-moistened eyes. He was about to go outside for some fresh air.

Then the shed door opened and in came Phillip. He had only known of him as the boy who threw stones up until now, but he innately knew now that this other boy was called Phillip. He was similar in height to Harry, with piercing blue eyes and straight black hair. He had dressed in short trousers, a shirt, a woolly jumper and brown Clark's shoes. His pockets were bulging, full of stones, no doubt.

"What you are doing, Henry?" He had been christened Henry but liked to be called Harry; Phillip used to call him Henry to wind him up.

"They told me to paint the shed. It's punishment for messing about at dinner last night and dipping Sharon Chambers' pigtails in the gravy."

Phillip laughed. "Piggy Chambers probably went home and licked it off. Fat little bitch."

"Stop being vulgar Phillip." Harry winced; he never used those kinds of words, but Phillip was always far more

scathing. He swore a lot. He was more violent towards others, he liked using his fists. He was always smoking behind the sheds. Probably why he was here and had smelled the creosote.

"Want to help?"

"No."

Harry continued to paint the rest of the inside of the shed. As he did so, he heard the first of the stones plop into the creosote pot. It splashed him and although he had a grown-up's shirt on, his legs were not covered. He felt the runny liquid reach his ankles, covering his new socks. It would stain his new plimsoles.

Plop. In went another.

"Phillip, please. I'm trying to do this quickly; you'll ruin my shoes and I'll be punished again. When I've finished, we can go and have a game of rugby if you like. One on one."

Plop. "Rather play football." Plop.

"Stop throwing the stones and I'll play footy with you."

Plop.

"Stop it or I'll tell the Headmaster. Or they will stop Edith visiting or worse, expel us again."

Plop.

"Phillip. NO!" he screamed this time, but Phillip was just smiling. It was a slimy broad smile; one you would think a human Toad of Toad Hall might make or the Joker from Batman. He really had had enough. He dropped the paintbrush back in the tray he had been using, took off the grown-up shirt and then ploughed headfirst into Phillip, with the best of his cheek-to-arse rugby tackles. Phillip gasped as he was bowled over.

Harry got back to his feet, but Phillip was quicker. He swung a punch at Harry, which almost connected. With his boxing training, Harry was able to step out of the way of the arc of the punch and block it. Harry took a swing himself and although he wasn't near, his reach was long, and he caught Phillip just on the end of his nose.

Phillip took a shocked step back.

"Bathtub!" Phillip cried clutching his bloody nose. Phillip staggered back and fell into the wall that was racked with high shelves full of different bottles and jars.

As Phillip collided with the shed wall, it rattled the whole fabrication. Rows of bottles wobbled and chinked like they were in a minor earthquake. As Phillip fell back further, one of the bottles fell and spilt its contents all over Phillip's head. He screamed.

Harry was paralysed with fear. That shelf held all the bottles of hazardous chemicals. He had been told to be careful. He felt like doing a runner when he saw what had happened. Phillip's face looked severely burned, like acid had scolded his face, dissolved his hair. One of his eyes was fizzing in its socket. He was gurgling now, rather than screaming.

Oh dear, what had he done? Harry set off at pace out of the shed, but not to run away; he went to get help.

The dream then cut to Edith arriving. He knew now that she was his older sister, but he thought she had died, or at least disappeared.

She was sitting at the end of his bed. He had been confined to it by Matron, after he had been given a tea laden with brandy and sugar for the shock of what he had seen.

"Phillip is in hospital, Harry." Edith had begun quietly, as if she still had not come to terms with what had happened.

"Is he okay?"

Harry knew the answer already. He felt like he had to ask. All the concern and terror building in his chest until he almost felt he would burst, or have a heart attack.

"Phillip has really bad burns. The peroxide has affected his eyes and has burned his face. He will be in hospital for a long time." She sobbed and Harry felt more sadness at that moment for her than Phillip. He had come in causing trouble after all, although he hadn't meant to injure his brother.

"He may be partially-blind for the rest of his life." Edith said.

It was then that he started to cry.

Harry awoke. Ellen was at his side. He hadn't remembered her coming in. He had gone straight to bed, he was knackered. Edith was his sister. How could that be? He also knew she had disappeared, presumed dead, when he was younger. The dates seemed strange, though. He had been in school in the nineteen forties. And if Edith was his sister...

He got up and put the coffee pot on. He checked his emails, and he drank first one, then two cups as he did so. It tasted good, but he was wide awake after. He decided to go down to the gym which was a couple of blocks from his apartment.

It was four-twenty a.m. and believe it or not, there were a few people in there. Did they dream of a strange childhood as he did? Had he had a brother called Phillip who Harry had seriously injured, burned? He could not for the life of him retrieve more of those memories. If they were indeed memories, rather than subconscious representations.

Living in a children's home seemed right, although it would have probably been called an orphanage. His parents had been dead. He had felt it. Although he had also remembered there being a headmaster there, so maybe it was a boarding school.

It gave him a little more to go on. He would google families with Ediths and Phillips in, as well as Harrys. He would investigate census records again. Just to look for clues. Was he having some sort of race memory? He had seen lots of references to the kind of anthropomorphic traits of memory being innately passed from one generation to another; for example, how did young animals know how to stand up and walk after birth or swim and hide from predators?

He ran ten kilometres, rowed a further six and did a few weights, then headed home. It was six o' clock when he got back and as he let himself in through the door, Ellen was coming down the stairs in her underwear. Lovely, beautiful Ellen. The most beautiful woman in his life, he thought, well aside from Maisie Price.

He paused, horrified with himself. Where had that thought come from.

Ellen was his love, the one he thought about every day. He gave her a big hug and they eventually fell into bed. He made love to Ellen vigorously and didn't think of Maisie at all.

Until just before he came.

He lay awake for a long time, guilt ridden and numb.

Grace Hodgson was leaning against the Institute frontage, smoking one of her regular cigarettes as Maisie pulled up in the BMW. By the time she had parked and made her way to the building, Grace had lit up another.

"You, okay?"

"Sick of doing post-mortems."

"Isn't that kind of your job, though?"

Grace shrugged. "I've done other amazing things in this job. Just a bad couple of weeks. How are you? You shouldn't be here after what happened to Teddy. Thought that he would keel over from a heart attack rather than be murdered."

Maisie luckily knew how blunt and impersonal Grace could be, so she just raised her eyes.

Grace dropped her fag and put it out with a heel. "Sorry, was that a little too brutal?"

Maisie nodded slowly.

"Sorry, Yorkshire. I don't do communication unless it's to the point. You take it or leave it. Coming to see this box of bones?"

"Yep, why not?" Maisie followed Grace into the Institute building.

There was a full female skeleton laid out in the viewing room.

"No signs of trauma. A little natural curvature of the spine, nothing that would have caused pain or proved physically challenging. Nancy obviously broke her left femur as a girl, a clean break at the age of ten or so. Other than that, it's fine. Corroborates George's diary. There are clear signs of

239

dismembering, but it was carefully and medically done. The remains were buried, likely disinterred, put in this box and reinterred. Again, this is what George's diary said."

It was also what George had said, Maisie thought, but Grace was not in their closed circle of almost-ghost seers.

"Right, I'm just going to finish typing the report for you. Tea and coffee in my office. Builders' tea, no sugar for me, Inspector."

Off she went. Maisie made her way back to the office. She said hello to weird Horace, who waved back, his head in a book with some very gruesome pictures she had accidentally glanced at when she walked by.

She made the tea and coffee for herself and went and sat at Grace's desk.

Whilst carefully putting down the cups she noticed a folder labelled Complex Case Team DNA results. A sheet of paper fell out. Maisie probably shouldn't have looked, but it was there clear to see. Her name was on that page. It was the results of a secret DNA sweep. She looked at the match. It said Harry Morton's name too. Why was Grace checking samples for their DNA? Harry had said they should volunteer, but they would have to check with the unions first.

She quickly put the sheet of paper back as Grace returned from the PM rooms with a similar buff folder to the one Maisie had just moved.

"Cheers. Wow, that's good. I knew a Yorkshire lass such as yourself would be able to make good tea."

Maisie smiled, but it didn't reach her eyes.

Chapter Twenty-Two
Another Random Factor

Pain.

Lady Bell sent painful memories to the Magpie. She was constantly in his head now and because he had chosen to do things he shouldn't be doing and she had found out, she was visiting him with his worst once-forgotten memories.

He then had a sudden and all-encompassing urge to kill.

It was an almost sexual urge to go out and find himself a random victim. At the time he could feel her unpleasant warnings from a distance, but his needs had briefly seemed to have overridden her will; when her control had receded, he set out to find someone. It needed to be random, to cut across the plan, to mirror the witch's ability to ask for a random kill.

Ever since he had killed Daisy, Lady Bell had grown in power. They were his victims, his collection of eyes, why was the fucking witch (he was now calling her a witch on a regular basis) getting more out of it than he was?

Yes, Lady Bell had supported him when he was at his lowest, yes, she had helped with all his disguises; she knew how to make one face resemble another, however different they may have been in the first instance. He still felt such jealousy at her gaining from his planned attacks. He knew his bespoke ones gave her nothing. That was why he suddenly needed to kill randomly. It went against all his planning and procedures, his OCD brain was boiling. He needed it though. Needed it so badly. To piss Lady Bell off.

He was sitting in the Walkabout pub looking to see who caught his eye. He wasn't looking for sex - he didn't have the urges for a sexual relationship. In his disguise, he had had plenty of sex in order to play his part; as himself he had had very little. The Magpie liked sex, but more as a means to an end. His real persona had always shunned it. Why would anyone look at him, let alone touch him?

The Marcus disguise was handsome, very handsome he had found. Both men and women looked at him in *that* way. They all eyed his fit muscular body, young and old alike. God forbid if Lady Bell stripped it away now. He would be lost. Back to his crippled self. Back to the self-hate and loathing. This murder was a gamble.

A handsome man of no more than twenty years was looking at him awkwardly, but longingly. Hardly more than a boy, he was with another group of boisterous men, probably his friends, who didn't realise their mate harboured same-sex thoughts. Tapping the sexual confidence of the real Marcus, he winked at the man when his friends' attentions were elsewhere.

The Magpie went to the bar, ordered a drink, and made sure he passed the young man. A trailing hand brushed an inside thigh, touching the bulging crotch. He tried to exude the nature of the man he had taken over, the self-confidence leaching through his every pore. He glanced back at the young man and then took his drink outside. It was a muggy evening. It had threatened to storm, but nothing had come of it. He immediately felt better; as usual, his heightened senses came upon him during the pre-kill, the pub now smelt strongly of sweat and cheap cologne. The fresh air was invigorating, purifying.

"Hi. I can't stay long. My mates don't know I'm queer." In the orange light cast by the streetlights, he looked even younger. Handsome, but a little grubby around the edges, a missing tooth, cheap tattoos.

"Will you be hanging around after they have gone, then?" The Magpie asked.

"Might be. Don't normally do older blokes."

"I'm hardly old."

"You got to be in your thirties." He laughed. He had peroxide blond hair. One ring through his nose.

"Thanks," The Magpie said, bitterly. The Marcus disguise -whilst years older now - had never aged past twenty-seven. The age Constable Marcus Vincenzo had been when he had been put into the furnace.

The young man leant towards him over the table. He felt a hand, at the top of his leg, near his balls. "I'll say my goodbyes in an hour or so. Got to show willing as it's my brother's birthday. My place or yours?"

"Yours," The Magpie said. "Where do you live?"

"Just over the Mexican in a flat. Number sixteen Bridge Street. Ring the bell, sexy old man."

The Magpie had never had sex with a man, and at the end of that evening, he still hadn't. The Magpie had got partially undressed, and had undressed Danny in turn and the lad was getting quite in the mood; his reaction clear by the size of the manhood that poked out of his underwear like a tent pole.

Danny had lasted a while after the Magpie had stabbed him, strangely the almost boy had laughed, blood pooling on his lips and called the Magpie a fucker as he died. "I knew you were going to kill me. I just knew it. There you go, not only was my life shit, but I could also see into the future, and I saw my own death. You fucker."

The last word was said with rattling sarcasm as the Magpie applied a lot of strength and plunged the knife further in. Danny's beautiful eyes would be his prized possessions. The Magpie quickly removed them, with the surgical tools from his pocket, putting them in the small transport jar he used for quicker kills.

Things were a mess and not just because of the blood covering him. He would borrow some of Danny's clothes to get home.

The Magpie did not want his latest kill discovered for a while, so in a departure from his usual cleaning up technique, he decided to light a vanilla Yankee candle, which sat on Danny's coffee table, before putting the gas rings on. All four of them. It smelled quite nice at first. Until the scent of gas cut through the custard like tones.

He was nearly back at his own flat when the explosion ripped a hole in the night, and the roof of the Mexican restaurant spraying Danny and his possessions to the four winds.

What have you done?

The witch asked as he shut his front door and leant back upon it. With her words came pain.

"Just mixing it up a little." He winced defiantly as he locked his front door.

There are to be no more spree killings. The Magpie cannot be discovered before the end of the planned killings. You know that. Everything I - no, we - have worked for will be for nought.

"I have to kill. I do it sometimes without thinking. Do you know how many I have killed?"

Three hundred and seventy-four in eighteen years. I know where you keep all those eyes. I know how cleverly you got rid of their bodies. The lonely, the people who were just moving out, going away, being deported. I was there to pick you up when your madness got the better of you, remember; that night when your guilt started to count each one of them. The three children too. You killed long before you came to me. All those nights you left the hospital, dressed in the clothes of the orderlies.

"Numbers do not matter to me. Only the kills. Let me kill when I want, and I will be able to execute our final plan much more precisely. Prevent me and I will become impatient and angry. You know how I can be. You obviously know."

He went into the toilet to relieve himself and washed his hands. He looked up in the mirror and she showed him an image of his own original, loathed face. She gave to him pain then, all-encompassing nerve-pain. He had to grip onto the sink to stop himself from falling to his knees. *Bitch. I will end you.* Then the pain increased.

Stand, he heard her say in his head and he stood. *Turn.* And he did. *Go to the kitchen.* He found himself walking mindlessly. He was not in control of his own body. *Fetch a knife. Put your other hand out.* He watched as he held the knife over his other hand. He was trembling trying to resist but he could not. *Slowly cut off the little finger on your left hand.* He watched as he put the blade onto his finger, felt it break the surface of his skin he was about to press down when she said. *Stop. Drop the knife.*

It clattered to the floor. She could take complete control of him now, as if he was a remote-control racing car. She could direct him at will. What had he done? The fucking bitch.

Shut up, my little Magpie.

Rollo had asked if he could come and see Claudine Taylor and Harry early. They sat in one of the small meeting rooms and he explained about the loss of his wife and daughter in the car crash and how he was drinking to try and forget the trauma. Whilst Claudine Taylor had known the reasons for his drinking, she had not known the extent of his angst, how he had been behind the car when it crashed, how he had found his little girl and wife dead.

"You should have said something," Harry said.

"Sorry sir. I'm not one for weaknesses. I thought I could control it. Coming to Lichfield was a new start. I was rebuilding my life. It's just these last few weeks with all this death, it seems it has surfaced again. I start to drink and that leads to other things, as you might have guessed. Trying to forget is making things worse. I've let you both down, I know. I'm willing to have some counselling. Constable Worth said…"

"No need to bring Hayden into it Rollo. You have suffered enough" DSI Taylor said. "It's been a tough few weeks. For all of us. Stay off another week. Then you can come back on phased duties. Yes?"

He nodded, that would be fine. His week would be up soon, and he could then carry on. And that was it - he was back in. He felt miles better for admitting he had been struggling. As he left the office, Hayden joined him, walking down the back stairs that also led into the car park. Rollo's Audi was parked in his usual spot. He pulled out a cigarette and handed one to Hayden, who refused.

"Body is a temple, gov," he said, pressing both palms together in supplication, biceps standing out from his arms even more. "I've just knocked off a night shift. Fancy a fry up at the up-all-night on the A5?"

Rollo was just mopping up his meal with a third slice of toast, when he heard another voice at the back of his mind. He immediately blocked it, but something had changed within him in the last few hours, and he felt it was important he listened to it.

If you kill again without my permission, I will destroy you. You will not have any notice, I will take you apart piece by piece, but first I will take that collection of eyes and I will squeeze every one of them to jelly with my bare hands. I will bite them in two or cook them in butter.

You touch my collection, witch and I will….

You have seen I can control you, Magpie. You will do my bidding and I will never set you free if you do not do as you are told. Once, but only once, you have delivered the breaking of that spell to me, will I then release you with your reward.

Lady Bell, I swear I will…

Lady Bell of Bell Manor? What has she to do with all of this? Rollo had seen her at a recent benefit ball held at her massive house. It was a wonderful place.

"You okay, Sir?" Hayden asked.

"Yes Hayden, I'm fine."

He wasn't. He felt like he had been losing his mind when his wife and daughter had been speaking to him. Now he was imagining a conversation between the Magpie and Lady Bell. Could she be his sponsor?

He might be mad, but he would like to prove he wasn't mad. He might spend some time looking into this woman. It may help them to eventually break the case. It might prevent him from drinking that evening.

Harry came out of his office after an exceedingly long day catching up on paperwork; it was late, getting on for seven o' clock and he noticed that Maisie's lights were on.

He told himself he was concerned for her following the loss of her fiancé Teddy. Harry couldn't forget the guilt of her face in his mind as he made love to Ellen.

He knocked on her office door.

"Hi, gov."

"Is she here?" He meant Edith.

"No. We have come up with some rules about when and how she appears. She might be my great aunt, but she can't just arrive without prior arrangement. It spooks me out more than anything. For so long I thought I was going mad and now it's just a bit of a bind. Like responsibility. Do you feel like that now you can see?"

He closed the door and sat in the chair opposite her.

"I am really struggling with all of this. The killer with links to both of us. The lack of any evidence until recently. This seems personal. The Morton references: he is getting at me. No doubt you feel like that about Teddy. He is baiting us. Both of us. Do you feel it? It's in the air, like a big supernatural cloud. There is a reason we can see Edith and George. They both suggest they are not ghostly in the sense we would understand. So, what are they, what is a nearly-ghost? The Moribund? Is the Magpie linked to

George and Legend Street? Is George lying to us? Was he really a killer? Evidence suggests he is telling the truth. Yet a lot of it does not add up, even when you take account of the other-worldly nature of things. Edith seemed so familiar to me. When she hugged me the other day, I felt complete. What links does she have to my past, to the reasons I am here doing this? The detective in me is screaming that my memory loss is also linked. I have a terrible feeling we will know who this Magpie is. I now know Edith is my sister, M. My fucking sister."

Maisie had nodded all the way through his long speech. He was normally a man of fewer words, but it had all just spluttered out. He hadn't told Ellen of his new skills. He hadn't told her that the headaches had receded. He felt he couldn't tell her yet as he felt she, as a nurse, would think he was having a breakdown.

"Have you told anyone about all of this?"

Maisie was particularly good at reading his mind these days, it seemed; they shared a bond through this business.

"No. I've kept it to myself."

"Not even Ellen?"

He shook his head.

"He is baiting us. Do you think we are next at some point? Daisy's one for sorrow, two for joy thing?"

"Kaden and Rochelle were three and four. Teddy is different though, there was no suggestion he was a planned kill. Grace feels it was a spur of the moment thing. No tableau. How's Daisy doing?"

"Oh, she's out in Spain with my parents. I haven't had time to Skype. Phone signal is rubbish, unless you are near to the local town. I'm not going to get the chance."

"And how is Pete?"

"That's over. It was a mistake. Nothing would come of it. He is a wonderful man. Just not what I need now." She sighed. "Do you fancy continuing this down the pub?"

Harry felt elated that Maisie wasn't with Pete anymore. Then he stopped himself and thought of Ellen, but she was on a late and it would be a shame to pass up a chance to have a conversation with someone who was feeling as he was feeling, or was also, possibly, bat-shit crazy.

The Angel was quiet, so they found a snug corner to sit in. Harry got a pint of pale ale and a cider for Maisie. Their round table was uneven and wobbly, so he fixed the lean with a folded-up beer mat.

"I so needed this," she said, slurping the top of her pint.

Harry looked at her as she did so. "I worry about you, Maisie."

"Snap." She laughed.

"We are hunting one of the worst criminals this country has ever seen. We have no real leads. We are obviously being targeted by someone who knows a lot about us. Any more to worry about? Oh yes, the link to six dead people who died eighty or so years ago. And we might both be targets."

"Do you think it's one of the team?" She had wanted to ask the question for such a long time, but had felt she could not.

"One of us?" he countered. "I'm not sure. What I am sure is however is that whoever he is, he knows a lot about us."

"I'm a bit scared." she admitted. "I have never been scared. I was about to be married to an armed response officer. I always felt safe with Teddy. Then that bastard killed him."

Harry saw she was starting to well up. She shakily put down her almost empty pint. Blinking back tears, she rifled through her pockets. He reached inside his and pulled out a pack of clean paper handkerchiefs. As he handed her one, she began to sob. He moved nearer and put his arm around her and pulled her close. Something he would not have done in a busier pub, or one where colleagues might have been.

"I'm scared, too. Not necessarily for myself, but the team. Why kill Teddy, what, other than baiting you was the reason for that? Could Ellen be in danger? Is he targeting particular people?"

Maisie blew her nose, but she did not break out of his embrace. "He would have killed us first if it was about killing us, surely."

"Maybe. I've talked with Taylor about protection, at our homes anyway. I might ask if it can be stepped up. Then I'll get Mo to sort it."

She nodded and settled back into his shoulder; she seemed comfortable there, like she had been there before. He felt complete suddenly.

"I'm going to go to Magpie Farm tomorrow. Pleasant's place on the Bell Estate."

"Want me to come?"

"No. I'll be fine. Edith will go with me."

"Be careful. We need to check for any links, any clues George may not be willing to share. Bring everything back as Owain Pleasant is okay with that. We will go through it with a fine toothcomb. Don't trust George until we have proof, he is not leading us astray."

She reached for her pint and sank the remaining dregs.

"We could be dead soon. Another pint?"

Gallows humour filled their conversations for the rest of the night, and they found themselves dissolving into laughter more than once.

Chapter Twenty-Three
The Spirits of Magpie Farm

Maisie pulled up the drive to Magpie Farm. It was set back from the road at the lower southern end of the Bell Estate. You couldn't see the mansion house from her approach, but she had heard from others that it was mightily opulent. Lady Bell was an enigma, but a generous one where the police were concerned.

Edith had been quiet as they approached. She had talked incessantly on the short journey, but had immediately ceased as they pulled up. It seemed even the Moribund got nervous.

The day was stupidly warm again. It was almost the end of October, for God's sake. Maisie wasn't normally one for sweating, but today she felt a little damp around the edges.

She opened the gate; it was a small entry at the side of a cattle grid. This led onto the yard where the farmhouse sat off to the left. The open barn to the right - where the cellar lay - shaded most of the yard; beyond that was the set of barn buildings that Pleasant was in the process of renovating to turn into his bed and breakfast rooms. Further beyond that, according to the map she had looked at, was Magpie Wood.

She had attempted to look up where she was going on Google Maps, but there had seemed to be a glitch; the picture was pixelated, un-focused like in the old days of dial-up connections, when there was poor internet bandwidth, and it took half a day to download any semi-decent picture.

Maisie walked into the shadow of the barn, the temperature dropping significantly. Her body's response - goose pimples - was becoming a regular occurrence. She shivered, although it was nearly twenty degrees Celsius, at nine in the morning.

"Has it gone cold?" Edith asked her. She was in her smart yellow dress and cardigan. Hair pulled back immaculately in a ponytail.

"Can you actually feel the cold?" She looked at her dead youthful looking great-aunt, who shook her head.

"No, but I can see it. It looks horrible."

Maisie tutted. It was bad enough she had to go down into an underground cellar.

There was a screech from the distant woods, and she jumped - some creature or another, a fox perhaps. Hope they fared better than those twins who were found at the bottom of the old well shaft. What were their names? Broad, that was it! Terrance Cobden's lackeys, the modern-day Kray twins of rural Staffordshire.

She could see the hatchway in the ground and wondered why Pleasant had not had it filled. George O' Neill had been found down there 20 years after he had been cemented into a living concrete block by the Broads at Cobden's behest. Their journey down the well had been karma no doubt, although they had found that O' Neill had killed more than twelve girls in his life and four of them had eventually been found on this farm. How could Pleasant stay here, live here? Maybe he was attracted by the fact he had rid this place of evil. She shivered. Had he rid the farm entirely of evil? It didn't feel like it to her.

Opening the hatch was easy. Climbing down into the cellar was not. She had been advised by a thorough read of the case notes to wear gloves and trainers for grip. One of the rungs of the latter was missing, it had broken when Jennie Cobden, who had covered up her father's crimes here, had fallen and struck her head. That was shortly after she had tampered with the brakes on Frances O'Neill's car. Evil bitch. Chip off the old block, no doubt.

"She didn't do any of that," Edith insisted, as Maisie had navigated the ladders and turned on a light switch at the base of the ladders. "Jennie was innocent. Owain framed her. He will get his comeuppance; I can feel it. There are spirits here. They can communicate with me, although they hold back. I don't think I'm good enough for them."

Thanks. Not making me feel any better.

The lights flickered and Maisie jumped again. She had told Pete not to bother coming with her as she wanted to have a chat with Edith. Maisie wished the big man were here now.

"A spirit comes."

Oh shit, she hadn't even got into the main chamber.

"Hello, dear. My name is Frances. Why are you here?" It was a disembodied voice.

Maisie didn't have time to respond.

"I didn't think anyone would return here after what happened. Why are you with this woman, Edith? Why aren't you dead? You should be dead."

The lights flickered again and a diminutive woman belonging to the voice appeared. She was light of frame with hints of hardened beauty, red streaks in mostly white hair suggested her ancestry as much as her Irish lilt.

"Frances O Neill?"

"Yes, dear. Now answer my question. There are restless souls here; we should have moved on, but the witch has grown in power, and she has dragged us back." She spoke with her voice now, not in Maisie's head.

"Witch?"

"Up at the Manor. The Usurper, the Curser, the Hate."

"Lady Bell?"

"Yes, that is her name these days, although I know her by others. And before you ask, I would not be stupid enough to reveal her real name now. Names are a power to a witch, for control and to control. A curse upon the speaker."

Maisie was struggling to comprehend the fact that this "ghost" knew Edith. What did that mean? Not to mention Lady Bell being a witch. A real witch? What the fuck was a witch anyway but a mistrusted wealthy woman, a midwife/healer blamed for stillborn children, or an old woman who was supposed to have blighted the crops? Being labelled a witch always said more about the accuser, across all of history. Having the witch burnt, drowned, or pressed meant some man or woman could covet her

253

land or possessions after she was dead. Exerted control.

"I'm here to find information about a group called The Cordivae. I believe, if I have this right, that George Wright sold this farm to your parents, who in turn handed it over to you, soon after, when you married. George was mixed up in a group called The Cordivae in the 1930s and 1940s; they were dabbling in scientific research that rendered people like zombies."

"I know nothing about that, but I remember Nancy. Yes. I remember Nancy. George Wright was a stupid man, but he did not kill her. He loved her. They came to meet with my parents, I was a young girl at the time. Somewhere around 1945, it was after VJ day, if I remember correctly."

"Nancy was my best friend" Edith offered, but Frances ignored her.

"I can't talk to her, it hurts me." Frances looked away from Edith. "Whereas you can see me without me using energy from the spirits. Look in the cellar rooms. George's spirit is mostly gone, so he should not trouble you."

"Would it be okay if I summon George Wright? He is like Edith."

"Yes, but I will not talk to him. I cannot waste my energy."

Frances then vanished. "Come and see me soon. After all this blows over. I might have more information about the girls my husband has killed. I have taken it upon myself to track them down, help console them beyond the grave. You are going to be able to set them free. If I tell you where they are."

Maisie nodded. Was this her future? Talking to ghosts and finding tortured, murdered souls.

It is an honour. To find souls and release them from their suffering.

Frances, lingering on in her mind, kind of had a point.

Lady Isla Bell was troubled. She hadn't been troubled for more than six hundred years, yet she felt, as corporeal as she was now, physically threatened. She cast her will out to the Magpie. He was getting the Daisy girl's body ready for transportation, so his mind was on his cleaning, as he called it.

There was suddenly a flare in her power net. What was Frances O' Neill doing, appearing again after all this time? She could feel her insufferable presence like a blind boil on her chin, all painful and difficult to get rid of. Frances and Terrance Cobden had foiled her plan to use George O' Neill in the way she was currently using the Magpie. George had been one of many Magpies, but the nearest to bringing her the total sacrifice she needed to finally break away from the estate. Yet, he had ultimately failed. Her spirits had dealt with those twins too late. George had been imprisoned in his concrete box and he could kill no more. She had tried the Pleasant man, but whilst he had set his wife up so he could inherit her money, he was not a seasoned murderer. Only murder gave Isla Bell power. Pleasant had never been an option. Luckily, a few years prior to Pleasant's involvement, she had met the man who now looked like Marcus Vincenzo.

Isla Bell - or Isabelle of Stafford -had been born in 1467. She had been born to another Isabelle and her husband Michael. At fourteen, Isabelle the younger had left Stafford to take up an occupation as a nurse to the children of Peter De Lacey, late of Stowe. Late by her hand. He had touched her too many times. His wife never found out who had killed her husband; she was only glad to inherit her husband's fortune. She had taken Isabelle under her wing, teaching her the arts that would make the men of the cloth have apoplexy, and start calling for the witchfinder pursuivant.

However, this had changed when the widow had married her second husband; he had found out their secrets and blamed them all on Isabelle, who was put out of the house after six years in service.

Isabelle had hoarded money taken from her mistress's fortune and had enough to set up an apothecary. She bribed a young homosexual man to marry her for convenience. She became respectful again, but she also had a habit for the drink by then, caused by seeing a procession of beautiful men who only had eyes for Stephen and not herself.

One day, she had been contacted by Sir John De Vere, who had been rid of his wife and daughter by a killer. When she met him, she had wondered why they had not just walked into the sea to drown themselves. He was an insufferable man and so she did not prepare the spell at all well. She just wanted his money. In addition, she had been under the influence of alcohol and instead of making it impossible for evil to set foot upon Magpie Farm, as it was known for the number of those birds who once congregated there, she had joined the spell with the words of a cupid's curse. It had become a tangled evil mess.

Luckily for her, she had - in early death - found her first Magpie, Sir Norman Belle, who had built the mansion on the same parcel of land as the farm. He had died too soon. The Bells soon established themselves and at one point had been Dukes under the stewardship of both the Charles.' Isabelle had lived there ever since as the ghostly guardian of the family who shared part of her name.

Isabelle came back to the present. There was another flare in her power net, but this time there seemed a hole in it; however, much she tried to cast it, she couldn't see the results. Come to think of it, there were three such holes. The two people who seemed dead, yet very much alive. She could disperse them once she was corporeal, she thought.

Isabelle cast her mind into that other one. Maisie Price. The would-be wife of Teddy. Finally, she was here. *Yes*. The noose tightens.

***

At the point George appeared, Maisie felt something prick her mind. Whatever it was, *it* was searching for something within her. She looked at George Wright grinning and felt like she wanted to kill him. Take a knife and cut his damned…

Wait - what the hell was she thinking? She blocked the presence. Was it that simple?

"Morning, George." she said, after the prick in her mind had gone. As if George was bothered if it was morning or night.

He was grinning inanely. "I don't like it here anymore, there are dead all around us."

"I didn't get all that from your grin."

"Nervous habit. Life in threat. Got me into a lot of trouble with senior officers as a boy during the first world war."

"Can you feel something else probing us?" Edith asked. Maisie thought of responding that she did, but she really wanted to get out of here as soon as possible. She'd noticed that recently Edith had the habit of fixating on something and then talking for Britain.

"Where's the stuff, George? Let's find it."

They went into the main underground room. The remains of the concrete sarcophagus remained, how ghoulish was that?

George started to look around. "I hid all my Cordivae notes and letters in a safe here. It's concealed. I didn't want to be caught with any of it. Paul Beaton often said that they would kill me if I divulged even one of their minor secrets. I had most of what I knew written down. And I was on the fringes of their work."

He scanned the room.

"Here," George said. He walked over to a door in the corner of the room. Some sort of cupboard. "This has not been opened since I was last here in 1948. I'd agreed with the Birds - Frances' parents -and then the

257

O'Neill's to still have access. I paid them a healthy stipend to enable me to do so."

Maisie went over and turned the knob. It did not budge.

"It's not a door," he said. "I don't know why I did not remember this as I entered the room. My memories are really selective."

"You are lucky to have memories," Edith said. "I only get them when Harry dreams."

George messed about with the handle. There was an imperceptible switch that helped him free the doorknob; he was then able to click it one way and then the next in a complex pattern.

With a final click and the door opened to reveal a safe behind it. George was about to open it when Maisie...

...found herself in the body of someone else, another young woman. How she knew that she wasn't sure, but the young woman was called Helen, Helen Marsh - and she was running.

Maisie, no Helen, looked back over her shoulder to see the Bell mansion behind her. Helen was panting, trying to get away, away from who? George? George Wright? No. George O' Neill.

He had captured Helen, and had taken her to see the strange woman up at the house. The beautiful woman, who looked both old and young, alive and rotten. Lady Bell?

Helen was barely a woman, she was only fourteen, but she knew her life was in danger. She ran as if the hounds of hell were snapping at her heels.

Helen's mother had forbidden her to leave their house. She hadn't told her mother where she was going, but if she had stayed at home, then her stepbrother Michael would have been pawing at her every time her mother was out of the room.

George O'Neill had promised her a handsome sum of money to clean his house after Frances had left him. He wasn't the monster many had said he was, he was a charming generous man. No way he was guilty of beating his wife to a pulp on more than one occasion.

The first few days looking after George O' Neill had been fine. Then he had started to paw her, like her stepbrother did during her chores. He had taken her up to the Bell Mansion on a pretence of introducing her to the grand lady.

Helen had become so frightened that she had run away, run away from George, as fast as she could. Still, she could hear him behind her, grunting, puffing like the old man he was. Dirty old man, she revised.

She had made it to the outskirts of the Manor grounds and was just swinging past the farm to go out of the gate and up the lane. Once on the main road, she would have more of a chance. Going across the fields or through the woods would get her horribly lost.

Helen swung the gate open, ran up the narrow lane and out onto the main road, where cars were flashing past in the bleak cold darkness of a winter's night.

She was so scared; it had got so dark. She stood there on the verge, near a bus stop, puffing and panting like her heart was fit to burst. Helen felt like a rabbit, choosing whether to stay where she was and face the owl, or race across the tarmac and risk being flattened by a car.

Just as she was about to dash across, a hand caught her shoulder. It was an iron-like grip. Big hands. The hands of a strong man who had farmed all his life. George O'Neill.

"Come here, you little bitch," he exclaimed, just before he hit her with all his force.

Helen suffered several beatings and sexual assaults in the room he had locked her in, below the farmhouse. She had wandered in and out of consciousness for two full days, as best as she could judge. She spent a further two days sobbing, then the attacks had begun anew. Then the day came where he had had enough of her. And she had known this day would come, if she did not get away.

As Maisie became aware of her own self again, she felt the knife drawn across Helen's throat as George killed his first victim on Magpie Farm.

In the here and now, Maisie instinctively pulled her hand to her throat to check if her lifeblood was leaking away. Of course, it was not, but the vision, for that was what it clearly was, had felt so real, so vivid. Her heart was hammering its way out of her chest. She gagged and vomited there and then. The act of being sick strangely calmed her.

"Maisie, are you okay?"

"Has George got what he needed?"

"Yes, he has. It's there on the table. He has just suddenly disappeared, though."

"Well, let's get the fuck out of here."

Maisie went to pick up the box, but there was a scream from Edith. It was blood-curdling, a long-drawn-out scream as if she were being killed herself.

"Edith, what is it?"

There was no reply. Edith was fading and fast. Still screaming, so much screaming.

Then she was gone. All that was left was the faint sound of a man laughing.

Maisie knew that voice. It was the voice of George O'Neill; she had heard it in her vision.

Maisie ran up the ladder, leaving the underground bunker behind.

Chapter Twenty-Four
Kiss of Death

Maisie was a quivering wreck when she returned to the office. Her heart was hammering as if she were still running from George O' Neill as she knocked on Harry's door, her memories of being Helen stark in her mind. Poor girl.

"Come -" Harry began.

Maisie didn't wait for Harry to finish though. She had slammed the door and sat straight down before he had managed the "in."

"What's up?" He could obviously see the terror writ large upon her face. She was shaking, no, trembling uncontrollably.

"That place is evil."

"Magpie's Farm? Well, a lot of evil things happened there."

It took Maisie quite a while to compose herself, so Harry poured her a coffee.

"I felt Helen Marsh die. Like it was me, experiencing her death. It was horrible. I've just checked the records. She was reported missing in the 1990s -an unresolved case. He killed her. George O' Neill killed her, after he had assaulted her several times. I felt it, Harry, I felt him pull the knife across her throat. She was only fourteen for Christ's sake. Fourteen, the bastard."

"Hang on. You felt her die? What does that mean?"

"That somebody, something, made me experience her last moments. I felt him kill her. The terror, Harry. There is something at that big house. Bell Mansion is linked to something truly evil. There must be more of his victims there. He took them there to kill them, I am sure of it. I think George O'Neill might have once been called The Magpie too. Its Lady Bell. She controls them."

261

"I knew you shouldn't have gone there on your own. It's out of bounds for you now, Maisie."

"It just caught me unawares."

"It's out of bounds, Inspector Price," he reinforced with a smile.

She looked at him, regaining some of her feistiness. She smiled back.

"You know how to push my buttons, *gov.*"

Harry sat back at his desk. "Just take me with you if you go there again."

"But *Harry*, you might be susceptible too. Don't you understand? I think it's because we can see. See *them.*"

He knew she meant George Wright and Edith. At least he was thankful he couldn't always see the dead, like Maisie could.

"When I took on the Complex Case Team, this was not what I expected. A few late-night exhumations perhaps, discussions with ancestry experts. Not this. Not nearly-ghosts. The Moribund. Not to mention the dead themselves revisiting us."

"That word has become a collective noun. We need to understand more about the Cordivae, don't we."

"I've got Mo looking through the papers and I'll get him to look through what you have brought back too."

"Whatever happened scared Edith away, and George. I can't seem to get them back."

Harry shrugged whilst taking a sip of his coffee. "We haven't even got to the bottom of who she is, by what she is motivated. I know nominally she is your great aunt and allegedly my sister, but as I've said before I would be careful when you are with Edith and George. Just until we know more."

Maisie nodded as she raised her cup to her lips. She was still shaking. She wanted him to hug her, but she knew it was not advisable, not in the office with his blinds open. Rollo would have a field day if he were about.

Harry's phone rang. He asked Maisie if she minded if he took it.

"It's Rivers," the Chief Constable said. "You are needed tomorrow to help me face the press. Get your shit together and we will give them something that won't set them running for the best conspiracy theory possible."

"Yes, sir. Do you...?" The dead tone of a hang-up halted him. "Rude bastard."

Maisie raised her eyebrows; at least she wasn't shaking any more.

"Rivers. I've got to face the press in Birmingham with him tomorrow. Wish me luck."

There was a knock at Harry's door. He went to open it. It was DCSI Taylor. She rolled her wheelchair in.

"Harry. Inspector Price. How're things?"

Harry looked at Maisie with a wry smile on his lips. Maisie knew they couldn't talk about the nearly-ghosts with her or what Maisie had just witnessed at Magpie Farm.

"Still a little perplexed, Ma'am. He is really good at covering his tracks."

"Do you think he is close to us? Could he be acting on information from one of the team, or God forbid, work here or in some other capacity in the force?"

"We are thinking a little along those lines, but we have no proof. There's no way we can be matching the DNA of our staff to his without permission. I am still exploring whether to ask the staff to agree to have the sample matched to their records. You know what the unions are like. We need to do it properly."

"True. As ever, you are right Harry. As you were. Rivers is after you, you had better give him a shout."

"He's already called."

"He's really grumpy."

"Hadn't noticed." He was grinning.

"You little shit. He's a bastard and you know it. Needs to retire." She nodded at Maisie, a wry smile etched on her face, turned her chair in little space and wheeled off.

"Lucky you," Maisie added. "Thanks for the coffee and chat. I'm going to see if I can catch up with Grace about Nancy Wright's remains."

Harry nodded and watched her leave. He was worried she was floundering, but he just had more appreciation daily of her strength of will. Just over thirty and she had lost her fiancé, however estranged and today she had coped with some sort of psychic, or supernatural attack; she had come through, scared but stronger.

Harry would have to keep an eye on Maisie Price; so long as nothing else went wrong, she would, he thought, be fine.

Harry glanced at his room clock. Then realised it was a date night with Ellen and he needed to get his arse back as they had a reservation at Ego's restaurant.

Ellen looked lovely as usual, dressed casually in an off the shoulder green silky top and petrol blue jeans. It was warm in the restaurant, even with the fold-back windows open. He could see the bottom end of Cathedral Pool and had a good view of the Cathedral itself. The towering, ancient building filled him with awe every time he looked at it, a sense of calmness and serenity, despite his accident within its walls.

They were waiting for their coffee; the meals had been great, and both had refused a dessert.

"Penny for them, sweetie." A smile lit her eyes. He really hadn't seen much of her recently, they lived such opposing lives. She was always on shifts; he was always at work for one reason or another. He put his hand on hers.

"Sorry. Miles away."

"You've got a lot on." She was professional enough, even in their private life, to not discuss cases in the open where the walls had ears.

An awful lot I can't tell you too. You should tell your life partner everything. Yet here he was, holding back secrets. Secrets he shared on a regular basis with Maisie.

"I need to tell you something, Harry."

He was immediately both concerned and intrigued. "Go on?"

"I found your records the other day. Prendergast's records actually, of your treatment."

Okay, well, Ellen worked at the hospital, usually in A and E and granted not outpatients in the Maxillo-Facial department.

"Well, you work there, I'm sure there's no data protection breach. You are named as my next of kin; with Dad in a home, they would inform you." His face probably told her he was mulling this over. She was dating a detective, after all.

"I deliberately went looking for them, Harry. No. What I mean is I went and took your files and read them without permission. I wanted to see if there was anything I could do to speed things up. To help you get your memories back. The dreams. They haunt you. You seem to never have a good night's sleep..."

"And you thought doing that would help. How?" He wasn't going to lose his temper, although they both knew she had committed a criminal offence and one that could end in a gross misconduct dismissal and her career down the toilet.

"I'm so sorry." Tears started to roll down her face, creating trails of mascara. "I shouldn't have. I know the position it might put both you and me in, but..." She paused to pull in a breath. "I couldn't help it. I had to know."

"What if they have camera footage of you breaking into the office? They will have your whereabouts from the smart ID cards you all wear."

She hung her head and said something almost imperceptible.

"Sorry?" he asked.

"I didn't think about my access badge."

"They will have a record of your movements. If they see that you have been into the files, if you were caught on camera? Oh God, Ell."

"You have nothing in your head, Harry. Prendergast has been lying. He sent a referral to community psychiatry, but it was never responded to. The block is psychological, not physical. You were found in the cathedral with a severe head wound, but it did not involve any skull fracture. I can only guess from what I saw that you had fallen from a height, but not a life-threatening one."

He was getting angry now. He could feel the heat rising, his face reddening. He now knew it was a psychological or a supernatural block, but Ellen had put herself in danger of losing her career by doing so. And she had endangered his, by association.

The biggest issue was however that he had spent years thinking every day could be his last. He had stayed away from commitment. He had never proposed to Ellen because of this - he had not wanted to leave her a widow. He had not wanted to hurt this perfect woman. Then she had gone and revealed his secret, but unlawfully. *His secret.* By means that would be inadmissible, should he need to use them in a negligence case.

"You have probably set me back years, Ellen." He could hear the bitterness in his voice, which wasn't him, but it was there, leaching out of him. Years of frustration. Or was it something else. This case. He felt so bitter.

"If I wanted to litigate the hospital or Prendergast, they would check every link to me before releasing the facts. They know you are on the staff. They will know you accessed those records. They will know." Harry banged the table. A few pairs of eyes looked towards him. "So, my search for the actual truth may never reach a legal conclusion."

266

Ellen was almost sobbing. She had probably rehearsed his reaction for days since she had carried out her spying deed.

"I thank you for proving beyond doubt that I do not have a ticking time bomb in my head. I also praise your loyalty to me, over and above your professional standards, it seems. This could ruin you and me."

"I was…"

"Nurse breaks into the office to look at her boyfriend's confidential medical records prior to a litigation case. Her boyfriend, a senior member of the police force… Ellen, did you not think for a moment? One fucking moment."

"I was trying to help you!" Her angry response was one of defence. He hadn't raised his voice, but she did. Faces of nearby diners looked around at them. Some were shaking their heads.

"I know you were trying to help, but you haven't. I'm not sure if knowing I'm fine, but realising I can't do anything about it, is worse than not knowing at all."

Harry necked his wine. "I'll get you a cab ordered. I need to be on my own, Ellen. With the stress of the case and now this, I think it might be a good idea to spend a bit of time apart."

She looked horrified. He wasn't going to back down though. "I'm not talking about forever. I love you Ellen, but this. Shit, mate, this is seriously out of order. You could lose your job, be struck off. How stupid!"

"Please don't start the patronising parental speech. Are you saying you never cut corners, never take a risk? I'd rather not have you, than have you knowing you are going to suffer every day as if it was your last. I'd happily give up my profession to give you some inner peace. Because I love you."

She grabbed her phone her bag and phone and stood. "I understand you are angry. I get that. Yes, I've been an idiot. Just don't think of me as you think of those criminals. I just wanted to help the man I love."

Then she left him. He didn't feel any remorse though. He was furious with her; rightly or wrongly, he was angry.

He got up and paid the bill and left the restaurant.

Instead of turning right out of the restaurant to go home, Harry decided to turn left and walk-through town to the Angel pub. He needed more to drink. He ordered a pint and sat in the same booth as he had sat with Maisie.

He was probably two-thirds down a glass of ale when he heard a familiar voice. "Penny for them."

It was exactly what Ellen had said only an hour or so before to him. When he had been happy, despite his shit few weeks. Just before the reveal that she had carried out a criminal act.

Maisie sat down next to him. "Budge up, gov. I have a fat arse."

He laughed. She was far from fat arsed.

"Needed a beer too?" He knew the answer.

"Yep, mind's on overdrive. Of all things I'm worrying why I can't see the ghost I've only just got used to seeing. Is that fucked up or what? Phoned all my girlfriends, they were all out with their alive fiancés. Phoned Mo, he doesn't drink and has Muslim charity and community stuff on, and Allah loves him. Couldn't reach Hayden for some reason, engaged all the time; and well Pete and Rollo, which one of those two should I have got drunk with, then?"

Harry laughed. "I've just had a massive row with Ellen."

"Oh sorry. Why? You two are perfect for each other."

"She's broken my trust, Maisie." And he didn't want to say any more. Thankfully, Maisie picked up on the pregnant pause. Clever girl.

"I've been there recently. I wanted to punish Teddy, and now he is dead."

Harry suddenly went cold. His head was beginning to hurt again. He shrugged it off, blaming the cold ale.

"Fancy another pint?" He asked Maisie, she nodded, draining her dregs, so he went up the bar.

Harry was really feeling cold. He turned and saw a man approaching. A tall giant of a man. Bowler hat on his head, starched collar. He was walking down through the bar into the back area. Harry watched him go, past where Maisie was sitting and towards the toilets. He didn't say a word and no-one else in the pub noticed him, particularly when he walked through the wall instead of opening the ladies' room door.

"Can I help you, Sir?"

Harry snapped out of it and turned to the barmaid. She had a badge that said Megan; her hair was pink with green highlights, she had a friendly warm face.

"A pale ale and a scrumpy cider please." He was still a little shaken and cold having seen the tall ghost; something was telling him this was the thin end of the wedge.

After he paid, he collected the drinks from the bar and turned to head back. He saw Maisie coming out of the ladies.

"Did you just see someone walk through the wall?"

"What, a tall bloke?" Maisie said casually. She really was getting used to all this.

He nodded.

"Yes, he's having a ghostly wee in the ladies. I was washing my hands and nearly wet myself again. Harry. Why us? Why can we see them?"

He placed the drinks down, let her get seated, then sat next to her.

"I can see the dead now too, It's all linked, isn't it?" He took a swig. "To the case. The Magpie, Edith,

269

George Wright. Now I know Lady Bell might be involved in this, after what you said about your visit to Magpie Farm. But she is just a reclusive philanthropist. A little crazy when I met her. Nothing more." He took a sip of the cool bitter drink.

"I'm not so sure," Maisie said. "Anyway. I spy with my little eye, something spooky beginning with G."

"Glasses."

"No, a ghost's willy."

"Was it insubstantial Inspector?"

"No, it was quite big actually."

That got them laughing and a little more relaxed. They had three more pints and then decided it was probably a good idea to leave.

"I'll walk you to your flat, " he offered, as they stood. "At least I'll sleep sound knowing you got home safely."

"Ah, gallant sir. I will take you up on your offer of help to a maiden in distress."

"Madam. You are not in a dress."

"Bub-bum-tiss." She mimed a set of drums, which made her stagger a little.

"I can see more ghosts," he said, as they passed Dr Johnson's Birthplace and headed for the market square. There were transparent figures all around them. Different people from different ages, all traversing the square and surrounding streets, walking where old cobblestone pathways had once been, unencumbered by walls or obstruction. In his drunken haze, he felt it was a marvel, a gift, rather than anything sinister.

"We could turn this to our advantage, gov." Maisie slurred. "Currently we can only interview live suspects, but in the future, we could also probably interview the dead."

"I think that would be inadmissible evidence," he laughed, struggling over his words. Harry grabbed hold of Maisie as she drunkenly veered away to the left. A small child with a stick tapping a rolling hoop ran through them and they both turned to look where she went, but she had already disappeared.

They staggered on, arm in arm, until they reached Maisie's flat.

She fumbled for her keys and eventually found them. Harry was feeling very light-headed, and Maisie had obviously had a bit too much, too. He was glad of the distraction. Ellen had seriously upset him.

Maisie turned to him "Harry. Thanks for a wonderful evening. Just what the doctor ordered."

She grabbed the lapels of his jacket and pulled him close. He felt her hot fruity breath, then her lips touching his lips and her tongue snaking into his mouth.

Harry knew it was wrong. He pulled her close and kissed her back. He would regret this.

For now, however, he felt so betrayed and alone, so he just did not care.

Chapter Twenty-Five
Rollo Gets Arrested

"What do you want you bastard?"

Harry somehow knew that it was almost three months since Phillip had been blinded by the peroxide in the shed. Harry had been punished by the Headmaster at school and the Matron at his children's home. He had spent a lot of time in his room and in detention. He had also had to speak to the police. That had made him really cry. He felt like a criminal.

Phillip was sitting up in his bed when he entered, his head bandaged everywhere above the nose. He looked a little like Boris Karloff in the Mummy, but he didn't say that to Phillip; it would have been cruel.

Ever since Harry had been allowed to visit Phillip, his brother had been even more horrible. Harry fully accepted the bitterness and carried on as if nothing had happened. Phillip was right to feel hatred for what Harry had done to him. Harry had, after all, nearly blinded his brother.

"I just wanted to see if you are all right." Harry said, sitting on the end of Phillip's bed. Phillip kicked his legs until Harry had to stand again.

"Of course, I'm not all right. My eyes are near boiled in their sockets. I've had skin transplant after skin transplant and it really fucking itches - you wanker. I can eat nothing but soup and pulverised fruit. I'm shitting every five minutes."

"I didn't mean for it to happen. We were just fighting. You shouldn't have been mean."

"Mean. Mean!" He screamed this time. "Look at me. I look like the Elephant Man, and you are calling me mean. You arse-shitting cunt."

Phillip utilised profanity in a very childish way. He really did not know what the words and phrases had meant, or how harmful they were. Harry wouldn't have known what the last one meant, unless Giles Parton had told him.

He was quite shocked to hear Phillip say such a word. Good job Matron wasn't about.

"I came to ask if you wanted me to take you around the garden in your chair."

"Oh yes, please. And maybe you can take me to the shops. Ask Mr Patel if he stocks new eyes. Get out, you fleabag."

"Phil." Harry almost whined.

"Fuck off."

Harry sighed and left the room. It had been the same every time he had visited. He was unsure if he would be able to do again unless someone else was there. Phillip was never like this when Edith was there.

He came out of Phillip's room onto the landing and was about to go down the front staircase, when a figure approached.

"Master Morton. I wonder if I might have a word, please."

Judging by his dress, this was a schoolmaster, but not one he had ever seen before. He was tall, overly broad. Looked a little like a circus strong man, he towered over Harry.

"Could you come with me to one of the classrooms? We do not want to disturb the poor infirm students. Matron would have my guts for garters."

They trailed down to one of the science labs. As they entered, the master shut the door behind him. The room smelled of burnt gas and oxidised chemicals.

"My name is Dr Prendergast."

Harry looked up; the man's face was leering and hateful.

"I've come to put something in your head."

Dr Prendergast reached in his pocket and brought out a big Bowie knife. It glinted in the sunshine that was now flooding through the windows.

Harry screamed and then ran. Fight or flight. The man was too big for a boy to punch. Harry reached the lab door, but Dr Prendergast had locked it somehow.

"I might also take your eyes."

Harry turned as the big man approached. He screamed. Then the bell rang.

Harry awoke from the fog. He turned to try and grab his ringing phone that screamed from his bedside table. It wasn't easily within his reach, so he had to sit up.

"Hello?"

"Is that Detective Chief-Inspector Harry Morton?"

Harry glanced at his bedside clock. It said six twenty a.m.

"Speaking."

"My name is *The* Magpie. Do I have your attention?"

Harry went cold. He had no way of triangulating the call without alerting the man on the other end. The voice sounded auto-tuned, very distorted.

"You do. What do you want? How have you got my number?"

"Let's just say I'm *very* resourceful." The voice was indistinct, male, deep even, considering the sing-song nature of the masking software. "Got any questions? I'll allow you two."

A showman then. No amateur here, it seemed. Well-spoken, therefore well-educated. Doctor, professor, or policeman?

"Why are you killing people like this? Fathers? Wives? Children?"

"Ah. It's been a long-standing hobby. I like it. I enjoy it. Well, actually, I don't like killing per se. It's a means to an end, you see. I like collecting eyes. The windows of the soul. I have quite a collection. Well, that's question one gone, Huzzah!" There was a giggle - he couldn't tell if the man was mad, or trying to approximate madness through his showmanship.

Harry thought hard. What would the best question be? He thought about all the twists and turns of the case.

"Come on, H. I don't have all day; I've got a special delivery to get in the post."

Okay. Pause, delay him as much as possible. Then he knew what he wanted to ask.

"What is your link to the six people of Legend Street?"

"Ah. Good question. Let's just say I used to play up there when Daddy went to meet Mr Wright."

"How old are you?"

"Sorry. Time's up. No more questions. C'est finis. Kaput."

"You really are a sad wanker." Harry couldn't help it. This was a man who had killed five people at least - probably a whole lot more. "I will get you."

"Ooh, name-calling time. I *like* it. Not if I get you first. I might phone again soon, if we have time. I have a present for you. I'll let you know when you can unwrap it. By the way, when I get your eyes, I will talk to them every day, and I will call you names too. Oh, and by the way, five for sixpence." The last line was an almost-scream. Then the phone went dead. His ears rang.

That was when he remembered he had kissed Inspector Price.

Maisie's head hurt. Whilst she had told the gov she was going to see Grace; she was almost certain the pathologist was out at a conference.

She walked through the entrance of the Institute and made her way to the reception. The girl at the front desk was new, but after Maisie flashed her warrant card and badge, she let her through.

She made her way down the corridor of offices. She passed Horace's, but his lights were off. Then she was at Grace's door. Doctor Hodgson was inscribed in copperplate on, ironically a copper plate.

She tried the door handle. Once inside, she located the file she had seen before easily. She opened it and rifled through the details on the sheet. There was more information now. It listed all of her colleagues who had allowed their DNA to be matched to the sample. And there was a match. The Magpie's blood was a confirmed match to Steven Rolleston.

Shit.

No. Not Rollo. It can't be.

Then she remembered kissing the gov. She smiled briefly. It was a great kiss. She had held herself well, considering five pints of scrumpy.

Then she snapped back to reality.

What should I do? Should I tell him about Rollo?

"Edith, what should I do?" Unfortunately, there was no answer from her Moribund relative.

Harry approached the press conference with his usual laid-back nature, whilst Chief Constable Martin Rivers was about to go off like a bottle of pop going down a set of rapids in a spin dryer.

Grace Hodgson had had about five cigarettes in the time it had taken them to set up the room and for the press to arrive prior to the start of the proceedings. She wasn't coping with the chief very well. That was unusual for her.

"He's going to die of a stroke very soon if he does not retire or calm down," she offered as if her expert opinion was critical to Harry's well-being.

"You get used to him. He usually berates me even if I've done a good job, or got him out of the shit. To be honest, he does want to retire. The Magpie hanging around at the close of his career is far from convenient. Well, I'd be a little wound up too to be honest."

"You are too good to be true. Why did I let you go?"

"You were more interested in cigarettes."

"Bit harsh. Spoken to Ellen?"

Harry had told Grace about their spat earlier that morning. He hadn't told her about kissing Maisie.

"She betrayed me, Grace."

And I think I might be about to betray Ellen.

Eventually, everyone and everything was in place. The BBC were right at the front, the usual reporter in pride of place; ITV and Sky were there, Five Live and a few others.

The press officer who was facilitating asked for order and the cameras started to metaphorically roll.

"Michael." Rivers invited the *Midlands Today* reporter, to ask his question.

"Chief Constable, is it fair to say that this investigation is a bit of a failure? Six historical murders with rumours of a seventh in Birmingham, along with five murders in the Lichfield district, one of which was an armed response officer. Can you tell us what you can offer to the scared people of Edgbaston and Lichfield?"

Rivers smiled. *Shit, not the best response,* Harry thought.

"Well, Michael, I do have some news. It seems we have had a breakthrough. We finally have a suspect."

Harry shot a glance at Grace. This was heading in an unexpected direction. Harry didn't know they had a suspect. As SIO he should have known. "What the fuck?" He mouthed at the pathologist.

"I'm sorry," she mouthed back. She scribbled something on a piece of paper.

"Detective Super Intendant Claudine Taylor is, as we speak, arresting the suspect with a team of officers. The man is a resident of Lichfield District, and he *does* have links to the police, although he isn't on active duty. He has allegedly covered his tracks well, hence us struggling to make progress. However, I'm sure you will agree it's good news."

There was a round of muttering and chatter.

"But what about the links to the bodies in Legend Street Edgbaston?" This was Clark Gaines from Radio Five Live. A bit of a slimy so and so. He was a walking comb-over bouffant, like the love child of Donald Trump and Margaret Thatcher

"The dead at Legend Street are not murder victims. Let me repeat that. Not murder victims. They are historical in nature and the results of some sort of scientific tests. We are liaising with the Home Office about that side of the case. We will have more to come in due course."

As there was a flutter of heightened muttering, Harry sat fuming. How dare they go over his head and make an arrest on his case without informing him?

Rivers held both his hands up.

"The bodies from Legend Street seem to be the remains of bizarre post-war scientific experiments. Although I would like to make it clear the perpetrators are long dead, even though their legacy was only discovered in the last few weeks. There will be no further investigations beyond working with the University and already-identified family members."

"And what about you DCI Morton, the original lead officer in this case? Surely the victims who, it seems, all share your surname have been bait. Why have you not been removed from the case yet?" This was a strikingly beautiful, tall woman from Sky News, Alex something or other, judging by her badge.

Rivers momentarily glanced towards Harry, but it was imperceptible. You would have to be well trained in body language to pick up the look.

"As you suggest, having DCI Morton targeted in this way does mean he will not be senior investigations officer from now on. It will now be up to DCSI Taylor to assign him to other duties."

Harry couldn't believe what he was hearing. Why couldn't they have told him? His phone pinged. It was Ellen.

So sorry. So sorry. I've been suspended.

His phone pinged again. *Gov. Grace seems to have evidence linking Rollo to the Magpie's kills. Is this the case?*

And there it was. Stitched up by the chief, his gov and one of his oldest friends, although he was hoping Grace did it under direct orders, or the threat of not having her invoices signed. Ellen had fucked up her chances of a career in nursing too. The world was going to shit.

He got up, not inclined to be bothered about consequences and he walked out.

He texted Maisie back. *Meet me at the Angel tonight. I may not have a job once I've had a showdown with Taylor.*

In Lichfield, Rollo was cleaning his house and boy did it need a spring clean. He had felt better in the last few days than he had for ages. He'd refrained from the drink and there had been fewer visits from his late wife and daughter although Chloe did wish him a good night, most nights. It was more of a comfort now than a fearful apparition when either of them appeared.

He had wiped down the surfaces of the kitchen and put a couple of beer bottles away from last night. Hayden had come over; and because he was such a fitness freak, he had drunk hardly anything at all.

He was just about to put the rubbish out in the blue recycling bin, when there was a loud thump. "Open up. Police."

He raced to his hallway.

"Wait, I'll open up."

It seemed there was quite an ardent team on today as within moments of Rollo reaching his door, it was bashed in, coming off one hinge. The neighbours would be pissed off about the noise. Rollo stepped back

"Hands up. Do not move." The armed response officer who came through to his lounge first aimed his gun at Rollo who backed up, immediately raising his hands. Two taser-wielding colleagues flanked the armed officer. The armed response officer was Patel. He worked for Chris Compton, a man both he and

279

the gov knew well and both had supported them on the Leek case. He didn't know Patel's first name and now didn't care to know it. Why were they pointing guns at him?

"On your knees."

Rollo did as he was asked.

"Lie down," Patel said. He knew the officer would be pointing the gun at his prone form. One of the taser officers must have come forward with their cuffs and he was roughly bound.

"Fucking scum." The officer spat, under his breath. "The nonces will love you. I'll make sure they know you are coming."

Then there was another voice he recognised.

"On behalf of DCSI Claudine Taylor, I am to inform you, Steven Rolleston, that you are under arrest for the murders of Angus Morton, Chrissy Parsons, Edward Robson...."

Everything then blurred. It was Mo Hyatt's voice. Mo was the arresting officer.

Silly bastards. They thought he was the Magpie. Rollo, not believing his luck, just as he was on the up, again tipped over the edge and started to laugh maniacally. Luckily, Chloe was there to hold his hand and smile at him.

Ellen was escorted into the car park at Queen's Hospital by James Witton, Director of People for the Hospital Trust.

"It's just while we carry out the investigation, Ellen," he informed her calmly. "It might come to nothing. You know what these things are like."

She did and that worried her. "How long will it take?"

"It is quite an allegation. It will be looked at appropriately and not rushed. Go home, get some sleep and we will be in touch after the weekend." He left her with a vacant smile and walked away. In another life she would have hit him.

The tears came again. It was late in the day now, almost dark. They had come in specially to suspend her, and it had taken hours to get the preliminaries out of the way. James had been nice to her, but he was playing the game. She knew how it worked; Human Resources, as she had known it, enjoyed playing good cop, bad cop. Her union rep had been a useless tosser too, no help at all. Everything Harry had said to her had come true - or was about to, no doubt.

She struggled to open her car with all her work stuff in her arms. They had made her clear her desk, despite the fact she was innocent until proven guilty. Employment hearings were not like a court of law though, as her union representative had helpfully informed her; you didn't have to prove a case beyond reasonable doubt to make a dismissal. However, there was always right of appeal.

"Nurse Roux," a voice called. Dear gods - it was Prendergast. What did he want? He shouldn't be talking to her. It would affect their investigation. She dropped her stuff unceremoniously on the back seat, reached into her pocket and clicked her phone to record mode.

"Mr Prendergast. I'm sure that you should not be speaking to me. You're the lead accuser in the case of my suspension."

He huffed and puffed, his jowls wobbling like an extra-large Christmas turkey. He was sweating like he was about to be slaughtered, too. Still in a suit in this heat. Storms were coming they had said. She laughed inside. The storm was always coming - eventually.

"I just wanted to let you know I'm sorry."

"What for? For this? Or the lies about Harry?"

He moved his sweaty bulk towards her. She hadn't noticed he'd had one hand behind his back. He came nearer and she could smell him, an aroma like stale biscuits. He grabbed her with his arm. He was surprisingly strong, more muscle than fat - cleverly disguised. His grip was like a sweaty vice.

"What are you doing. Don't you realise...?" Then his other arm had come forwards and she then felt a sudden sharp scratch.

She looked down at the hypodermic he had injected her with. The bastard had given her a shot of something.

She suddenly felt very weird. Like the time she had been anaesthetised after she had broken her leg. That was the day her sister had died, she remembered. Why did she remember that now? She thought she had blocked that trauma out.

Then the ground reached up to devour her, and hell had her sister's face.

Maisie knew that kissing was a foolish idea. However, as Harry had said, they were both off the case, would likely be permanently removed for having had the murderer - Rollo - under their noses all the time. Not that they believed it one bit.

"Penny for them?" Maisie asked. Harry looked pensive on the journey back to her flat. He was probably thinking about Ellen. Maisie pushed the jealous thought away. *Silly cow.*

They made it back to Maisie's flat just after the heavens opened. The thunder had been growling like an angry lion for some time. They still got a soaking.

They continued to kiss on the steps of her flat entrance as she fumbled for the keys. She found them and dropped them whilst laughing. They had drunk an equal amount of beer to the night before, so they were both very tipsy. She picked the keys up, giggling.

She got the door open, and they went up the stairs, past the concierge desk and arrived at number 14.

She opened the door. They went inside. It was dark. She didn't flick the light on. Instead, she grabbed his head with both hands and kissed him some more. She took his wet jacket off him and then took her own off. She undid his shirt effortlessly and

282

took it from him. She felt her gooseflesh, all pimply and rising in response to the coolness of her air-conditioned flat. She kissed his neck, but he pushed her back and he started to undo the buttons on her blouse. They were both soon topless and he was kissing her breasts and she pulled him into the lounge. She dropped her trousers and so did he. She was aware that he was hard, and she grabbed at him with one hand through his trunks as the other wrapped around his neck, pulling him towards her.

Soon they were on the sofa, and they were moving together as if they had been lovers for years. Her hands were strong on his back, almost digging in, holding on so he wouldn't stop.

Then he gasped. "Daisy."

Shit, what was Daisy doing there? She was meant to be away in Spain with their parents for at least another day.

It wasn't actually Daisy.

The look in Maisie's eyes as she peered over Harry's shoulder was one of pure, unadulterated horror. He moved off her and looked around. Just to try and gauge the situation.

He stopped cold. It wasn't Daisy, but it was an insubstantial image of her, flickering, as if she were a ghost - as if she were dead. Daisy was beckoning with one ghostly hand. Then he noticed Daisy's eyes – or lack of them.

"No." Maisie cried. "Not my sister. Not Daisy. Harry, she's got no eyes. Harry, he's got her. He's fucking got her" Maisie grabbed his arm. This time, her grip hurt.

The flat was suddenly colder, much, much colder than the air conditioning should have made it. Preternaturally cold. The ghost of Daisy was patient enough to wait whilst they at least put on their clothing. She continued to beckon, with one ghostly hand, but she wasn't pointing outside the flat, she wanted them to go further in.

Daisy led them down the long hallway, past the kitchen and utility room to a bedroom.

"No. He hasn't. Not here. No."

"Stay there, M," Harry said. He had guessed what had happened.

"Would five for sixpence mean anything to you and Daisy?"

Maisie shook her head at first, and then another look of horror crossed her face. She pulled at the necklace and pulled it from beneath her blouse. And then he saw the pendant on her. It was half a sixpence. Why had he never noticed? For the love of Christ, Morton! You were just looking at it on Maisie's naked chest.

"I need to see her." Ghostly Daisy walked through the door of the bedroom on their left.

Harry reached out and opened the door. He was worried the Magpie might still be there. To pull a stunt like this meant he had knowledge of their movements. Meant he had time to follow them. Maybe it had been Rollo. Maybe killing Daisy had been his final act?

Harry's phone pinged. He looked at it quickly. A lone message.

"Got you a present! Hope you like it. Love, The Magpie"

Harry pocketed his phone as Maisie tugged his bare arm. Slowly he pushed her bedroom door open.

Chapter Twenty-Six
The Magpie's Finest Work

The Magpie had created his finest tableau yet with Daisy's corpse. He mulled over his previous night's work, as he travelled to Solihull, wrapped in his disguise.

He had killed her a few days prior to the arrangement of her body and had kept her in one of the big freezers at the Manor House.

Lady Isla Bell, or Isabelle of Stafford, as she had once been called, was in a better mood. Lady Bell was not assaulting his mind so often now that Daisy was dead. Two more deaths for the wizened bitch and he would be free of his loathing of her; permanently changed into the body he now had.

For the death tableau, he had ordered a two-kilogramme box of daisies which, it turns out, was a surprising number. He had also liberated his personal deposit accounts to buy some unbelievably expensive silver coinage, some dating back to the Roman invasion of Britain.

In finishing the tableau, he had reinserted the knife, and my, he was really getting through them. The knife shop owner Carl must have thought he was a murderer with the amount he was buying. He chuckled, ever so slightly insanely, at that thought.

He had lain Daisy on the left-hand side of Maisie's double bed where he had slept so often recently. He then left a space on the right, to symbolise were Maisie, as her womb twin, should be.

He had arranged the silver coins in a representation of the Gemini horoscope sign, for that was, ironically, their birth month. What a nice, serendipitous touch that had been.

Daisy was naked, but again he felt no sexual gratification. He had found Maisie attractive, but only deep within in his character, when he had come across her from time to time at the water cooler and other places. Daisy, however, was a plain Jane, all flat where her sister had nice curves. Nothing special about Daisy in life but much more special in death, surrounded by the daisies and the silver coins.

He had found out, during one of his long evenings of research, that Maisie meant pearl. So, he had purchased an antique set of pearls and arranged them into a teardrop, to finish off the piece.

The Magpie had known for a while who "five for a sixpence" would be; he had planned for it to be Daisy without too much influence from Lady Bell. The witch had banged on about the power of the rhyme to him since they had first met, because of something about using a Magpie symbolically in another spell. Strange woman.

One day he had seen the fine chain about Daisy's neck and noticed the half a sixpence. He had then noticed her sister's too. Maisie did not always wear it, but he had seen it on her one day when she had worn a top that was lower cut than usual.

Now he was off to carry out the "six for gold" murder. This was also his idea; Lady Bell had laughed for the first time in years in his company when he had told her who he thought it should be.

Seven for a secret had been Lady Bell's own decision. She had known all along whose life they would take for number seven, and it was very, very clever. He'd had to hand it to Lady Bell once she'd told him. It was like a dream come true. How much heartache could he pile on Harry?

The previous morning, he had nervously watched Maisie go to work - he had already pulled in a favour from an acquaintance to borrow a private ambulance. The acquaintance would not be found for quite some time hopefully, but he would talk to the man's eyes later and apologise. Donal had been a gullible Irish

286

fool with deep-sea blue eyes and a private undertaker's licence.

He'd broken into Maisie's flat – well, he had expertly picked the lock with un-shaking hands, which was good considering he'd just carried her sister's gurney single- handed up the stairs. He was thankfully strong in whatever guise he chose, Marcus, The Magpie, even his own. His strength was another legacy from another time.

He'd laid out Daisy's body efficiently. He was used to working quickly and under pressure. If Maisie had returned, he would probably have killed her, but thankfully it didn't come to that. He wanted her to see Harry dead. The icing on the cake.

"You can kill who you like when my quota is done and I can walk in the light," Lady Bell had said.

As Pete Miles, the Magpie had texted Maisie to see if she wanted to go out for a drink, knowing she had a prior engagement, probably with Harry. He had seen how they had become close in recent days.

His text bought him the information he needed: the knowledge of how long he had to lay out Daisy that evening.

Maisie was cagey on the phone; he gathered she had something to hide and other plans for most of the night, because she said she would be happy to see him the next evening. Normally Maisie was up for a late nightcap.

Shame she would have other things on her mind tomorrow, he thought. The Magpie/Pete might go and console her, if he remained undiscovered. But it was unlikely. The witch had said he would be revealed to them soon. How the fuck she knew was a mystery.

Once he had paid a visit to his sixth victim that afternoon, he would probably be revealed. Grace Hodgson might piece it together, eventually – she was the clever one.

Earlier the previous day he had been clever enough to switch Rollo's blood sample for his own, just to buy a little time. The silly bitch Grace had asked him to put his own sample in the fridge when he had been to see her to give his blood. His bloods were not on record, which would have been stupid. However, Rollo's had been, so he switched the labels. It had been so easy. He was surprised she hadn't worked out there was one sample left that had no links on the police database.

Which was why it made it even more pleasing that he, or rather, his current disguise Pete Miles, beefcake, was on duty on a Saturday, volunteering to take the test results over to the Chief Constable himself. Rivers had requested the test results after they had decided to take in Rollo. Something to do with showing the assistant commissioner on the golf course.

Claudine Taylor was more than happy not to have to pitch up at the weekend.

As he pulled up in his yellow car, he could see that Martin Rivers' house was grand. The Chief had said it was a good time to go over, as his wife would be out shopping all day. However, he was playing golf from two until six, so could he time it for about half-past one?

Well, as the Magpie, he arrived much earlier, early enough to see Chief Constable and Mrs Rivers leave to go shopping and gold respectively, which they did every Saturday morning, and he had entered the house and made his way to the study.

The study was where Rivers spent most of his time when his wife was out, looking at pictures and videos of young Japanese girls. Rivers always went straight to the crime scene when he returned, to check his notifications on the dark web. Just to see if he had been sent new files. Habitual. They all played into the Magpie's hands. He'd installed the cameras weeks ago as he had planned all his tableaux thoroughly.

The study was on the second floor of the demi-mansion. It was decked out in plush drapes and pictures of four children in degree robes, who had

288

long since flown the coop. They would never see their dad alive again. *Shame.*

The Magpie made himself at least two cups of tea. It helped him to relax.

Nearer the appointed time of the Rivers' return from Morrisons, the Magpie washed everything in bleach and went to wait in the room Rivers would not enter. His wife's dressing room. He thought about dressing in some of her clothes to kill Rivers. Like he had dressed in his mother's that time, all those years ago.

That would have just been a bit too weird. He wasn't unhinged - although the myriad silk robes were luscious to touch. Instead, he just stripped naked.

Eventually, Gold Command, as he had been known at times, returned home. Rivers immediately went to his study, and as expected, had stripped to his underwear to search for his favourite websites and drop box accounts via a couple of servers in Russia and Columbia.

The other thing the Magpie was good at manipulating was technology. He had come to it late in life, but had become quite adept after spending all that time researching the first thirteen murders he had carried out for Lady Bell.

He had taken control of the webcam on Rivers' laptop and had slaved it to his phone via a clever little program he had spent at least a month designing, just in case it ever came in handy one day.

Whilst Rivers was masturbating his tiny member tightly to get himself off in the only way, he could these days, the Magpie flicked the content to the master channel where a clever little magpie animation came on. It squawked and said, "stop looking at kiddy porn, because we're coming to get you, Rivers."

The Magpie reckoned either of two things was going to happen. Rivers was either going to jump up with a wilting cock and quickly turn of his computer.

Or, because his wife was not yet home, he would most likely sort out the mess. You didn't look at illegal porn when you were a senior police officer if you didn't know a trick or two. Rivers would attempt to fix it. He had done it before when the Magpie had trialled an internet blackmail scam on Rivers' computer, threatening to send a captured picture of Rivers' gurning face to all his police contacts.

Rivers started to type on his keyboard to try and re-boot his machine. The Magpie stepped out of Mrs Rivers' dressing room and pressed another button on his phone. The folk rhyme of the magpie played one for sorrow up to six for gold, as a little animation appeared on Rivers' screen.

Then, quiet as a mouse, the Magpie opened the study door stepped up behind Rivers, who was desperately trying to stop his laptop crashing. The Magpie was wearing nothing but a Donald Trump mask, it was a last-minute touch. He was getting frivolous in his old age.

Then, quickly with two hands, he plunged the knife in a reverse thrust into the Chief Constable's chest. Just like that. It had taken a few seconds.

Easy.

With his strong vice-like grip and preternatural strength, he held Chief Constable Rivers in place using pressure points in the senior policeman's two shoulders, to prevent him from standing, narrowly missing the spray of blood that gushed forwards onto the computer screen like a final deletion.

As he held Rivers in place The Magpie could see the chief's face reflected in the bloody screen, panic-ridden, but unable to speak. Rivers shivered as if he had suddenly felt someone walk over his soon-to-be yawning grave, and then started to twitch, arterial spray slowing as blood pressure dropped and his body started to go into fatal shock. He gurgled as his lungs slowly filled with blood. Then the pumping stopped. Heart failure, it seemed, before he drowned.

The Magpie wasn't bothered about all the blood this time, he didn't plan on cleaning-up. A mess was his intention.

He left the recording going for a while before he stopped it; he would savour the chief constable's death tape.

Quickly, he removed Rivers' eyes and put them in one of his small portable containers.

Then The Magpie walked through to Rivers' walk-in shower. He was going to get washed and dressed. Then he heard a noise on the landing.

"Martin. Are you okay? I've cooked you a bacon butty, but you aren't answering your phone and I know you do not like being disturbed when you are playing your computer games."

Before he could get to the door, the handle turned, and Bernice Rivers opened the door. Shit - he hadn't locked it. When had she got back?

Mrs Rivers screamed, although not for long.

The Magpie managed to get to her after retrieving the knife from her husband's corpse. But in the crowded room, he wasn't at the right angle to put the knife in her chest, so he stuck it up under her chin and into her brain.

She looked incredibly surprised. His first reaction was to laugh. Then the light went out in her eyes, and she dropped as he withdrew the knife. Hot blood soaked his lower legs and feet. It was now a very crowded study.

He moved across the landing to a larger bathroom, where he showered and changed into his police uniform.

He put his other black clothes in a bag and then left with them, but not before letting the dog in first.

Banjo would be found lapping at a pool of his owners' blood shortly after the video of Rivers' death hit the Commissioner's email account.

291

Later that same evening, Harry was pacing in his flat, beside himself with grief and anger following the death of Daisy and the gruesome way in which she was discovered. He couldn't work out what would have been worse: Maisie discovering her sister alone, or her ghostly appearance hovering over them as they rutted.

The Magpie was ripping his team, no - their lives – apart. His own guilt was stifling him, increasingly convinced that the evil bastard was after him and no-one else. As the clock neared midnight, Harry was still disturbed, he needed to see the remaining members of his team. They needed to close ranks. Protect each other, but more importantly, see if they could make head or tail of this mess.

Could they work out who the Magpie really was? There was no way it was Rollo.

Was there?

Maisie was in bed, asleep on the mezzanine. It would be weird if Ellen turned up but hey, he would cross that bridge when he came to it. It wouldn't be the strangest situation they had found themselves in of late.

There was a knock at the door. It was Mo Hyatt. He looked dreadful. Daisy had been as much of a good friend to the diminutive man as Maisie was.

Harry held out his hand to Mo, about to shake his hand, but then gathered him in for a hug.

"Gov, what is going on? First Teddy, now Daisy. Is he out to get rest of us?"

"He's baiting *me*. I've had another call from him just now. Let's wait for Grace and Pete."

"So, it can't be Inspector Rolleston. He was in custody." Mo murmured, in a voice that suggested he had never believed that even as arresting officer. "God, what have I done?"

Harry patted his Acting Inspector on the shoulder. It was all he could manage.

He made Mo a coffee and they sat, almost in silence.

Another knock at the door; then another five seconds later as Grace and Pete arrived.

Karol was off duty, and he couldn't get hold of the Polish officer, but there was someone else he had suddenly remembered, someone he had talked to for the first time in an age last night. Hayden Worth. He had asked the rugby player-turned-copper to stake out Bell Manor. Why did that feel strange, though? Could either Karol or Hayden be The Magpie?

No. Surely not.

Grace was in and out for the first hour as they chatted, chain-smoking like a set of industrial cooling towers. Pete was in the kitchen making tea, as ever. He was always drinking tea.

Pete kept looking upstairs in between brews. He was probably wondering why Maisie was in Harry's bed. Although the young officer was being an angel, putting Harry's washed-up pots away; then, he was drying the knives very carefully. Harry watched Pete as he worked, looking at the kitchen knives as if they were his prized possessions, weighing one of the long and thin utensils in his hands. Pete placed it back in its wooden block delicately, like it was a sword going back into a mythical stone.

"Right. Who thinks its Rollo?"

"The DNA is a match," Grace offered immediately. She had never really liked Steve; perhaps this was clouding her judgement. Harry couldn't blame her though; Rollo's recent behaviour really did not help his situation.

"But it could have been switched. What did the Chief think, Pete?" she added.

She took an imperceptible glance at the young officer. Harry might have missed it if he was less tense. He grinned back at her. Did he wink? Was there some tension there, Harry wondered? His team was too small now, he could do without any more loss or divisions.

"Harry..." Grace started, then Harry's phone rang. He looked at it. Claudine Taylor.

"Hi, gov," he said, wearily. The last thing he needed was another bollocking.

"It's not Rollo," she said, simply.

"How do you know?"

"The Magpie. He got Rivers. Martin was found with his eyes missing, Mrs Rivers was killed too. *He* sent a video to me, a file that also contained some of the chief's extracurricular hobbies. Six for Gold Harry. I've just come off the phone to Rivers' brother. Did you know he had a brother? A twin brother. Has Mo spoken with you?"

"Dear God, Rivers?" He took a big breath. "Mo is with me. We haven't got around to that. I've got Grace, Pete, and Maisie here too. She is out of it, on doctor's orders."

"Speak to them, but no others. The fewer who know at this point, the better." She paused. "Harry, I've got some disturbing news; the victims are all twins. That's the link. We have traced the families of the six from George Wright's list. All had surviving twin brothers and sisters. Angus, Chrissy, the kids were twins. Daisy was a twin. He's targeting twins. Twins with your name, or linked to you. We need to know why? Do you know any other twins, other than Maisie? Think carefully."

He didn't need to. "Ellen. She had a twin sister, she died when Ellen was nine."

"Do you know where she is?"

"No."

"Then find her. And Harry - I didn't know Rivers was taking blood samples from the team until I was asked for mine. He threatened my career if I let you know."

"It's okay. I know you wouldn't have done it behind my back. I need to go."

"Find Ellen."

Harry swiped his phone to read. He looked at the faces in front of him. There was no love for the Chief in this room for one reason or another, but that was no reason to not feel sorry for the man, moreover his dead wife and their poor children.

"Rivers is dead. The Magpie got him. He took his eyes. On camera. Killed his wife too, poor Bernice."

There was a definable silence in the room. Except for Pete who carried on putting plates away in cupboards. Harry heard the *ching* of a knife pulled from the drainer. He thought nothing of it. Good old Pete, doing the pots again.

"Was he a twin, gov? The other victims were all twins." Mo almost vomited this out. "I forgot to say. We never had the chance to discuss. Poor Daisy. What about M?"

Harry nodded. "Pete. Can you stop for a minute?" The banging and crashing of porcelain plates was getting louder.

"I need to go and look for Ellen. She is a twin, too. He is going to go after her. Anyone else in the room a twin? You guys will have to look after Maisie."

"Harry, stop," Grace was in the kitchen looking at Pete, her eyes wide.

"Grace, what's up? You look like you have seen a ghost."

"I had the remains of a twin removed from my stomach when I was a child."

"My twin died too, but as a baby in the womb," Mo admitted. "I didn't want to say anything because it didn't seem relevant. Until...."

They settled a little and Pete washed more pots. Harry phoned Taylor back to get her to find out where Karol was. Grace kept looking over at Pete. What was going on there?

"Harry. Can I have a quick word?" Grace whispered, he noticed she still had one eye on Pete in the kitchen."

"What is it, Grace?"

"We need to get Maisie and get out of here. Get rid of Pete. Now."

Harry went cold, like someone walked over his grave.

"What? Maisie's asleep."

"I think the Magpie is here." She looked towards Pete.

"What?"

"Pete went to see Rivers. Today."

"What are you whispering about?" Pete called from the kitchen. "Mo, what are they talking about."

Mo looked from Pete to Harry. Pete was grinning, he had a big knife in his hands that wasn't from Harry's kitchen block.

"Back up Mo." Harry shouted. Realisation hitting hard.

"Pete went to see Rivers today." Grace hissed. "He swapped the samples. It could only have been him. Pete's The Magpie." Grace said, as unconfident as he had ever heard her.

"Speak up there Gracie." Pete laughed in a chilling way. He flashed the knife about in the air. Harry had his eyes fixed on the police constable.

"Yes. Who would have thought it? I'm a twin too. What's the coincidence of that? What a merry dance. What a collection of twins. How did we all come to be together? It's like magic. Focused death magic."

Pete's tone. Same as on the phone. Same as the Magpie.

"And the penny has dropped, Henry? Clever Grace. My second mistake. My first was underestimating Teddy. Fat fucking Teddy. My second was not killing Gracie instead."

Pete suddenly flickered, like a digital television image breaking up. Where he once he'd had dark hair, he now had a shock of white over his left eye where it parted. He cackled like a crone – an incongruous sound coming from such a handsome young man. It could well have been someone else's laugh.

In one quick move, Pete Miles flipped the large knife in the air, caught it, took three long paces across the kitchen and rammed it into Grace Hodgson's sternum.

"In one," the Magpie laughed.

Grace dropped, making a moaning sound Harry would hear in his nightmares for the rest of his life.

Mo went for Pete with a wine bottle that had been on Harry's counter, but Pete pulled the knife from Grace, stepped back with a fighter's agility and rammed it through Mo's left eye. "In two."

The little man went down quickly, like a marionette with his strings expertly cut. The Magpie withdrew the knife with a ghastly sucking sound.

It had all happened in seconds.

Because of the acute shock of seeing two good friends and colleagues cut down, Harry didn't even have time to react as Pete came at him and hit him hard with his left fist. It knocked him across the room, as the knife clattered to the ground. *Such strength. Dear God.* Harry got back up, but Pete hit him again.

"She said I can't kill you yet, Henry. But I will. You horrible shitting cunt."

Harry reeled under the strength of that attack, and he fell, the wind thoroughly knocked out of him, his head cracking off the floor under the weight of The Magpie, before the world around him went black.

Maisie. He'll get Maisie. Then, Ellen. I love them...

"Wake up. We need to get back. I need to go and meet Nancy. I think she has gone mad; she has spent a fortune on our Hallowe'en costumes, now she's behaving like a monster."

Edith was sitting beside him as he woke, but he was in the dream world again. Why did his head hurt here? Then he realised it usually did.

"What year is this, Edith?"

"It's 1948, silly. October 31st. It's Hallowe'en. Hence the Hallowe'en costume. Duh."

Harry sat up, looked at his arms and the rest of his body. He was for the first time the Harry of the waking world.

"I need to get back to my own time."

"No. You are remembering, H. I need you to remember." Edith said.

"I need to go back. Ellen is in trouble. Maisie is on her own with a murderer."

"No, wait. We have to remember. It's not 2022. It's 2005 for you and I'm in 1948. Hallowe'en. You said you would take Phillip to the Cathedral Tour. It has a new interactive exhibition; it's geared towards the sensory impaired. You had lived so long in secret you both needed to get out."

"So, you take Phillip to the Cathedral, and I'll take Nancy to the party." Edith smiled at him like any big sister would when they are trying to take control of a situation.

Big sister.

"Yes. I'm your long-dead big sister, Harry. Phillip is our brother too. Although you might know him as Pete. You are twins."

"You are not making sense."

Yet he could feel the resemblance to Pete not in looks but glances, actions, and thoroughness.

"Edith. I think you might be dead," he said, remembering the moribund woman in yellow.

"Oh yes. I am dead. I have been dead a while," she repeated, almost crying.

"They've killed Nancy, she was a monster, Harry. Phillip had to get them to kill Nancy. Phillip took her eyes. I think they are coming for me afterwards; I am a liability. I know too much. Oh, dear God, Harry where are you? You are fading. My brave soldier, you would have saved me. Had you been there, but you and Phillip would have been too Morton? Wouldn't you?

"Harry. Wake up."

Maisie was shaking him, in between sobs. Shaking him awake.

"Harry. Wake up. Edith's just been here. She woke me up. Oh God, what is happening?"

Her tears were peppering his face.

"Harry, Mo is dead. And it's not fucking fair. His lovely children? They will grow up without a dad. Grace is dead too. Why didn't I hear all the noise? I must have been so out of it... Oh no. Daisy too."

Harry sat up. The room was too calm. The smell of blood was thick in the air. Maisie was hugging herself, sobbing. It was warm even with the air conditioning in the room. He sat up despite the pain in his head, then crawled over to his first prostrate colleague. Harry put two fingers to Mo's neck, but his eyes were dull. There was no pulse.

Mo was dead.

Grace.

He crawled over to the forensic scientist and placed two fingers on her pulse point on her neck.

"There's a pulse, but it's faint. Maisie, have you called it in?"

"Yes. I spoke with Claudine. She is on her way; she is bringing back up with her too."

Maisie stood, wavering. "We can't wait though, Harry. The Magpie has taken Ellen. Edith has gone to look for her. She said we must go to Magpie Farm and talk to Frances. Edith said if Ellen dies, the evil will come."

Dear God. Ellen. I had almost forgotten.

"What do you mean the evil will come?"

"Edith said if Ellen dies, the Witch will have the power of life. She will allow the Magpie to kill you. She will then use her magic to infect the world. Infect life. With death. The birth of the Magpie Universe."

That was a bit prophetic, Harry thought.

"Witch? Do you mean Lady Bell?"

Maisie nodded.

"Phillip will kill me. I can see it in his eyes. But his eyes were blinded. I blinded him."

"What?"

"Maisie, it's Pete. Pete is really my brother Phillip. Phillip is the Magpie. Phillip is my twin brother. The one from my dreams. Throwing the stones."

But Maisie wasn't listening - she was throwing up.

299

Chapter Twenty-Seven
The Witch Rises

"Time is of the essence," Isabella sent her thoughts to Phillip - also known as Peter, also known as Marcus and The Magpie.

I wish she would get out of my fucking head, he thought.

"Not a chance, my Magpie. No chance at all. We are linked now and forever. You will always be here to do my bidding. The conflagration approaches. The Age of the Magpie Magic will soon begin. I will be alive again. Corporeal."

Yes, and I'll be able to cut your throat and take your eyes. Once I have restored myself. He thought this whilst keeping an image of Harry at the front of his mind.

There, she didn't hear that bit, the bitch.

He had practised building a wall in his mind in recent days, where the things he did not want Lady Bell to know were stored. He had been testing this theory during their last few encounters, imperceptibly.

Despite her claims, he had been able to hide more and more things behind the wall. He had hypothesised that the more she became corporeal, the less ghostly influence she had over him. Quid pro quo.

Despite his mental success, the Magpie was not in a particularly good mood. For the first time in many years, he had not been able to collect the eyes of two of his victims. How would he be able to talk to Mohammed Hyatt and Grace Hodgson before he slept, as was his habit?

"The pathologist is not dead," Isabella informed him, and he felt more disappointment, both at the fact she had heard his thoughts again, as well as his failure to kill.

The Magpie wanted to go back to finish the job; but with the knowledge he would more than likely end up in custody, he needed to put his disappointment to one side. They knew he was Pete. They would be looking for him.

"Do not worry, my Magpie. The Edith woman is here somewhere, and she has called them to us, the silly bitch. We have Ellen. Harry will want to rescue his love. His angel. Ha!" Lady Bell actually cackled. "They will soon realise Ellen is the true secret. The key to my spell. The key to your full restoration. And the key to mine too. Let them come and I will kill them. Then we can both dance on their graves."

Harry, it is time, once I have your eyes I will kill the witch, the Magpie thought, behind his psychological wall.

Steve Rolleston walked out of the station on Eastern Avenue a free man. They didn't let him know why they had released him. In fact, the station felt like it was all at sixes and sevens.

Taylor had looked at him with such sad eyes and had told him she would brief him once it was over, but he was to go home and get some rest. He was just about to do that, but then George had appeared and told him he was needed at the farm.

The Moribund man was sitting next to him in his car.

Moribund? For fuck's sake. What did that even mean?

One part of Rollo's brain still thought he was quite mad. Whilst he had regularly imagined his wife or daughter visiting him and he could still feel their presence, he was baffled as to why he was seeing this spiv bloke from the 1940s.

George had first come to Rollo in the house in Cornwall. Harry thought Rollo couldn't see the man. Rollo, however, was drunk and unsure whether what he had heard was a figment of his imagination at first.

Until George had come to see him later, to tell him he would at some point be needed.

Rollo had also seen the woman in yellow, Edith, George had confirmed. He would have to apologise to Maisie, for pretending he hadn't seen her; he thought Edith had been just another aspect of his fractured mind and dismissed the vision as being further proof of his mental collapse.

Rollo had the sight, according to George.

The sight: he could see dead people, like the little boy out of that film with Bruce Willis.

You can *see*, George had said, so Rollo could help defeat Isabelle. Who, in turn, allegedly controlled the Magpie?

When Rollo had explained to George, he had heard Isabelle/Lady Bell talking to the Magpie, George had been convinced.

"We must go to Magpie Farm," George had insisted earlier that day, when he had appeared in the cell beside Rollo.

"But why are we going to the farm? Isn't it the house we want? Lady Bell, Isabelle lives *there*."

George had then fully explained that he was half-alive.

"How the fuck can you be half-alive? You are either dead or alive. There isn't a place in between."

George had sighed loudly. "Are you going to listen, or not?"

Rollo apologised.

George continued, "I wish it weren't true. I so want to rest. Yet I can't. They have seen to that. The Cordivae."

George told Rollo how they had secretly worked out of a Birmingham University department, testing ex-military subjects -mostly twins - throughout the late 1920s to the late 1940s.

George also explained that as willing subjects became rare, they started to force civilians into being tested.

"Why are you telling me all of this?"

"They killed Nancy. Not me, not the person who eventually ended her. The Cordivae group killed Nancy. Although I worked for them. I also hated them."

George outlined that the Cordivae Group named in the Magpie investigation was allegedly still going. Experimenting on people to this very day.

"My Nancy had been a serving nurse in the army, she wanted to enlist as a soldier too, but she had seen such horrible things; and those nightmares kept her up at night, screaming. When she had heard I was supporting the Cordivae's work, she had asked for the formula herself. I managed to swing it because they had wanted more test patients. However, my business partner Paul Beaton allowed it. He'd made a deal with the scientists.

"It had gone well at first. The formula had healed her of her night terrors, then her scars all started to heal. She found that any injuries she subsequently sustained were soon non-evident. She even cut herself deliberately with a knife - it healed in minutes.

"Eventually, the significant side effects began to appear. Nancy became like a creature possessed.

"On the 31st of October 1948, after a day spent with Edith, Nancy had gone for my throat."

Rollo shivered.

"The only way Nancy could be stopped was to take out her infected eyes." I took her to Beaton.

"What?" Rollo said, nearly driving off the road. "Is that why the Legend Street Six were without their eyes?" He remembered at the autopsy that Grace had mentioned the strange ganglia at the back of the optic nerve.

"The formula had initially been provided via a research grant from Lady Bell. Paul had negotiated the finance with her when the University Dean refused additional grants. Lady Bell had insisted, however, that Paul Beaton was to discuss certain specifics with the scientists. She was very learned, he had said. Lady Bell had given Beaton a formula the scientists said accelerated the healing process.

"It was during those later tests that they noticed the growth of cell clusters at the back of people's eyes. Like little glands. The glands stored healing enzymes; enzymes unknown to have ever existed in the human body. Those little glands became linked to some of the most important functional parts of the brain. If they were removed, the person would effectively be rendered brain dead.

"In most cases, the subjects became rabid. A few survived and they were enhanced, although I never got to find out how.

"Nancy's treatment hadn't worked. So, I begged them to take her eyes. Even though they really wanted to experiment on her. One of their agents took her eyes eventually to prevent her killing them.

"So, I had her surgically dismembered. There were stupid rumours that if I didn't, she may come back to life. Then I buried her in the garden.

"I made sure that I paid the disposal surgeon enough money to acquire the six bodies I put into the tanks. They were my fall back. However, I couldn't have stored Nancy like that. I kept the six, so I had some evidence, some leverage should this connection with the Cordivae Group prove illegal. I knew soon after Nancy's death they were watching me. Watching my house. They knew I had taken test subjects that had been meant for dismemberment or cremation. However, they didn't suspect I would keep them in the hidden attic in my house even though some of the early experiments had happened there. The scientists thought they were gods. They overlooked the obvious.

"I put my finances in order and ran away from it all. But not before I had taken a dose of the formula. I was out of my mind at that point, and I wanted to die. I wanted to end myself in the most violent way. Although nothing happened after I plunged the contents of the syringe into my leg. I went to

Cornwall, where Paul Beaton met me and killed me. Bastard shot me in the head for knowing too much about the Cordivae, To prevent me from revealing their secrets. Secrets way beyond Whitehall's comprehension.

"As you can see, I didn't die. I phased into the Moribund state. I didn't understand why this had happened. Now I realise it was probably due to Lady Bell's interference. It was magic, rather than science, which helped their formula. Lady Bell may well have unleashed a plague on man.

"I need to find out the eventual results of their tests. I need to stop them. I want you to help, Steven."

Then after his long monologue George fell silent.

Rollo struggled to believe the story at first, but as they continued their journey to Magpie Farm, it began to make sense. It fitted with the Legend Street Six and the discovery of Nancy's body in the gardens. Rollo wished he could have his night terrors taken away. He still had bad dreams. Night after night, he re-lived one awful assault on a factory in Helmand Province in Iraq, where he had discovered one of Saddam's bespoke killing machines and the half-shredded man who was still caught up and desperately screaming in the crushing jaws of a waste grinder. He could understand the temptation of taking a formula that healed the mind only too well,

After pulling onto the drive, parking up, Rollo allowed himself to be led into the farmhouse, where George outlined their next steps.

Had Ellen known how slimy Prendergast really was, she would have looked at the records sooner. She had no regrets; it proved that Harry was not physically affected by whatever had happened to him at Lichfield Cathedral. She had suspected all along that he might have some sort of mental block caused by a traumatic event. Possibly a form of PTSD.

After she had sat through two days of revelations from the strange woman she was incarcerated with, she realised there were others worse off than Harry.

The woman, Jennie, was convinced she herself was dead and had been dead for a few years. Jennie had then explained that she would prepare Ellen for the worst that was to come.

Ellen suspected it was unlikely she would leave this place alive; and Jennie had helped to soften the blow a little. But Ellen understood the situation she was in. The power Prendergast had over her. You did not capture and imprison women to let them go. Not when you were a perv like him.

Ellen had felt sorry for Jennie when she explained how her husband, Owain Pleasant, had betrayed her.

"He had been the Chief Inspector of the Cold and Complex Team," Jennie had stated.

That had stopped Ellen cold.

"My Harry is the Chief Inspector of the Cold and Complex Team."

"I know. Where I am, you tend to find out more than when you are alive."

Jennie had filled Ellen in on her tale: the beatings she received in prison and the loss of the child who she had miscarried because of those beatings.

It was surreal, like a dream. Ellen had said so and that was when Jennie had told her they had been drugging her food.

"That's how you can see me," Jennie had explained, just after breakfast had been delivered that morning. "Hallucinations. Only those with sight, or those who were suffering trauma and associated mental health conditions could see the dead. Those medically induced could only get glimpses of beings who were beyond the veil if they had the right concoction of drugs. You seem to see me really well, even under inducement. I wonder why that is?"

Ellen wasn't sure and frankly she didn't care. She had an individual view of life. Enjoy it - when it was over, it was over. When Harry had stormed out the other night, she realised their relationship was probably over. Much like her life. It was coming to an end. She could feel it. People like her knew death and how it approached.

"Did anyone close to you die? Do you have close links to the spirit world?" Jennie had then asked.

Even in her drugged state, Ellen's mental robustness would not have revealed details about her late twin. She had blocked Ailsa out of her mind when Ailsa died; it was better that way. Thank goodness that it was not Ailsa appearing now.

Jennie suddenly flickered in front of Ellen and her image was replaced with that of a young girl. The girl looked genuinely like Ellen might have, if she were the same age.

"Hello, Ellen."

Ellen gasped. Her worst fear. Ailsa.

"They want our secret, Ellen. That's why you are here. Not because of your love for Harry. They want our secret, a secret never to be told."

Ellen went cold, but she was still composed. Despite the realisation Jennie had been a ghost. That Ailsa was here with her. Ellen would never reveal their secret, never.

"Go away please, Ailsa, you are dead. The dead can neither help nor hurt me."

Ailsa just cackled as she flickered like decomposing celluloid film.

Harry and Maisie pulled up onto the driveway of Magpie Farm. Harry had received at least three calls from DCSI Taylor, maybe more. In the end, a text came through.

"If you are after him, be careful. Grace is going to be okay; the knife missed her vitals, but punctured her lung, that's all."

There was still the chance that if Taylor realised, they were out this way, she and whatever was left of the Cold and Complex team would come lumbering in, destroying any chance they had of getting the Magpie, discovering the reason he was baiting Harry and rescuing Ellen.

Why did Lady Bell need Ellen -what did she have to do with all of this? Other than being a twin, like all of the Magpie's victims, Ellen was on the periphery. The link could only be that she was Harry's fiancée. The Magpie and Lady Bell wanted to really twist the knife, culminating in his death, too.

"Seven for a secret never to be told."

"What?" Harry asked Maisie.

"Daisy's words have just come to mind. The Magpie is piecing together the rhyme. Possibly Lady Bell. If that secret involves Ellen, then you can guarantee it's going to hurt Harry."

Now that was blunt, but he could forgive Maisie's mood after the loss of so many of their friends, a sister, and a fiancé.

"This is a bit too much like one of those tense TV murder dramas, where most of the cast get wiped out." Maisie said. And he was then worried for her mental health, not to mention his own, because he laughed.

They both got out of the car and then jumped as Edith appeared. She flung herself at Harry.

"Harry, my brother," she said, covering him with kisses.

"Sorry, but if Harry is your brother, he would be over ninety years old."

Harry hadn't really thought about it like that. He had the memories of the past, he had been a little boy in the cell, maybe thirteen or so.

"We do not have time to dwell on that. We need to return to the farm cellar. It was built over the ground where Isabelle of Stafford created the first magpie curse."

"What?" Harry had put some of it together, but it was only now making sense.

"Isabelle the witch of Stafford, or Lady Bell as we know her. Dead a long time. Trying to come back to life. The Magpie is killing for her. Making her corporeal again. I can feel the veil stretching."

"And why do we need to go down to the cellar?"

"I don't want to go down there again." He knew Maisie's experience of that cellar had not been good.

"I need both of you to come. The cellar is where the spell is the strongest."

"Spell?"

"The spell that started all of this. Harry, do you not remember coming to this farm when we were young? Don't you remember meeting George Wright and my friend Nancy here when you were about twelve, in early 1947? Nancy and George had just got together."

Harry could not. He hoped that this was because it had not happened in his dreams. He felt secrets and past events had been leaking out there, but not in order. He was over ninety years old? How?

"We need to go into the cellar. Now." Edith led the way to the hatch level with the floor in the big-corrugated barn, disappearing down the shaft without answering his question.

Maisie went next and Harry followed. They both started down the rungs, carefully.

"I am not quite sure what is going on, but I know we need to do this."

"Yes, I know, Harry. I can feel it too."

Maisie was trembling when they got to the bottom of the ladder in the half orange light. The lights were blinking intermittently. Harry gave her a quick hug but could see Edith beckoning. Edith was flickering again, and he could feel a dull ache in his head. He thought he could hear women chattering. They were all young, by the sound of it. As Harry watched, the lights flickered in time with the nimbus around Edith, his supposed sister.

Maisie felt physically sick. She could feel a pressure building in her head. Voices, like untuned radio stations flitting across her thoughts. Her fear of this place was immense.

Could Harry not feel it? It was like the sensation when she had seen Nanna Price, amplified a thousand-fold. She would be brave. She owed it to Daisy and to Teddy. This was a nightmare they needed to see through to the end. They needed to bring the Magpie and Lady Bell - Isabelle - to justice.

However, Maisie couldn't help but feel they were in far too deep. Ghosts, magic? It was beyond her. She felt out of her depth.

But Ellen was in danger, and they needed to rescue her. Harry had always called Ellen his angel. They were rescuing an angel.

Maisie knew at the back of her mind that her dalliance with him was probably at an end. They would rescue Ellen and he would go back to her.

Or they would all die.

Edith appeared fully, again. Maisie jumped; she still wasn't used to that.

"Could you not just announce yourself with a ringtone?" Maisie asked, angered.

"You modern-day people talk nonsense. Clara is laughing at our predicament. She was always a wicked bitch."

"How did you become her half-sister?"

"I ran away when I was fourteen. Abusive parents. Phillip and Harry were just infants, or I would have taken them too."

Edith disappeared then re-appeared.

"Edith, I may be a bit too old for this, and I am going to die quite soon of a heart attack if you are going to keep appearing like that." Harry warned.

He was worried for Ellen, Maisie thought; he needed more answers about Edith and Phillip and how they were connected.

"How can Harry be that old? It doesn't make sense, Edith. Look at you , what are you? Twenty-two, twenty-three years old?

310

"Harry will remember soon. Then so will I. It's not for me to force his memories out."

They walked down the damp corridor to the room at the end with the large door.

"Wasn't this where George O' Neill was encased in concrete and killed by the Broad twins?" Harry asked, knowing Maisie would have a better memory, having looked at all of this only recently.

Maisie nodded, and she shuddered again.

"He didn't die. George O'Neill stayed just a hairsbreadth away from death for twenty years, until Jennie Pleasant came down here and released him. Jennie was able to get past the original spell. She was pure," Edith explained.

"You keep talking about a spell. What the hell does that mean?"

"It means there's a witch, who you now know is called Isabelle. She wants to kill your girlfriend, Harry. She is up at the house."

The Irish accent belonged to a very petite woman who appeared out of nowhere, her image dancing like flames in a hearth - like Edith.

"I am Frances O' Neill."

Maisie had seen an older version of Frances on her last visit.

Frances came over and placed a caring hand on Harry's cheek. He began to feel his head hurting again. It was getting quite painful. Then Frances spoke again as he faded.

"We ladies need a chat. You need to be reacquainted with your past, Harry. Hold on."

Harry stood in the farmyard at Magpie Farm, looking up at the creepy farmhouse with some trepidation. He was glad he didn't live here. He was looking forward to his birthday on the 31st of October. The other boy, Phillip, who he now knew to be his brother, was with him and – unusually - Edith. Edith was ten or so years older, maybe more, a young woman. She had been staying with the

Keats who had adopted her, when she had run away. They had not wanted to take on twin boys, who had instead gone into care later, after their parents had disappeared.

It had only been in the last couple of years that Edith had come to visit Harry and Phillip at their state funded boarding school. Over the last year, they had joined her in the holidays and stayed with her. That was why they were at Magpie Farm. They had come to meet Edith's friend, to look around at their new property. George Wright had bought it on a whim to redevelop, but then felt he had too much on.

Harry looked at Phillip, who had a handful of stones he had collected from around the yard. Knowing Phillip, he would go and throw the stones at the farmyard animals. Phillip wasn't a nice boy.

Edith had said that to Phillip quite often, when she had spotted him throwing stones at Harry.

One day, on school hols, Harry had found a dog with broken back legs. Phillip had pretended to want to look after it, but he had tortured the poor animal. He had poked it with sticks in the places where the flesh was broken, and the blood was flowing. Harry had guessed that the creature had been hit by a car. Phillip had eventually killed the poor thing with a house brick. It had made Harry sick to see the creature's brains exposed so, its two eyes perfect and undamaged next to the mangled mess. Had Phillip removed them?

Harry looked at Phillip again, but he was suddenly different. Phillip had bandages over his eyes, although he still had a pocketful of stones; despite being near-blind, he still threw them at Harry. Harry remembered he had caused the blindness when he had shoved his brother in the shed, when the peroxide liquid had fallen from the shelf and burnt him.

Isabelle of Stafford could feel her power growing, her corporeality strengthening. Once the final secret was revealed, she would hold sway. She would be the dominant creature as Lady Bell. The Alpha Witch.

Lady Bell knocked on the door in the attic, near where the servants' rooms had been, before she had shunned them.

She had come a long way from that girl who had died choking on her own vomit, after delivering a spell that was both surprising, in that it worked in some ways, and was an utter failure in others.

It had taken her a hundred years to realise that the way in which she had approached the spell had caused it to mutate, caused it to have properties that its creator could turn to her own favour. She used the preternatural power to attract her Magpies, then she had tried to bend them to her will. This current Magpie had been an astounding success; although he was resisting now, he had, at first, fallen hook, line, and sinker for her mutually beneficial offer to help him with his revenge, and her promise of renewal.

Lady Bell took the set of keys from her pocket and opened the door, but without using her hands. Her ability to physically manipulate objects just with her mind was improving by the hour.

Ellen Roux - the final piece of the puzzle - sat upon her makeshift bed as Lady Bell entered. There had been a spirit here too; judging by the sickly-sweet smell it had been Jennie, but she had dissipated.

She looked at the beautiful young woman before her. Ellen was her secret, her secret Magpie. If things went well, she would no longer need Phillip. Mad, warped Phillip and his jars of eyeballs. He had been an excellent killer. However, his time was almost up. She could feel it in her dead bones.

"My darling. How are you? Prendergast didn't mistreat you; I hope?"

"Aside from sticking a hypodermic needle full of a tranquiliser in me and kidnapping me on your behalf, no."

"Good. You are strong-willed. We need you to be fit and strong for the endgame."

"Endgame. What do you mean by endgame? You need to let me go. My boyfriend is a Police Chief Inspector, he will be looking for..."

"Harry is here already, dear." Lady Bell pulled a creaky chair from under a tatty table that was the only furniture in the room, other than the two dirty mattresses. She sat straddling it. "He has come to rescue you, but he will not be able to help you. I know your secret, Ellen. And you will never tell another soul."

The young woman looked down, breaking eye contact, but she was still defiant, it seemed. "I have no secrets."

"So, pray, do tell. Why did you become a nurse?"

"To help people." The response was quick, just quick enough for it not to be mistaken for a lie.

"Did you really? You are forgetting I know. I know what you have done, Ellen. It is the reason you have ended up here."

"I do not know what you are going on about. I have been a nurse for years. I am good at it."

"Yet you broke into Prendergast's office and looked at confidential records. That would suggest you are less than honest."

"I wanted to help Harry find out what was wrong with him."

"Ah, his mental block? Did you know I put that there?"

Ellen was starting to get agitated. *This was excellent*, Lady Isabelle thought.

"What do you mean, you put it there?"

"I put the block in Harry's head. I told Prendergast to lie. I paid him handsomely. Would Harry save you, knowing what I know?"

"I do not have any secrets." Ellen replied.

"You are a dirty liar," Isabelle half-whispered. "It's no good if you reveal the secret. The spell will not work. Secret. Never. To. Be. Told."

Then, as expected, Ellen made a dash for the open door. Isabelle knew she would. With a wave of her hand, the door crashed shut and Ellen crashed into it. Dazed, she hit the floor and started to sob.

Then, Isabelle pulled the knife from inside her jacket. She had sharpened it that morning.

Isabelle said a few ancient arcane words and Ellen stuck out her tongue. Not in childish spite, but because she had been bidden and she couldn't resist. A simple compelling spell.

As Ellen's breathing became more and more strained and the nurse's spittle rained all over Isabelle's face, the witch slowly cut out the woman's tongue with two hacking cuts.

Then she part-healed the wound by magically cauterising it. It would be no good if Ellen lost too much blood. Ellen needed to die. Just not quite yet.

Oh, Isabelle thought, *I am so good at this.*

Prendergast was waiting for Lady Bell when she came out of the room in which Ellen was being held. He was puffing and panting, having climbed all the stairs to the attic rooms.

He grimaced as she opened the door and exited with a blade held out before her that was dripping with blood.

"You need to see to her wound before it becomes infected. You said you would be able to cut out her tongue. It seems you are a coward. Make sure she has antibiotics. I do not want her dying before the ritual."

Chapter Twenty-Eight
Phillip

Harry's first firm memory was of being eight years old. It was year before he and his brother had started to fall out, before their parents had disappeared in the USA. They were sitting in the main reception room at Legend Street. Wait. Had he lived at Legend Street? It seemed so. Was this a memory or an amalgam of remembrance?

Yes, they had lived there, until his parents had disappeared the night after George Wright had bought the family home from the owner, Robert Waterfield from whom his parents rented. That name again.

In the memory, a woman came into the room. She was beautiful. Tall, red hair and dressed in quite matronly clothes despite her beauty.

"Hello, my little boys. It's time for your medicine."

"Medicine?" Phillip had asked. He had a die-cast toy Model T Ford that he was repeatedly rolling down a slope at another car, which it crashed into. He dropped it and got up. You did as you were told where Mummy was concerned.

Harry stood up at the same time as his brother. His twin brother.

There were four flights of stairs - the main ones, the first, then second floor flights and then those up to the attic. They had the full expanse of the attics for all the properties in the terrace, as they had apparently been connected by Mr Waterfield before they had moved into the house.

They walked almost the whole length of the attics and halted near the door which led into the secret room, where Daddy had a laboratory.

Daddy was there beyond the door, smiling. Mr Beaton was there, too. He and their daddy worked together at the University of Birmingham.

"Hello, Phillip, Hello Harry. How are you both?" Paul Beaton asked. He was a very tall, thin man who looked like he needed a pie or two. Thick horn-rimmed glasses sat on a beak of a nose.

"I am well, thank you," Harry answered. Phillip said nothing.

"Where's Edith?" Phillip asked.

"I am afraid she has ran away a long time ago. They have stopped looking for her. No doubt she is dead." His father added so very matter of fact.

Harry just accepted this news with his new knowledge of the past and the future. Edith wasn't fully dead.

"Jump up on the table, boys," Mummy said, then she left the attic and went about her business. She did not often come up here. Daddy did not always allow it.

Daddy lifted first Phillip and then Harry and put them onto the metal table. It had a hole at the end your feet would be if you were dead; the hole led to a drain. Daddy had been a surgeon of the Royal College - a pathologist. Until he was, what was the phrase he was never able to use? Ah yes, that was it: "struck-off."

Mr Beaton had a syringe in his hands and as he moved toward Phillip, his brother started to cry.

"Inject me first," Harry said to Mr Beaton. Phillip would be calmer if he did it first. That led to his dad ruffling Harry's hair.

"Brave lad," his daddy said.

It stung and he watched as the liquid disappeared from the glass syringe into his arm. Phillip was still sobbing.

"Don't be silly, Phillip," his dad had said.

Mr Beaton picked up another syringe from a kidney dish on the table. A little spray of liquid flicked out. Then he advanced on Phillip.

"Right young man, be brave."

"No. No. No. No." Phillip almost whimpered his words.

"Phillip, you must."

"But what is it for, Daddy?" he asked not defiant, but inquisitive. "Will it kill us? Mr Beaton is an architect, not a doctor."

"Mr Beaton is whatever I tell him to be. This medicine is special. It will make you live for an awfully long time. An exceedingly long time. It is a longevity serum. It is perfected... Well, nearly. Its magic."

Mr Beaton stifled a laugh.

Their father then held Phillip down, who screamed. "I do not want to live for a long time, Daddy. There's something in my head. It needs to die; it can't live forever. It says I am a Magpie. I don't want to live a long-time, Daddy, not with a Magpie in my head."

Mr Beaton stuck the needle into Phillip's arm. That was when he started to fit. Harry remembered now that this was what had triggered Phillip's bad moods. When he was working up to his fits, he would be bad-tempered, would throw more stones; he would hurt Harry, he would be generally unkind. Afterwards, he would blame the thing that woke up in his head on Harry. If I had gone first, you would have had the seizure. The logic of a child.

Harry shook himself out of the daydream. Ellen was in danger, and he could not contemplate staying in this damned cellar much longer.

As he came round, he noticed that Frances O' Neill, who had been haunting them had gone, but Edith had returned and was standing next to Maisie.

Hayden Worth was there too. It would be good to have some strong arms with them if they were going to catch the Magpie. Who knew what sort of entourage Lady Bell had at her behest?

They had dashed to Magpie Farm as soon as he had come around. Maisie was in a daze but had seemed to gain focus when Frances had appeared in the cellar. Frances had warned them that they needed to rescue Ellen from the house as she was about to become the next victim. There had been a tremor and Frances had suddenly vanished.

"It's Lady Bell. We need to go up to the house soon," Edith said. "Quickly. I can feel Lady Bell growing in power. I can feel the witch picking at my mind. She is so connected to this place; she almost *is* this place. Her will instils all around us. It is like the taint of promised death. We need to purge it."

Maisie looked at Harry, then Hayden.

"Such a good day." the big managed a grin, as nervous as they were his sarcasm a little off pat.

318

They left the cellar via the ladder and began to make their way up to Bell Manor. It was stiflingly hot; there was a rumble of thunder and a flash of lightning above them as they wound their way around the scrubby forested area and into the grounds.

"We need another good storm to get rid of this heat," Hayden offered. No-one disagreed. He was talking, Harry thought, to detract from the tenseness of the situation. Wise lad.

They made their way past the farmhouse. There were lights on inside shining through every window. Harry strolled over and peered through one of the windows; he could see a familiar shadow. *Was that Rollo?*

There was a shout from inside, then suddenly the front door swung open.

"Rollo. What are you doing here?"

"I bumped into him. He heard her speaking to the Magpie. He has brought weapons, Harry." This was the voice of George Wright.

"I don't use guns." Harry snapped. He was surprised to see Rollo, but more surprised to see his suspended Inspector could see George.

"I'll hold onto it then, gov," Rollo said, but he did pass the other gun to Hayden. "Do you know how to use one of these, Hayden?"

Hayden nodded. "I have nothing left to lose, Sir, of course I do."

Harry looked at him. The young officer had everything to lose. Hayden could be killed. Then he did a double take. He looked again at Hayden.

Hayden flickered. Like an old, doubly exposed super-eight film.

"You died." Harry's head twinged painfully. He remembered Hayden being injured when they went to arrest Leek. He remembered the phone call to say Hayden had bled out later that day. Hayden's femoral artery had been cut. They'd been invited to a memorial service. How could he be here? How could they have forgotten?"

319

"He what?" Maisie and Rollo said this at the same time.

It was George who answered. "Hayden worked for Cordivae. He has been working undercover in your team for quite a while. You served together in the army Harry. Way back in the nineteen sixties. You played in the same rugby team, at Twickenham. Army versus the Navy."

"What?" Harry was befuddled.

"Look I am sorry. I was one of original soldiers the Cordivae treated. I am surprised I lived as long as I did before becoming Moribund. The more I have found out though. Well, this all sickens me. They used Isabelle's magic in the formula. We are all infected – aside from Maisie."

"So, they told you I had been infected?"

Worth nodded, not making eye contact with Harry.

Harry just shook his head. Maisie was unusually lost for words.

"We will discuss this later. Hayden, I need to know you are with us."

"Yes gov. I am sorry. They hypnotised me. I lasted the longest out of the University experiments. When I died, my memories returned. I didn't know I was working for them. Honest. My memories had gone."

"Like mine have?" Edith sighed. "Poor Hayden."

"Are we really immortal?"

"Nancy was injected from the old batch." George explained. "It had been a mistake. Beaton had brought the wrong phials. He was a fine architect but a bad medic. Battle medicine didn't prepare you for the work your father and Cordivae were doing Harry. The next batch of the vaccine had been touched by something else. It started to turn those of us made near-immortal into nearly-ghosts when we died. The Moribund. It seems you and Phillip are something else however."

"Immortal?" Harry asked. Then remembered his daydream. The injections his Daddy had given him and Phillip.

"That's why I am so old. Why can't I remember – George, is this the case? Why can't I remember all the things that have happened to me?"

"You had your own block as well as Lady Bell's. You have compartmentalised your memories, Harry."

"Why have you not told me all of this before, George? How come Edith only remembered what I dreamt?"

"I did not tell you because I wanted you to come here. I do not know why Edith doesn't remember things unless you dream them. I hadn't seen her since 1948. I still work for Cordivae, my contract did state afterlife too. I recently had a visitor, from the group, in a place only a few of us can go. They want to recruit you Harry, but they can feel your links to the Magpie and Lady Bell. It's the same with Steven here. He has the vision too, like Maisie."

Harry turned to Rollo. "You too? That's why you looked so spooked. All that time."

"You should have said something." Maisie cried.

"Long story, Maisie. And I am sorry for my behaviour. I will explain as soon as I can."

Harry saw that Rollo's eyes were alight again. The dullness caused by his addiction had almost faded.

"George has brought me up to speed, Sir. I'll help in any way I can." Rollo explained, as if knowing Harry's military past had changed the way he responded as a former squaddie himself.

"Me too." This was Hayden.

COME

They all jumped.

"What the hell was that?" Maisie asked. "Did you all hear that?"

It hadn't been spoken, but it had been felt.

Harry saw them all nod.

"It's the Witch." This was Edith. "She knows we gather."

"Give one of the guns to me, Rollo," Maisie said. "I want to kill that bitch. Then the Magpie."

She didn't say Pete. Harry looked at her. Brave lass, all of this shit and she was still fighting. There would come a day where they would be both chasing the stress away.

"We need to bring him in alive, as a priority. He needs to atone, by rotting in a secure cell for the rest of his days," Harry said, grimly.

"Ellen is in there. We need to get her out. That's your priority Harry, isn't it?" Maisie said. "The guns are protection. We hardly understand what we are facing. A supernatural threat. Ghosts? Nearly-Ghosts? The Moribund. A witch? Who knows what might happen?"

COME.

"Ellen is important, yes, but not more important than taking the Magpie off the streets," Rollo added.

Harry took a deep breath. He nodded at Rollo. They at least agreed.

"You are right. Claudine Taylor is playing a blinder keeping our colleagues away from this place. She is going out on a limb for us, and we need to repay her. We have two hours. She has sent me the ground plan for Bell Manor." Harry flicked his phone around horizontally. "As I suspected there is a way in the back, what would have been the original servant and trade entrance. Hayden and Rollo, you and George go in via the rear, find Ellen, get her out. Maisie, Edith and I will go in the front. As we have been so very nicely invited."

They all took a little time to study the layout of the building, then the two groups went their separate ways in dreadful silence.

As Harry, Maisie and Edith neared the grand drive to the mansion that wove through lush gardens and lawns Edith gasped and staggered. Maisie caught her.

Edith started to flicker. She was going in and out of focus.

"It hurts. Isabelle's influence hurts me. I am not sure how much help I will be. Her power is rooted in the earth around us. We are in her lair. I am struggling to remain here. I have part of her in me. That is my only anchor."

Edith was almost translucent by now.

"Edith what do you mean part of her is in you?"

"I can't answer that really, not until we are inside. I'm guessing it's the magic in the serum. I'll do anything to save Ellen, but we must get him too before he kills anyone else."

"Your brother. Phillip." Maisie said, her voice trailing off as if she had uttered the worst of profanities.

"It would explain a lot. Pete knew our every move."

Maisie visibly shuddered. " And what's the thing with the eye removal?"

"He got so close. I need to know why he does what he does. When I was out unconscious that last time, I saw him as a boy. We were both injected with something - the thing that has allegedly made us near immortal and what caused Edith and George to be Moribund. I saw our parents, Maisie. I don't know how time works in my dreams, but we were young, and they were fucking experimenting on us. He was petrified. He asked them to kill the thing in his head, not inject him. I think even then Phillip knew there was a monster within him. He even called it the Magpie"

Maisie put her hand on Harry's shoulder. "If he is immortal, if Lady Bell has made him the way he is, how can we kill him?"

"I think we can die. I just don't know how. I repeat, however, he is not to die. He needs to face justice."

"This story isn't going to stand up in a court of law Harry," Maisie said.

"Then we will have to write a story that will," Harry responded angrily, but his ire was not directed at Maisie.

COME

Harry was broken out of his pensiveness by the mindfuck that was Lady Isla Bell. Maisie touched his arm again and they continued.

As they neared the Manor, the many flickering golden eyes that were its front-facing windows leered out of the darkness. Large topiary animals looking like the worst of monsters, flanked their path as they hit the threshold of the grand marble steps that led up to stout oak double doors of Bell Manor.

"It looks about as impenetrable as the force of her will," Edith whispered, still flickering.

As they approached the massive doors, they swung back with a set of creaking-thuds. A sense of horror yawned from within, overwhelming them with trepidation.

"Why would you ever enter such a place?" Maisie asked.

"To catch evil and to rescue the good. I don't want to enter. But I think we have to." Maisie offered him a supportive, if nervous smile.

"Sounds like the opening lines of a cheap film," Edith muttered more substantial now.

It lifted the mood a little.

Rollo, Hayden, and George sensed nothing as they approached the tradesman's entrance. If Lady Bell had servants within these walls, then they were awfully silent. It was as quiet as the grave.

Rollo smashed a side window and opened the latch from the inside. They entered and Rollo signalled for them to be quiet.

324

The house looked untouched by time. Like Legend Street had been. An absence of modernity, technology, or furnishing.

They walked down a long corridor. Even in the half-light of the candles in their sconces, Rollo could make out the intricate patterns of the Victorian tiles under their feet.

Then it started to go cold. Rollo's breath, being the only one still alive, misted.

Suddenly a creature woven from nightmares appeared.

A man of rags and pustulating sores stepped out of the darkness ahead of them. He had no eyes; his face was burned; the skin stretched in places broken and cracked in others. He screamed, even though he was a half-dead ghost Hayden still jumped.

George stepped forward. "Leave us be. We have been summoned."

"You are not wanted. Lady Isabelle does not want you three here."

The creature reached out a hand, grabbed George by the throat and lifted him effortlessly.

George whimpered. Rollo aimed the service pistol and fired, but the creature was smoke and mirrors, an illusion, although corporeal enough to interact with George, not solid enough that a bullet could stop it.

The creature squeezed and continued to do so, until there was an audible pop. It sounded like George's ghostly spinal cord had been severed. His body fell away from his head; the creature had effortlessly separated them.

There was no gore nor mess. George just dissipated. Head and body. Rollo presumed you couldn't kill a nearly-ghost, but could you destroy it? Could George recover from that?

"Shit. I thought if you were a ghost, you wouldn't be afraid of anything but that is evil," Haydn swore.

The creature turned to them and with the speed that amazed Rollo, it approached him and slapped him across the face. It did not connect with him, but

325

some sort of force did. He was flung into the nearest wall.

Hayden had decided that attacking the creature was the best form of defence and he threw himself at it. He grabbed it about the neck, and he squeezed, trying to give it a taste of its own medicine. It changed, however, to sand and just poured through Hayden's hands to the floor.

Rollo watched in horror as the creature coalesced into its original form, but this time slightly different. One arm was a massive, sharpened stake.

Hayden went in for the attack again. He dropped his shoulder as an only a good rugby player could, but the creature speedily stepped back. Hayden righted himself in preparation for another attack, but the creature drove the stake into him. He screamed - and then, like George, he dissipated.

As the creature was distracted by Hayden, Rollo scrambled to his feet and despite his injuries, he ran up the back stairs of the house, in the tradition of a servant who was late for his master's bidding. The horrible apparition thankfully did not follow.

The Magpie - aka Marcus, aka Pete Miles, aka Phillip Morton - had constructed quite a shield around his mind. As Prendergast helped to bring out Ellen Roux and tie her to the platform, he built his defences further. As Prendergast lay the faggots of wood at the feet of poor Nurse Roux, who was in some sort of feverish trance, the Magpie cemented the final brick of his defence. He did not know how he did it, but he knew he suddenly had help. He silently thanked the previous myriad of murderous Magpies who lined up behind him in spiritual solidarity.

Soon, he thought he heard a voice reply.

He didn't, however, expect that by building one wall, another would come down.

He started to remember.

Their parents often locked Phillip in the attic of Legend Street. He was difficult it was punishment. After all, he might run away like their disobedient daughter.

Once, he had worked at the lock of his cell for some time, to try and get out.

He was whittling away at it with a sharpened shard of metal that had once been a spoon. He had loosened the wood around the hinges and with a thunk, as he kicked at it, the door banged open, careering off the adjacent wall, then falling from the frame.

He had noticed shortly after the last injection that his strength had increased. He wondered if Harry was this strong. He would have to try and punch him, if he saw him again.

He moved down the tight gap between the rooms in the attic. He moved towards the noise. A sucking, hissing noise, coming from the room where he and his brother had their injections.

The voices he could hear were Paul Beaton's and George Wright's. Beaton was his legal guardian now and had brought him back to Legend Street. It was 1948. Not long after his parents had gone missing on their trip to Chicago. He didn't know where Harry was.

The hissing and gurgling continued, even as he cowered in a corner as they went past and out of the attic laboratory, locking the door behind him.

He moved into the lab, even though fear was strong, and he could feel his mouth going dry and the dampness of sweat under his arms.

The lights were still on. Strapped to a gurney was a woman. She seemed familiar, but only glancingly.

She was naked; he had never in all his years seen a woman naked before. She was thrashing and spitting. She stopped as he approached. Her breasts stopped jiggling and her face turned to him slowly, her grin inane.

She was beautiful. He felt his belly and lower parts flutter. He presumed she hadn't always been this feral, though, the injections must have changed her in different ways to how he and Harry had been changed. What was in those jabs he and Harry had been given?

327

Wait - he was a child? No, an adult. Remembering the past.

"Hello, sweetie," the woman said as if her nakedness was so ordinary. "My name is Nancy. What is wrong with your face?"

"Hello, Nancy," he replied to the beautiful woman as matter of fact as he normally communicated. There wasn't much room for emotion. "I was burned. Or will be. I think. Time seems funny here. My brother did it. Why are you here?"

She laughed, but it was more of a gasp than a raucous gesture. "I am an abomination. Their experiments went slightly awry. Instead of creating a superbeing that would meet the next German attack head-on, they created un-dead things like me."

"I'm not sure I understand."

"Come closer, my mouth is dry. I cannot shout."

He went nearer. She started to whisper, but he did not hear it at first.

"Sorry, you are very quiet."

"I am a monster."

In one movement she sat up, breaking her bonds. She turned her body toward him. Her beautiful, naked body. She smiled and that's when he saw her hands. They were glowing. The ties that bound her pinged apart. Then, Nancy flew at him and as she hit, he could smell the musk of her. It was intoxicating. He felt his knees go weak. There was a pain in his neck, and he felt her hands grasping each side of his head sucking at him.

He flung her away and she crashed into the gurney. She stood and smiled, her body glowed, her breasts were translucent, same as her belly and down near her sex, she was glowing.

Phillip could feel himself drawn to her again, then she screamed with laughter again and launched herself at him, blonde curls like a halo around her head as she hit him. He was knocked back.

She was on top of him. Then he grabbed her and held her. He had his hands around her neck. Her teeth were gnashing, getting closer, like the blades on a mechanical lawnmower.

Then he remembered what she had said. This wasn't a dream, but a memory. "Take my eyes. Please. It's the only way to kill me. I am Vivore."

When Paul Beaton crashed into the attic, he had the beautiful woman in his arms, she looked perfect in death, like a China doll. Except for the bloody tears and the holes where her eyes had been.

Prendergast hadn't been the first to tell The Magpie how to remove eyes, Nancy the eye hospital nurse had. Nancy the would-be female soldier.

Nancy Wright hadn't been buried with her eyes; they had never found them. Phillip had kept them in his pocket.

Vivore eyes. He still had them in a jar.

Chapter Twenty-Nine
Lady on a Pyre

"Welcome. I am Lady Isla Bell, but I was originally Isabelle of Stafford." The beautiful woman was nothing like the Lady Bell Maisie had seen before. That Lady Bell had been nothing more than an aged cripple.

"Put that gun away, dear, it cannot harm me. I live between reality. Substance cannot affect me."

"I'll take that chance. "Maisie didn't move a muscle. Click, she pulled the hammer back. It was an old gun.

Harry, Edith and Maisie had been led to the large ballroom on the second floor of the massive house. The room was impressive. It was curtained off at one end and standing in front of the curtain was a large, fat man.

"Why is Prendergast here?" Harry asked, puzzled. The big, bulky man gave a little wave.

"Oh, he's been my servant for years. Let's just say William likes his dollar bills and his ladyboys too much to run too far from me, like all the other servants did over the years. William has been useful, especially as your medical specialist. He diagnosed that terrible piece of moving bone in your head, did he not?" She smiled like a raptor bird. "He also had a very serendipitous meeting with your lovely lady, Ellen, in the car park at Queens. It was after her disciplinary panel, where they began proceedings against her for revealing the fact you were totally healthy. Your block was nothing more than a result of too many mental traumas. With a little cursory help from me."

Lady Bell waved a hand; Harry gasped, and he fell to his knees.

"What the fuck have you done?" Maisie screamed.

"He might dream for a bit; I have just returned all his memories. All that angst in one fell swoop from the 1930s or whenever he was born, until now. It might send him mad, like his dear brother Phillip."

"You have been controlling Phillip. Or should I say Pete Miles." Maisie's grip on the gun out in front of her wobbled with a mixture of anger and fear. She knew pulling the trigger would be useless, but it gave her some feeling of protection, even if it was nothing more than a placebo.

"Ha!" Isabelle laughed "I named him Magpie, like all the others before him. I own them all across time. Soon the future too. You see my spell has mutated over time. It has become exponential on a quantum level. I set the Magpie's tasks. They bring me life. Phillip is just one step away from being like me. One step away from power. Unfortunately, he does not get it. Neither he nor Harry or their stupid sister understand what power those injections their daddy gave them will eventually bring."

Whilst Maisie had got the witch talking, Edith had moved behind her. She wasn't sure what her adopted great aunt, Harry's true sister, was up to, but she seemed to have a plan.

"Phillip. Come here," Lady Bell screeched.

And Pete walked out from behind the curtain. He smiled at Maisie; aside from the shock of white in his hair, it was the same beautiful young man she had shared her bed with. Like the grief for Teddy and her sister had been held at bay, so too had the revulsion at finding out Pete was the Magpie. It flooded into her now and she shivered; she could have thrown up there and then. *Hold tight Maisie. There will be time for that.*

"So, Ellen's the secret never to be told then? Or is it, Harry?" Maisie asked braving the situation, holding back her gorge. "Who dies next Isabelle? Have you lured Harry here to kill him with Ellen? Or make him watch. Presumably, you can't reveal the secret, by virtue of the stupid rhyme, it doesn't work?"

Isabelle cackled. It was a strange sound on one so young looking and perfect in every way. "Oh, you are clever. Daisy worked it out after the first two deaths, didn't she? I told her what I was doing before my Magpie killed her. Now you have tried to complete the rhyme. Unfortunately, you are not clever enough. William, open the curtains."

Prendergast did as he was bidden and pulled on a long gold cord and another tableau was revealed. This one belonged to Lady Bell and not her Magpie.

Maisie let out a little desperate gasp, the gun wavered.

Ellen, Harry's fiancé was tied to a wooden stake on a platform. Below her was a base of well-packed wood and kindling.

"Ellen!" Maisie called, with a sickening revulsion as she noticed the blood on Ellen's chin. "They cut out your tongue, didn't they?" This was said to herself as much as anyone else in the room. "So, you can't reveal your secret. Well, that's it, then."

Maisie knew it was all over. This evil woman, Isabelle, witch, whatever you want to call her, had won.

Then Edith flew at Lady Bell. Time stood still for a moment. But Lady Bell turned preternaturally fast, and with a squeezing motion, she caught Edith and dissipated her. The Moribund woman screamed as she vanished. Lady Bell turned back to Maisie.

"Sorry about that. Tiresome woman. Now, where were we? Once upon a time, Maurice Morton, and Paul Beaton made a pact with a witch, who came to them as a vision during a drunken weekend at a farmhouse they wanted to buy off George Wright, for development and re-sale. But he sold to the Rogers' my last servants for the soon to be wed O'Neill's.

"Beaton hated Wright for that. They thought by having a piece of my land they could harvest my power for themselves. The witch said she could make even the dead heal, after all. That witch was yours truly. They didn't want to deal with me, eventually they had to.

"Funnily enough, that little agreement was made in this very room, Maisie. You and Harry were destined to come together. I orchestrated it all locating Harry after his accident. Bringing Ellen into his life, and then linking you to your dead aunt and through your Nanna, that another insufferable bitch.

"And do you know what is funny? None of that is the secret. Nothing at Legend Street was ever the secret, even what the government know about the Cordivae group, or what the Cordivae Group know about themselves.

"No, the biggest secret is the one that Ellen will take to her grave, unspoken and unwritten. I found her by accident. A little girl, who on a holiday trip from France to Lichfield, stumbled onto my farm."

"Harry, why don't you take Phillip to the Cathedral. He likes the sound of the Choir," Edith said. She was standing with Harry; Phillip was in his wheelchair next to them.

It was 2004 and Harry had returned from Afghanistan, where he had been serving as part of an elite SAS team in a joint operation with the US Navy SEALs. He had only just got out alive and had decided to retire from military life, to come home for some R and R and before his commanding officers realised, he wasn't ageing. He had been on tour for years; they would suspect something soon. Why Edith was there, he couldn't quite comprehend. She had gone missing in 1948, never to be seen again. Time and events were still very much mixed up in his mind.

"We are all together again now, this is happening then and now and at other times. Isabelle has broken nature, even in the world of dreams. They do not realise what they have done making pacts with Isabelle. The Vivore will come."

"Vivore?"

"An ancient name. Life Eaters. Their DNA has ancient magic within it. Evil magic."

Phillip had been silent. Harry had picked him up from St Mark's Hospital, where he had been since 1999 and they were only just decommissioning the hellhole. He had written to Phillip to say he was coming back. Poor Phillip. Harry still felt guilty about his brother's continual breakdowns and successive escapes and re-capture.

Harry started to push Phillip towards the grand Gothic cathedral. The wonderfully carved stone figures that adorned the front face of Lichfield Cathedral were a glory to behold.

Up a disabled access ramp they went, into the cool near-silence. There were muted voices all around, but they were displaced, indistinct, swallowed by the space around them. He heard the organ strike up and the first few bars of Jerusalem which then led into a full rehearsal it seemed.

"I want to go above the choir, where I used to go as a boy, when I was first blinded by you." That was the first thing Phillip had said to him. Harry thought that was probably fair as he hadn't seen Phillip for years. "The ghost-bitch can't come."

He meant Edith, who nodded as if to agree that she would stay below.

The steps to the balcony were narrow and it was difficult to lead someone up there who had poor sight. They managed it eventually and they walked onto the balcony just as Jerusalem ended and Amazing Grace began.

"I used to lean over the balcony a little to get the best sound, Harry. Lead me to it please, then you can leave me for a time. I'd like to listen. It is so... beautiful."

Harry led Phillip across and placed his hands on the low rail.

Harry was just about to leave his brother to his music, when Phillip grabbed hold of a wrist. It was a vice-like grip and it held Harry fast. The serum had affected them in different ways. Harry could go for days without sleep, enhanced stamina, great in combat situations.

"Why do you never come back to see me?"

Harry sighed; this conversation was always inevitable. "I don't want to live anymore; I never want to come back.

I have been waiting for the final moment, when I can die and rest forever. I am really tired."

"You blinded me and left me for years, Harry. So did she."

"That was a mistake. An accident. Edith died. She told you that she struggled to return. The serum worked differently on her."

"She never told me any of that. She looks at me like I am a monster. After you left, after school, I couldn't cope with University; I broke down. I was left to rot in different institutions, over time I was moved from one place to the next – without choice. Every place I went to was worse."

"I couldn't help our parents dying, Phillip."

"They didn't die, fuckwit. They went to America. I heard someone talking, someone who thought I was mad. One of Beaton's cronies. Father and Mother were still alive in 1949. They had also taken the serum. They abandoned me. Edith abandoned me, although at least she had the manners to die. You abandoned me. Left me. I could almost forgive you for taking my eyes, but you left me for so long."

"I didn't take your eyes, Phillip. They were burnt."

"Losing my eyes was just the start. What I can't forgive you for is all the time I was abused, felt up, buggered in the shower blocks by the nurses. Even though I had my strength, I could never have overpowered three or four of them. Time after time. My mind rotted and now I must kill to keep it from rotting further. I had to go and find friends. I had to take their eyes to make them my friends. Not even the witch truly knows how many I killed in between relapses of the psychosis, when I escaped. I couldn't let any of them try to suck out my life force like Nancy. So, I killed them and took their eyes. I could talk to their eyes. They were all going to suck my life away, and you, my brother, you left me to them."

Harry felt Phillip's grip tighten, then he was shoved, propelled towards the low stone rail. Harry knew at that moment how he had ended up in a coma. Then he heard her voice....

"Hello Harry. I am Isabelle."

....and how he had been injured....

335

"I can speak to you through the connection I have to the serum in your veins."

....Harry hit the rail, tumbled over and fell to the stone floor of the Cathedral....

"Let me just put a little block into your head."

...Harry then realised, before he lost consciousness, that Phillip was right; it was he who was the monster, for abandoning Phillip in the first place. For not catching the Magpie when they were boys. Instead, Harry had let it out.

Harry came to; it took him a while to get his focus, then he wished he hadn't. He'd always had good eyesight and he could clearly see Ellen upon a pyre.

He didn't move, he wanted to judge the situation before acting. That was the years of military training and exercise coming through. All the memories had nearly drowned him in those few seconds of download as the block was fully removed. Isabelle thought his mind would break. It had just got stronger.

He realised he had naturally performed a very clever trick. He was able to compartmentalise years of memories and store them in the higher functioning parts of his brain. He put them all in his memory box. It had always been there, it seemed. He had constructed it a long time ago during his first battle experiences in the Korean War.

He could hear Maisie engaged in conversation with Isabelle.

"And if she dies without giving up her secret, what happens to you, what happens to Pete?"

"Good question. I live my corporeal life again. I have been dead for hundreds of years; it's been so very lonely. As for Phillip, The Magpie, as I named him, well, he gets his sight back."

"Sight? What do you mean sight? How could he have committed all those crimes without vision?"

"His "Marcus/Pete" disguise is made from loose strands of the spell that infuses this land. I wove them into a cloak and made him see again through a mask. I gave him a purpose."

"Giving him a purpose to kill? Surely, he had that trait already. You cannot take the credit for all that is The Magpie."

"I presumed he had that in him, didn't you dear?" Lady Bell looked over at Phillip, as he was being called now and smiled. It was a sickly smile one might give a moment before you vomited that ever-so special birthday meal.

"Harry made me what I am. Edith made me what I am. So did my parents. Abandonment." Phillip looked at Maisie.

"How did that translate into you killing people and taking their eyes?"

"I did it to save myself. My first eyes were taken in self-defence. I still have Nancy's eyes. I still talk to her, I still talk to the rest of them, *they* became my friends."

Harry knew that Phillip was insane. Maisie had shared her bed for all that time with an insane killer. Poor girl.

"But did you choose that path, or did she control you all along?" She asked Phillip.

Isabelle started to laugh.

"Stop laughing, bitch. I asked him a question. Pete or whatever you are called?"

"She *has* controlled me at times," was Phillip's quiet answer.

Lady Bell waved one hand and Phillip was picked up and held into the air by some invisible force. As Harry watched, Phillip started to flicker around the edges, his face changing from that of Pete Miles to disfigured Phillip, so genuinely like Harry but with darker curly hair, as opposed to Harry's ash-blond locks. His real face was revealed: the occluded left eye, the scarred right.

"Why twins? Why Daisy?" Maisie needed to know it seemed.

337

"Ah, my clever darling. All the right questions. Double the power. I was a twin; I have used the essence of my Ann to empower me further. She was such a sweet, sickly thing. Pathetic. I have woven the birth of twins into the land. Your families have all been here. Even the Mohammed boy - his father once plastered my ceilings when he first came to this land, after the Partition of India in 1948."

Lady Bell, Isabelle, let the Magpie go. He landed well; his visage had reverted to that of Pete, with the lock of white hair in amongst the black. Now the Magpie again, he reached inside his pocket to get a large Bowie knife, just like the one he had carried out his killings with. He seemed to glow with confidence once more.

"Let me kill Harry, Isabelle, I am tired of this charade."

"Not yet. Kill the policewoman, get another set of lovely twin's eyes for your collection and we will then kill Ellen, we no longer have need of either of them."

Lady Bell nodded to Prendergast and William held up a brazier, then he set the pyre alight.

That was when Rollo appeared, cannoning into the Magpie just as he was about to advance on Maisie with his knife. She heard the knife clatter to the ornate ballroom floor. She saw where it had dropped and once, she reached it, she kicked it towards Harry. Harry sprang up and ran for Prendergast as fast as he could.

Then Maisie stopped. She was caught, held fast in that vice-like supernatural grip - and then, she was taken elsewhere.

Maisie appeared in the dream world Harry had just vacated. It was 31ˢᵗ October sometime in the 1400s, she was in the market square again in Lichfield. It was close, very warm. Thunderhead clouds crowded the sky dirty, like billowing smoke.

There was a pyre here too and a crowd of people. In distance, she saw a familiar yellow blur. Edith was there. Her great aunt, Harry's sister, put her finger to her lips. Do not let on.

As Maisie watched, a cart pulled by a dray-horse parted the crowd with a clip-clop. She expected to see a screaming woman or man aboard it, but instead, all she could see was a rotted corpse of a young woman. As it neared her vantage point, she could sense it was Isabelle. Or what was left of the witch.

The cart pulled up and a voice spoke from the crowd the other side of the pyre.

"Here today we burn the cursed remains of Isabella of Stafford. A witch."

And that was it. Two unfortunate fellows had the tricky job of tying the bony corpse to the pyre. They did so with thick ropes.

A priest led a service of absolution following an exorcism and the pyre was lit.

The flames grew, then strangely stopped.

Another silent figure had appeared next to Maisie. They had been joined by a red-headed woman dressed in the garb of the locals of that time.

Isabelle was suddenly reanimated, alive looking again. She looked directly at Maisie, looked at Edith and cackled.

"Jesus, she got that witch thing going early, she can't be more than twenty." Maisie spat.

"My sister always had delusions of grandeur." The red-haired woman said. She was always beautiful and evil in equal measure."

"This is Ann, Isabella's sister, she is the link." Edith said. "Isabelle used Ann's remains as part of the cupid's curse that went wrong, the spell that draws the evil to Magpie Farm and now the Bell estate. Isabelle then acquired her sister's bones as an anchor for her future spells. A reliquary."

Then Isabelle was standing before them.

"Get out of my past," she said, with a flick of her fingers.

And suddenly they were elsewhere.

Harry reached Ellen, who was screaming in a tongueless manner. Prendergast had lit the fire and it had taken hold, but then, for some reason, the flames had stopped. Like they were a television picture, and someone had paused the flames. With a remote.

Ellen still screamed.

He was distraught, despite her betrayal. Was it a betrayal? Ellen always had best intentions at heart.

His angel.

Behind him, he could hear the fracas between Rollo and the Magpie, but for now, he turned his back on Ellen just for a moment.

Prendergast barred his way.

The fat, sweaty doctor was a big man, but Harry had his measure. He had remembered things only minutes ago and accessed a set of those memories pertaining to his advanced hand to hand training.

I don't use weapons. What a joke.

That was the false Harry. The one without the memories.

Prendergast had raised his hands to prevent Harry's coming past, but as he neared the tall, bulky man, Harry kicked at one of the Prendergast's knees. It gave with a loud crack. The big fellow went down with a scream. Harry followed up with a kick under the doctor's chin. He didn't care if it broke his neck - he deserved it.

Harry hadn't needed the knife, after all.

He turned back to Ellen, the fire was still, paused. He looked up at Ellen; she was conscious, despite the pain she must have been in. Tears formed at the corners of her eyes, but soon dried. Isabelle had taken her tongue to keep her silence. To end the rhyme. A secret never to be told.

My poor angel.

340

Who could do this to a human being? Who could light such a fire in an enclosed space, unless they had magic to be able to contain it, pause it? Did Lady Bell have magical means to put it out? Or would she let her home burn? Harry cursed.

Then he too went elsewhere.

Rollo grunted as the Magpie kicked him in the stomach, winding him terribly. He heard the snap of a rib; luckily, he knew it was too low to affect his lungs, but it could do other damage internally.

"I'd quite like your eyes for my collection, Steve," The Magpie stated. "I'd like to talk to you long after you are dead. Your eyes look quite troubled. Like they have seen a lot and regret much. Am I right? Your name isn't Rolleston, is it? Your name is Chambers."

"You are such a fucking comic book villain The Magpie. What if it is? I took my mother's name when I joined up. My father was as fucking mad as you. Always talking about prophecy. Claiming one of his descendants would be a goddess on another fucking planet. You are a fucking nutter like he was."

"Why. Thank you."

Sense of humour too, it seemed, behind the madness. Rollo got to his feet as the Magpie came at him. The guy was strong. Rollo managed to avoid two punches, then one landed on his left shoulder and he was rocked back. Steven Rolleston had seen some shit in service in his time, but big bastards fell just as well as weaklings. You just needed to find their Achilles heel.

The Magpie had no idea of his positioning, because he was lost in his earlier mummery. Rollo knew, however that he was right in front of a plate-glass window that opened over a balcony, forty feet above the courtyard below.

Rollo had rather a good understanding of physics; he knew that if he managed a decent enough speed, the momentum would take the Magpie and himself through that window and out into the air. Thirty feet or so up above a concrete driveway.

Rollo had never felt a concussion as painful as the one he felt when they both went through the plate glass, lead and wooden frame – well, not until, they both hit hard ground.

Fuck. That hurt. Rollo though for a moment.

The he heard a giggle, and Chloe grabbed his hand. She smiled. He was joining his girls. *At last.* He took one last living glance at the start of his breath, and he could see the Magpie, who lay just to his left, neck at just the wrong angle to have survived. Then he sighed his last.

Steve Rolleston had finally joined his family.

Chapter Thirty
Never To Be Told

"My Magpie!" Isabella screamed. She felt the latest in a long line of Magpies die, the psychic link disconnected. So much for his immortality. His father's efforts were wasted, it seemed.

She might have shed a ghostly tear at another time. She had rescued Phillip, took him under her wing. She couldn't bother with all that now, however. Phillip was no longer essential to her plan.

Her attention turned to Ellen, another Magpie. Ellen needed to die to end the spell. The final twin. The ultimate power was hers.

Isabelle had reappeared from the Nothingness in the ballroom of her house. The fire had been paused; Ellen was screaming. The fat form of Prendergast lay prostrate on the floor, writhing about crying and mewling. On the ground next to William, she could see Harry, out cold again, under the influence of someone else with the long sight.

Who was it? She had dissipated the woman in yellow, the only woman she feared. She had been lucky she had caught Edith at a point where she could not anchor. There was more to Edith than the others knew. Isabelle would have to eliminate her, or Edith would be such a threat when she was human again.

She paced over to Harry; she needed him to watch his girlfriend burn. He was linked to all of this, after all - not revealing the secret was key, but having people witnessing the secret not being revealed was the point. She could kill him then for her Magpie. If Phillip could die, so could Harry.

On the floor, next to Harry, was Phillip's knife. She quickly picked it up, went over to Prendergast and stuck it in his throat. With a wet rattle, the mewling stopped, and William stopped. *Fat leach.*

She walked over to the broken window and looked over the balcony. She might have been irritated at the mess, but she didn't have the time. Below was Phillip, his head at such an odd angle and the other policeman lay next to him, skewered by a large shard of glass, his face white as the now-burgeoning moon.

Thunder rattled the windows, the conclusion to her spell was close. The lightning hit a tree in the grounds, exploding it as she watched. Like a giant torch, steam from the sap and smoke rising into the sky. The heat of her influence was building. It was all leading to the moment. Her moment. She smiled.

As the thunder smashed again, Maisie reappeared. She was obviously strong in the gift to be able to move between the worlds of life and death so easily. Edith then appeared too, the Bitch in Yellow. Isabelle could feel her power. Then others appeared. A beautiful woman with red hair, who she hadn't seen for such a long time, with her skin on at least, her sister Ann, then the O'Neill bitch and finally Jennie Pleasant, who had come so near to unravelling her power most recently.

She smiled. None of them was a match for Isabelle of Stafford. Even together they were no match. This was her domain. She was almost corporeal. A full witch was infinitesimally more powerful than any number of ghostly ones.

Isabelle felt their joint psychic attack and realised that even at her vast age, one could be so naïve. She reeled and was knocked backwards. That was irritating. Reaching out a hand at Frances O' Neill, she squeezed her fist. The old woman did not dissipate, however.

"Ann is the link. Her bones and blood, Isabelle. The biggest of your mistakes writ all the way through this mess of a spell," Jennie Pleasant smiled.

That didn't matter. Isabelle turned all her amassed will towards Ellen on the pyre. She could feel the intensity of the secret linking to the spell as the girl

344

burnt. She dropped the knife and held both arms out. She stoked the fire with her power.

"Stop, Sister." It was from Ann. "We must let her speak. You are going to open the gates of hell. The Vivore cannot come."

"I cut out her tongue. She will not speak."

Ellen screamed. It was a horrible, garbled sound and Isabelle loved it.

As soon as she reappeared in the ballroom at Bell Manor, Maisie could feel Ellen's secret. Like a gaping void before them. Ann had opened her up to the power, the power that linked back to Nanna Price, to Edith, to all her female relatives back in history who were strong in the power.

She stepped into Ellen's mind. She took Harry with her. He did not want to go. He wanted to capture the Magpie.

"He is dead, H. The Magpie is dead."

"Where are we?" Harry asked, as if moving through the planes of reality were the most normal thing to do.

"We are in the Nothingness. And also, Ellen's mind."

"No. This isn't right, M. Let me out. It's not fair. She is out there, dying. I need to save her. Get Phillip."

"We need to know her secret," Maisie reminded him. "If her secret isn't revealed, then Isabelle wins. Ellen is lost, Harry. Phillip is lost."

Harry could suddenly hear laughter - two little girls were playing in their room, having fun. Twin girls, Ellen and her sister Ailsa. They were playing hide and seek; Ellen was running away from her sister, trying to hide as she counted.

"Stop running about!" came a shout from downstairs. Grand-Mere. Gran was such misery; she spoiled all their fun. Ellen had once thought.

She and Ailsa continued to race about, ignorant to how it might sound below, the banging and the chinking of the chandelier lights would be enough to try the patience of a saint.

"Stop it, girls. Zut Alors!"

They could hear Grand-Mere stomping up the stairs again. It meant trouble. Gran wasn't old by any measure, so she still had a powerful slap, and she was free with it.

They saw Ellen stop and watch as Grand-Mere approached. Ellen stood her ground though, as the older woman slowly climbed to the top of the stairs. Grand-Mere arced her arm back and hit Ellen with the mightiest slap she had ever felt as an adult or a child.

Ellen screamed. She looked at her grand-Mere and shouted, "bitch."

Grand-Mere hit her again, but ended up losing her balance.

Ellen laughed, and in response, swung her fist back and connected with her Gran's chin. Gran tottered in surprise, but she tottered too much and fell backwards into the air, down the stairwell like a marionette sans string. Her fall was arrested by her head; Gran's neck snapped sideways with the sound of dry wood thrown upon a fire.

"She killed her Nan?" Harry gasped. Was that the secret?

Then the image flipped. Different house...

"No!" Isabelle screamed.

"We can get her secrets as she dies, Isabelle," Ann's ghost said. "Your reign of terror is nearly over."

Isabelle thrust her will back at her sister, but Edith countered, along with the woman, Jennie Pleasant.

346

No, she couldn't fail here not when she was so near to living once again.

Isabelle stopped sending her power out and instead retrieved the knife for the second time that evening - and dashed towards Ellen.

She leapt at the girl, knife in hand, but then she stopped. Held in place. They were blocking her again. She thrust out her will in a series of pulses. One of them, she didn't know who, weakened and she managed to break through. Isabella jumped onto the pyre and thrust the knife into Ellen.

Nothing happened. The knife would not penetrate. She could not un-pause localised time.

Isabelle was a ghost still, but soon she would be whole. She would defeat them all. There had not been such a powerful witch alive or dead for centuries.

She tried to step away from Ellen, but then the tongueless woman's arms locked about her.

Ellen and Ailsa were older now, they looked about nine years old. They were tidying their room whilst arguing.

"Not sure why I have to do this when you messed it up," Ellen shouted.

Ailsa told her where to go and opened one of the windows because it was so hot. The château was in Normandy, not far from Rouen. They were spending the summer there again and it was boring. The weather was just hot, day after day, no pool or river to swim in and they were not near the sea either. Their mother and father were always busy with their marketing business, so the girls were left to their own devices for long periods of time.

"Shut the window."

"No, it's too hot," Ailsa replied.

"Take off your jumper then, you silly bitch." Such a grown-up swear word for nine-year-olds.

"Shut it," Ellen repeated, moving over to her sister.

"No - make me."

"I don't need to make you; I just need to end you."

And, with a shove, Ellen pushed Ailsa, who fell out of the bedroom window - but not before she pulled Ellen with her. Ellen landed on her dead sister and broke her own leg in three places. They thought at first that she had been screaming because her sister was quite obviously dead. Ellen felt nothing for her sister, but her leg was on fire.

"Oh my God," Harry gasped, "that was intentional." Maisie lay a comforting hand on his shoulder.

The scene changed to a hospital...

"We have her secrets, Sister," Ann said.

Edith could feel the secrets leaching out of the screaming girl. The fire was pausing, then burning, then pausing at regular intervals.

Isabelle laughed as she struggled in their grip. "Do you think I would create a situation where all this hinges on a few silly little deaths? It's only the tip of the iceberg."

They were on a hospital ward. Harry and Maisie could see an old man in his bed. His name was written on a board: Arthur Peterson. The words "Nil by mouth" were added messily, scrawled in doctor's handwriting next to Arthur's name. The man was obviously close to death.

The door opened and Nurse Ellen Roux entered.

"Morning, Arthur." She said in a whispered voice. "Time to die you pervert, no one cops a feel of these bad girls without permission, even if you are at the end of your life, my boy."

As Harry watched, Ellen checked her watch and went over to the morphine syringe driver linked to the drip. With a little twist, she opened the valve up. Then she went on her way.

The scene changed, the same hospital, different ward…

A child lay in bed, obviously poorly but not in a life-threatening state.

Ellie sat on the edge of the girl's bed. They were chatting about music and girly things. Ellen had such a nice smile. A smile that hid secrets so well.

"You don't normally work here, do you?"

"No," Ellen said. "Just helping out. Do you want your lunch now?"

"Yes, please," the girl said.

There was a selection of dishes on an over the bed tray. Ellen lifted the lid off the meal and the pudding.

Ellen was blocking the girl's view of her actions; she secretly reached into her pocket and brought out what looked to be a peanut. She crushed it between her fingers and added it to the food and stirred. Ellen left the tray, then left the room. She was a good few yards away when the anaphylactic shock kicked in. Jessica Long died from asphyxiation due to the narrowing of her airways and the resulting drop in her blood pressure.

Harry could not believe it - there were tears in his eyes. Not Ellen. Not his wonderful Ellen.

His angel was an angel of death.

Cut to a park. Ellen running. It was not a park he knew and judging by the surroundings it was abroad, the Mediterranean, by the look of the architecture. It was spring, fresh leaves on the trees. It was before they had met but probably not long before, judging by Ellen's outward look. There was a man approaching, another runner; he wolf-whistled at her and stopped to chat. Within minutes, Ellen had pushed a concealed knife through his right eye.

Harry dry retched. It was surprising that could happen in the dream state. Although he'd not eaten for hours though and there was nothing to come up.

"Are you okay?"

"I'm not sure how much of this I can watch."

"You need to continue." Ann said.

***

Isabelle screamed. Things were unravelling, Ellen's secrets were coming out. She had to kill the woman before the biggest of her secrets was revealed.

Isabelle clenched her fists. She took hold of the power that sustained her sister's spirit and cut it off at the source. Ann dissipated. Then she did the same to Jennie. The woman in yellow, Edith was stronger, so she pulled her to the dream state.

Isabelle and Edith appeared next to Harry and Maisie.

"She has killed thirty-seven people. Thirty-three of them patients. How much more of this is there?"

"That is her secret. She needs to keep it."

Isabelle screamed. The scene changed. Yet Isabelle was gone. Edith soon followed.

They were in Harry's flat. He was asleep upstairs.

"Edith. Edith. Edith," he was saying in his sleep.

Harry looked at himself; it was bizarre to see yourself from the outside. He probably needed to hit the gym when this was all over.

Ellen, in her sexy underwear, a vision that he loved so much, made her way up the stairs to the mezzanine level. She looked around at the real Harry who was watching and winked at him. She mouthed the word "Sorry."

Then Ellen Roux placed a pillow over Harry's face and killed him by suffocation. As they watched and the scene changed, she did it to him seven or eight times.

"Why won't you die, Harry?" Ellen from the past asked his sleeping form. "You are so hard to kill, sweetie."

Edith reappeared next to Isabelle who was triumphant. Ellen was dead, a charred corpse, affixed to the smouldering stake. She had not been able to reveal her final secrets before she died.

"I did it, bitch," she spat at Edith. "I am alive. And if my poor Magpie were alive, he would have been whole again by now."

"Oh, but I am alive." came a voice.

Harry and Maisie reappeared next to Edith to witness the Magpie, or Phillip, now looking his Pete Miles self, walk across to his mentor to ram his bowie knife into Isabelle's chest. He stepped away and the short-lived rejuvenated body of Isabelle of Stafford fell to the floor, dead once again, blood spraying, fanning across the beautiful ballroom floor like the finest of hosepipe sprinklers.

Harry let out a sob, but it wasn't for Ellen. It was for his brother. He knew what was coming.

Maisie had raised her revolver; she aimed it at Pete Miles. Harry snatched it from her and aimed it at Phillip.

"Harry. Don't."

"You'll never pull the trigger, Henry, you coward."

Harry shot The Magpie, his brother through the head.

DCSI Claudine Taylor arrived with Karol Wosijc and an armed team soon after, but it was all over. It was a scene of carnage.

Taylor counted the total of men and women lost from her team, including her senior officer and would later that night sob for every one of them, including Rivers.

Harry had been found sobbing in the arms of Inspector Price. His fiancée Ellen Roux a charred mess, killed apparently by Lady Isla Bell, who now lay with a knife in her chest on the ballroom floor.

They had found Rollo first, glass piercing his stomach. He had bled to death probably quite quickly. DI Hyatt was dead, Grace Hodgson seriously injured. Not to forget poor murdered Daisy and Hayden Worth, who had died of his wounds a few weeks ago. Claudine had meant to ask Harry why he had been talking about Worth being on the team for so long after, but for some reason it always fled her memory.

At least they had the Magpie's body. She didn't know how she would write this one up; she would have to call Peter Silas the Chief Constable of Somerset Police who was leading the Police Complaints Committee review of Rivers' death.

A sorry mess.

She eventually got some time with Harry and Inspector Price, but they were both exhausted, and with a heavy heart, she placed them both on open-ended sick leave.

The Final Chapter
Conversation in A Graveyard

Robert Waterfield stood on the brow of the cemetery and looked down over the small valley of graves.

It was a cold November day, three weeks after the events at Bell Manor.

There were funerals aplenty. The skies rained tears. Mo Hyatt had been laid to rest within days of his death because he and his faith expected it. They mourned him first. Gentle Mo.

Then two weeks later the bodies of Rollo and Daisy were released. Ellen's body was still at the morgue. It would remain there until preliminary investigations had begun into the allegations of her being a serial killer.

Harry and Maisie had gone to Chief Constable Rivers' private funeral the previous day. He had been buried with his wife; there was little ceremony because of what had been found on his computer.

There had been a quiet but formal internment for the six Legend Street victims and Nancy Wright. Robert had also attended Chrissy Parson's funeral as well as Angus's, Kaden and Rochelle's, as the story finally unfolded.

Robert watched Harry Morton; the DCI had stayed back with Maisie after her sister's funeral, which had taken place just an hour or so before.

Both police officers had needed a little time on their own before they went and joined the guests at the wake.

Maisie's distraught parents had immediately left for Spain following proceedings, blaming Maisie for not telling them that she had received a message from Daisy, nor checking that she had got to Spain.

Maisie would have been disconsolate if she'd had the strength.

Suddenly, as Robert watched, George Wright, the slimy arsehole from the Cordivae Group appeared. It was the first time Robert had seen the man in years. I bet he was telling them he was estranged from the Cordivae Group. He was a liar. Edith Keats appeared too, as lovely as when he first saw her, on the day she had died.

"Hello." George said to Harry and Maisie. "How are you both?"

Harry raised an eyebrow, so Maisie had to answer. "We are a bit battered. As you would expect."

"We need a little of your time."

Maisie sighed angrily.

"Can't it wait?" Harry spat. "Are even the dead so impatient and insensitive these days?"

George bowed his head. "I'm sorry, Harry. This is important. I have currently been tasked with tidying up the whole Cordivae affair. Penance and reward for bringing down Isabelle."

"You did very little George. You were conspicuous by your absence. And, by the way, who had tasked you with that?" Maisie asked. "Someone from the past? Someone else who is Moribund that we have yet to meet? Who the fuck are the Cordivae anyway?"

"The Secretary of State for the Home Office has tasked us with it." Edith added.

"Marcus Rounds?"

"The very same."

"Really?" Harry asked. "You too Edith?"

"Rounds has asked for cooperation from me too," said a voice.

A beautiful red-haired woman stepped from behind the trees. Her hair was fiercely wound about her head. Her clothes were smart but functional. The woman seemed no older than forty.

Harry knew who it was immediately.

"Mother," he said, flatly. "The same mother who led Phillip and I up the stairs to have our injections. The same mother who abandoned us. You know what you have done to us all?"

354

"Henry," his mother said.

Robert saw Maisie grab Harry's hand tighter.

"What do you want? I was told you and father were dead. Then Phillip said you were alive. We had a memorial service. Do you know what it is like to attend such a thing as a child? Speak a eulogy at nine years old?" He shouted the last.

"Your father isn't dead either, Henry." The words seemed strange coming from such a young-looking woman. "But he has gone missing."

"My real father is dying in a care home. *He* was just a lab tech who stuck needles in monkeys. *He* is no more my father than you were a mother."

"You don't understand. I'm not here to revitalise an ancient familial bond. Your Father has gone missing and has taken your brother with him."

Harry shook his head. "My murderous so-called brother is dead. I shot him through the head. His body is in storage, pending a formal investigation."

"Oh, don't be silly, Henry." Harry's mother said "He's evolved. He lives again. And he will be far more dangerous now. If we do not find them, then the fate of humankind will be in the hands of a maniac, not to mention his evil son. He is Vivore."

Harry Morton looked at Maisie Price and he began to laugh, but a flattened laugh with no humour.

"That's your problem, then. I have a police team to re-build, depleted due to your insane experiments and their legacy. Unless you start to commit strange crimes on my patch, I want nothing more to do with you. I have no interest in you, the Home Office, Cordivae or you, George. I'm a local cold case policeman, not MI6 or the CID. Edith, you are welcome to visit us in the future any time, but the rest of you can go and get fucked. Especially you, *Mother.*"

Harry led Maisie away so they could have time to grieve, leaving his mother standing open mouthed as the rain began to fall.

Robert had witnessed enough endings to know that this wasn't one.

A week later, Robert knocked on Harry's office door. One hand was thrust in his pocket, mainly because it was glowing.

"Come in." Harry's voice sounded louder, more confident, just weeks later.

"Superintendent Morton? My name is Robert Waterfield."

Harry looked agape, he was obviously too tired for a response.

"Mr Waterfield. I've been dying to meet you. You name has dropped into case notes and conversations for the last ninety years. Welcome, please take a seat."

Harry's tone was one of resigned sarcasm.

"It is good to meet you too. You are looking well for a man in his nineties. I am also an old man who looks nothing like his age. Would you believe I was born in the 1860s. You are a young man, compared to me, Harry."

Harry sighed, then visibly relaxed, but only slightly. He was used to the strange, it seemed, but not fully at ease with it. Not like Robert, who had worked with it since he had been a seven-year-old boy.

"Are you another Moribund? You would have been old by the time the serum was developed. How could you look so youthful?"

"It changes you." Robert said remembering the time he had broken into the Cordivae laboratory and stolen the serum, near to the end of a long life. When he had wanted to live longer, to match the lifespan of the love of his life.

"Harry, Look at me."

Harry looked up at Robert. Robert took his glowing hand out of his pocket.

"This is the next evolutionary stage of those who took the serum successfully. I *am* truly immortal - like you. I am also Vivore. It is affecting my mind. I dream of conquest. Although I can mostly hold it at bay. I can feel it devouring me."

Harry looked on wide eyed.

"Harry, as you fight your bizarre crimes, I want you to know you have a helpful benefactor in me. I also need your help. We need to have a reciprocal relationship. You will also become Vivore unless we find the antidote. The Vivore will then become Whampyri."

"What?"

"Different stages of evolution. Eventually bringing the death of mankind. Look Harry I have spent most of my long life investigating the bizarre. My early cases will helpfully shed light on some of those you investigate today. Isabelle, or her influence, has appeared in my adventures, more than once. For I was a detective of sorts, at the turn of the century, of the arcane, mostly. In the basements of Legend Street are my secrets. One day I will share them. They will help to banish the Vivore before they can mutate again."

"I am not sure I can cope with any more secrets. I am not sure I want to end up glowing, or living a hundred and sixty years. Or fighting these Vivore. I am already very tired of life."

"You need to find out more about the Cordivae, Harry. Find out their secrets and how the effects of this serum can be reversed. I suspect they have an antidote. Your mother has clearly taken it, *she* is alive. She is not Moribund. I want to live again as a man. I should never have taken that serum. The magic in it curses us all. Unless you have the antidote, you will become like me. If you do not find it and share it, I have seen a time when humanity will fall to the Vivore. You need to be cured then we can break down Isabelle's hold on the past and the future."

Robert touched Harry's face with that glowing hand. Harry gasped. Harry would suddenly feel weak. Robert was sucking energy from him after all.

"So, Superintendent. Imagine if the likes of Phillip or your father could do that. Suck the life from people like an energy vampire. Thousands would die. My past cases will help our fight to end this."

Harry looked shocked then he sighed. The man did that a lot.

"Send them to my Inspector, Maisie Price. She can read them, and we can then look how you might help. She is just up in Lincoln at the moment, beginning another case"

"Indeed," Robert said, knowing exactly where Maisie was. Isabelle's taint was all over Lincoln too.

"It's too early to talk about all of this Robert. Please go away. Come back in a few weeks. I have a new case to solve."

Robert nodded at Harry.

"Goodbye for now. Here's my card. Please do not hesitate to contact me."

Harry picked up the card and then nodded at Robert.

Harry looked afraid.

Robert smiled, then left Superintendent Morton's office, but did not leave the building. Instead, he dropped through to the Nothingness. It was a place he had been accessing since he was a boy. A purgatory of sorts, between life and death.

He was going to visit a Raven. She might be able to help Maisie in Lincoln.

THE END.

To be continued in Price and Morton Book 2:
The Raven's Message, out in 2023

Robert Waterfield's Early Adventures will be revealed in
The Ghostly Menagerie, a Magpie Universe Novel, out very
soon.

Acknowledgements

Wow, this book has been a while in the making. At the time of writing, I have completed five other novels in the time it has taken me to get this out. There has been a catalogue of issues, mainly mine, which has delayed this book. My other books will flow at a faster rate, for a time, I promise you. The sequel, the Raven's Message, is due Summer 2023 at the latest.

I'd like to thank my wife for being patient. I was made redundant in the autumn of 2017 after a period of potentially fatal illness (yes, they did) and began to formulate ideas then. Soon in early 2018 I found myself living most of the week in Gloucester as a self-employed management consultant. It was during those nights that the Magpie Universe was born, and this book and Impossible Fruit were completed. Jacey kept the family afloat through those difficult times. So, I thank her again, immensely, for that.

There was a group of very good friends and family who helped to read this book as it developed. So, thanks: Jacey, Carol and Jason Saunders, Sam and James Alcock, Sam and Mark Baker-Smith, Stu and Sophie Dunn and John James Dadd. This book has been improved tenfold by their feedback and advice. I also want to thank Catherine Cooke my editor/script doctor, and David Collins my cover artist - for professional jobs.

Finally, I would like to thank Harry Morton (not Henry) my grandfather – just for the use of his name – he died in 1989, a closed book. He isn't the Harry of this novel, but he was a World War I hero. I've honoured him the only way I can.

GJM 5/9/22

About the Author

Gary J. Mack, yes, his real name, was born in Birmingham and now lives in Staffordshire with his wife and three teenage lads. He is an avid fan of 1970s and 1980s science fiction and fantasy novels, and will be watching Doctor Who until they nail his coffin shut. He is the author of many published stories collected in the Impossible Fruit series, and he also writes fan fiction on a regular basis, published in Doctor Who and Blake's 7 anthologies.

Printed in Great Britain
by Amazon

85949082R20210